THE MEASURE OF THE RULE

THE MEASURE OF THE RULE

Literature of Canada

Poetry and Prose in Reprint

Douglas Lochhead, General Editor

The Measure of the Rule

Robert Barr

Introduction by Louis K. MacKendrick

UNIVERSITY OF TORONTO PRESS

Preface

Yes, there is a Canadian literature. It does exist. Part of the evidence to support these statements is presented in the form of reprints of the poetry and prose of the authors included in this series. Much of this literature has been long out of print. If the country's culture and traditions are to be sampled and measured, both in terms of past and present-day conditions, then the major works of both our well-known and our lesser-known writers should be available for all to buy and read. The Literature of Canada series aims to meet this need. It shares with its companion series, The Social History of Canada, the purpose of making the documents of the country's heritage accessible to an increasingly large national and international public, a public which is anxious to acquaint itself with Canadian literature — the writing itself — and also to become intimate with the times in which it grew.

DL

Robert Barr, 1850-1912

Louis K. MacKendrick

Introduction

Robert Barr was born in Glasgow, Scotland, on 16 September 1850. His family moved to Wallacetown, Ontario, in 1854, and then to a farm in Kent County before settling in Windsor. Barr later professed (probably politely) to recognize his own youth in his friend Stephen Crane's *Whilomville Stories.* He attended schools in Chatham and afterwards taught on a provisional basis in the Chatham area; he was later to marry the daughter of a trustee of the township school which was his first position. Barr entered the Toronto Normal School in January 1873, in its forty-ninth session, and took a standard syllabus: spelling, composition, grammar, algebra, arithmetic, history, and geography.

After graduating from the Normal School with a second-class certificate, Barr began teaching for $218 per annum in Wallaceburg; he soon moved to Walkerville and eventually attained the principalship of the Windsor Central School (salary $600). It was during his tenure at Windsor that Barr attempted to secure a teaching position for his friend Alexander McNeill.

Barr had met McNeill in Toronto, where they had shared the same Normal School-sponsored boarding house of a Mrs Rammer at 248 Church Street. (As a private joke, the names of Barr and McNeill appear on the School rollcall in *The Measure of the Rule.*) The two were frequent correspondents, Barr being particularly eloquent on the subjects of women, teaching, and boating. His letters often looked back nostalgically to Normal School experiences and associates; once he wished that Mrs Rammer had treated 'her victims more like gentlemen & less like children.' He continually urged 'Mac' to attempt the First-class certificate with him.

Barr's early writing took the form of facetious correspondence to the Bothwell, Ontario, *Advance* and humorous squibs to the satiric paper *Grip*, published in Toronto. His pseudonym was 'Luke Sharp,' the name of an undertaker near Mrs Rammer's establishment. The first major submission, however, was a punning, mock-heroic account of a boat trip taken with McNeill around Lake Erie in the summer of 1875. 'A Dangerous Journey' — 'a thing to blow about for years to come' in the author's opinion — was eventually accepted by William E. Quinby, managing editor of the *Detroit Free Press*, for inclusion in a Sunday supplement. (Barr's difficulties in placing this serial are outlined in the appended essay, 'Literature in Canada.') On the strength of his sketches Barr was offered a position with the paper. He rose from reporter through columnist to exchange editor by 1881, even once accompanying the minister of the interior on a mission to conclude a treaty with the Iroquois. In 1881, with characteristic opportunism, Barr established a British edition of the *Free Press* in London: it was the first American paper in Europe. His writing included interviews, obituaries, political assessments, and travel notes.

In 1892, in London, with Jerome K. Jerome *(Three Men in a Boat)*, Barr started *The Idler*, a successful, lavishly illustrated men's magazine. It carried serialized novels, poems, articles on literature and theatre, memoirs, an 'Idler's Club' of repartee, and short fiction by an impressive array of contributors; these included Bret Harte, Sara Jeannette Duncan, Mark Twain, Israel

Zangwill, Gilbert Parker, Rudyard Kipling, Arthur Conan Doyle, Grant Allen, Rider Haggard, and R.M. Ballantyne. Every Friday saw an 'Idler at home' party at the journal's offices on Arundel Street. Though Barr lost control in 1895, and was forced to sell out after an expensive libel action against Jerome, he later re-joined the magazine and edited it until its finish in 1911. Though journalism and short fiction constituted his best work, by 1895 he was a committed novelist who also enjoyed a considerable reputation in London as a clubman (the Vagabond, Devonshire, National Liberal, Savage, and Cecil). In addition, he claimed to have 'discovered' the writing talents of G.B. Burgin (sub-editor of *The Idler*), Israel Zangwill, and Anthony Hope Hawkins.

Barr achieved a considerable financial success which enabled him to build his home, 'Hillhead,' in Woldingham, Surrey, in sight of Stephen Crane's Ravensbrook Villa at Oxted and, later, within walking distance of Crane's Brede Manor. He was a frequent guest at Crane's, along with such figures as George Gissing, Henry James, and Joseph Conrad, and was a familiar of Arthur Conan Doyle (whose Holmes he satirized as 'Sherlaw Kombs' with some skill). Crane, Barr, and the writer Harold Frederic (to whom the Barr's house was lent at times) comprised a trio which played cards, exchanged 'yarns,' and roistered at 'Baron Brede's.' In the face of Crane's many petty financial crises, it was Barr who helped him and his wife by coping with summonses, lawyers, publishers, and tradesmen, often while himself afflicted with rheumatism. Barr also completed Crane's posthumous novel, *The O'Ruddy*, a task initially rejected by Barr himself and then by Kipling, Henry Marriott-Watson, and A.E.W. Mason.

Barr travelled widely, to Algeria, Germany, Italy, Scotland, Switzerland, and often to America. In 1900 he was awarded an honorary MA by the University of Michigan; in that year he also opened 'Hillhead' for the nursing of wounded Canadian volunteers in the Boer War. His last voyage was in 1910; he spent his final winters in Italy, in ill health, and died on 22 October 1912, of heart failure and the effects of dropsy.

By nature, Barr was bluff, hearty, and ebullient; he had a reputation as a raconteur and as a generous, unusually energetic and sociable man. He was burly and bearded, and was a constant smoker of imported American cigarettes. His hobbies included travel, golf, cycling, and photography. He had a vast supply of spontaneous plots, anecdotes, and amusing stories which, along with his club activities, must have given others the impression and atmosphere of a men's smoking-room personified. He was said to have 'a violent manner' and a 'wealth of strong adjectives' by his friend Arthur Conan Doyle, and many reports agree on Barr's frequent and fluent oaths. He was inclined to wear tweeds and a fedora, and it was in this outfit that he was most often caricatured by several contemporary magazines.

As a writer, Robert Barr considered himself to be ' "merely a commonplace plugger" '; Stephen Crane thought him 'a shrewd, capable, journalistic writer.' Eric Solomon, a Crane commentator, calls Barr 'a gifted hack' and a 'competent journeyman.' Arnold Bennett confided to his journal that Barr was 'an admirable specimen of the man of talent who makes of letters an honest trade,' though at another time he denied that Barr's mind had 'any actual distinction.'

There is no doubt that Barr recognized popular taste in fiction and catered to it with profit. By experience and inclination he was a journalist; his best work was in the form of the short story, and many of his novels were hardly more than episodes loosely connected by the same principal character. Barr relied on formula heroes or heroines, stereotypes who were differentiated by little more than sex, occupation, and wealth. His writing almost uniformly depended on the elaboration of incident, not character, and his creations had no inner complexities. He had two models, or idols: Sir Walter Scott, after whose example Barr fashioned many historical romances (and whose daily output he attempted to equal), and Mark Twain, whose brand of whimsy underscored much of Barr's other work, including non-fiction. Barr's chief property was a bemused narrator, to which was added elementary love-interests, sentiment, and sensation. Barr's protagonists were invariably articulate, resourceful, optimistic, and given to badinage. Within such general specifications Barr wrote the majority of over twenty books with a comfortable facility.

Barr did have several artistic successes. In *The Triumphs of Eugene Valmont* (1906) he capitalized on the current popularity of detective fiction, and in Valmont created a droll and distinctive character with more than a passing suggestion of Agatha Christie's later, celebrated Hercule Poirot. (Stories from this book were anthologized for years following in collections edited by Harry Haycraft, Ellery Queen, Vincent Starrett, Dorothy Sayers, and others.) Further, in *The Mutable Many* (1896) and *The Victors* (1901), respectively the stories of an industrial strike and metropolitan politics, Barr showed a remarkable and uncharacteristic talent for gritty social realism. Dismayed reviewers, however, declared that his forte was light romantic comedy, and urged that he return to it; *The Critic* asked, 'why should one of Mr Barr's novels be burdened with a purpose?' These elements of romance and realism underscored *The Measure of the Rule*, the nearest Barr came to writing an autobiographical novel.

The details about the operation of the Toronto Normal School given in *The Measure of the Rule* are accurate. In Barr's time, a quarter of a century after its foundation by Egerton Ryerson, the School also housed the Education Office, the Educational Depository, and a museum. Observation and practice teaching were done by teacher trainees in the attached Model Schools where the students, like their novice instructors, were segregated by sex. The School was only empowered to grant a document acknowledging the prospect's attendance, good conduct, and rating as a teacher. The actual certificate of teaching was granted by the government; those of the first and second class were tenable for life. After the School Act of 1871 a third-class certificate could be issued by a County Board; it was valid for three years in an area under the board's jurisdiction. Local Model Schools were later established for the observation and practice of area teachers, who could then proceed to the Ottawa or Toronto Normal School to complete their training. Eventually the Normal School became the linchpin of a provincial system for licensing teachers; this satisfied Ryerson's requirements of uniformity in the preparation of instructors, and co-ordinated efforts which had formerly been left to individual County Boards.

At one point in *The Measure of the Rule* Tom Prentiss, a self-confessed novice at story-telling, shows a naive view of the relation between literature and life:

> I come now to a chapter which a writer of fiction would dare not use. The freaks of chance ... play such a part in the incident

I am about to relate that such a narration would be useless anywhere else than in a true story.

This was a mannered gesture in many of Barr's works; perhaps he considered his writing as pure journalistic fact, or was protesting against the heavy stylization of contemporary romantic fiction. Nevertheless, he did use the device of chance or coincidence in his novel, even in obscure ways. Aline Arbuthnot, the heroine, is unofficially engaged to a civil engineer, Tom's one-time ambition; her father, the judge, removes her to Paris, Tom's own artistic goal; and the land from whose sale Tom realizes enough to subsist in Paris for several years is too convenient to be credible. Yet the overriding fact is that Barr was drawing on much of his own experience for *The Measure of the Rule*, and this very nearly dominated the trappings of conventional fictional romance.

Barr was no exacting stylist. Here as elsewhere his expression can be uncluttered and uncomplicated, but in a great many places it carries a heavy freight of rhetorical and melodramatic flourishes: 'I held her with a palpitating fervour which thrilled me with the delight of life...' *The Measure of the Rule* has little realistic dialogue; rather than being colloquial Barr's young persons are stilted, gravely sententious at times, possessed of a wisdom beyond their years, and grammatically impeccable. Aline, 'a picture of comeliness glorified by dark eyes,' seems to mingle art and life when Prentiss observes, ' "Her name is Aline Arbuthnot, which sounds like the title of a heroine in a cheap novelette, but she is worthy to be the heroine of the most expensive novel" ' — an at best quixotic standard. She is the typical Barr leading lady: anonymously pretty, competent, bright, cheerful, skillful at repartee, disarmingly practical, and self-possessed. She is consistently described in the language of romantic idealism, as much a reflection of Prentiss' infatuation as of Barr's slim characterization and the demands of saccharine romance. It is only appropriate that, before Tom becomes aware of his true calling, he sees in Aline a resemblance to 'a renowned picture by some great artist.'

Barr manages the conversion of Tom Prentiss from engineering by way of teaching to art with limited finesse and little narrative preparation. Tom's transformation at the sight of Aline in the Normal School art gallery is dramatically self-sufficient:

A potential civil engineer entered that gallery, and was never seen again. A potential painter came out. ... Dr Darnell had blotted out a bridge-builder and produced, if we are to believe certain art critics, an indifferent painter.

Tom only perfunctorily admits, ' "I find myself rather ambitious to become a painter." ' Barr's meager attention to his hero's inspiration and change of heart (accentuated by that undemonstrative 'rather') is again apparent when the artist *manqué* resolves that 'my first picture, *when I had learned the rudiments of the art*, should be Aline as a sister of charity ...' (my italics). In short, Tom's desire is scantily motivated and only functionally realized — though Aline does note that he figures 'artistically' on a blackboard. Prentiss' romantic-artistic sufferings, malnutrition, and triumph in Paris show Barr's writing to formula, in this case one suggested by Henri Murger's *Scènes de la Vie de Bohème* (1851) and many subsequent fictional treatments. The Parisian episodes have a negligible sense of place; by contrast, the vivid ice-boat scene in Toronto harbour has a compactness and interest that show Barr's best control of his material.

As suited his academic subject, Barr employed thematically appropriate epigraphs for his chapters from such sources as the Bible, Byron, Otway, Shakespeare, Milton, Scott, Chaucer, and Waller, as well as from Horace Smith, Nathaniel Parker Willis, and John Trumbull, among others — examples of genuine literature mingled with indifferent verse. In a sense the epigraphs parallel Barr's dual impulses: keenly felt autobiographical experience subjected to and at times overwhelmed by a sentimental and formulaic romanticism. *The Measure of the Rule* also contains a persistent undercurrent of Biblical references and imagery, perhaps an unconscious echo of the Normal School's founding philosophy: 'Designed for the Instruction and Training of Teachers upon Christian Principles.' (In reality, religious instruction was given in the School for one hour every Friday, to each according to his denomination.)

The Measure of the Rule vividly conveys the several repressive and regimentative pressures, both academic and sexual, associated with the Normal School. As Prentiss complains of Dr Darnell, he

> almost made me believe that the drastic rule of the Normal
> School was made by the Lord, and not by a body of fussy old
> gentlemen in high places, who had forgotten their own youth,
> and never suspected they were contravening the will of the
> Almighty as expressed in the impulses of His creatures.

In actual fact, men and women could communicate only with the Principal's permission. Barr invests the eloquent Sam — Samson? — McKurdy's resistance to Darnell, the emblem of the system, with heroic terms:

> [The students'] whole sympathy went out towards the quiet
> young fellow who stood the target of this grim man clothed

with authority, a man of power, free and untrammelled, confronting an opponent hampered by all the restrictions of discipline.

Sam is a literate muscular opposition, yet it is the sombre and sardonic figure of John Henceforth through whom Barr achieves greater realism, interest, and intensity of characterization.

In *The Measure of the Rule* it is clear that the Normal School's concern is academic drilling, not training in methodology. The operative principle in Barr's time was thorough training in the subjects to be taught to children and the example set by the master-teachers, rather than practical pedagogy. The writer's bitterest and most personal comment in the novel is directed against this insufficiency of preparation:

> Contempt and dislike for this hurried manufactory of half-formed teachers flung out upon the public every six months, this farce of scholarship, filled me with regretful longing for the leisurely methods and the picturesque surroundings of the older school [the University] whose gates were closed against me.

In 1871 severer licensing regulations tended to produce an abundance of transient and lower-certificated teachers. However, with the reorganization of Ontario's secondary schools in that year the Normal School began to concentrate less on purely academic matters, though the results are not immediately apparent as filtered through Barr's fiction. His scornful and articulate opinions of the school system itself and of the level of its educational operations may be found in the essay following this introduction, 'Literature in Canada.'

Several figures in *The Measure of the Rule* were modelled on actual teachers with whom Barr had been familiar when he was a teacher trainee. The 'bald-headed, red-whiskered, thick-pated, florid-faced, hot-tempered' Dr Darnell is a caricature of the authoritarian minister and grammarian H.W. Davies, third Principal of the Normal School (1871-84). Inexplicably, the doctor loses force as the novel progresses, and becomes a rather gentle old man — perhaps because his heart was 'as kind as his face was severe.' Dr Cardiff, teacher and physician, was drawn after James Carlyle, MD, a relative of the English writer and mathematics master at the school from 1871 to 1893. It was Cardiff whom Barr consulted early in 1875 about teaching prospects in British Columbia. Professor Donovan, 'lovable' to Tom Prentiss, was Thomas Kirkland, science master from 1871 to 1884 and Dr Davies' successor as Principal. Finally, the satanic John Brent was suggested by James L. Hughes, Head Master of the Boys' Model School from 1871 to 1874, afterwards a youthful Inspector of Public Schools for Toronto, and author of such works as *Mistakes in Teaching* (1877) and *How to Secure and Retain Attention* (1879). Hughes' biographer, Lorne Pierce, quotes an admission relevant to Barr's otherwise severe portrait:

> I was trained to believe that my supreme duty was to *criticise destructively* the teaching of the Normal School students while they were teaching their practice lessons in the Model School. I was told to point out to them the errors they made as the best means of making them good teachers.

However, Hughes's immediate qualification would have encouraged Barr: ' "I have no sympathy with such a course now, and I am glad that I saw the great evils of this method of training before I was appointed Inspector of Schools." ' Perhaps fortunately, with the improvement of the secondary school system in 1871, teachers' examinations were put in the charge of a committee; judgement of the individual candidate was no longer in the hands of his immediate instructors.

Reviews of *The Measure of the Rule*, which had been first published as a standard six-shilling novel, were contradictory. The story was felt to reflect 'a singularly colorless phase of social life, colorless at least so far as fictional uses are concerned' *(New York Times)*. It was nonetheless 'original in its subject and treatment' and 'certainly readable,' though not 'of tremendous power' *(Outlook). The Dial* bluntly considered the book 'puerile.' *The Nation* ambivalently found the work to be both 'solemn reading' and 'extremely humorous,' criticized the 'certain magnified non-natural horseplay,' and confessed bewilderment about the change in tone after the opening comic treatment of 'aged school-boys.' Yet in *The Measure of the Rule* Barr was exorcizing a very real situation and memories which no romantic fiction, nor the expectations of his public, could entirely submerge or invalidate. It is interesting to add that the Normal School jubilee volume (1897) noted Barr as 'a well-known *litterateur*,' while the centennial memorial (1947) observed of his novel: 'The book is pleasantly old-fashioned in style, and is somewhat melodramatic in its ending.'

Barr's attitude to Canada was curious, as the essay 'Literature in Canada' shows. He was a disappointing literary critic, though the satire in his analysis went unremarked, and one earnest reader wrote, 'Naturally we might expect an author by the name of Barr to lug whiskey into a discussion on literature. Whiskey and bars go together.' (Interestingly, the second part of 'Literature in Canada' was in the issue of *The Canadian Magazine* which contained a prose portrait of Barr as a 'Canadian Celebrity.') Despite his frequent visits to his family in Canada, Barr's former associates were in Detroit, and it is significant that in later years he invariably thought of himself as an American writer.

Nevertheless, Barr's first novel, *In the Midst of Alarms* (1893), was a sardonic and high-spirited rendition of the 1866 Fenian 'invasion' of Canada near Ridgeway. Not only was one of the protagonists, a journalist, an extended self-portrait, but Barr had actually served with the St Thomas volunteers against the Fenians. In his *Handbook of Canadian Literature* Archibald MacMurchy admired this book's 'Canadian color.' Another book, *A Woman Intervenes* (1897), which had been serialized in *The Idler,* concluded at a Canadian minehead amid some conventional national scenery. Other strictly Canadian material appeared in a very few short stories, chief among which was 'An Extra Turn,' ironically published in *The American Magazine* in 1909. The story demonstrated how a university-trained rural schoolteacher required both academic superiority and muscle to manage his students – a situation similar to experiences Barr had undergone in Wallaceburg and had communicated to Alex McNeill. Though Barr was acclaimed in *The Canadian Magazine* of September 1899 as 'the prince of Canada's storytellers,' the accolade was a pious exaggeration.

Only occasionally did Barr write of Canada in non-fictional terms, and 'Literature in Canada' was by far his most important work in this area. Even this apparently well-meant essay suffers at times through Barr's fondness for whimsical hyperbole. In an earlier *Idler* article he had celebrated Montreal as 'the one perfect city in the world,' adding:

> The Montreal man is a good all-round specimen of humanity, an athlete, temperate, resolute and hardy, a boon companion and a staunch friend: an Englishman — with modern improvements.

Again, his reflections on 'The Future of Canada' (1905) considered the country's position on 'the great pathway of commerce' between east and west, her possession of vast natural resources, and concluded:

> I therefore predict that Canada will become the chief manufacturing nation of the world, as well as the chief wheat-producing nation, and will therefore be in time the most prosperous of all countries.

Barr was on surer ground with fiction than with nationalistic prophecy, however, and *The Measure of the Rule* can stand as the authentic product of a genuine Canadian experience.

Canadian reviewers and commentators who wrote of Robert Barr were either bitter over his apparent disassociation from the country or were all too quick to claim his writing, without qualification, as that of a Canadian author who happened to live in Britain. In an effort to be impartial, the anonymous contributor of the 'Canadian Celebrities' article on Barr wrote:

> His works are extensively read and eagerly sought after by those who knew him as a school teacher and reporter; not because they are 'Bob Barr's,' but because the people feel they are well written, interesting and worth reading.

xx

Even here, the clash of loyalties to national personality and literary product which bothered Barr's Canadian critics is apparent. In retrospect, however, *The Measure of the Rule* is as much a social document as a novel, complicated by Barr's sometimes imperfect objectivity about his sources. Yet, apart from the interest inherent in the educational system described, the book possesses a frequent intensity which romance cannot hide.

Select Bibliography

A Woman Intervenes New York: Stokes 1896
In the Midst of Alarms Philadelphia: Lippincott 1893
The Mutable Many New York: Stokes 1896
The Speculations of John Steele New York: Stokes 1905
The Triumphs of Eugene Valmont New York: Appleton 1906
The Unchanging East Boston: L.C. Page 1900 2v.
Young Lord Stranleigh Toronto: McLeod & Allen 1908
The Victors New York: Stokes 1901

Allen, C. Stan 'A Glimpse of Robert Barr,' *The Canadian Magazine* IV (April 1895), 545-50
Brown, Walter James 'Robert Barr and Literature in Canada,' *The Canadian Magazine* XV (June 1900), 170-6
Burgin, G.B. *Memoirs of a Clubman* London: Hutchinson 1922, 95-103
'Canadian Celebrities IX: Robert Barr,' *The Canadian Magazine* XIV (December 1900), 181-2
Crane, Stephen *The O'Ruddy* (completed by Robert Barr), ed. Fredson Bowers, intro. J.C. Levenson Charlottesville: University Press of Virginia 1971, xxvii, xlviii-lv, lxvii-lxxi
Halsey, Francis W., ed *Authors of our Day in Their Homes: Personal Descriptions and Interviews* New York: James Pott 1902, 247-54
Jerome, Jerome K. *My Life and Times* New York: Harper 1926, 166-95
MacMurchy, Archibald *Handbook of Canadian Literature* Toronto: Briggs 1906, 143

Pierce, Lorne *Fifty Years of Public Service: A Life of James L. Hughes* Toronto: Oxford University Press 1924, 66

Solomon, Eric *Stephen Crane in England: A Portrait of the Artist* Columbus: Ohio State University Press 1964, 12, 29

Toronto Normal School 1847-1947 Toronto: School of Graphic Arts 1947, 30 (48 in expanded edition)

Toronto Normal School Jubilee Celebration (1847-1897) Toronto: Warwick Bros. & Rutter 1898, 184

Literature in Canada

Robert Barr

Part One

In the May number of *The Canadian Magazine* there appeared an article by the editor entitled 'The Strength and Weakness of Current Books.' The article deals largely of Canada and its literature, and thus it is interesting to all of us who have an affection for Canada, especially as the subject is treated with illuminating restraint by Mr Cooper.

As the matter is, strictly speaking, none of my business, I naturally desired to say something about it, but the year has grown several months older before I could snatch time from more pressing work than the delightful task of lecturing Canada, and even now I must treat this important theme with a haste and superficiality it does not deserve.

Canada, from its position on the map, its hardy climate, its grand natural scenery, its dramatic and stirring historical associations should be the Scotland of America. It should produce the great poets, which I believe it is actually doing, although I doubt if their books are selling in the Dominion. It should produce the great historical novelist; the Sir Walter Scott of the New World. Has the Sir Walter Scott of Canada appeared? And if so, is he unrecognized? If he has not yet come forward, what are the chances for his materialization? If Scott came to Canada, to change W.T. Stead's phrase, how long would it be before he starved to death? It is towards the solution of these questions that the jumbling remarks which follow will be directed, although I do not guarantee to keep to the point, and reserve to myself the privilege of wandering all

The Canadian Magazine, XIV, 1 (November 1899), 3-7

over the place if I want to. I have felt for some years that it would be desirable for a writing man to take upon himself the odium of telling the truth to Canada, as far as literature is concerned. It is so popular to be eulogistic, that the average man's address or article touching Canada, on literature and that sort of thing, has a tendency to strengthen the delusion, already too wide spread, that Canada is an intellectual country. For an excellent example of this fatal habit, turn to Mr. W.A. Fraser's address before the Press Association, published in the May number of *The Canadian Magazine*. The chief fault which I find in this address is that it embodies an underestimation of Canadian men and women writers, which is so typical of Canada itself.

Mr Fraser is addressing a body of Canadian Pressmen, and one of the duties of a Canadian Pressman should be to foster Canadian literature. Does Canada possess a literary man or woman? Not so far as may be learned from Mr Fraser. Here are the names of the persons mentioned to the Pressmen – Zangwill, Baring Gould, Robert Burns, Talmage, Shakespeare, Goethe, Kossuth, Dickens, Rudyard Kipling, and G.W. Steevens. In that oration there is not a single Canadian mentioned, or even hinted at, unless the phrase that 'Canada is the abode of wicked French priests, who are only kept from ruining everybody by the gallantry of the hero,' is a sneer at the charming romance of Charles G.D. Roberts, 'The Forge in the Forest.' The Bible tells us that a prophet is not without honour save in his own country, and this eternal truth is exemplified in Canada to-day, and has been for years past. Mecca cast out Mahomet, and it was only when he was driven from its gates that he founded the religion of which Mecca is to-day the centre.

Mr Fraser says, 'So far, literature has done little for Canada.'
This remark, which, by the way, is untrue, recalls to my mind the
much more striking phrase of the late John Sandfield Macdonald.
'What in hell has Strathroy done for me?' What has Canada done
for literature? Little or nothing. Her greatest literary man would
live in squalor, if he remained within her boundaries and depended upon her for support. Canada does not buy books to any
extent worth mentioning. Apologists for the Dominion have said
that life in Canada is strenuous; that there is the inevitable struggle in conquering a new country; that money is scarce and that
books are not a necessity. Is this true? Is it the lack of money
that makes Canada so poor a book market? Or is it because the
Canadians are not a reading people? Is it lack of intellect rather
than lack of cash? In writing this article here in England I have to
admit I am not well supplied with statistical volumes relating to
Canada, and any statement I make in the line of figures is subject to
correction. I have at my elbow the statistical 'Year Book of Canada'
for 1889, and so whatever I glean from it will be at least ten years
old. I find (page 191) that in the year 1885, for instance, Canada
drank 1.12 gallons of whiskey per head, as against 1.01 gallons per
head in Great Britain and Ireland. That is to say, the Canadian drank
eleven hundredths of a gallon more than the Britisher, who has
never been held up to the natives of this earth as a strictly temperance individual. I find that in the five years ending in 1889,
Canada consumed annually an average of two million eight hundred
and ninety thousand five hundred and eight gallons of spirits.

Now, when I was in Canada last year, five bottles of whiskey
went to a gallon, and they charged me a dollar a bottle; so,
putting the gallon at the low figure of three dollars, this would
mean that Canada's liquor bill was something under nine millions

of dollars, more than double of what Ontario paid during those years for education. We used to have a phrase in Canada to this effect, 'Talk is cheap, but it takes money to buy whiskey.'

I find that in those years Canada transformed something like a hundred million bushels of good wheat into spirituous liquor, but her production of books during the same time seems to have been so infinitesimal that the statistical Year Book does not even mention the output.

It will be seen by these statements that it is not the lack of money that makes Canada about the poorest book market in the world outside of Senegambia.

It may be said that I am putting literature on a low level when I place it on a cash basis; but an author must live if he is to write, and he must eat if he is to live, and he must have money if he is to eat. Cash is the magic wand of modern life; it will conjure up nearly anything you like. Recently a music dealer in Italy offered a substantial prize for an opera, and the offer brought forth 'Cavalleria Rusticana' and 'Pagliacci,' two musical efforts which became instantly successful all over the world. The *Youth's Companion* once offered a large prize for the best short story, and the taker of it was an unknown writer in Toronto. The Toronto *Globe* some years ago offered tempting prizes for short stories, and actually hooked in one of mine, and if mine did not take the first prize it was because there was a better story ahead of it.

The bald truth is that Canada has the money, but would rather spend it on whiskey than on books. It prefers to inflame its stomach, rather than inform its brain. And yet there are people who actually hold that Canada is an intellectual country. The trouble is that it adds stupidity to its lack of intelligence. This sounds somewhat tautological, but a person may lack intelligence and still not be stupid. Commercially, nothing pays a country better than lavishly to subsidize an author. A Sir Walter Scott would bring millions into Canada every year. Scotland could well have afforded to bestow on Sir Walter Scott a hundred million dollars for his incomparable Waverley Novels. His works have made Scotland the dearest district in the world in which a traveller can live, and have transformed it from a poverty-stricken land into a tourist-trodden country, rolling in wealth. The reason I choose Sir Walter Scott as an example is, first, that he was the man whom the six gentlemen mentioned by Mr Cooper chose to lead their list of desirable authors; second, because no Canadian writer has ever been made wealthy by Canada, and so I can't go to the Dominion for an example; and, third, because I am myself an adoring admirer of Sir Walter Scott's works.

Now Sir Walter Scott was not writing for laurel wreaths; he wrote entirely and solely for cash. He began his Waverley Novels to support his lavish expenditure on Abbotsford. I doubt if he had any idea how good the books were. I think it was a canny precaution of Scott when he refused to put his name on them, fearing they were bad, and that he might jeopardise his already well-won reputation as a poet; yet whether they were good or bad he resolved to write them if they would bring in money. He continued his output of novels afterwards to pay his debts, incurred in a disastrous commercial speculation, the object of which had been to make money. If Sir Walter had thought he could make more money by planting trees or raising stock he would undoubtedly have turned his attention to those pursuits, and the Waverley Novels would have been unwritten.

One of the first recorded utterances of Sir Walter Scott's, touching upon books, that I can find, was made to Ballantyne just a hundred years ago, where he says:

'I think I could, with little trouble, put together sundry selections of them (Border Ballads) as might make a neat little volume that would *sell for four or five shillings*,'

You see, he does not say that it would be well to collect these ballads in case they might be lost to the world, or that their publication would give deserved fame to ancient writers, but that the book would sell for four or five shillings. It is the four or five shillings that the average literary man is after and must have, if he is to continue in the business.

What chance has Canada, then, of raising a Sir Walter Scott? I maintain that she has but very little chance, because she won't pay the money, and money is the root of all literature. The new Sir Walter is probably tramping the streets of Toronto to-day, looking vainly for something to do. But Toronto will recognize him when he comes back from New York or London, and will give him a dinner when he doesn't need it.

I would like to say before going further, that although Mr Fraser's address to the journalists filled me with resentment, because of his ignoring Canadian literary men, I am, nevertheless, a great admirer of that gentleman's stories, and, if I am not very much mistaken, he got his start in somewhat the same manner as I did myself. In the Philadelphia *Saturday Evening Post* of June the 24th, are two items side by side which ought to be pondered on by Canada. One paragraph says: 'Mr W.A. Fraser sent his first sketch to *The Detroit Free Press*, and it was at once accepted. The cheque for it determined Mr Fraser to regular writing, and his success has been pronounced.'

The second item is about Charles G.D. Roberts, and reads: 'Professor Roberts is in future going to live in England. It is understood that he goes abroad by the advice of a well-known publisher, who assures him that he can make much more money in London.'

Mr Fraser had to go outside of Canada to secure his first cheque, and that was my own experience, getting the cheque from the same paper.

The first article of mine that was accepted by *The Detroit Free Press* had been sent to every paper in Ontario, without exception, and unanimously declined, although it was offered for nothing. The preacher in the story, said 'Thank God' when he got back his hat after passing it round a very stingy congregation, but I was not so fortunate as the reverend gentleman, for many of the papers not only kept the manuscript, but the stamps enclosed for its return as well. I never expected to get pay for anything published in Canada, but was always glad when editors did not send me in a bill for publishing my contributions.

The Honourable Mr W.E. Quinby, editor and proprietor of the *Detroit Free Press*, who gave Mr Fraser and myself our first cheques, has himself done more for literature than all the editors from Quebec to Vancouver, and his literary judgment is infallible. He does not care from whom the manuscript comes, so long as it is good, and again, he is willing to back his opinion with money, and that, as I have said, is what counts in this world, whether in a horse trade, in literature, or in an election. I know men and women in England, in Canada, and in the United States, now in the front rank of literature who owe their start to Mr Quinby's appreciation of their early efforts. There is little merit in recognizing genius when all the world recognizes it, but to select a winner when no one else knows of him is a feat to be proud of.

One winter, during a visit to Atlanta, Georgia, I had the pleasure of meeting the late Henry W. Grady, one of the most remarkable journalists that the United States has produced — a man who would certainly have been Vice-President of the United States had he lived, and probably President. In speaking of the beginning of his successful career, he said his starting point was a cheque from Mr Quinby, of Detroit, received when he was out of employment, with no hope of gaining any.

'My assets were, one wife, two children, and three dollars,' he said. 'That was all I had in the world. The encouraging words of Mr Quinby to me, then an unknown, no-account young man, and the substantial nature of the cheque he sent, raised me from despair to hope, and I have never had an uneasy moment from that time.'

Kipling, himself an early contributor to the columns of the *Free Press*, said to me once, 'The reading of the *Detroit Free Press* was about the only pleasure I had in my newspaper work in India; what a splendidly edited paper it is.'

As one good turn deserves another, I believe the *Free Press* was the first paper in America to call attention to Kipling's genius. It is something for a man to have produced a paper like that, and more, that he paid generously for the contributions he accepted, whether the sender was famous or unknown.

My advice then to the Walter Scott tramping the streets of Toronto is:

'Get over the border as soon as you can; come to London or go to New York; shake the dust of Canada from your feet. Get out of a land that is willing to pay money for whiskey, but wants its literature free in the shape of Ayer's Almanac, in my day the standard work of reference throughout the rural districts, because it cost nothing. Vamoose the ranch. Go back when all the rest of the world is acquainted with you, and you may find that Canada has, perhaps, some knowledge of your existence. Anyhow, when you return you will have a good time, for there are some of the finest people in the world in Canada.'

This proves a very much larger subject than I thought it was when I took it in hand, so instead of dealing with it in one article I propose to devote two to it. It would be useless to scold over a state of things for which there was no remedy. I believe there is a remedy; I believe that Canada can be claimed from literary darkness and rye whiskey; therefore, in a future contribution, I propose to point out what this remedy is.

Part Two

In a previous article I devoted some attention to the somewhat benighted condition of the average citizen of the Dominion who, according to his own statistics, loves whiskey better than books. I now turn with equal horror to the contemplation of the educated Canadian.

Canada has suffered much at the hands of her cultured class. Mr Cooper, in his article in the May number of this magazine, says the educated Canadian is conservative. This is putting it mildly, but I believe the statement is accurate as far as it goes. The educated Canadian is conservative because he has no opinion of his own. In literature he waits until a definite judgment is pronounced outside of Canada; then your educated Canadian knows it all. He retails this second-hand estimate to admiring listeners with all the confidence of a man exploiting his own discovery. This is a very happy state of things for the educated Canadian, for if you contradict him he waves you off by saying, 'Oh, the London *Times* agrees with me,' or '*The Athenaeum* has given expression to my view,' and thus you are floored. But the unfortunate thing for a young Canadian endeavouring to make his way in literature is, that until he leaves his own domicile and has achieved commendation from other people, he has no chance whatever of making any impression on the second-hand opinion of his educated fellow-countrymen. The cultured Canadian glosses his ignorance with a hard polish, which is utterly impervious to thought that is Canadian in origin. He says of Canada as

The Canadian Magazine, XIV, 2 (December 1899), 130-6

they of old said, 'Can there any good come out of Nazareth,' and it is not until Jerusalem has deified, or crucified the Nazarene, that he becomes of honour in his own land.

Mr Cooper tells an interesting story which is not related for the purpose of confirming my argument, but which, nevertheless, goes some distance in that direction.

Six men of education and culture, he said, were taking dinner in a private room in a Toronto restaurant. Being cultivated persons their talk naturally turned towards literature, and the good old stock question came up. If all the books were to be blotted out with exception of the Bible and Shakspere and one other volume, what should that one other volume be? Please note the conventionality of the exception. There are many men of culture and education who are not in the habit of reading either the Bible or Shakspere, yet when this stock question arises, this stock exception is invariably made; sometimes Milton and Homer are lugged in, usually suggested by a posing man of education and culture who has never read a line of one or the other. Here then are the authors preserved to us by the six men of culture and education in Toronto — Scott, Dickens, Carlyle, Kipling, Macauley, Parkman, Thackeray, Ruskin, Elliott, Pope, Lecky, Stevenson, Browning, Tennyson, Goldsmith and Arnold, in the order named.

Imagine, if you can, the depth of decadence into which critical judgment has fallen in Toronto, when there can be found half a dozen men throughout that ill-fated city who actually place Dickens before Thackeray, and who, at this age of the world, seriously consider Macaulay, when right in their own town, doubtless within a street car fare of where they were dining, lives Goldwin Smith, a writer incomparably superior to Macaulay, whether considered as a literary stylist or as an accurate historian. If cultured Canadians would only import their opinions with reasonable celerity, such mistakes could not occur, and there is really no excuse for this tardiness when there are several lines of steamers running from England to Montreal each week. Doubtless the distinguished diners themselves will be shocked to learn that, to use a commercial phrase, Dickens stock began to decline on the day of his death, and has been declining ever since, while in like manner Thackeray stock began to appreciate and has continued to do so.

But there are six prigs in other places than Canada. The editor of an English magazine told me a while since that six English novelists dined together and the usual question came up with the usual exception. It took this form: 'If you were sentenced to a term of imprisonment and could get only one book to read, which book would you choose, Shakspere and the Bible excepted?' The answer was unanimous; the six novelists chose George Borrows' book *Lavengro*.

I sat silent for a moment or two when this was told me, and then said with deliberation, 'I think I should have chosen *Lavengro* too.'

'So should I,' replied the editor.

Thus there were eight of us, like the little niggers. On leaving my editor friend I went at once to my favourite book-store on the Strand, and said to the man in charge: 'Have you got a copy of a book entitled *Lavengro*?'

'Well,' replied the attendant, 'there isn't much call for it, but I think I have a copy. Yes, here it is; two shillings; by George Borrow.'

I paid the money, took the book home with me, and since then I have read it.

Now these six English prigs differed from the six Canadian prigs in this; there was at least some originality about their choice. Without knowing who the six were, I surmised that probably an article on George Borrows had appeared in one of the reviews, and each man supposed he alone had read that article, so he thought he would surprise the others by naming a book of which they had never heard. I take some delight in imagining the long faces pulled by the six novelists when the poll was declared. Next year, Mr Cooper, when your six men are dining again in their private room, I'll bet you a year's subscription to this magazine that they choose *Lavengro*.

Rather more than a year ago, when I was in America I had the pleasure of listening to a lecture by Mr James L. Hughes, Inspector of Schools for Toronto. The lecture was the last of a series on the same subject, and the subject was Charles Dickens. I sat entranced, listening to the rounded periods of Mr Hughes. For the time being the years rolled off my shoulders, and I was once more a boy of seventeen listening to the estimate of the noted novelist whom I had cherished at that period of my existence. It staggered me at first, I confess, to learn that any educated man considered the exaggerations of Charles Dickens worthy of six discourses, but once in the auditorium all that was forgotten, and I bathed in the eloquence of the Inspector as if I had discovered the fountain of youth which Ponce de Leon failed to find in Florida.

I quote here from an inaccurate memory, and so cannot reproduce the exact words; but this was their substance:

'Murdstone'! The sonorous voice of Mr Hughes rolled out the cognomen, dwelling thrillingly on the 'r's.' 'Think of the significance of that name! "Murd," the first syllable of murder, and "stone," typical of the hard heart of this wonderfully drawn character.'

This was most impressive, but still, if Mr Hughes had wished to get names with meanings, he had only to go back a little further in literature to the old dramatists, and there he would have found Mr Lovemore, Mr Bashful Constant, Mr Brilliant Fashion, Mr Lively, Mr Sombre, Mr Moody, Mr Joyful, Sir John Reckless, Lord Graball, a miser; indeed he might have had a more recent example, for an American novelist once wrote: 'Mr Winterbottom was a cold, stern man.'

But after the discourse was over and I had removed myself from the magnetism of the lecturer's presence, I began to ponder on the disquieting position of things which this oration displayed. If the chief educational official in the largest and probably the most enlightened city of Ontario, held literary opinions which perhaps it would be too harsh a term to call infantile, what must be the state of mind of the ordinary teachers throughout the Province, and what chance is there of any of their unfortunate pupils becoming a Judge Haliburton or a Gilbert Parker, an Archibald Lampman or a Dr Drummond? The fact that the country does produce such men is merely an example of the amazing fertility of nature. To expect it to do so as a matter of course, would be as absurd as if a farmer looked for fall wheat to sprout in the spring, when he had neither ploughed the land nor sown the grain the year before.

During all my school days in Canada, whether in the humble log chalet of the backwoods or the more imposing educational halls of Toronto, I never once heard the name of a literary man mentioned. Never once was I told that I lived in a country containing the grandest scenery the world has to show. Never once was the information given to me that the history of the deeds which won an empire from the wilderness was more absorbingly interesting than the most thrilling romance ever penned. And here I come to the chief indictment I have to bring against the conservative educated Canadian. The school books which he compiled for his unhappy victims throughout the Province reflected his own second-hand state of mind. Unfortunately I have not in my possession the school books at present in use in Ontario, but the third, fourth and fifth books of my day were as bad as if I had compiled them myself. Canadian history was represented, when I first went to school in Canada, by a little yellow book, which was as dull as a page of logarithms. Later we had a larger book containing many bad wood-cuts, and this volume was even duller than the other, because it was bigger. The selections for the reading books were mostly chosen from English sources, and if we saw Canada at all, it was through English eyes. There were some turgid poems on Niagara, if I remember aright, but they were all by Englishmen, and I think the prose description was by Charles Dickens himself.

The other night I was invited by the Whitefriar's Club to attend a dinner given to Mark Twain. One of the speakers was Dean Hole, of Rochester, celebrated alike as an orator and a bookmaker. He told a story which he credited to Dr Conan Doyle, but which, nevertheless, was my story. Discussing the very point I am endeavouring to throw light upon now, I told this story to Dr Doyle, to emphasize my remarks, and he asked permission to use the anecdote on his lecture tour, which permission

I most cheerfully gave, and now Dean Hole has got the story in one of his books, and if my name were only attached, I should have some chance of going down to posterity. Here is the yarn:

As a boy I worked my way from Detroit on a schooner to the Welland Canal. The schooner was the *Olive Branch*, and I believe her bones now lie exposed to the winds on the shore near Toronto. My objective point was the Niagara Falls, and as soon as I got off the schooner I tramped from the canal to the cataract, one hot, dusty summer's day. I sat and looked at the Falls, but was bitterly disappointed with them. No reality can ever equal the expectation of a boy's lurid fancy. However, I consoled my-self by saying, 'Never mind; some day I shall have money enough to go to England and see the Falls of Ladore.' In the third, or the fourth, or the fifth book, which was than used in all schools throughout Canada, Southey's poem, the Falls of Ladore, was given:

Recoiling, turmoiling and toiling and boiling,
And steaming, and beaming, and gleaming, and streaming,
And dashing, and flashing, and splashing, and clashing.
All at once and all o'er, with a mighty uproar,
And this way the water comes down at Ladore!

Naturally I thought such a cataract must be the greatest down-pour in the world, and sure enough, neither money nor oppor-tunity being lacking, I had a chance of viewing the wonder of nature which inspired Southey's muse. I landed one summer evening at a lakeside town two miles from Ladore. My impatience would not admit of my waiting till daylight, so I started on foot along the beautiful well-made road which skirts the lake, then almost as light as day under a full harvest moon. After I had tramped about two miles I began to fear I had lost my way, for, pausing every now and then, I could hear no sound of water, so I sat down on the rocks by the wayside until some belated passerby should happen along and give me more definite directions. At last a countryman came slowly down the road and I hailed him.

'Can you tell me where the Falls of Ladore are?' I asked. The man paused in astonishment.

'Why, sir,' he said finally, 'you're a-sittin' in 'em.'

The fact was the falls had gone temporarily out of commission because of the dryness of the summer. Now, however picturesque the surroundings of a cataract may be, I maintain that a little water is necessary as well, and yet, thanks to our Canadian school books, I had waved Niagara contemptuously aside for this heap of dusty stones!

Canada always underestimates her own, and my reason for writing this article is to enlarge, if possible, her bump of self-appreciation; self-conceit, if you like. I have done it before in an instance which I shall relate, and so I do not despair even with so large a handful as the Dominion. Once when spending a winter in the lovely English watering place of Torquay, I took my map and walked towards the village of Babbacombe. Nearing the place I met the local policeman and asked him if there was anything worth seeing in Babbacombe.

'No,' he said slowly, 'there isn't. You ought to see Torquay, that's a great place.'

'But, I objected, 'I have just come from Torquay. You don't think it would be worth my while then to go on to Babbacombe?'

'Oh, no, sir,' he said, 'there's nothing a-goin' on there. I was born and bred in the place, and nothing much has happened ever since.'

Nevertheless, I continued my journey across the wind-swept down and came to the edge of a precipice, where an astonishing view burst upon me. The cliffs were of red sandstone, resembling in colour the Esterel mountains in Southern France; the water was as deeply blue as the Mediterranean, and down the densely-wooded Devonshire Combe, embowered in foliage, straggled the thatched roofs of the quaint old cottages of Babbacombe, the floor of one house level with the peak of another, and so on to the edge of the glittering sand, and the white line of foam from the rippling tide. On returning I again met the leisurely policeman.

'Look here,' I said, 'Babbacombe is the loveliest place I ever saw in my life. The next stranger you meet, tell him that whatever else he misses, he mustn't miss Babbacombe. The cliffs are the colour of the mountains of Judea, near Jerusalem; the water is as lovely as the Golden Horn at Constantinople.'

'Do you mean to tell me so, sir?' he asked, opening his eyes wide in astonishment.

'I do, and I don't want you to forget it either. A man who was born in such a place should be proud of it.'

When I looked back from away down the hill the policeman was still standing where I left him, gazing after me.

Six years passed before I met that policeman again. He did not recognize me, but I recognized him.

'Well, officer,' I said, 'I'm tramping on to Babbacombe. Is it worth while going there?'

'Worth while?' he cried, with enthusiasm, 'it's the prettiest village in the whole world; them as travels has told me so. Part o' Babbicom is just like Jerusalem, and another part is like Constantinople. You mustn't miss Babbicum, sir, for I was born and bred there.'

Now I should like to do for Canada what I did for that policeman. He got his similes rather mixed up, but he was on the right
track, and I believe he will remain on it until he is superannuated.

The thing that seems to me to stand in the way of the Canadian Walter Scott, is Canada's persistent undervaluation of her
own men and women. Mr Cooper in his article commented on the
fact that his six prigs dining in a private room had included no
modern author except Kipling and Stevenson, but what strikes
me as emblematical of their limited minds is, that not one of the
half dozen gave any chance to a Canadian. Mr W.A. Fraser, in his
address to the newspaper men, to which I took exception on this
same count, said that above all else we must have Truth, and he
spelt it with a capital T. I think there must be truth in fiction,
otherwise it will not live. It is probably the absence of truth in
the writing of Charles Dickens, all his pictures being exaggerations, and his character sketches, caricatures, which accounts for
his gradual decline, and which will account for the ultimate ex-
tinction of his work. Stevenson is another of the men chosen by
the learned six, and in some of his books he has ventured on American topics, which he treats with a lack of truth which must ever
distinguish the work of a foreigner writing of a country not his own.

'A man should write what is in his bones,' said Kipling once,
and the phrase has stuck to me ever since I heard it. Kipling
himself is the exception which goes to prove his own rule, for he
has written truthfully of a life which, so to speak, was not in his
bones, as is shown in his story of the fisher folk in 'Captains
Courageous.'

'The Master of Ballantrae' is generally admitted to be one of
Stevenson's most notable books, and the character of the Master
is drawn by a vigorous and sure hand, while an even more subtle

creation is the old servant, MacKellar, who tells the story. But the moment Stevenson brings his people across to America the element of truth escapes from his novel, and it goes to pieces. He has his company wander blundering through the north woods from Albany for something like three weeks, when anyone who knows the Indian and the time is well aware that every member of that company would be decently scalped and dead before they were half an hour in the forest. Stevenson has his Indians do what no Indian ever thought of doing. He has the aborigines stroll listlessly along the valley with the white foreigners gazing down on them from the ridge, when in reality the incident would have been the other way about.

This is what comes of dining in a private room in a city restaurant instead of camping out in the valley of the Don and learning the ways of Indians. I hope Mr Cooper will take his six, next time they are hungry, to the city limits on an electric car and treat them to a picnic where they may see the methods of the wilderness. If there had been a single original idea in the brains of the six they would have given a vote for at least one Canadian book, and so against their next meeting in a private room, I'll bestow upon them a hint. I shall not go to any author so well known as Gilbert Parker, whose splendid array of books is now heading the lists both in England and in the United States. I shall take a writer much less famous perhaps, but no less deserving of fame. In a book written by Mrs Harrison, of Toronto, entitled *The Forest of Bourg-Marie*, there is a chapter describing an ancient ruined chateau in Canada which has been made a store-house for furs by the grim old man who is the striking hero of the book. Not only has Robert Louis Stevenson, nor any one mentioned by the six, never written anything so striking as that description of the furs, but, to find its equal in literature, you will have to go back to the time of the Arabian Tales. I know nothing of Mrs Harrison beyond what may be surmised by a reading of her book, but I stake whatever little reputation I have on the statement that *The Forest of Bourg-Marie* is a notable work of genius, a book superb in its character drawing, noble in diction, thrilling in incident, and so strongly constructed that it dispenses with conventional love-making, without losing an atom of its interest, a feat which has not been accomplished, to my knowledge, since Robinson Crusoe, and I doubt if there is a novelist living, however famous, who would have the courage to put forth a romance without a heroine in it.

I must apologize to the immaculate six, for mentioning a work which emanates from mere Toronto.

Now what is the remedy; what can be done to get Canada out of the literary slough of despond in which it wallows? I think it will help to clear the way if we admit that, with the present generation, all effort is useless. The six cultured and educated men who dined in the private room are hopeless, and perhaps even I am not able to convince them that they are six egregious asses, holding the same literary opinions now to be found only in the colliery districts of England; opinions which have been discarded by men of intelligence everywhere else in the world. Our endeavour at reform must begin with the rising generation and so, if possible, an attempt should be made to civilize the school teachers of Canada. I am taking it for granted that the school books are nearly, if not quite, as bad as they were in my day, and I arrive at this estimate of them because the Inspector of Public Schools in an imperial city like Toronto holds good old matured literary opinions that are of the vintage of 1876. I doubt also if the Normal School has improved, and so it were useless to look to that institution for help in reclaiming the teachers. In my day the Normal School was a sort of educational pork-packing factory. It gathered in to itself the raw material from all parts of the Province, rushed it through the machine, scraped off some of the ignorance, but not much, and there stood the manufactured article, produced in so many minutes by the watch. I was captured from my native lair, soaked, scraped and so flung upon a defenceless Province, certified as being of correct weight and size, all in something less than four months.

We must get at the teachers direct. My plan is to place *The Canadian Magazine* into the hands of every teacher in Ontario. To expect the teachers to pay two dollars and a half a year for it is absurd; because Canada, although willing to lavish millions on railways or on telegraphs to the other end of the earth, is graspingly penurious where her teachers are concerned. She pays them meagre salaries, so that every woman among them is looking towards the day when she will get married, and every man is anxious for the time when he can step into something that will bring him in more money. My statistical hand-book of Canada shows that in the year 1887 there were something like five thousand schools in Ontario. I suppose that by this time the number has doubled. Placing the figure then at ten thousand, how are we to get the magazine into those ten thousand schools? Of course it would be a small matter and quite unnoticeable in the tax list if each school section in Canada were to appropriate two dollars and a half a year for the magazine, but to look for that is to look for an impossibility, although this would be the natural way out in a civilized community. I propose, therefore, to start a fund. I will place a hundred dollars in the hands of the Editor of

The Canadian Magazine if forty-nine other prigs, educated and cultured, will put up a like amount each; that would be five thousand dollars. I should expect the ten thousand teachers to subscribe on their own account fifty cents apiece, and I should expect the proprietors of *The Canadian Magazine*, on getting an order for ten thousand copies, to let us have them at a dollar a year, each subscription.

Then if I were the editor of the magazine I would get a number of the bright young people to write articles on the stirring historical events of Canada. The war of 1812 alone is a mine of wealth, and in the United States, not to mention Canada, there is a vast amount of ignorance regarding the outcome of that historical episode. What writer could wish for a more attractive hero than General Brock, or a more romantic character than Tecumseh? Where, even in the history of Scotland, is there an act of more womanly devotion than the night excursion taken by Mrs Secord through swamp and forest to warn her countrymen of the enemy's approach? Literally, the woods are full of incidents like these.

The recent success of *McClure's Magazine* in New York shows what can be done on these lines. Miss Ida M. Tarbell, a girl unheard of before the magazine was founded has been, as it were, the backbone of that publication. She began by writing a life of Abraham Lincoln, and is still at it, having sandwiched Napoleon between the two histories of the Martyred President, and I must confess I read the account of that great plain man's life with as intense an interest as I did some years ago, when the articles first appeared.

Now, in Canada there are hundreds of girls who are as bright, as clever, and as well educated as Miss Tarbell, but there is no opening for them in the Dominion. The United States' publications are closed to them because readers on the other side of the line are not interested in the historical annals of a foreign country. When I offered my first book, which dealt with the Fenian Raid in Canada, to a New York publisher he refused it, but said if I changed the venue of the incidents over to the States he would publish the book. 'We have no interest in Canada,' he added. Well, as I was unable to transport the Fenian Raid from the Province of Ontario to the State of New York, my book had to be published by another fellow, who took it with some reluctance, having exactly the same objection to it. This shows the disadvantage under which Canadian writers labour when they seek an outlet for their wares across the border.

Last year, when I visited one of the High Schools of Buffalo, I found on the desk of each teacher files of every New York magazine. Stories and articles from these magazines were read to the classes, explained and commented upon. Such a course not only interested, but brightened the pupils, and made them alert and up-to-date. I propose then that *The Canadian Magazine* be read in the Canadian schools; that the children should be taught something about the leading writers of the day, especially those who belong to Canada, or who write about Canada; that they should be taught something of the grandeur of their country, of its scenery and its history. They should be told that the important things of life are right around the schoolhouse door, and not over in England, or on any other distant shore. To this end I am ready to contribute a hundred dollars a year for the next five years, if there are forty-nine men in Canada willing to do the same. In such a way I think the chances of Canada producing a Sir Walter Scott or a Jane Austen from among the present boys and girls of

Canada will be considerably enhanced, and, perhaps, when the boys now in school grow up, they will be willing to buy more books and less whiskey.

The Measure of the Rule

Robert Barr

THE MEASURE OF THE RULE

CHAPTER I

Perhaps thou wert a Mason, and forbidden
By oath to tell the secrets of thy trade.
'ADDRESS TO AN EGYPTIAN MUMMY.

THE short winter day, increasingly cold, was drawing to a close as the train, ninety minutes late, came to a standstill under the lofty canopy of the Union Station. For hours and hours it had crunched along over a frozen land, losing time because of slippery rails and accumulated snow. With the ending of that railway journey a section of my own life had reached its conclusion; for, like the train that carried me, hitherto I had been losing time. On the previous day an ambitious friend, solemnly bidding me farewell, suddenly realized to the full the importance of the plunge I was making, and put the question—

" How old are you ? "

" Twenty-three," I replied. " How old are *you?*"

" Thank God, I'm only nineteen," was his fervent answer.

To-day, I being well on in years, there seems an element of humour in that brief conversation, but it was serious enough at the time, and, for a moment, this four years' handicap pressed its weight upon my shoulders.

I

Heretofore my life had been spent first in the labour of tilling a backwoods farm; second, in the labour of teaching a backwoods school. It is delightful to read in books about farming, and even the periodical press contains now and then articles upon agriculture so charmingly written that the reader is soon convinced of the simplicity, healthfulness and independence which a rural existence presents to its votaries, and as I peruse these contributions I am filled with a vague longing to go back to the land. Candour compels me to state, however, that at the time I was engaged in this vocation the prospects which look so well in print had not been presented to me. I was quite willing to leave to others the delights of raising wheat while I earned my bread in some other manner. Being thus determined to exchange the complex existence of a farm for the simple life of the city, I spent my evenings and wet days in study of one kind and another, reading everything in the shape of a book that came to my hands, discovering thus a very pretty taste for mathematics and science, finding algebra as interesting as the puzzle column in our weekly paper, while Euclid's problems seemed to be much better constructed than the average short story, with conclusions that were invariably more logical and satisfactory than the efforts of even our best authors, and thus it came about that one day I journeyed to our county town, passed certain examinations inflicted by the State, and emerged from the ordeal with a third-class certificate, licensing me to teach school for the term of three years from the date thereof.

I now got my first lesson regarding the nonsense talked by those charming writers who show the advantages of farming life. My day's work, instead of beginning anywhere from four to six o'clock in the morning, started at nine, and ended at four, while my recompense was half-a-dozen times the amount I could have earned at farm work, though I toiled all day and half the night. I have owned farms since that time, but laboured on them merely by proxy, earning my bread, as Artemus Ward said, by the sweat of the hired man's brow.

The forced economy of the farm was part of my nature, so I determined in that three years covered by my teacher's certificate to save enough money to enable me to grapple with a college. I knew that my future lay along one of two paths: mathematics or science. Science fascinated me, and on more than one occasion I had nearly blinded myself with premature explosions. A young man with a lean purse, and thirty miles between him and the nearest chemist's shop, one would think had little opportunity for research, nevertheless so successful were some of my experiments that the inhabitants of the house where I boarded were compelled on several occasions to camp out in the green fields while the breezes of heaven blew noxious vapours through the open windows. I achieved in some sort a local reputation, but the desire to have me board at some one else's house became exceedingly general throughout our neighbourhood. I dreamed of ultimately receiving the thanks of the Royal Society by discovering some new and particularly objectionable compound.

On the other hand, there was a chance that I might be a success in mathematics, perhaps as a grave college professor, or who knows what else. A young man whose taste for light reading is such that he goes through six books of Euclid like a ravaging bush-fire, and yearns for more, seems adapted for progression along that line.

At the moment when the respective claims of mathematics and science swung in equal adjustment, there was slowly approaching me across the fields and through the woods a young man of my own age who was destined to settle the matter. Looking out of the window of the white school-house on the hill one afternoon, I saw this young man with bent back and wide-spread legs in the field below, peering through a little telescope on a tripod. He was making incantations with his hands, waving now the right, now the left, and far down the valley stood another chap, holding upright a red and white wooden pole taller than himself, which he adjusted this way or that in response to the manual signs made by his chief. I knew at once what was afoot. These were the advance scouts of the railway which had been talked about for years and years. Nobody in the neighbourhood believed it would ever be built, and yet the other day I read that the world's record of railway speed had been broken along the line this young man was surveying.

It was nearly four o'clock in the afternoon, and as no pupil is likely to complain if the school is dismissed a few minutes too soon, I let the class go, climbed a fence, crossed a field, and struck up an acquaintance with the civil engineer. The young man was as glad to meet me as I was to meet him, for as the sun declined he became anxious about a stopping place for the night. On this point I was able to relieve his mind. I lived at a house some two miles further west, and there I assured him he could secure a room, and something to eat, such as it was. He was accompanied by a retinue of axe men who slashed their way through the forest when tall timber intercepted the line. The choppers were a rough crowd, given to profanity and chewing tobacco. Their days were employed in cutting a straight and narrow path, but not necessarily in following it. This gang slept in barns, with or without permission, or in the woods if night overtook them there. So, indeed, did the civil engineer and his super, who carried the wooden pole, when they could do no better, but the two young men preferred more civilized environment when they could get it.

We spent a red-letter evening after supper. The engineer was an excellent story-teller, and he recited extract after extract out of a book then just published, entitled *The Innocents Abroad*, written by a man I had never heard of, named Mark Twain. I resolved to buy the book, for the author seemed to have touched on several points overlooked by my ancient comrade, Euclid. But the most startling thing I learned that evening was the compensation received by an engineer running a railway line. The sum seemed incredible in its hugeness, and I resolved at once to join so lucrative a profession. I wrote to the University several hundred miles away, asking particulars of the civil engineering course, and received a printed slip of paper which gave a list of books, and various interesting items from which I gathered that two years from entering the University I might, if reasonably diligent, write C.E. after my name. And thus it was that on a particular evening in the early part of January I found myself one of the crowd emerging from the train at the Union Station of the city that contained the University.

Leaving my trunk in custody of the railway company, and taking only a small hand-bag, for I should need to stop at an hotel for a night or two, until I learned whether I should be assigned rooms at the University, or be directed to lodgings outside, I walked up a slight hill, and came to the main street of the town, the crisp snow creaking under my feet. The weather was intensely cold, but very dry, and the air seemed as exhilarating as if some magician had taken all the nitrogen out of it. I needed no stimulant, however, for I was already in a state of such exaltation that the snow I trod might have been the clouds of heaven. Although the lamps were lit in two long lines, stretching so far that they seemed to merge into one another, on either side of the main street, darkness had not yet set in. I stood for a moment, and gazed down past the Union Station to the great lake upon whose shore the city stood. To the eye it was as expansive as the ocean, for in the clearest day no man can see to the other side. Motionless it lay, and sailless; frozen, and pure white with the wreathed snow that covered it to the horizon. Along the water front rose innumerable masts of ships locked in the iron grip of winter. A mile or more away a curved island partially enclosed a bay that faced the city, and the surface of this bay, dark as slate, was of smooth, clear ice, from which the wind seemed to have swept every vestige of snow.

In the deepening gloom it looked like a liquid lake forgotten by the frost, and this illusion was strengthened by two or three belated ice-yachts skimming over its surface, their huge sails, out of all proportion to the hulls, making them, in the haze of distance, to resemble low-flying gulls of incredible swiftness. The street cars were gliding along on runners, tuneful bells jingling on the necks of the horses; the rails temporarily abandoned under the snow. But I did not patronize the company. My tip for the next two years was rigid economy, and it cost nothing to walk. On my right hand I passed a huge hotel, which seemed to me the largest in the world, occupying the greater part of a whole city block. That hotel might be mine some day after the letters C.E. had been attached to my name, but not to-night, yet poverty seemed simply a good joke, a merely temporary inconvenience. Life was full of such amazing possibilities. I had just stepped across the threshold of the world, so I snapped my fingers at the big hotel, and cried aloud—

"Some day, my friend, we'll meet again."

Reaching the market square, I found the tavern of which I was in search, and there, with an overpowering feeling of being a prince at large, I ordered a room, and hanged the expense. After securing the room I enjoyed the evening meal in a dining-room so huge and gaudily lighted that it gave me the feeling the Prodigal Son must have experienced when he first set out to squander his share of the property. Often have I looked at the outside of this commonplace commercial hotel since the time of which I write, and have restrained the inclination to approach the cook, and say to him—

"If you can give me what I had when I first dined with you twenty years ago, I will pay you unquestioned the rates of the most expensive hotel in the world."

The astonished man would probably reply that the fare of to-day is infinitely superior to that provided in the last century, and such may be the case, but he could never supply the delicious sense of semi-wickedness which his hostelry formerly bestowed upon me: a thrill which belonged to twenty-three, graphically described by Magda as being "on the loose." Many morals have been pointed from the career of the Prodigal Son, but no one has yet pictured the young man's hilarious sense of freedom while his funds lasted.

After dinner I went out to view my newly-acquired kingdom. The clear-cut moon had risen glittering and cold, and seemingly so near as to be neighbour to the city and part of its municipal lighting scheme. The streets presented all the splendour of an Arabian tale transported north; the shops were ablaze with light; the pavement thronged with an effervescent people. The street was musical with the tinkle of silver-tongued bells, and alive with the swift motion of spirited horses and gliding sleighs. This capital was a city of hilarious youth, with the riches of the world displayed behind sheets of plate-glass, transparent as curtains of dew.

As I had already traversed the main streets from the Union Station to the market-place, I now broke new ground and struck north along a thoroughfare scarcely less distinguished than the one I had left. This, I knew vaguely, led to the University, whose building I had never seen except in a picture. As I wandered farther and farther north the pavement became less and less crowded. The shops out here were beginning to close, and by and by I found myself alone. The name of a side street attracted my attention. It was Park Avenue, and I turned to the left, walking underneath a canopy of trees through which the moonlight filtered, and came at last to the entrance of an extensive park, beautifully undulating, with its coverlet of snow, dazzlingly pure under the ascending moon, its million points of frost scintillating in the cold radiance, like diamond dust on the gown of a bride. Gigantic trees were grouped here and there, as if they formed the rear-guard of the ever-retreating primeval forest which, within the memory of living man, had covered these plains; or, rather, they seemed sentinels forgotten, standing frozen at their posts, like Napoleon's veterans in the disastrous march from Moscow. The night was intensely still, and I stood there as much alone as if I had never left the frost-bound farm in the west. The cultured park, with its formal gravel walks, its trim parterres and beds for summer flowers, had lapsed back to Nature under the all-covering mantle of snow, until now it was very brother to the farm. It seemed impossible to believe that but half-an-hour ago I had been jostled by the multitude.

And yet in this solitude the works of man over-topped the works of God. Above the tall trees rose the taller Norman tower of University College, strong and staunch in solid stone; square and battlemented, with its round turret in the corner, like a military castle set up on the battle-ground, where savagery and ignorance had waged its in-effectual warfare with civilization and enlightenment. I pressed through the miniature forest to the other side, and there before me stood the most magnificent structure I had ever seen: the centre of a landscape almost blinding white, with the moonlight shining full upon this noble edifice. I fancy I was enthralled with the same emotion that agitates a devout pilgrim when from the hills he sees for the first time the dome of St. Peter's in Rome. Here, like a dream-palace, was the fulfilment of dreams, and as I leaned against a tree and gazed upon it, my eyes filled with tears, until the vision became dimmed as if a cloud had overcast the moon. It all seemed unreal, and unreal it was, so far as I was concerned, for another man had once stood as I was standing there: his name was Moses, and he viewed the Promised Land.

All along the extended front no light was visible; its numerous windows gazed blindly at the moon. These sightless panes, without a friendly gleam behind any one of them, began to oppress me with a loneliness that was almost intolerable; my exaltation subsided, and gradually died in a shiver of desire to hear a friendly voice. I retraced my steps down into the bustling city once more, yet, strangely enough, the loneliness was not lifted. All these gay, laughing people were conversing with each other on their mutual concerns, and I was an outsider. I had merely exchanged the lonesomeness of the solitude for the greater lonesomeness of the unknown crowd. Thinking of absent friends, I remembered a note written before dinner to announce my safe arrival in the city, and inquiring for the nearest letter-box, was directed to the post-office itself, into whose maw I dropped my missive. Near the post-office stood a striking building of stone, with flat pillars running from the pavement to its very eaves, giving to it an unusual appearance, which may or may not have been good architecture. Asking its purpose of a passer-by, he told me it was a temple of a noted fraternity. This secret organization I had joined the day I was twenty-one, and eligible. I asked if a Lodge met there that night, and the man laughed, taking me doubtless for what I was, a green countryman.

"There are probably two or three in session at this moment, as it is the home of many Lodges.

The porter in the entrance hall will give you more exact information if you wish it," and so the stranger passed on.

I stood there gazing at the Temple as a while before I had gazed at the College. Inside were sworn brothers of mine, so why not pluck up courage, enter, and greet them? I had every right, and was well up in the ritual. A reluctance to thrust myself thus upon strangers held me back for a few hesitating minutes, but I said to myself that a civil engineer should be a bold man if he is to succeed; so I crossed to the Temple, and interviewed the custodian. He gave me the choice of several Lodges, and when I had made my selection, conducted me into an ante-room, where, presently, two brethren came out, asked me a number of questions, shook hands, and invited me inside.

An initiation was going forward, so I tip-toed to the first seat available, and there sat until the end. When the function was finished, a general movement and mix-up of members immediately took place. The two who had introduced me now sought me out.

"We are all about to adjourn from labour to refreshment," said one. "Is there any friend among our members with whom you would like to sit?"

"No," I replied; "I do not know a soul in the whole city. I came up to-day from the western country, and expect to begin attendance at the University to-morrow."

"Ah," said my new friend, "then that's why you came to this Lodge. We call ourselves the Educational Lodge of the city."

"Then I hope that's a good omen," I replied. "I must admit I made my choice in ignorance.

The man down-stairs mentioned the Lodges in session, and I chose this one purely by accident."

"In that case," continued the one that had spoken, "we'll place you beside Professor Bruit."

"Nonsense," cried the other, "if he attends the University for the next three or four years, he'll see more than enough of Bruit, who's as dry as a stick. We can do better for him than that. Let us introduce him to Dr. Darnell. He has some sense of humour."

"You forget," objected the first, "that the Doctor's own institution opens this week, and he is always like a bear for several days before."

"Oh, come now," his colleague protested, "I never knew the Doctor bring his renowned discipline into a Lodge-room. He is a Prince of School-masters and a Doctor of Divinity, but he mixes with us *incog*. and leaves the pedagogue at home."

I threw a dash of oil on the waves of discussion.

"I am myself in a small way a peasant of school-masters, so I insist on meeting my Prince."

The two men laughed, and the one who had demurred, said—

"That settles it; you are the victim of Dr. Darnell," and with this he hailed a man whom I had already differentiated from the rest, wondering who he was. The crowd in the Lodge-room was filtering through an open doorway, which gave a glimpse beyond of a long table, set for supper. Dr. Darnell seemed to have forgotten all about the call from labour to refreshment, for, quite alone, he paced up and down the emptying Lodge-room with head bent and hands clasped behind him, meditating on some problem, with a deeply-marked frown on his broad brow, seemingly as oblivious of companionship

as if he were alone in his own study. The dome
of his head was bald, and on each side of his face
stood out bristling whiskers of an aggressive red.
His features were strongly marked and clean cut,
and his eyes, when he raised them from the floor,
seemed to scintillate with chilly grey light that
penetrated me like X-rays. When he was aroused
from his reverie, introduced, and had turned his
regard upon me, I felt, under that flash of appraise-
ment, that I was instantaneously judged, condemned,
and cast aside. My sponsor gave me a genial
introduction.

"Dr. Darnell," he said, "I want to make you
acquainted with Brother Thomas Prentiss, who
comes from the western land, and has journeyed to
the East, like a true member of our fraternity, in quest
of wise men, and so we instantly thought of you."

"Ah," said the D.D., and if brevity is the soul
of wit, the Doctor of Divinity had scored in his curt
salutation. He shook hands with no undue cordiality, and bestowed upon me another lance-like
glance, which the two men simultaneously inter-
preted. and one of them hastened to reassure the
Prince of Schoolmasters.

"Mr. Prentiss is not coming under your tutelage,
Doctor, but aspires to be an undergraduate at the
University."

"Ah," said the Doctor again, giving a slight
inflection of relief to the exclamation.

Our quartette now moved towards the dining-
room, my conductors vying with each other in
cheerful conversation about nothing in particular,
probably to mitigate the frigid reception accorded
me by the learned schoolmaster, while one at least
may have cherished a hope that the Doctor himself

would thaw even slightly, and merit the reputation
he had received of being a humorist, but he walked
in silence to the table, and contented himself by
indicating the chair adjoining him, with a wave of
his hand. Upon this chair I seated myself, as
tongue-tied as he, and we were left by the other two
to make the best of it. I deeply regretted that I had
paraded my University aspirations to the examiners,
who seemed to be cheerful, commonplace persons of
a companionable nature, and therefore blithe company, whom I should have preferred to the taciturn
pundit seated beside me.

The feast was very simple; sandwiches of various
kinds, white and brown bread, and pressed beef.
For drink we were given the choice of coffee, beer,
or Rhine wine, and I saw that the majority of my
brethren on each side of the long table took the wine
in glasses of a peculiar shape that was new to me.
Up to this point in my existence I had never tasted
any beverage that was intoxicating in its nature, so
I bespoke a glass of wine without the least intention
of emptying it, resolving to satisfy my curiosity with
a sip, and then fall back upon the more familiar
coffee. I had an idea that wine was a seductive fluid
of such enticing qualities that if once a man indulged
in it he needed great strength of mind to withstand
the liquid lure that would ultimately draw him on
to destruction. I was sure I possessed great strength
of mind, and therefore might with safety dally for
one brief moment with the charmer, and so gather a
new experience. I expected it to taste like a glorified, sublimely sweet lemonade, and was certain that
a thimble-full would not make an inebriate of me.
If there was exhilaration in the cup, I wanted it
then, for a deep depression weighed upon me, and

the loneliness of the streets had returned. I was with the brethren, but not of them. Every man there except myself was acquainted with the others, while I was a stranger within the gates, and as the very name of the Rhine possessed an aroma of romance; of old-world medievalism; I took to the cup, hoping in my moderation that it would cheer but not inebriate me.

" So here's to the brew of history and of fiction," said I to myself.

Another disappointment awaited me. Could this sour, otherwise tasteless stuff be the Rhine wine celebrated in song by the great poets? I could scarcely swallow it. The Doctor on my left was comforting himself with a tankard of beer. He asked me curtly how I liked the city, and in the midst of answering, I saw he was not listening, and he paid no heed when my sentence stopped abruptly in the middle. I suppose some problem was occupying his mind, but every now and then a consciousness that he was by way of being my host seemed to prick him, arousing him momentarily to a sense of duty, whereupon he shot a quick question at me, and relapsed into his reverie during my answer.

" Do you go to church?" was his unexpected demand.

At the time I was feeling particularly wicked, because of the glass of wine at my elbow.

" Yes," I answered, so shortly that he had not time to slip into his brown study again.

" I am Rector of Holy Trinity," he snapped. " Many University students attend. I shall be pleased to see you there any Sunday."

" Thank you," said I.

So he was a clergyman. I had gathered from

what the two men said that he was connected with some educational institution, but the discipline they spoke of doubtless meant church discipline. In calling him the Prince of Schoolmasters they probably referred to a former occupation, for many of our ministers had graduated from the teacher's desk. I caught myself wondering what sort of sermons he preached, and arrived at the conclusion that he would come out strong in the denunciation of his fellow-creatures. Never before had I met a man who made me feel so absolutely worthless, and of a consequence, so despondent and gloomy. I knew I was going to fail in this city. My place was in the rural community which I had so heedlessly deserted. How could I hope to compete with such alert and capable men as lined this table? An air of prosperity surrounded each. I had heard more than one called by a well-known name, and others I recognized by having seen their pictures in the newspapers, but instead of being inspired, I was humbled and crushed. My lips were dry, and my throat parched with the hot discomfort that filled my frame at being unable to say a word or a sentence that was worth listening to, and although half the glass of Rhine wine was gone, I took another sip, for sour and noxious as it was, it still moistened the vocal cords if my benumbed brain should give them any work to do. The confusion at my own unworthiness was masked by the ever-increasing volume of conversation up and down the table. There broke out bursts of laughter every now and then as some one told a good story, and I could not but smile in sympathy, wishing luck had placed me in one or other of the groups to hear the tales. Imperceptibly my spirits began to rise. After all, the hope of the city lay in its diet of youth from the country. The man whom they called Senator, at the upper end of the table, one of those I had recognized from his portrait, I remembered now had worked as a lad at the carpenter's bench, and there he sat, a rubicund millionaire, and a power in the political world; stout, it is true, but laughing with the heartiness of a boy as he tossed off his Rhine wine. Gazing intently at him, his eyes met mine, as is so often the case. With a smile he raised his glass.

"I drink wine with you, sir," he said.

I noticed my own glass was full again. I lifted it, saluted him in return, and drank. After all, it wasn't so sour as I first thought it to be. Why should I allow myself to be depressed by the discourtesy of any Doctor of Divinity, and mentally I used the two "d's" to indicate an adjective before the term. Curse his patronage and his estimate and his sizing up! A man's a man for a' that, and I was as good as he, and probably ran as great a chance of salvation.

"Are you going in for a B.A.?" I heard him say.

"No, C.E."

"But they don't teach civil engineering at our University College."

"I beg your pardon, sir, they do. I wrote to the University and received printed particulars of the C.E. course. It takes two years."

"You are mistaken," said the Doctor, with the frown of a man who does not like to be contradicted. "The University examines, and confers the degree, but University College does not teach civil engineering."

I laughed, and patted him on the shoulder. He

2

seemed to stiffen under my touch, and an expression came into his face that would have frozen an ordinary man, but it seemed to me as comical as that of a clown in a circus.

"My dear Doctor," I cried, "there are still a lot of things for you yet to learn in this world."

I had conquered him at last. He drew a deep sigh.

"That is true; that is true," he said almost in a whisper.

"After all," thought I to myself, "there's nothing like standing up to these chaps who think they can put other fellows down. I have shown him I am not such a fool as I look."

A group opposite, who had noticed my condescending salutation of the Doctor, at first with amazement, as if they were witnessing something never seen before, which indeed was the case, now shook with laughter, raised their glasses, and we drank together. At last every one rose to his feet. The Master had given a toast, and we all drank.

"Gentlemen, you may smoke," he said, as we sat down again. And now a tall man was on his feet amidst a great rattle of tankards on the table, and he sang, in a deep, strong, bass voice, of which I had never heard the equal; never heretofore had suspected there could be such singing—

> My home is in the cellar here,
>   Upon a cask I'm seated,
> And every wine that heart can cheer
>   To me is freely meted.
> The cellar-man deserves my praise,
>   From duty never shrinking,
> He deftly fills the glass I raise
>   When I'm drinking, drinking, drinking.

Good lord, this was glorious!   Here was where the city outdid the country. We had nothing like it where I came from. As he sat down amidst well-earned applause—

"Bravo!" I shouted; "Bravo!" and the cry was taken up.

"Encore!" I roared. They would see I understood one French word at least.

"Encore, encore!" shouted the rest, and the singer with a smile of gratification was on his feet again, bowing diagonally along the table to me. I held aloft the Rhine wine, and spilled a little down my sleeve. Again we were favoured with a magnificent bass song.

"By Jove! that was good," I said to the Doctor.

The tobacco smoke had become so thick that it seemed to obscure my vision a little, but the Doctor's face reminded me somehow of cast iron. This being funny, I quite naturally laughed, but my attention was turned to the Master, who was on his feet again. He said something about their hospitable Order, and their delight in welcoming the stranger. All men were brothers. It was his pleasure to propose the health of their guest, coupled with the name of the gentleman from the West.

I was about to rise, when I felt a grip of steel on my left wrist. For some reason the Doctor was holding me down in my chair, and when he himself rose he placed his right hand on my shoulder that I might be kept there. They drank, there was a cheer, and they all sat down again. The chairman spoke my name, and a cry of "Prentiss! Prentiss!" echoed along the table.

This was not the first time I had addressed an assembly, with more or less success. On former occasions I had spoken on my feet to uncritical gatherings composed of friends, neighbours and acquaintances, yet I had always approached the platform with a feeling of trepidation. Here I was to hold forth to a much more important audience than I had ever before faced, yet all diffidence had vanished. Never had my mind been so diabolically clear. Never before had such barbed shafts of wit lain ready for my use, and probably never again would such a store-house of humorous anecdotes to emphasize my points hold its doors open for me. For once the hour and the man had coincided. Fear and humility had vanished, and in their place had come a malignant determination to show Dr. Darnell that I was a person to be reckoned with. All the rest of the audience were merely the strings of the harp I would play upon, but Dr. Darnell, D.D., I would make sit up as surely as he had held me down physically a moment before, and held me down mentally the whole evening. In this mellow glow of self-satisfaction there was only one thing that troubled me. My knees had become universal joints, and I knew if they got the slightest encouragement they would certainly give way in some unexpected direction; backwards, for instance, like the hind legs of a horse. It was annoying that at the very moment I had reached the apex of mental perfection, my legs should unexpectedly show signs of refusing to support a brain animated by such genius. However, by holding them excessively rigid, I hoped to control those joints which had so surprisingly developed ball-bearings during the evening. The silence showed me it was time to begin. My voice, although it proved far off, was nevertheless as flexible as my knee-joints, and much more under control. I do not remember a word I said, but I knew from the second sentence that I had gripped my audience. Then there was a ripple of laughter, and a few moments later a roar, and from that time on until the conclusion, my address and my stories were given in the intervals between laughter and applause. I had my hearers on the run, and knew it, exultant, monarch of all I surveyed. At last I launched my supreme story. I had intended that for the end, but now I saw I was so great an orator that I could speak to them all night. In the tempest of sound that followed the narrative, I again felt the steel grip on my wrist, and a slight downward jerk. I had no intention of taking my seat, but that jerk was something my knees had not calculated upon, and they spread. Seated thus, entirely contrary to my intention, I turned round fiercely to the Doctor, and was astonished dimly to perceive that those eagle eyes were moist, and yet sparkled with that indication of humour with which he had been accredited, but all sign of which had hitherto been lacking. In the tumultuous uproar which continued and continued, his whisper came sharp as a lancet to my consciousness.

"It's all right, my boy. The success of a speech depends on knowing when to sit down. Don't open your mouth again to-night either to drink or speak, and you will have scored one of the finest oratorical successes I have ever heard."

I drew a deep breath of satisfaction, partially realizing that it was this man's commendation I had been working for, and not the boisterous applause I was receiving. I heard the strains of "For he's a jolly good fellow," and then came hand-shaking which chased away for the time a languorous desire for going to sleep. They helped me on with my overcoat, which was unduly heavy, and I doubted if it were mine. I think there was some friendly competition about seeing me to my hotel, but drowsy as I was, I remember Dr. Darnell's decided dictum that this pleasure devolved upon him. When we reached the street the keen, cold air roused me for the moment, but the increased frost had made the pavement underfoot slippery and difficult to stand on.

"You'd better take my arm," said the Doctor.

"Then we'll both fall," I laughed. "The ground is as slippery for you as for me."

"Not to-night," replied the Doctor grimly.

The street was silent and deserted. I was still baffled by the trouble with my knees, and was seized with a great desire to collapse and let it go at that. A wave of oblivion came over me like a whiff of laughing gas, and unexpectedly I found myself standing in the dimly-lit hall of the hotel, and by a mysterious necromancy, which I could not fathom, the Doctor had been transmogrified into a porter, who seemingly wished to conduct me to my room, an offer that I rejected with some indignation. The man, in a huff, said—

"Oh, very well. No use of making a fuss about it," and I walked, stiff and dignified, in a straight line down the hall to the stairway, humming nonchalantly, "My home is in this cellar here," to show the porter, who was undoubtedly gazing after me, that I knew what I was about; then, fearing a trap door, for there is more wickedness in cities than in the country, I cautiously climbed the stairs on hands and knees, thus anticipating Mr. David Balfour's ascent of his uncle's ruined stair. I reached my room triumphant.

CHAPTER II

Down came the storm and smote amain
The vessel in its strength.
           'WRECK OF THE HESPERUS.'

THE annals of next morning have frequently been written, and are sad reading. I regret, for the sake of the warning they might convey, that my experiences differed from those of the printed word. Perhaps my strenuous rural training had warded off the effects I was entitled to, for I had no headache, no parched throat or woolly feeling in the mouth, and no remorse. I confess to some uneasiness regarding what I had said the night before, of which not the faintest recollection remained beyond a misty remembrance of being on my feet, having trouble with my knees, and talking. Not one of those who were gathered round the table could I recognize if I met him again, except Dr. Darnell, who remained in my mind vivid as chiselled marble, and I prayed I might never more on this earth encounter him; indeed, the chance of a future meeting was so remote that I brushed my uneasiness aside, and set my face towards the future. One conventional thing I did, which was to resolve I should never look upon the wine again, when it was white or red, and thus obey the Scriptures.

I was astonished to find myself with my clothes and boots on. The wonder was that I had escaped freezing, for the morning was intensely cold, and although the sun shone brilliantly outside, its rays made no impression on the frosted pane, and my pitcher was full of solid ice. I rang for something more liquid, and took a long draught of it when it arrived, with a keen enjoyment of its cool refreshment. A wash and brush-up, a clean collar and tie, prepared me for the hot breakfast down-stairs, to which a rural appetite did ample justice. Yesterday was a day that did not count; a mere interlude between the end of one section of life and the beginning of another, and so out into the street, breathing an air so crisp and exhilarating that it almost became competitor to the Rhine wine. Early as it was, the streets were already thronged. This thoroughfare appeared to be the busiest in the world, and the huge commercial buildings on either side spoke of unlimited wealth to a young fellow with very little money at his command. I was keenly enjoying the novelty of my environment when suddenly I became aware of a beaming face and an outstretched hand.

"Good-morning. I'm glad to see you looking as fresh as a snow-drift."

"Not as white, I hope."

"No, you're all right, and a good healthful colour. I say, my son, you did rub it into old Darnell last night. I never enjoyed myself so much in my life. You see, he's rather sarcastic sometimes, and to tell you the truth, we're all a little afraid of him. They say his books on education are A1, though I've never read any of them myself, and to see you take him on his own ground, and simply mop the floor with him, was too rich for words, and I tell you, my boy, I agree with every word you said, and so did every one there."

"Did they?" I gasped.

"Yes, your comparison of the teacher and the preacher was masterly. Of course, as you said, the future of the nation rests with the teacher, and not with the preacher. The one works with humanity at the malleable age, the other attempts to influence those whose characters and opinions are hardened and fixed, but the moment we realized old Darnell was having some home truths thrust upon him, which many of us had thought but none dared say, the interest was intensified. You should have seen his face. It was a study in conflicting emotions. You see he is not only one of our leading clergymen, but also perhaps our most notable teacher, so while you were scoring off one half of him, as it were, you pleased the other half, and I could see the old man didn't quite know how to take it. I saw a look almost of terror come into his eyes when you began to tell stories. I suppose he thought that finding yourself in the company of men—— Oh, well, I don't know what he thought—but as the stories were all right, he laughed just as heartily as any one. You must join our Lodge. Get a demit from the Temple you hail from, and be one of us while you're in the city.''

I shook my head. '' I've no money to spare,'' I said. '' I have two strenuous years ahead of me at the University, and just barely enough to carry me through with the strictest economy.''

'' Are you on your way to the University now ?''

'' Yes.''

The man looked at me with that expression of envy with which elderly middle-age sometimes regards ambitious youth.

'' Lucky devil,'' he said.

'' Are you on your way to business so early as this ?''

'' Yes,'' he replied. '' I generally get there before

my clerks do. That's my establishment," and he waved his hand towards an immense block that housed a hive of retail industries.

"Are you the owner of that name?" I asked, nodding towards the huge sign across the end of the store towards us, familiar in big letters on the advertising pages of the daily papers.

"Yes," he replied.

"Lucky devil," said I, and we laughed and parted, never to meet again.

So now I knew the subject of my discourse, and it frightened me to think that a man might lose touch with his brain and remember nothing of what he had spoken. Again I resolved to leave wine alone in future, thanking my stars that I had seemingly got off so cheaply in my first encounter.

All was bustle and rush when I reached the University. The splendid edifice seemed to me as soul-satisfying in the sunlight as it had appeared in the mystery of the night before, and the interior was no less impressive and medieval than the outside. Just within the hall a group of young men were studying written and printed communications tacked to a notice-board against the wall. Another boisterous company besieged the door of some official near the entrance, who, breathless and worried, was answering questions. I wished to put a few queries to this official myself, but I thought I had better wait until the present scramble was done with.

Groups of three and four stood here and there exchanging greetings after the Christmas holidays. Solitary, studious individuals paced slowly up and down reading, or sat with books in the embrasures of the mullioned windows.

I had come from a land of wood. The houses were

of wood smoothed by the plane; the much larger barns were of rough wood from the saw, the former painted white, sometimes with shutters of green, the latter rarely touched, even by whitewash. Here and there the log house still existed, and the framed house was considered a long stride towards a more perfect civilization. In our building out west there had been little attempt at ornamentation, except, perhaps, at the cornices. The architectural aspect of the western landscape was strictly utilitarian, and the houses were so much alike that they might all have been built by the same man, which indeed, within the range of eye, they usually were. Every carpenter was his own architect, an art in which he had received not the slightest training, nor did he or his clients feel the least need of it. To-day, in the same district, there is an era of brick, supposed to be another step forward.

Here, then, I stood in an edifice of hewn, rough, and carven stone, with stained-glass windows, with cloisters, with long echoing halls, with ceilings of timber. The architect, I was told, had wandered in Europe, visiting ancient seats of learning, and here, from the Aladdin's lamp of his experience, had conjured up in the new world a dream of the old. I had always loved to read of bygone times, and in spite of the modern young men around me, in spite of my own modernness, and in the teeth of the fact that I was about to begin the study of the most unromantic, practical profession in the world, the glamour of medievalism was over me, and I felt as if I were taking part in some pageant of the past in a mouldering castle or college or monastery. It seemed incredible that such luck should be mine, and I found it difficult to understand the nonchalant air with which my fellow students bore their great privilege, feeling certain it would never become common to me through months of custom.

In the midst of my exultation a deep bell tolled in the Norman tower. The solemn sonorousness of the peal was in keeping with the character of the place, falling mellow on the ear like the note of a distant cathedral chime.

While the air still quivered with melody the hall emptied itself, the scholars, active and passive, trooping off in one direction or the other, until I found myself deserted. School had begun. I sought the man in the little office to learn my own part in the programme, but he also had disappeared. I went down the hall, and caught a glimpse of a belated student's coat-tails whisking up a stair. Him I followed, and came at last through an open door into the upper part of what looked like the gallery of a theatre, where I sank unobserved on the end of the uppermost semi-circular seat. The class was all assembled in curved terraces step by step below me, and at the bottom, on a little platform, stood a middle-aged man talking in an easy conversational tone about Roman history. I had evidently got into a room that I should not see again, for, excellent road-builders as the Romans undoubtedly were, the record of their strenuous lives would be of small assistance in aiding me to pass an examination in civil engineering. However, the lecture was interesting, and I sat out the session even though I had no blank book in which to take down those notes that kept all the others busily employed.

I next drifted into a class-room devoted to chemistry, and there felt more at home, for I was reasonably well versed in the subject. I was fascinated by the personality of the grim old man whose spectacled eyes glared upon me now and then, for he was of sinister celebrity in our land. Something of the mantle of the hangman fell in invisible folds from his shoulders. In murder cases where poison had been used, his unerring analysis had sent many a criminal to the gallows. On a table by his side stood some instruments of glass, and a servitor handed to him this or that as he needed it, or brought from the laboratory whatever had been forgotten, or was suddenly required. I think it was not imagination that gave me the impression of his glasses flashing oftener at me than at any one else in that gallery, for at last he whispered to his underling, who disappeared at once, and returned shortly after empty-handed. The keen-eyed old professor had detected a foreign body in the human mixture before him.

Absorbed in an experiment, I was startled by a slight tap on the shoulder, almost as if the analyst before me had passed upon my case, and now I was arrested in the name of the law. Looking round, I saw that the official of the little office near the entrance had tip-toed in. He motioned with his finger for me to follow him. I did so without disturbing the class, and caught another dazzling glance from the spectacles as I departed. That glance sent a shiver of apprehension down my spine, for the grisly professor, with his long claws and his hooked nose, looked like some ill-omened bird of prey that would yet be my undoing unless I used the pistol instead of poison.

My conductor, without a word, led me along the hall, and knocked at a door, opened it softly, ushering me in with a slight wave of the hand, closing the door in silence when I had entered. I found myself in a small, extremely cosy library, oblong in shape, lined with books in rich leathern bindings. An open fire burned brightly on the hearth, at the further end, and before it stood a man who was, I surmised at once and correctly, the Head of the University. His face resembled that of Mr. Gladstone, and was surrounded by a plentiful crop of hair, pure white. His whole attitude and expression may be summed up in the one word, benign. Instinctively a person liked him and trusted him. His feet were set well apart, his back to the blaze, and with the forefinger of his right hand he was tapping the lid of a snuff-box, looking at me the while over the top of his glasses with a most benevolent regard. A slight smile hovered about his lips, aiding and abetting an equally slight twinkle in the eye, as if the snuff were particularly good which he was now partaking of by shaking forefinger and thumb alternately at each nostril.

" I think I have not had the pleasure of meeting you before," he began, and his velvet tones gave one the impression that this had been a great deprivation, now happily ended. He tapped the snuff-box again, and treated himself with an air of distinction to another duplex inhalation.

" I am here," I said, " to begin a two years' course in civil engineering."

" Ah," said the old gentleman, the exclamation long drawn out, the pinch of snuff arrested midway between the box and the nose. " The University grants the degree, but civil engineering is not yet taught in the College. Not yet, not yet."

He lingered over the words with an intonation of regret. The smile faded from his lips, and the twinkle from his eye, for my face must have shown my bitter disappointment. It was the same information that I had so light-heartedly received the night before from Dr. Darnell, and to which I had paid so little heed that it had not served even to soften the blow which now authoritatively fell.

"Thank you, sir. Good-day," was all I could bring myself to say. I reached for the door-handle, and had some difficulty in finding it. He saw I was hard hit.

"One moment," he said, and I faced him again. He was taking great pinches of snuff with reckless extravagance from the open box, and the powder was descending from finger and thumb in a drizzling brown mist.

"Excuse my indulgence," he continued. "The infirmity of an old man. Ah, my young friend, beware of traffic with tobacco in any form. At first it is an insidious, stealthy friend; then a domineering tyrant."

Between every few words he was shaking the stimulant into one nostril, then into the other, bending his attention to this rather than to what he was saying, but I knew that he was merely giving me a chance to recover my composure. Real sympathy and the odour of snuff permeated the air. At last he closed the box with a click, and placed it with some force on the mantelpiece at his back.

"Get thee behind me, Satan," he murmured, with that winning smile of his, as he dusted off coat and waistcoat with his fingers, and at last he drew an old-fashioned brown silk handkerchief from his coat-tails, and blew into it a blast like a trumpet call. When once more he looked at me over his glasses, and saw something remotely resembling a smile on my own face, he cried heartily—

"That's right, that's right. We are a new country, you see, and must creep before we walk. We take the name of University although our teaching is not so universal as it should be. All will come in time, no doubt. With our undeveloped west, civil engineering is doubtless one of the great professions of the future, and there are those who say that instruction in this and other similar branches is much more to the purpose than the study of Latin or Greek which we are so fond of here. Perhaps so, perhaps so. I am old-fashioned, and love the classics. There is a bright side to everything if we can but see it. If you apprentice yourself for two years to a civil engineer or a land surveyor, you will get an education such as no college can bestow. You will learn the things by doing them, and when you come up to our periodical examinations, your pen will describe in your own words the actions your hand has already performed, and that, I assure you, is better than learning from books. But study the books in your spare time. I will give you a list of them."

"I already have it," I interrupted. It was the printed slip that had originally caused the trouble.

"Very well. Study those books diligently, and come up for your exams. when you think you can pass them."

During this useful and kindly exordium his right hand was searching nervously, and doubtless unconsciously, for the snuff-box at the rear.

"Sir," I said, "I thank you very much for what you have told me. I shall need to think a little over the situation before I decide what to do. And now, if I may carry away with me the knowledge that your hand has found the snuff-box, I shall bid you good-bye with a lighter heart than I possessed a few minutes ago."

The old gentleman laughed heartily, and with a sigh of relief turned to the mantelshelf, but the snuff-box was not there. The laugh stopped abruptly, and a look of consternation came into his eyes.

"Can I have knocked it down?" he cried, glancing at the empty hearth beneath him, then he suddenly opened his left hand and disclosed the little box.

"However did it get there?" he exclaimed. "Surely a case of the right hand not knowing what the left did." But he refrained from indulging in his infirmity, as he called it. Coming forward, he clasped me by the hand.

"I am very sorry," he said, "that we lose you for the moment. Perhaps some day we may see you here again, going in for the Arts course if the apprenticeship should prove disappointing. And now, good-bye."

He held the door open for me, and as I walked down the echoing hall, I heard the vigorous tapping of his fingers on the lid of the snuff-box even before he closed the door. So ended my University career of half-a-day.

CHAPTER III

Independent as a hog on ice.
                                        PACKINGTOWN PHRASE.

IT was nearing noon when I slowly retraced the
steps I had so jauntily taken that morning. I did
not look over my shoulder at the noble University
building, even when the solemn bell boomed after
me that it was twelve o'clock. Although the benevolent principal had enheartened me while he spoke,
I was now the more depressed in that, added to everything else, I should never come under his gentle
governance. Life had suddenly become an ill-timed
practical joke; I seemed to hear the cry of " April
Fool " in the depth of winter. Vaulting ambition
had overleaped itself. I was but a countryman come
to town with the usual result of being ensnared.
I seemed to hear the roar of rural laughter when my
neighbours learned that my University career had
lasted less than half-a-day, but this thought, at which
I winced, had one decisive effect; it determined me
not to retreat even if I had to take service in the
hotel of which I was now a " guest." Like Nanky
Poo, there might be much fun at my expense, but I
would not be there either to enjoy or to endure.
Slowly as I walked, I at last reached the busy
thoroughfare up which I had come so buoyantly a
few hours before. Its activity was even more dis-
couraging than the silence of the park, for every

one was hurrying with some definite object; I alone
had nothing to do. To be free of this absorbed
populace I turned down a side street. I must think,
plan, formulate a course of procedure, yet my facul-
ties seemed to be numb, as if the air, previously so
bracing, had developed anæsthetical qualities. Suddenly my attention was arrested by a phrase,
"College of Technology," which, painted in large
letters, designated a square, commonplace, ugly
edifice, vastly different from the towered and pinnacled
University building from which I had been so
courteously dismissed. I stood and looked at it, for
in architectural terms it expressed the downfall of
my hopes. Here was one alternative, the head of
the University had said, and, after all, the profession
I had chosen was as practical and commonplace as
a keg of nails, so why should it not be learned in
a house so frankly matter-of-fact? I entered and
received from the porter some printed leaflets giving
particulars of the various useful courses taught therein, with the hours, the amounts of the fees, and
what not.

Perhaps one cause of the exhilaration of youth is
that no matter what happens, a good healthy hunger
develops at stated intervals. As I emerged from
the College of Technology the bells of the town
were announcing one o'clock, and, remembering that
from one until three the festival of luncheon was held
at my hotel, I walked briskly towards the market
square. The clerk behind his counter accosted me
in a most friendly manner.

"What luck to-day?" he asked.

I shook my head.

"Very poor," I replied.

He glanced up and down the entrance hall, which

was empty, the lunch bell having gone some minutes before, then he said—

"You look a little down in the mouth. Have a drink with me. I keep some of the right stuff under the counter here."

I surmised that my reputation as a talented and indefatigable drunkard was in danger of becoming fixed upon me at this hostelry, probably through the report of my actions by the night watchman, so I nipped the same in the bud, recognizing, nevertheless, the kindly intention of the clerk.

"Thanks," I replied, "I don't drink. I never tasted anything intoxicating but Rhine wine, and that was last night, when I imagine I took enough to last me for a year."

"Oh, don't say that," protested the genial clerk, "the year's young yet, and we never know what may happen before next Christmas. What's your line?"

The hotel was a commercial house, frequented largely by commercial travellers and out-of-town traders.

"My line," said I, "is the supply of materials to colleges. I called in at the University this morning, but they have everything on hand they need."

"Oh, well," he counselled soothingly, "the University may be the biggest educational shop we keep in the place, but it's far from being the only one. We have more schools than taverns in this town, and I believe it's the only city in existence which totters under so unequal a balance of things."

He seemed to feel the disgrace of this position so bitterly that he fished out a bottle and a glass, helping himself.

"Sure you won't join me?" he inquired.

"Not to-day, thank you."

"Well, here's luck to you," he cried, tossing it off. "There's the Norman School, the Presbyterian Theological College, three medical colleges, a Methodist seminary, the College of Technology, and plenty of others that can use up a lot of material in a year. You've only been at it one forenoon, and you'll do a lot of business before the week-end."

"Thank you," I replied. "I have been to the College of Technology, and think I shall make a deal with them to-morrow."

With that I walked into the dining-room, and consumed a substantial meal, quite convinced that the clerk did not believe in the least that I was a shining example of temperance principles, for I knew I had risen in his estimation through having been conveyed home the night before.

After lunch I wandered down to the Bay, and there, in the brilliant sunshine, saw an unaccustomed sight —three miles or more of dismantled shipping frozen in at the wharfs, as if they were all Arctic schooners that had lined up against the North Pole. But the Bay itself, with its glittering surface of clear ice, showed an animated scene in striking contrast to the frozen ships. Near the wharfs hundreds of skaters were disporting themselves, and even further out adventurous parties were gliding along the glare ice, a feat not without its dangers in spite of the expertness with which the swift ice-boats were managed. These ice-yachts, which seemed to consist of one huge white sail, flitted here and there at incredible speed, like dragon-flies, each a dragon-fly shorn of one wing and therefore kept from bearing aloft its dot of a body. The single wide-spread wing was out of all proportion to the tiny hull, and flying across the breeze these winter gulls shot through space at a rate considerably in excess of the wind that supplied the motive power. The paradox can be proved both in theory and in practice, and in my case the practical experience of the mystery came first.

The wharfs were crowded with spectators enjoying the unique out-door exhibition. In the shelter of the pier on which I stood three energetic young men were preparing their ice-yacht for a voyage. The immense sail had been raised to the peak of the tall, slim mast. The body of the yacht consisted of a triangular platform, made of pine scantlings joined together like a proposition in Euclid, the floor consisting of rough pine boards nailed thereto. This triangular frame-work rested on three huge steel skates, one at each corner, two of which were fixed, while the third acted exactly like the rudder of a canal boat. The young men were making everything taut and snug, looping ropes tightly round cleats, and seeing generally that there were no loose ends about. I was watching these preparations with interest when the young fellow who stood ready to take the tiller glanced up at me.

"This kind of craft seems to be new to you," he said in a very friendly manner.

"It is," I replied. "Until yesterday evening I had never seen an ice-yacht."

"In that case you'd better come with us," he invited me with the utmost cordiality. "The pleasure of seeing a yacht is as nothing compared with the enjoyment of being aboard one in a good breeze such as we have to-day."

"The deck seems rather small, and there are already three of you."

The young man shrugged his shoulders.

"Oh," he said, "I've had nine aboard at one time. We don't walk about the deck of an ice-boat, you know, and so, like a tin of sardines, it will carry as many as we can pack. We could run you over to the island and back in a couple of minutes, if you can't spare the time for a longer voyage."

Now the island was more than a mile away, but from what I had heard of the speed of ice-boats, the steersman was not exaggerating the capability of his craft.

"You're sure I won't incommode you?"

"Oh, not in the least."

The unaffected good nature of the young fellow, the evident sincerity of his welcome to a stranger, quite won my heart, and I accepted his offer with gratitude and alacrity.

"Don't go," whispered a voice in my ear. I turned round quickly. If any one had told me that the person I saw would exert an influence on me that very evening which was to change the whole course of my life, I would have laughed in scorn. There stood a young man, a year or two younger than myself, I judged, whose clothes were so badly cut and fitted, so coarse in texture, and so ill-made, that they proclaimed aloud the rustic, and his face corroborated the testimony of the costume. He was a youth of tremendous muscular power; one could see that at a glance. A hard customer to tackle in a struggle, I surmised, but the smooth, broad face, vacant of all definite expression, showed that Nature had protected humanity from the power of the frame by placing it under the control of a mind good-humoured and of extremely limited capacity. It was a moon face, of youthful smoothness, completely devoid of intelligence, I assessed it, and the owner stood with hands in his pockets, gazing listlessly at the kaleidoscopic interweaving of the winged shuttles in the distance. If any one else had been close to me I should never have suspected this unique individual of the whispered warning. The outer end of the pier was crowded with sightseers, but we two stood practically alone at the shoreward portion, with the three busy men and their yacht on the ice below us. Although so much more stalwart in frame than I, no one could have convinced me that both in mental equipment and personal appearance I was not his superior. My face was adorned with a moustache big enough to proclaim the manhood of the owner, and, if I must say it who shouldn't, even without the moustache my countenance never proclaimed such cherubic innocence as that of this country bumpkin with his hands deep in his trousers pockets. That this bucolic Reuben of the backwoods should have ventured to address me, who had been a city man for nearly twenty-four hours, roused my resentment. The polite and cultured tones of the yachtsman, combined with a deferential manner, had shown me the superiority of city life over that of the farm, and I was quite anxious to make friends with him, but I had not come to the city to make rural acquaintances.

"Did you speak to me?" I asked, in a voice several degrees below zero.

He turned upon me an inane smile.

"No," he said, "I was just whispering to myself. It's a habit I have."

"I beg your pardon, I thought you were addressing me."

"Oh no," said the youth, with the most pacific humility. "I shouldn't think of taking such a liberty. You see, I arrived in town only this morning.''

The steersman, seeing us apparently conversing together, said generously—

'' Perhaps your friend would like to come along too.''

'' He is no friend of mine,'' I protested, but the countryman ignored my disclaimer. His face lighted up with a boyish joy he took no pains to conceal.

'' May I come ?'' he asked.

'' Certainly,'' replied the yachtsman. '' There's plenty of room; she'd hold double as many.''

The stout stranger sat suddenly on the edge of the wharf, reversed himself, put his strong hands on the ends of the planking, and lowered himself as gently to the ice as if his body had weighed no more than a feather. His action betokened muscles of steel in the arm under the most perfect control. Although a lighter man, I clambered down much more clumsily, but got there ultimately with some puffing and a final fall.

'' By Jove,'' said the townsman, glancing at the other fellow with admiration, '' you've done some gymnasium work, I take it.''

'' Oh no,'' replied the hayseed, '' merely the swinging of an axe in the backwoods.''

'' All ready, Jack ?'' inquired another of the trio, coming from behind the big sail.

'' Yes. Here are a couple of friends who are coming with us to the island and back,'' said Jack, with a wave of the hand that took the place of a more formal introduction. The third man appeared, and both nodded acquiescence.

'' Crouch down here,'' said the man at the wheel,

indicating my portion of the platform. "Lie as flat as you can, and look out for the boom when I bring her round. Keep your head down at the turn."

My fellow passenger crawled in beside me with an awkwardness which showed how unaccustomed he was to an ice-yacht, his actions contrasting strangely with the agility that had won the yachtsman's admiration a minute or two before. Jack had his arm on the tiller. The other men on the ice, one at either hand, pushed the boat along with scarcely any visible exertion, the polished steel runners passing practically without friction over the smooth ice.

"All aboard," cried Jack, and the other two jumped on forward. The sail caught the breeze, and instantly we were off, with a peculiar ringing sound of the skates and an ever increasing momentum. The yacht seemed to have a hair trigger sensitiveness to the touch of the tiller, and Jack steered her among the groups of pleasure-seekers with a deftness that won my utmost admiration. Once clear of the skaters the man at the helm drew in his sail until it caught the breeze to the best advantage, and then, for the first time in my life, I realized what the word "speed" meant. The city retreated from us as though some gigantic hand were pushing it back and back so that, from a resplendent city, it rapidly shrunk to the proportions of a toy village. I found myself unable to breathe, and just as I was wondering what I should do to fill my lungs, I was projected head first like a shaft from a cross-bow. High into the air I shot, poised for a moment while I spun a double-somersault, then came down on one shoulder with a thud that jarred every tooth in my head. Next began a terrific slide, head first and full length, along the smooth ice, and a shiver of fear ran through my frame as I saw that I was likely to have what little brains I possessed dashed out against the island now so rapidly approaching.

But even a moment of peril presents its mitigation. My companion in misfortune had come off the ice-yacht in a sitting posture, and we were running our desperate race on parallel lines, but, whereas I lay at full length, he sat as on a pivot, legs outstretched, whirling round and round and round while flying in a straight line through space. Alternately I saw that expressionless face and the back of his head, but although I had given a shout or two of dismay, he had maintained a rigid silence, the meaningless smile seemingly frozen on his countenance. Luckily the edge of the island was protected by a ridge of snow, and into this feathery medium I ploughed head first, while my companion took it back on, as it were. He piled up the snow and stopped, while I won by two lengths at least.

" Are you hurt ?" I gasped.

" Not in the least," he replied, with that smile. " The sole of my trousers seems to have worn a little thin. I felt the situation becoming colder and colder as we came on. How is it with yourself ?"

" I seem to be all here, but I am not sure. I ought by right to have dislocated my shoulder, but," swinging my arm, " it seems to be in working order."

We dusted the snow from our persons, and I looked abroad to see where our ice-yacht had gone, but it was impossible to distinguish it among the dozens gliding here and there in the distance. Then I opened up my vocabulary and gave, in the vigourous western tongue, my opinion of the three yachtsmen, more especially of the man who governed the tiller. The stranger looked at me gravely, and over the face, hitherto so blank, came an expression, first of grief, then of dismay. Seeing that my imprecations shocked him, I pulled up.

"I beg your pardon," I said, "but sometimes I am taken that way, and find a relief in language."

"Do you actually think they did it on purpose?" he asked, with childlike innocence.

"On purpose? Of course they did."

He thrust his hands in his trousers pockets, which seemed a favourite habit of his, and then in calm, even voice began to heap maledictions on the heads of the trio, maledictions so intense and far-reaching that his language, compared with mine, was as a Californian dialect poem to one of Dr. Watts' most blameless hymns.

"Oh," I said at last, "I'm sorry I spoke. If I had suspected your genius in that line, I'd have left the whole contract in your capable hands. What's your name?"

"Sam McKurdy."

Although he showed no curiosity regarding my own appellation I volunteered: "I'm Tom Prentiss. Here's my hand, Sam, and the next man who asks me if you're a friend of mine, I'm going to say yes. I apologize for having misjudged you."

"Oh, that's all right," said Sam. "I know my clothes don't fit; which is because I'm so abominably poor that they are hewn out with an axe. I've been through this game before. I'm up at the Normal School, but this is my second session. Thus, I'm a veteran so far as the city is concerned, although I don't look it. Possessing luxurious tastes without the money to gratify them, I indulge in ice-yachting by coming down to the city front and standing like a moon-struck owl, and before five minutes I receive an invitation to come aboard. There seems to be something irresistible in my appearance so far as the city man is concerned, and he plays games with me. The first time I think I must have slid a mile on two elbows and the back of my head. Since then they've got me off once or twice, but I always took one of the crew with me. Once I carried away the steersman, rudder and tiller, and wrecked the boat, but that was exceptional good luck. I'm afraid that by and by they'll get to know me along the front. Still, there are enough ice-yachtsmen to last me until spring."

"Then you didn't need to come off when I deserted the ship?"

"Oh, bless you, no. I saw on the wharf how green you were, and resolved to stand by you."

"Thanks. Is my origin so apparent as all that?"

"It's pretty plain, Tom. Your clothes fit better than mine, but you can't pose as a member of the Stock Exchange for some little time to come. The stock farm is stamped all over you."

"Oh, hang it, Sam, it can't be quite as bad as that. If you're at the Normal School you intend to be a teacher, but I have been a teacher for the last three years, so the stamp of the stock farm should have become faint by this time."

"God gi'e us a guid conceit o' oorsels," said Sam, in the accents of lower Scotland. "Still, we have no time to discuss the subject just now. These chaps will be back again directly."

"What makes you think so?"

"Oh, they always return. I know them. Not personally, of course, but I know their class. Their style of joke is what I call muscular. It is the mechanical brand of humour, for when you go down to the eternal foundations of things there's really nothing funny in risking a stranger's neck by shooting him over the ice. Still, they think it's funny, so it's not for any man from the grocery store at Muggins' Corners to dispute with them. They haven't brains enough to let well alone, so they will be here shortly, and will apologize in most polished sentences. I saw that that young chap's mellifluous accents took you in as completely as he threw you completely out a few minutes later. Now, your name's Thomas, therefore you ought to act the part of doubter to perfection. I'm the innocent cherub from the back-lot, who believes no ill of his fellow creatures. You will accept their apologies with dignity, but refuse to go on board again."

"You can bet your boots I'll refuse. You will never catch me on an ice-boat again until they are practising the sport in the lower regions."

"Nonsense. You listen to me, and pay attention. I swallow their story, and step on board. You stand here and refuse. Our friend Jack will stick to the tiller, and I'll get beside him in a friendly manner, trying to persuade you to do likewise, but you are as firm as a man can be on slippery ice. Then the other two will come off, and endeavour in the choicest language to convince you it was all an accident, pleading to be allowed to take you back to the city. If you still remain firm, they will jump at you unawares, fling you on, and then, springing aboard themselves, off they go. You'd be shot out over the lake next time, and would never stop sliding until you bumped your head against the horizon. Now you keep your eye on them, and edge away as they approach you, edging, however, toward the

yacht. At the critical moment I will let out a yell
that will momentarily paralyze both them and the
steersman. I learnt the yell from an Iroquois Indian.
The moment you hear it, spring on the boat and lie
down. Leave the rest to me.''

" But if they were coming back they could have
been here long ago.''

" Yes, they're watching us. They're waiting for
us to start across the ice towards the town. That, of
course, gives them more fun than getting us aboard
again. They will come flashing down upon us soon.
A stranger tries to avoid them, which, of course, is
futile. He sprawls and slips and flounders, and
comes down, and behaves generally, as the saying is,
like a hog on ice. They are so clever with these craft
that they can come within a thousandth part of an
inch of you at two miles a minute, and yet never
touch you. William Tell with his bow and arrow
wasn't a circumstance to these chaps. Now, we've
stood here long enough. Let us tramp along the
edge of this snow-drift as if we intend to reach town
along the margin of the island. That will fetch 'em.
You see, we're too close to shore for them to
manœuvre and have sport with us. The moment an
ice-boat runner touches the snow the craft's done
for. We've only to step over into the snow, and
they can't even scare us. The average greenhorn
usually makes the mistake of attempting to cross the
ice to his boarding-house, and so delivers himself
into their hands. He is mad as a wet hen anyhow, at being flung off, so the lads have more fun
than a funeral.''

By this time we were trudging along together like
friends of some years' standing, making rather tardy
progress on the slippery ice by the margin of the

snow-drift. We had not proceeded thus for ten minutes before we saw the sail of an ice-yacht, which had detached itself from the fleet, grow larger and larger as it swooped down upon us with all the celerity and silence of the Magic Carpet in the *Arabian Nights*. The steersman whisked the boat round beautifully, bringing it to a standstill within ten feet of us, sail flapping in the eye of the wind.

" I hope you are not hurt," said the steersman, in tones of deep concern.

" Oh no, thank you," said Sam. " Not in the least, but we have both had enough of ice-boating."

" I'm sorry to hear you say that. I had forgotten for the moment that you were unused to the sport. It is entirely my fault; I should have shouted for you to hold on. But one becomes so used to having a crew that understands all about it that one forgets. I warned you of the boom, but quite overlooked the equally important caution to catch hold of something when we turned round."

" Oh, it isn't your fault at all, as I was just this moment telling Mr. Saunders here. He thinks you did it on purpose."

" He is quite mistaken, I assure you. I ran a little too close to the island, and if I hadn't turned when I did, we would have been piled up on shore before one could say ' knife.' "

" That's all right," I said crisply. " I've no complaint to make, but I'm going back to town by the shore."

" Oh, I say," pleaded the steersman, " that's hardly fair to us. I said I'd take you to the island and back, and you really must give me a chance to carry out my promise."

" I'm very much obliged to you, but I prefer to

walk. I make no imputation on your good faith at all. You kept half of your promise at least, and delivered me head first on the island.''

Sam was standing beside the steering end of the ice-yacht, gazing at me with a look of deep reproach.

''Oh, come, Saunders,'' he cried, ''don't get on your ear about it merely because you've slid to land in that attitude.'' Then I heard him say to the steersman, ''I'm sorry he takes it that way, but I'm not to blame; don't know him at all, never met him before.''

The other two members of the crew now got off, and came gingerly towards me with uncertain footing.

''I hope you will come with us,'' said one, ''and I'll guarantee to deliver you on your feet this time at the spot where we picked you up.''

They manœuvred clumsily to place themselves between me and the island, and I moved closer to the ice-yacht.

At that moment a most piercing war-whoop rent the air, a whoop that must have startled the city a mile away. Sam shoved round the corner of the ice-yacht, flung the steersman from the tiller, and, with astonishing activity, pulled the sail to catch the wind. I had barely time to fling myself face downwards on the floor when we were off. The steersman was taken so completely by surprise that he lay motionless on the deck until Sam had given a couple of twists of the sheet round a cleat, then, while one arm lay along the tiller, he stretched the other out, dragged the steersman towards him, and sat down on him.

''I always like a cushion to sit on while I'm steering,'' he said to the owner in benevolent tones, as if

4

he loved him. The latter struggled and cursed, but he might as well have tried to remove Mont Blanc as to shift the ponderous person seated on him.

"Keep quiet, Johnson," said Sam, spreading his gigantic paw over his face, and rapping the fellow's head once or twice against the boards. "Keep quiet, or I'll smother you. Just look aft, Saunders, and see what the other two are doing."

"They seem to be making across the Bay," I replied, for we were now a long way from them, and they were difficult to distinguish other than as black dots on the black surface.

"Then Lord help them," said Sam fervently, "if they haven't sense enough to keep close to the island. Now," he continued, "I'll teach you how to hang on. Lie down on your front, and get a grip with both hands on one side of the yacht. Brace your feet against the other side, if you think you'll need their help."

I followed instructions, and Sam, lifting himself for a minute from his cushion, swung the yacht round with a suddenness that strained every muscle in my body. And so we came about before the late cushion, lying on his back, could reverse and get a grip; thus he departed into space.

"Look at our friend gyrating for the lake!" The steersman was whirling like a Catherine wheel toward the mouth of the harbour, two or three miles from the spot where Sam had taken the helm.

"Reverse and hang on again," cried Sam, and a moment later I thought there had been a collision, for I felt a shuddering thump, and heard a shriek, then I had all I could do to keep my place as the yacht swung round again.

"Good man, Saunders," cried Sam. "We'll

make something of you yet with anything like luck. You hung on like a tax-collector. You can sit up now, and watch me cast this bread basket on the waters.''

He had picked up one of the three on the fly, as it were, and jerked him aboard with a bang. The man was so paralyzed by his swift transition that he lay in a heap, face upwards, without a struggle, Sam's strong right hand grasping the belt round his middle. When we had traversed about half the length of the Bay, McKurdy lifted his victim as easily as if he had been a baby, and placing him gently on the ice, sent him like a curling-stone skimming over its surface.

'' There,'' he said, with the deep sigh of one who had accomplished well a task set to him, '' I have scattered those three so that each one of them is a mile or more away from either of the others. I shall now cease calling you Saunders, and we may proceed to enjoy ourselves like rational beings.''

'' I don't know how it is with you, Mr. McKurdy, but I will enjoy myself much better once we are quit of this raft on skates, and I find myself safe in the seclusion of my tavern. I fear we have qualified ourselves for appearing before a police magistrate, if not in the dock of some higher Court.''

'' There's just a glimmer of sense in that remark. I'm glad you made it. I suppose I have been guilty of robbery, kidnapping and attempted murder. I propose that as we took ship at the upper end of the city, we leave it at the lower end; a search for the ice-boat will occupy our three musketeers for some time, and give us a chance of escape.''

'' I don't care where you leave it, so that you leave it quickly.''

McKurdy did not attempt to thread his way through the fleet, but headed for the mouth of the Bay until he nearly barked the shins of Jack the steersman, whom he greeted with a war-whoop. Then he swung round to the edge of the mainland, and came up along the city front, finally turning deftly into an oblong alcove where half-a-dozen ice-yachts were at their moorings. Here he laid the boat gently alongside. Half-a-dozen desperadoes in a more or less disreputable state of repair as regards clothing, came sliding and shuffling up, clamouring for permission to take care of the boat while we went ashore, for they saw that she did not belong to the coterie usually berthed there. Sam selected the most villainous-looking of the tribe, gently inquired his name, and receiving it, wrote the same on his cuff.

"We're going up town to get a drink. Can you recommend us a good place?"

"Pat Murphy's is on the second corner," said the man. "He'll treat you right."

"Very well; see that you don't let any one steal our boat."

"I'll look after it, sir, till the last dog's hung," replied the pirate truculently, and with that we clambered on the wharf and walked up the hill to the main street of the town somewhere near the Central Station at which I had arrived the day before.

"It is always well," said Sam, as if meditating, "when on a retreat to leave a pretty quarrel to the rear. Our jocular friend Jack, whose nose I nearly put out of joint a few minutes ago, stood where we passed him and watched our sail come to land. He has never lost sight of it, and I did not intend that he should. Doubtless at this moment he is slithering over the ice towards his craft. I don't think he will be in the best of humour; indeed, the chances are that he will have lost his politeness and likewise his tact. Now that garrotter in whose charge we left the boat will dispute possession, waiting quite honestly for the two men from Murphy's. Jack may make the mistake of attempting force, so all in all, I think I can promise him an exciting discussion, and we two honest men in this city of rogues; simple, warm-hearted countrymen, easily deluded by the snares of the wicked, may walk at leisure down this thronged highway, instead of having to take to our heels with the hue and cry behind us, all of which goes to prove my contention that mentality will beat muscle from the drop of the hat to the finish."

I laughed.

" I must say, Sam, you seem well provided with both."

" We are as the Lord made us, as my Aunt Jane used to say, and we should do our duty in whatever station providence places us, as my Aunt Jane usually added. You taught school for three years, you tell me, which means you won a third-class certificate good for thirty-six months, and I may further prognosticate that you've come here to better a defective education."

" Quite right."

" Then, proceeding onward, I take it you will attend the Normal School to secure a second or perhaps a first-class certificate, and so I shall have the pleasure of your further acquaintance."

" My dear sir, as your Aunt Jane might have said, you should learn to leave well alone. Your first two surmises were correct. The third is woefully astray."

" I see," replied the imperturbable Sam. " I

didn't know when to quit. A prophet should proceed with caution. What's your game, then?"

"I came here intending to put in two years at the University, but they treated me as Jack did on the ice-yacht; they slid me across the park into town again."

"Couldn't you pass the entrance exam.?"

"I wished to qualify as a civil engineer. They don't teach this at University College, and so, figuratively speaking, I am standing up and dusting the snow from my noble form, still a little dazed with the suddenness of the throw-out."

"Have you money enough to go to the University, then?"

"I've got enough to keep me for two years."

"Great heavens, I never met a rich man before!"

As Sam said this he stopped at a street corner.

"This is where I turn off," he explained. "It is Church Street, the most godly of thoroughfares, said to contain more places of worship than any similar mile of road in the world; therefore I chose my abode upon it."

"The clerk at my hotel was bemoaning the prevalence of colleges and schools in this city. You'd better come with me, and tell him of the multitude of churches. He'll be quite heart-broken when he hears of it."

Sam shook his head.

"The delights of hotel life are not for a pauper like me, and I refuse to accept a hospitality I am unable to return. Besides, I think it well to conceal this mug of mine from public view for a few days. School opens to-morrow, and I must be there at nine o'clock. Personally I'd rather go to jail, but I haven't the time to spare. I do not wish to meet our three musketeers until their anger tones down a bit. By and by they'll want to keep quiet about the incident, but to-day they're after blood, and I might be compelled to knock their three empty heads together, which is an action frowned down upon by the police of this law-abiding city. But you come with me; come and see how the poor live."

"Very good. I'm with you. You seem to be particular about the company you keep, while I'm not. If you won't come with me, I'll go with you."

"That's the proper spirit," said Sam, and we walked nearly half-a-mile up Church Street, when he turned in towards a rather pretentious three-storied house, with steps up to a platform before the door, which was surmounted by a portico. Sam pulled a latch-key from his pocket and let himself in.

CHAPTER IV

The best of Prophets of the future is the Past.
BYRON.

McKURDY conducted me up one flight of stairs, then, opening the door to his right, ushered me into a small room with two windows overlooking Church Street, giving a view of one of the numerous sacred edifices with which he had accredited that thoroughfare. The street was quiet and pleasant, lined on either side with trees, whose gaunt branches gave promise of pleasant shade when hot weather came. A heavy circular table, covered with a drab-coloured cloth, stood in the centre of the room, which in turn was littered by well-worn text-books, sheets of foolscap paper, an ink-stand or two, and numerous pens. Opposite the two windows were two doors, which I afterwards learned led to small bedrooms, each half the size of this study. A well-worn carpet covered the floor; two arm-chairs, a sofa under the windows, a bookcase and three ordinary chairs, completed the inventory of the furniture.

"By Jove, McKurdy," I said, "this squalor is far ahead of my luxurious room in the hotel."

The young man was on his knees, not because he resided in the straight street of the churches, but to light the fire already laid on, and presently he produced a merry blaze that added cheer to the gathering dusk of an early winter evening.

"Yes," he said, getting up on his feet again, and dusting off his knees—as if anything he might do could make those trousers more respectable! "we manage to get along here with lowly living and lofty thought, both of which come cheap. Fling yourself down in that chair. Do you smoke?"

"No," I replied, with virtuous firmness.

"Neither do I. Do you drink?"

"N—no," I faltered, with involuntary hesitation. "That is to say I drink tea, coffee, milk, or other stimulants of that sort."

"Same here," said Sam briefly, not noticing the feebleness of my answer.

He rang a bell, and presently there appeared in the doorway a tall, thin, angular, soured female, with iron-grey hair, who looked, not at the man that had summoned her, but at me, and if ever there is dislike at first sight this was a case, for I saw that in a glance she had weighed and found me wanting. Sam, who had thrown himself down in the opposite arm-chair, was on his feet in an instant, and a flattering deference came into his manner as he addressed this living ramrod.

"Oh, Mrs. Sponsor, I am so sorry. Is the servant not in?"

"This is her afternoon out," said Mrs. Sponsor, with a severity that at one and the same time cast censure on the habits of servants and on the requirements of lodgers.

"If I had known that I would not have troubled you, Mrs. Sponsor. Pray excuse me."

His tones were silken soft, and his manner that of a courtier. The severe face relaxed as it turned from me to my host.

"What did you wish, Mr. McKurdy?" she asked,

the iciness melting in the sunshine of the young man's urbane radiance.

"Well, really, I—we—that is to say, we thought of indulging in a cup of tea, but we can quite easily go out for it."

"There is no necessity for that, Mr. McKurdy. I hope I know my duty. You shall have tea within ten minutes."

With that she faded away, and McKurdy's form became upright again.

"Is that your landlady?" I asked.

"Yes. Like myself, she is not prepossessing at first, and has rather the air of a disappointed old maid than that of a most respectable widow. Although severe of aspect, I fancy she has a kind heart, and has had a hard life. Mrs. Sponsor is one of the licensed boarding-house keepers of the Normal School, and that alone is a guarantee of the primmest uprightness."

"She looks to me like a man-hater."

"On the surface only, I think. I am led to this conclusion by the fact that when she became licensed boarding-house keeper, she might have chosen to receive lady students, whereas she preferred men. A licensed boarding-house keeper cannot accept both, so I feel flattered to think I am one of Mrs. Sponsor's chosen, just as the late Mr. Sponsor must have been in her early days. She probably thinks you are a new tenant, and naturally is on her guard against you, for she recognizes you as a source of future trouble, because her duty towards you does not end with seeing that your bed is made up and your food properly served. If, for example, you remained out later than ten o'clock at night, she would be compelled to send a note to the head-master, informing him of your delinquency."

"Is she compelled to sit up most of the night so that she may know when people come in?"

"No. Mechanical devices have eliminated human labour in this instance. The moment ten o'clock strikes the door is bolted and barred, and your latch-key becomes automatically useless."

"But cannot one of the fellows who stops in admit the outsider when he gives a mild signal, say that Iroquois war-whoop of yours?"

"I see you are well qualified to take up the academic life. That device has been thought of before, and is put to nightly practice in other boarding-houses, but not here. Mrs. Sponsor is conscientious, and keeps a great big key, which we haven't been able to duplicate, never having discovered where it is hid. Upon occasion I have climbed the porch, and entered unobtrusively by the right-hand window; still, that has the disadvantage of exciting the police if they happen along at the improper moment."

"So you live under a state of tyranny and espionage?"

"No more so, I believe, than any under-graduate has to put up with at a University. The penalty is not severe unless you persist in wrong-doing."

At this point we heard steps along the landing. McKurdy jumped up and opened the door, taking the tea-tray from Mrs. Sponsor as soon as she appeared on the threshold, thanking her over and over again for the service she had rendered. The woman evidently liked him so far as her undemon-strative nature allowed her to show, but she darted at me a glance which seemed to carry a wish that the tea would poison me.

McKurdy lit the gas, drew the blinds, and poured out the tea, all with the dexterity of an estimable young lady. We drank our unexciting beverage in silence, and I felt, rather than saw, that McKurdy was looking me over, if I may so term it. I fancied he was making up his mind about me, perhaps apprehensive that he had been too friendly with a stranger picked up on the streets, as one might say. At last he placed his empty cup on the table, interlaced his fingers behind his head, leaned back in his arm-chair, and spoke—

"I see you think I'm rather a humbug in treating the gaunt Mrs. Sponsor as if she were something of a princess."

"My dear sir, you are quite mistaken. No such thought occurred to me."

"Then you are not so penetrating as I had supposed," he went on calmly. "I am a humbug. These blandishments I bestow upon her are merely practice. As I think I have deceived that sharp-eyed woman, I believe myself to be progressing, and in time who knows what may happen!"

"You may marry her," I suggested, but he went on without heeding.

"I noticed that you sized me up as no end of a country lout when you first set eyes on me to-day, but you ought to have seen me when I came to town seven months ago. It might be making too great a demand on your credulity to inform you that I have improved, but I assure you that I was constantly falling over my own feet, and from their acknowledged size, you may estimate the severity of my tumble. Are you a student of woman?"

" No; of mathematics."

" Ah, well, I may be able to assist you in that, for I am supposed to be no slouch at figures, but I thought that a man with a well-trimmed moustache might be able to give me some hints about the fair sex."

" I'm not a ladies' man at all," said I, with firmness.

" My Aunt Jane says they're the worst when the right time comes. Do you go all to pieces in the presence of a good-looking young woman ?"

" Certainly not."

" Well, I do. My hands grow to an enormous size, and I don't know where to put them, neither can my feet be concealed unless I hire a barn, and as for saying anything—well, if silence is golden, my riches ought to attract the ladies. The proper study of mankind is man, said the philosopher, and I think the prefix ' wo ' has dropped away from the last word in transit, because woe seems to come to me when I endeavour to make man embrace the woman, as the humorist put it."

" I understood you to say you were here to study for a teacher's certificate."

" Oh, did you ? We weren't so well acquainted when I told you that. However, I now recognize that you can bring a mathematical mind to bear on what one might term a social problem. Suppose that for six months, during one session of the Normal School, you sat within four feet of a very good-looking young woman. How would that affect you ?"

" It wouldn't affect me at all. I shouldn't look at her."

" You'd never glance across the aisle ?"

" No."

" You'd gaze at the teacher?"

" Yes, if the teacher were a man."

" I see. You're what they call immune in the yellow fever districts? But suppose that the most drastic rule of the institution was directed against the situation I am so lamely endeavouring to describe. Suppose that it meant expulsion, the loss of your Normal School certificate, and the wrecking of your career, if, happening to meet this girl on the street, you were so courageous as to take off your hat to her, and that simple act of courtesy were brought to the knowledge of the Normal School authorities?"

" Then I'd leave my hat on my head."

" Of course you would. I forgot. I may as well attempt to discuss the mystery of colour with a blind man, as expect to get counsel from you should I become involved in a love affair."

" Does this drastic rule you refer to apply only to the men?"

" It applies to all students, men and women."

" If, then, you lifted your hat to Miss Charming, and she recognized your salutation, would she also be expelled?"

" Yes, if we were seen by any of the school authorities, and he were mean enough to report the matter."

" In that case a chivalrous man should take care not to raise his hat."

McKurdy remained silent for a long time, then he drawled—

" I think we need you at the Normal School. Precept and example are so seldom partners that their union among us would be like a limelight in a lone land, if that is the quotation, which I think it is not."

" You ask for the precept, but the example I shall not have an opportunity of showing you. I fear you are making fun of me, Mr. McKurdy."

" No, I am merely envious. But why can't we have the benefit of the example? Why don't you attend the Normal School rather than the College of Technology ?"

" Because it isn't in my line. I have quit teaching, except in so far as I can bestow instruction upon you and others of my friends."

Sam laughed at this, then went on—

" I am not sure but that you are in need of a little instruction yourself, and perhaps you are not so impervious to a practical suggestion as you are to the glances of beauty. An acquaintance of mine, much more learned than you are, because he knew the distinction between the University and the University College, had been, like yourself, a teacher for some years, but came here to enter the College of Technology. For some reason he changed his mind, and entered the classes of the Normal School instead, but went also to the night school at the College of Technology. He was a tremendous worker, and at the end of the session had not only grounded himself well in drawing and the use of mathematical instruments, but secured into the bargain, at the Government examination, a first-class teaching certificate, good for life. Like yourself, he was a young man of irreproachable conduct, and broke neither the rules nor the heads of any of his teachers, and consequently left the Normal School with the highest possible commendation that institution could give him. This, with his Government certificate, got him an appointment in a western town, at a salary three times what he had ever earned before. While teaching, he became acquainted with a civil engineer, and apprenticed himself to him, working hard at his chosen calling every day after four o'clock, and all day Saturday. He passed his examinations one after another, and in two years received a diploma from the University. I need hardly add that he spent practically no money on himself, never went to a theatre, or even to a circus, and when he began the practice of civil engineering, he had a good sum of money in the bank; was a great deal richer, in fact, than when he began to learn the trade. I regret to add that simply because he did not look at the girls when they blushed red, and did not allow a kiss on the mouth to steal away his brains, he married the only daughter of the Mayor, who was the richest man in his town, and now he is city engineer, and has an extensive private practice which is rapidly making him as wealthy as his father-in-law. It grieves me to make a recital of this sort, for it sounds too much like a moral tract to suit my fancy, but this has always been an unjust world, and it is men like him who get along. Frugality, industry, and an eye to the main chance, my Aunt Jane tells me, will ensure my future, so I'm all right, and I'm merely citing this example to apply certain features of it to your case. One good turn deserves another. The weak feature of your plan of campaign is this. You have money, you say, to keep you two years. Very good. Suppose you attend the College of Technology for that time, suppose you pass every one of your examinations, and suppose there isn't a hitch in the scheme from matriculation to diploma, you will then need to set out in your profession of civil engineer penniless, and may, indeed, be compelled to drift back into teaching in order to buy bread. Any professional man who begins expecting to make his living from the first is usually disappointed."

" I should try to get a job on the survey of some new railway."

" I doubt if you'd get a very lucrative one with only theoretical knowledge in your head, but what I'm trying to impress on you is this: by following in the footsteps of the acquaintance I tell you of, you'll get your degree of civil engineer almost as soon as you would by attending the College of Technology, and whether you started on railway surveying or city work, you would save enough of money to keep you for three or four years. At the end of six months in the Normal School you can doubtless take a second-class certificate, and perhaps may go in for a first. You will spend your evenings at the College of Technology, which is as different from a lady's parlour as anything I know of. You will study the curves of railways rather than those on the cheek of beauty, and the rosy tint on the face of the fair shall in your case be reflected from the maps you colour."

" I fear, Samuel, that my remarks about the ladies are receiving more attention from you than they deserve."

" Envy, my boy, envy, as I told you before, and, by the way, my name is not Samuel, but Sam."

" All right, Sam, go ahead. You're making out a very good case."

" That is nearly all there is to say. By either method you get your C.E. degree about the same time, but in one instance it is given to a penniless person, and in the other to a man with money."

" Well, I'll think about it, and let you know."

" Now is the time, my dear fellow. The Normal

5

School opens to-morrow, and after that you cannot enter. Indeed, if you had to pass an examination you could not enter as it is, but your third-class certificate will give you admission. When you are surveying your new railway through the wood, and I am your chopper in chief, and happen to find one of my trees falling in your direction, and shout to you, you mustn't reply, 'I'll think of it and let you know.' As my Aunt Jane says, 'Mr. Now rides in his carriage, and Mr. Later-On takes the dust from his wheels.'"

"Your Aunt Jane should have had a nephew called Solomon instead of Samuel."

"Sam, if you please."

"I beg pardon. If I decide to enter the Normal School to-morrow, may I join this coterie here?"

"Oh, you can do that in any case, even if you attend the College of Technology. I don't know what sort of a crowd we'll have this term, because I'm one of the few that have come up again. Last session we had three medical students, one theological man, who said grace before meals, and four Normalites. Of the four, I am the only one who has returned."

"It is very good of you to give me the run of the ranch in this hospitable western way, so I will shift my belongings to this place to-morrow whether I become a student of the Normal School or not."

"Then that's settled," cried Sam, and as he spoke the door opened, as Mrs. Sponsor came in for the tea-tray.

"Your tea was so delicious, Mrs. Sponsor," said McKurdy, "that my friend, Mr. Prentiss, wishes to leave the luxurious hotel at which he is stopping, take bedroom No. 2, and share this study with me."

"I thought as much," snapped Mrs. Sponsor, bending a look on me that made me shrink further into the arm-chair.

"So you are sure of two roomers at least during the coming session," continued Sam cheerfully.

"Indeed," said the woman, with a toss of her head, "I have had to-day three more applications than I can accommodate."

"Good enough," chortled Sam. "I've always said this is the most popular house in the street, and lucky are those who find rest for the sole of their foot therein. I was just telling Mr. Prentiss before you came in how fortunate it was that he had applied in time."

The woman stood by the table and frowned. Clearly she had some premonition of the trouble I was to cause in that respectable abode.

"But he is not in time," she objected. "I showed a medical student this study and bedroom, and he said he'd take them."

"Surely, Mrs. Sponsor, you'll not endanger me with a medical student. He'd be certain to poison me before a month was past with some of his new remedies, and likely as not he would amputate an arm in my sleep. A full-grown doctor is bad enough, but a medical student is a terror, and a danger to the community. When was he here?"

"He called this afternoon at three o'clock."

"Ah, then, I am saved. You remember telling me just before the Christmas holidays, Mrs. Sponsor, that if I had any friend with whom I wished to share this study, you would see he was admitted."

"Yes. Still, it's first come, first served, Mr. McKurdy."

"Certainly. That's just the point I'm making.

Prentiss is the oldest friend I have in the city. To-day at seven minutes after two o'clock we were on the ice together going to the island. Prentiss is a very staid, sober, sturdy person, but through circumstances over which he had no control, he found himself leading a faster life than he liked, and he yearned for a place where there wasn't so much hustle, and where he could take better care of his clothes than he was doing, so I recommended this house, and he accepted. This, as I have said, was at seven minutes past two, so my friend was just fifty-three minutes ahead of your medical student, and, as you truly say, first come, first served. I, you see, with your authority, acted as your agent, and, when your medical student comes again, if he makes any sort of fuss, I will cheerfully throw him half-way across the street. Oh, it's no trouble at all, Mrs. Sponsor, I love throwing medical students half-way across streets."

"Humph," ejaculated Mrs. Sponsor, as she picked up the tray and left the room.

"She doesn't seem to take to you, my son," said McKurdy, "but time will reform all that."

I regret to say it never did.

CHAPTER V

He was a scholar, and a ripe and good one;
Exceeding wise, fair spoken, and persuading;
Lofty, and sour, to them that lov'd him not;
But to those men that sought him, sweet as summer.

'KING HENRY VIII.'

I REACHED my hotel for the last time through brilliantly lighted streets, passing the same Aladdin-palace wonders of the shops to which I was not yet accustomed. The deep depression of noontide was dispelled, and although the evening did not see me in that state of exultation which enthralled me when I trod the pavement in the morning, I was far from being the despondent castaway of mid-day. This casual acquaintanceship, which had ripened with tropical rapidity, gave me a new interest in life, and I pondered with interest on what the young fellow had said regarding my career, little realizing that my projected career was already done for; that I should never survey a railway or draw a map, or in any other way add to the material benefit of my country. The change was to begin before many weeks were past in a department of the Normal School which bore no relation to the scholastic side thereof.

I ruminated over what my newly-found friend had said, and all in all, his plan appeared to be the best way out of my difficulty. I could not bear the thought of returning to the district which I had left, and if I did return there was nothing for me to do except take a place on a farm.   There were two reasons why I could not engage in my old profession of school-teaching, and each reason final.   First, I had no certificate, second, all the schools were now in session, each with its quota of teachers. Not until the summer holidays would there be an opportunity for me to engage in the one thing I could do, and until that period I might as well attend the Normal School as the College of Technology; better, indeed, as McKurdy had pointed out, because at the end of six months I should doubtless acquire at least a second-class certificate which would get me into something better than a backwoods school, and, as first and second-class certificates were tenable for life, I had always a bread-winning occupation to fall back upon, if I failed in everything else.   So, before I reached the market square hotel, I had resolved to enrol myself next day as student at the Normal School, unless some unforeseen obstacle barred the way.

Next morning, having paid my bill, I walked to the Church Street boarding-house carrying my handbag.   The trunk would come later.   I had neglected to take the number of the house, but found little difficulty in recognizing it from its position opposite the church.   McKurdy gave me a cordial welcome, and seemed in no way to regret his hasty invitation of the day before.   Indeed, he appeared rather to enjoy meeting me again, and confessed that he dreaded the opening days of the school, where all, or nearly all the faces would be new to him.

We walked together up the street until we came to the Normal School, which, with its ample grounds, occupied a large square bounded by four streets.   I think the academic edifice was of classical design, and the effect was not so commonplace as that of the College of Technology, nor so ornate and romantic as that of the University buildings.

There were two large temples of learning, joined together by an enclosed corridor, like architectural Siamese twins. The front group contained an art gallery, and administration offices pertaining to the department of public instruction. Grounds with trees, shrubbery and flower-beds separated these offices from the street. To the rear stood the extensive buildings of the school, square and unornamental, and behind them the spacious playground.

There were certain formalities to be gone through, papers to be signed, and what not, before I became a student of the Normal School. When this had been accomplished, and we stood in the wide hall of the main building, McKurdy paused, an expression of hesitation overspreading his face.

"I am afraid you will think you are involved in a mass of prohibitions, and so you are. There is a forbidden corridor between where we stand and the waiting-room of the school. It is open to all the world except ourselves. It was open to you until a moment ago, when you signed the final paper. Shall I lead you through it?"

"What is the object?"

"Oh, it saves three-quarters of the distance; saves us going out to the street in front, along to Church Street, and then to the proper gate. The other object is that it is forbidden ground."

"It doesn't seem to me worth while. Let's take the unforbidden way."

"Good man," said Sam with a sigh. "I see you are going to exercise a beneficent influence over me."

"Is there plenty of time?"

" Oh, plenty. There's no excuse, of course, except that the other is the broad road that leadeth to destruction if we should happen to meet the headmaster, which is reasonably certain. You will find he has a nasty habit of omnipresence. I fully expected to meet him yesterday afternoon, when we had stolen the ice-boat, and I'm not sure yet he didn't see me."

" Is he such a terror?"

" Terror? Why, he'll snarl the name McKurdy as if it were an offence against the statutes. His very glance makes the cold chills run up and down my spine. I may conceal my misdeeds from my Maker, but never from the chief."

By this time we had reached Church Street, and thus joined the stream of students hurrying toward the upper gate. They were evidently all strangers to each other, for no two except ourselves walked along chatting together.

" New faces, new faces," growled Sam, " and I don't see a striking one among them. Well, I hope these lads will meet our luck of last session, for after all I have said about the chief, there were some few delinquencies which he failed to discover."

Once inside the building, we climbed a stair, and entered a large, square, crowded room, bare of all furniture; not even a chair or a bench was visible, therefore half-a-dozen of those present were seated on the window-sills swinging their legs. Holding so many, the room was nevertheless deadly silent, but the moment we entered, the stillness was abruptly broken, for Sam's stentorian voice rang out in a way that startled every one, myself included.

" Get down off those window-sills!" he roared in tones ringing with anger. Instantly every man there jumped, and the sills were cleared. They took this tall, smooth-faced, frowning stranger for some one in authority.

" So, gentlemen," he cried, glaring at them, " even before you enter the school-room you begin by breaking one of the rules."

" I assure you, sir, I didn't know," stammered one of the culprits, and the others muttered protestations of ignorance. The stern expression on Sam's face faded away, and a sunny smile took its place.

" As a matter of fact, boys, you *were* breaking the rules, but then nearly everything you do will constitute a fracture of some law or bye-law of this institution, so you needn't let that worry you. It was not breaking the rules I was thinking of, but breaking the ice. You may just as well fraternize and ask each other's names and thus save time. As a starter, my name's McKurdy, popularly known as Sam. My friend here is Tom Prentiss, a chap I picked up yesterday for nothing on the streets."

Somebody laughed, and then three or four more joined in. From behind us spoke up a hearty voice—

" Hello, McKurdy, is that you ?"

Sam turned round to greet an acquaintance, but met a sea of strange faces, and in spite of himself disappointment came into his own. The speaker cried out genially—

" You *said* you were McKurdy; so I thought I'd test the matter," and before Sam could recover himself there was a general roar of laughter which, as it were, welded the separate atoms of humanity into a corporate mass. The strangeness had somehow vanished.

" That's all right," cried Mac, " and one on me; and now, enacting the part of the person who knows, having been here before, I call your attention to that large gong at the top right-hand corner of the room. When that gong sounds one stroke it means that we go to class-room number one, presided over by the headmaster, who teaches grammar, English literature, and a few other subjects that at present you know nothing about. When the gong strikes twice we go to class-room number two, presided over by the mathematical master, who does tricks with arithmetic, algebra, and is supposed to have been a personal friend of the late Mr. Euclid. The signal of three bells does not bear the same significance in this room that it does at sea. It means that you will troop noisily down-stairs and visit the class-room with a laboratory attached, where you will be taught chemistry, natural philosophy, including statics and dynamics, and mysteries of that sort. These are probably all the signals that you will hear to-day, but there is a music-room, a drawing-room, not in the social acceptation of the term, and various other chambers of torture. In a few moments there will be one stroke of the gong, and I, the bell-wether, as one may say, of this innocent flock, will lead you through the right-hand door into the awful presence of the headmaster. The department of education has decreed this so that you shall know the worst at the very beginning. Those who escape from that room alive need fear nothing that is to follow, except one appalling department which will come later, and that is the Model School. Now the headmaster——"

"What is the Model School? Tell us about the Model School," cried half-a-dozen voices in different parts of the room.

"You will know nothing of the Model School for the first week, so why anticipate your fate? The headmaster will first read a chapter in——"

A roar arose that drowned Sam's voice.

"The Model School!   The Model School!" they cried.

Sam gazed around him, his face beaming with benevolence.

"I see, gentlemen, that the name McKurdy has conveyed no meaning to you. By and by you will know better, though I may have to toss one or two obstreperous persons through a window. I call your attention to the fact that we are one storey above the ground, which is frozen hard, not covered by enough snow to break the fall, which, they will tell you in room number three, begins at sixteen feet a second, and increases rapidly. Am I to be allowed to continue my remarks about the headmaster?" he concluded mildly.

"Go on about anything you like," cried a chubby man in the corner. "We were as lonesome as a cowboy on the prairie when you came in."

"Thank you.   The Head will read a chapter in the Bible, so selected that for the first time in your lives you will realize what miserable no-account sinners you are. Then he will make a prayer that sounds just like a malediction. After that the real trouble begins."

He paused and looked about him with his friendly smile, and met nothing but tense silence.

"Thank you, gentlemen, I shall now proceed to inform you about the Model School, although at any instant I may be interrupted by the crack of doom from the gong yonder. When the gong sounds the rest is silence and a quick march after me, and in case I forget it, kindly tip-toe into the class-room. That is another of the requirements. If you come clamping in, heel and toe, as if you were at a barn dance, you'll hear something not to your advantage from the Head. Now, gentlemen, although you would not think it from my appearance, I am from the country. Some of you come from towns and villages, doubtless, but perhaps not one of you was ever in so large a city as that in which he finds himself to-day. It is a mathematical fact not taught in room number two, that the ratio of human wickednesses increases in arithmetical progression according to the square of its population. There is something logarithmic about the natural cussedness of a city urchin. Attached to this institution, which I need not tell you is for the purpose of training teachers, there is what is termed, erroneously I believe, a Model School. I am a serious-minded person, and most of my similes are drawn from the Bible, in which I follow the example of my Aunt Jane. I have often wondered, when reading the account of the destruction of a certain pair of cities, that enough brimstone wasn't saved to wipe from the face of the earth the Model School of which I am speaking. It consists of four divisions, and supports a headmaster with three assistants. The fourth division is composed of little city chaps, who, if the Lord spares them, will ultimately develop into first divisioners. I rate the four divisions thus—bad, worse, worst, and damnable, the latter being the first division, made up of boys from sixteen to eighteen years old. Each day a number of us victims in the Normal School are chosen, by lot, I suppose, as pirates elect those who are about to walk the plank, and we are sent down to the Model School to teach first, second, third, or fourth division for one hour. You are left alone in some class-room, and before ten minutes have elapsed you will regret that you were not placed in a den of tigers instead. Tigers? They're worse than tigers—wild cats is the only thing I can compare them to. All these chaps are up to snuff. They despise you because you come from the country and your clothes don't fit. They know you dare not touch them, no matter what they do, because corporal punishment is not allowed in the Model School. The only power you possess is the right to send the boy out of the room if he misbehaves himself. But then, as they all misbehave themselves, you find yourself in a dilemma. If you send away more than half-a-dozen you are considered a failure as a teacher, and whether the boys are punished or not, which I doubt, you receive a black mark against your name and these count up as the session grows older. The unfortunate candidate for good marks tries to do his best by these lads, and sometimes makes pathetic appeals to their sense of fair play, which doesn't exist. To a sensitive man, or a conscientious teacher his hour in the Model School is simply torture. I may say, parenthetically," continued Sam, embracing us all with his innocent smile, "that I am not a sensitive man."

There was a ripple of laughter at this, punctuated by cries of "Go on! Go on!"

"When first I went down to the Model School and was alone with my class, one sweet little cherub asked me if I could dance, and then, meeting my reproving gaze, he added, apologizing profusely, that my feet were so well developed he thought I must have treated them to violent exercise of some kind, and merely wished to know what sort. Another chap begged to know if he might ask a question, and when I gave him permission, he requested me to translate the first sentence of our lesson into the language of the aboriginal tribe from which I came. I ordered him to leave the room, but he said to me reproachfully that he had asked permission to put the question, and it wasn't fair to punish him for what I myself had given him leave to do. There was such a sweet reasonableness about this assertion that I gave him leave to resume his seat. Now the best way to deal with the Model School is——"

" Clang !" went the great gong at the ceiling. We had forgotten all about it, and every man jumped as though it had been a musket-shot. Sam McKurdy, on tip-toe, led the way into the class-room number one.

CHAPTER VI

Give me the avow'd, the erect, the manly foe,
Bold I can meet—perhaps may turn his blow.
' New Morality.'

THE headmaster's class-room was of more than generous proportions, lighted by a row of tall windows along the north side. The floor was level, and we were not seated in the tiers of an amphitheatre, as was the case in the class-rooms of University College. Each man had a seat to himself, and fronting him was a desk with a lid, and a tank inkstand to the right hand of the level part at the top. So far as I can remember, we were not allotted any particular seat, but took what came, and yet I think this cannot have been so, otherwise I should have chosen a desk alongside or before or behind Sam McKurdy. In any case my seat was the last in the row nearest the windows, and Sam sat about the middle of the same row. On entering, I saw pouring in from the door opposite our own a troop of young women, who proved equal to ourselves in number, but I paid slight attention to them, and sat down in the seat I have indicated with my back to the feminine procession rapidly filling its half of the huge room. I recollected Sam speaking about sitting within four feet of a good-looking girl. If such was his position the session before, and if the choice of the seat he was to occupy rested with him, he had now placed himself further away from temptation, because row after row

79 "

of young men intervened between him and the first row of the young women. I wondered if he had been smitten the session before, and, once bitten twice shy, had put himself as far as possible from future complications. Perhaps my own comments on the situation when I refused to take the forbidden passage had produced some effect. However, he scoffs at scars who never felt a wound, and I dismissed the question from my mind, as one of trivial moment.

I gazed about the room at my fellow-students. They all looked alike to me, as was said of the coon in the song, and yet among them must be many unknown friends, from whom I should part with regret, and perhaps, who knows, an enemy or two. The survey of my comrades was interrupted by a strong, deep-toned voice enunciating solemn words, and their resonance struck a strange cord of memory that brought me to myself with a jerk. I turned my eyes with something like terror to the master's desk, and there (great heavens above us!) stood Dr. Darnell! Dr. Darnell, whom the night before last I had met in the Lodge room, and worse, ten thousand times worse, Dr. Darnell who had taken me to my hotel in a state of shocking intoxication, drunk on Rhine wine. Yes, I had tried to stifle the remorse, to evade the verdict, but that was what it amounted to; drunk, drunk, drunk. I could not even mitigate the disgrace by the more roundabout word, inebriety, and there, in front of me sat Sam, to whom I had spoken counsels of perfection. I was not going to break rules, pass through forbidden corridors, or sit on window-sills, yet I had talked like a babbling fool to this man now reading the Scriptures, and had lurched against him like a sot from the Lodge room to the market-square hotel.

Never did the severe language of Holy Writ fall on more unheeding ears. I was tingling with shame, and the rounded periods fell on my ears like unmeaning condemnation. If the door of exit had been at my back, instead of alongside the master's desk, I should have slipped out and bolted, but I dared not face the ordeal of passing down the whole length of the room. When the effects of the first shock subsided, two possibilities emerged from the gloom. First, among so many he might fail to recognize me; second, perhaps he was not, after all, Head of the Normal School, but merely a clergyman opening its exercises, yet a moment's thought showed me that the latter contention was improbable. If some one else was headmaster, that man would be standing beside the preacher. Dr. Darnell read alone at the desk. Much as I had disliked him at the Lodge, I saw that his attitude here was more militant and aggressive. He stood stiffly upright; his side-whiskers seemed redder than under the gaslight; the Shakespearean dome of his bald head indicated a power that was absent from any of those who sat before him, and the set of his mouth denoted a knowledge of this, and an ill-concealed contempt for his listeners. He knew so well the chapter he was reading that his eyes did not need to follow the lines, but under the heavy overhanging brows they swept us now and then like the swing of a search-light. The demeanour, tone, the very aspect of the man seemed to say, "You unlicked cubs, I will thrash you into shape before I've done with you." A great teacher they had said, but I did not believe it. A great teacher must show sympathy, and of that in Dr. Darnell there seemed not the slightest indication. Then a flash of remembrance came to me.

6

This must be the James Darnell, D.D., LL.D., with ever so many other letters after his name, whose text-book of grammar I myself had been teaching from for three years. The fly-leaf, as I remembered it, had not named the author headmaster of the Normal School, and, never intending to be a pupil at that institution, I had not been at pains to learn who were its responsible heads. Now, however, the gloomy conviction settled down upon me that this man was indeed the headmaster, and that my ill-luck had brought me into contact with him in most deplorable circumstances. And yet the very overbearing qualities of the man called into life a corresponding determination in myself; a rising resolution of resistance. After all, I had a certain right to be upon the earth, even if there were no letters after my name, and why should I be abashed because on one solitary occasion I had taken too much Rhine wine? Hang it all, if he was going to make it lively for me, I should probably make it interesting for him.

> Unwilling friend, let not your spite abate,
> Help me with scorn, and strengthen me with hate,

I might have said, if John Davidson had at that time written the words for me.

The chapter ended at last, and a short prayer followed. Dr. Darnell sat down, and drew towards himself some large sheets of paper. He said sharply—

"As I call out each name, let the person to whom it belongs stand up."

Then he began upon an alphabetical list.

"Aline Arbuthnot."

A tall girl stood, her face pale with the excitement of being made first in that assemblage of strangers.

"Have you ever taught school?"

"No, sir."

Slowly over those fair cheeks a roseate flush spread like an approaching dawn. Her clear-cut beautiful profile stood out against the gloomy background of a blackboard, and it seemed strange to me that womanhood in the mass proved so uninteresting as I came in, yet here the first figure called up out of it resembled a renowned picture by some great artist. I wondered why I had not noticed her in the feminine procession, for her seat at the front indicated that she must have been one of the first through the door.

"A relative of Judge Arbuthnot?" inquired the headmaster, leaning forward, and actually speaking gently and with a certain warmth of interest.

The girl blushed more deeply.

"I am his daughter, sir," she said, and at a nod from the doctor, resumed her seat. The roll-call went on, the next and the next, and the next were men, and all three had been teachers. Mr. Armitage was the last of the A's, and Barr the first of the B's, then Blakeley and others, until it came to McKurdy, and Sam rose with a leisureliness that somehow suited his giant strength. The doctor pronounced the name as if it were a sneer, but he showed no recognition of the student who had been there the session before.

"I see your Christian name is set down here as Sam. You were christened Samuel, of course?"

"Well, doctor, my parents didn't think so. They were very ambitious, and nominated me Sidney Alexander Maurice McKurdy, but when I learned I was fated to come to the Normal School I massed the initials and called myself Sam. If you place a full stop after each of the letters, you will get it about right."

Dr. Darnell leaned back in his chair, a light of recognition gradually dawning on his face. This was very well acted, because, as I afterwards learned, he knew Mr. McKurdy from the beginning, but determined to put the pupil in his proper place at the beginning of a new session.

" Ah, yes," said the doctor. " I recollect you now. You were here a term or two ago, were you not?"

" I was here last session, doctor."

" Last session, was it? I think you have never taught school?"

" No, doctor, I have not."

The atmosphere was electric. All the sharpness had gone out of Dr. Darnell's speech. McKurdy's replies were scarcely above a whisper, yet they were distinctly heard in the stillness of the room. Every one felt instinctively that here were two antipathetic men at daggers drawn, each wary of the other. The lecture which McKurdy had given in the waiting-room had made all the newcomers aware that he did not exactly love the headmaster, and now the headmaster's pretence that he had not instantly recognized so striking a figure as that of McKurdy gave the snap away, as the vulgar say. That McKurdy had expected this encounter I now felt reasonably sure, and I saw a method in the nonchalant discourse with which he had favoured us in the waiting-room. Of this discourse Dr. Darnell was, of course, ignorant, and therefore he could not know that McKurdy had already put himself *en rapport* with the male portion of the pupils. The doctor consequently was at a certain disadvantage in this verbal encounter. Besides this, McKurdy's graphic description of the Model School had not only filled most of his hearers with fear of the unknown, but had constituted himself a leader and a champion of them, so that their whole sympathy went out towards the quiet young fellow who stood the target of this grim man clothed with authority, a man of power, free and untrammelled, confronting an opponent hampered by all the restrictions of discipline.

"Then, Mr. McKurdy, you did not attend the Government examination for a teacher's certificate after you left us?"

"Yes, Dr. Darnell, I attended that examination."

The doctor raised his eyebrows in gentle surprise.

"I have looked over the list of successful candidates in this morning's paper, with an especial eye to those who had been students at the Normal School. I must have missed your name."

"No, Dr. Darnell, you did not miss it. Your acuteness is such that any name in a list to which your attention had been called, could not have escaped your observation."

Even Dr. Darnell unconsciously straightened up under this generous commendation. Every student in the room hung upon each word, although the girls evidently did not understand the subtle warfare, or the influence which Sam's discourse in the waiting-room had exercised over all of the male students.

"You don't mean to tell me you failed, Mr. McKurdy?"

The question was imbued with an almost tender sadness and regret. McKurdy perceptibly straightened himself up, and the cloak of humility dropped from his shoulders.

"I was successful in every subject taught in the Normal School except two. I gained the highest marks in chemistry, in natural philosophy, Euclid, algebra, arithmetic, history, geography, and all the rest, but failed miserably in grammar and English literature, and those failures were so complete that they nullified all the good the full marks in other subjects did me.''

Here fell an answer that even the women understood, for every one knew that Dr. Darnell himself was the teacher of grammar and English literature. Here, then, came a stinging insult flung at the headmaster in the face of his class, a veiled charge of incompetency, spoken as quietly as if it had been a compliment, for even when McKurdy squared his shoulders for the final thrust, he had not raised his voice a semitone. The master leaned forward over his desk, the light of unholy anger flashing from his eyes. His very whiskers seemed to bristle with electric rage.

'' It requires brains to understand grammar,'' he shot at McKurdy.

'' Yes, and to teach it, Doctor,'' was the suave reply.

We were now treated to an example of the triumph of common-sense over anger, a trifle belated, perhaps, but nevertheless, here at last. The severe set of the Doctor's lips relaxed into a smile; those eagle eyes softened almost to tenderness.

'' Well bowled, McKurdy. During this session I shall endeavour to make the intricacies of grammar plainer than I appear to have done in the past.''

'' And I,'' said McKurdy, '' will pay stricter attention to your instructions, Dr. Darnell.''

The doctor bowed, requested Sam to be seated, pushed the tally-sheet away from him, and addressed the class.

'' I wish to tell you, as briefly as may be, the functions of the Normal School, regarding which there is a very widespread misapprehension. When the Government inaugurated this institution, it intended to establish a school which differs from all others in existence. Its business is to train, not to teach. The Government took it for granted that all students entering these classes would come equipped with the tools of their trade, and we were supposed to show how those tools should be used. Experience has proved that the Government was unduly optimistic. Circumstances force us to teach as well as to train. The Normal School has no power to grant you a licence to teach. The Government does that, and you are expected to satisfy the Government that you possess the knowledge you are required afterwards to impart. The Normal School gives you a document which certifies that you have attended one or more of its sessions, that your conduct has been good, bad, or indifferent, and that your rating as an imparter of knowledge is so-and-so. Take, for instance, my own subject of grammar. It is no part of my task to teach grammar to you, but it is my duty to show you how to instruct your future pupils in this branch of knowledge; nevertheless, I shall be very glad, either inside or outside of school hours, to smooth away any difficulties you find in my subjects, no matter how elementary those difficulties may appear.''

This little speech made an excellent impression upon the class, and it extracted the sting from the final remark in which McKurdy seemed at the time to score so heavily against the headmaster. Either McKurdy knew the nature of the Normal School or he didn't. If he knew it, he had taken an unfair advantage of the headmaster before a class ignorant of the subject; if he didn't know it, then grammar was not the only subject he had neglected during the former session. Becoming better acquainted with

Dr. Darnell I was able to appreciate his action in provoking what I thought at the time to be an unwise controversy with a pupil whose strenuous quality he had previously experienced. The fact seemed to be that he was taken aback by seeing McKurdy once more before him. He feared Sam's influence on the new class, and, not knowing that McKurdy had already aroused the admiration of every man in the school, he endeavoured to discredit beforehand what he believed to be an evil example.

Shortly before the end of the former session, it became suspected that McKurdy was not only defying one of the strictest rules of the school, but was also leading others along the path of disobedience. Dr. Darnell had insisted that no charge should be made unless positive proof were presented, inwardly praying that definite evidence might not be forthcoming. His heart was as kind as his face was severe, and he did not wish to see any of his pupils cast out. The mephistophelian figure in the drama, the Nemesis on Sam's trail, had said confidently to Dr. Darnell that he was certain of McKurdy's guilt, and would be ready with the proof if given a month in which to watch the trap he had set, and Dr. Darnell doubtless needed to check the phrase that rose to his tongue: "Thank God there are only three weeks more of the session."

And now here was McKurdy back again, still suspect of course, but this time with the end of the session six months away, and John Brent, head of the Model School, determined to ruin him. It was a situation that wrung Dr. Darnell's heart, yet his devotion to duty was such that he could not call off the detective nor warn the culprit. McKurdy and others knew the rule, and if they deliberately broke it they must be prepared to take the consequences. Dr. Darnell, consumed with a grief of which he gave no sign, would utter the condemnation and pronounce sentence in an unflinching voice, without a quiver to show the agony within.

Again he picked up the list, and worked his way through the mass of names—McNeill, McPherson, and so on, until at last he came to one that made me quake—"Thomas Prentiss."

I rose to my feet, and met the steady gaze, the Doctor's overhanging eyebrows lowering and lowering as recognition came to him.

"Have you taught school?"

"Yes, sir, for three years."

He called out the next name, and I sank into my seat. A few minutes later the roll call finished, and shortly after, a gong, which none of us had noticed at the ceiling near the windows, struck twice with a brazen clang that startled us all. I could not help comparing this strident clangour with the mellow tone of the tower bell at the University, and a wave of regret almost overwhelmed me. The difference between the two centres of learning, from stucco to stone, from the commonplace to the ideal, were all against the institution in which I found myself. The contrast between this hot-tempered, sharp-tongued principal, and the snuff-taking, courteous old scholar, seemed typified by the modern factory clink of our gong compared with the distant cathedral-toned bell in the Norman tower. Contempt and dislike for this hurried manufactory of half-formed teachers flung out upon the public every six months; this farce of scholarship, filled me with regretful longing for the leisurely methods and the picturesque surroundings of the older school whose gates were closed against me.

At the summons of the brazen gong I stood up with the rest, and the crowd began pouring out of the two doors, men to the right, women to the left. Standing at the back of the hall, I now saw plainly, full face, the girl who had first been called to her feet by Dr. Darnell's summons. She, like myself, stood there immovable, until the converging crush of the lines at the narrow door had ceased.

I judged Miss Arbuthnot to be between seventeen and nineteen years of age. Her face was beautiful and sweetly serious. The mass of dark hair which surrounded it framed a picture of comeliness glorified by dark eyes that gazed unwaveringly at the crowded exit, as if she, too, yearned to leave this class-room, but disdained to mix with the pushing throng. Never once did those eyes deflect for the fraction of a moment towards the men in the room, and never once during all the session, as day by day I watched her walking with proud dignity the length of the room to her place in front, did I see her glance at one of us. So far as Aline Arbuthnot was concerned, man did not seem to exist, and I said to myself, "Here is one who will not infringe the cherished rule of the school."

Slowly as I walked towards my door, and slowly as she walked towards hers, I had ample time to admire face and form. Here at least was one feature denied to the staid old University which at that time did not admit women to its learned halls. Although those steady eyes of hers never wavered, I fancied somehow she was conscious of my scrutiny, for a delicate, and it seemed to me indignant flush gradually crept over her face. When we two had passed one another, I did not dare, after my boldness, risk turning round and watching her disappear. I was disturbed to find my attention drawn to a much less alluring prospect. I noted the gaze of Dr. Darnell fixed threateningly upon me. Beside his platform facing the desks was an individual so palpably an Irishman that he looked as if he had stepped from the pages of one of the comic papers. He, I learned later, was the genial Pat Boyle, janitor of the school, a diplomatic individual, who ran with the hares and hunted with the hounds, and was equally popular with the pupils and the masters. Boyle followed me into the waiting-room, and tapped me on the shoulder.

" Are you Mr. Prentiss, sir ?"

" I am."

" Then Dr. Darnell would be obligated if ye called upon him in his private room. Come this way if you please, sir," and with that Boyle led me once more across the now empty class-room, and knocked at a door opposite the headmaster's desk.

I entered a small room lined with books, and at a table Dr. Darnell was seated, looking, I must say, extremely forbidding.

" Mr. Prentiss," he began curtly, " I think we have met before."

I tried to carry off the encounter with lightness, and said—

" Dr. Darnell, I remember the meeting much more distinctly than the parting."

His face did not relax.

" Is it your intention to attend this session of the Normal School ?"

" I enrolled myself a student this morning for that purpose," I replied more gravely, realizing that in this room of soberly-bound books any attempt at humour might miscarry.

" I wish to say, then, that because you and I

belong to the same Fraternity, no favouritism is to be expected on that account."

" Dr. Darnell," I answered gruffly, temper rising, " I think you might have waited until I attempted to take advantage of our former meeting before giving me an unnecessary warning. I am as sorry to be here as you are to see me here. If I could bring myself to ask even the slightest favour from you it would be to beg that you place double punishment upon me whenever I am called up for correction. I hope to receive enough injustice at your hands to obliterate the humiliation of the night before last."

" Good-morning, Mr. Prentiss," said the Head in brusque dismissal.

" Good-morning, Dr. Darnell," I replied, and thus our unpleasant interview came to an end.

CHAPTER VII

He was the mildest manner'd man
That ever scuttled ship, or cut a throat.
'DON JUAN.'

SHORT as the interview with Dr. Darnell had been,
it nevertheless caused me to find the waiting-room
empty when I re-entered it. Remembering that two
strokes of the gong indicated the room of the mathematical master, I made my way thither, and was glad
that the vacant seat assigned to me stood so near the
door, for I was unused to tip-toeing, and should not
have cared to traverse the whole room making experiments with my clumsy boots when so many eyes were
turned upon me.

Dr. Cardiff was our mathematical master, teaching
arithmetic, geometry and algebra, but for some
reason, probably because he was a doctor of medicine,
and not a doctor of divinity like the headmaster,
physiology was also one of his subjects. I saw,
seated at the teacher's desk, a fine-looking man with
a long black beard, and I was somewhat startled to
observe beside him an unnaturally white human
skeleton suspended from a stand consisting of one
pole and four feet. This I was often to see the smiling Boyle carry back and forth from the class-room
to the closet, its abiding-place, as is the habit with
family skeletons.

The men were all sitting upright, watching the

quick and the dead nonchalantly, but I noticed that many of the girls persistently kept their heads down, and shuddered when the collection of bones rattled, as the doctor, in a familiar way, touched it here and there with a wooden pointer.

Prof. Cardiff's first lecture was a useful, easy-going talk on the care of our health, and although, as I have said, he referred to the human framework beside him, I think it occupied the platform more for dramatic effect than for service as an illustration. Dr. Cardiff was a very placid man, who, I imagine, had never been angry in his life. In every sense of the word a gentleman, he was courteous and kind, and just a little blind to any transgressions which came to his cognizance so long as the students kept order while receiving his instructions. I imagine he took the view that he was Professor of Mathematics, and not a private detective, and this knowledge gradually permeated the class as it grew better and better acquainted with him, and did not in the least detract from his popularity, even with those who were rigidly righteous.

Before the talk—it could hardly be called a lecture; school would not begin seriously until next day—before the talk was half-way done, the students were favoured with an excellent view of the most sinister figure attached to our academy; one who took a vastly different view of his duties from that held by the easy-going master of mathematics. The door nearest to the teacher's desk opened very, very softly, at first as if moved by some invisible agency, but later it disclosed, standing there, as if he had materialized out of transparent air, a smooth-faced man of about thirty. He appeared before us without a sound, and stood there, doubtless waiting for a pause in Dr. Cardiff's remarks before venturing further forward, but he came so silently that the doctor did not hear him, and although John Brent, head of the Model School, stood in full view of all the class, Dr. Cardiff, at the desk, was the only person in the room whose back was towards him, and thus we were so happy as to see for several minutes an absolutely motionless man awaiting his opportunity. This struck me afterwards as emblematical of his life. His cold gaze scrutinized the assembly, some members of whom, then completely unknown to him, were to be victims of his subtilty and their own fall from grace. He was one of the handsomest men I had ever seen, and might have stood model for a statue of Apollo. The position he occupied, as head of a school termed "model" by the Government, proclaimed him officially the best teacher in the country, an estimate with which I was entirely unable to agree; still, it is an undoubted fact that the pupils he taught would have laid down their lives for him, so there must have been something capable in the man, even though I failed to discover it, to call out such devotion from the young scallywags he ruled. Indeed, I cannot pretend to do justice to John Brent, for even the subduing effect of passing years has been quite unable to mitigate my dislike of him.

There came a pause in Dr. Cardiff's homily on health. He might much better have been warning us how to protect ourselves against model masters than microbes. Brent tip-toed over to the desk of the mathematical master, as noiselessly as if his light shoes were soled with rubber. He seemed qualified to be the model master of a tip-toe school, for his own tip-toeing was so perfect that in my mind it always conjured up a keyhole at the end of his glide.

I saw now to what a perfection I might attain through practice in this silent, surreptitious method of progression; which mystery I carried out awkwardly like a man on stilts. The whitest sepulchral skeleton was not so silent as John Brent. Occasionally its bones rattled in a companionable sort of way, but Brent was the embodiment of the inarticulate. I suppose this leopard-like tread came through constant habit and because of great strength, for Brent as an all-round athlete was admirable. At football he met few equals, and in the game of cricket he was a master indeed. His feats in the field of sport must in some measure have accounted for the dog-like devotion of his pupils. Indeed, I have seen a coterie of Normal School students, every one of whom loathed him a thousand times worse than ever the Devil was hated, applaud him in spite of themselves when, at a critical point, his keen judgment, backed by enormous strength and an almost satanic skill, saved the day for our city. Brent never played to the gallery, and received the plaudits of ten thousand spectators with calm indifference. The play was the thing with him: success at all costs, whether in the school-room or in the play-ground, but for the applause of the populace he cared not a jot. He would ruthlessly break a man's leg, if necessary, on the football field, and say suavely—

" I *beg* your pardon, sir," and as he played football, so he played Life : cool, relentless, and correctly polite.

The effect of Brent's stalwart, upright pose before the class changed as the line of sex was crossed. There was a low murmur of admiration among the girls, and I heard one whisper, " How handsome he is !" but the men knew instinctively that here stood the enemy so far as they were concerned, and a sense of danger seemed to pervade our section of the room; a sense which had nothing to do with reason or previous knowledge, being similar to that which animates a person who hears for the first time the signal of the rattle-snake, when (like the Light Brigade) he does not pause to reason why, but (like the schooner *Hesperus*) leaps a cable's length. I have often wondered why this man chose to make us his enemies rather than his friends, for we were all young, and therefore hero-worshippers, and he might as easily have led us as antagonized us. Once when McKurdy and I were leaving the football field after a magnificent and strenuous game, of which we had been the spectators, where the prowess of our city had proved triumphant against the somewhat brutal methods of a distant town all through the superb leadership and play of John Brent, Sam said with a sigh—

"I'll never go to another match where Brent plays. I fear I may come to love the man."

It was generally believed by my colleagues that Brent was as ambitious as Lucifer, intending to storm the throne itself and displace the hot-tempered Dr. Darnell. It was therefore thought to be his game to prove that we were undisciplined, breakers of rules, contemners of authority; that the school needed the laying on of hands, and Brent knew his hands were strong. Of course there is one chance in a thousand that the man was quite unselfish, a devotee to duty, but even in that case, which no Normalite would admit, his detective methods seemed to resemble those of the French police during the most tyrannical period of their existence. The pupils under his direction were supposed to be the most enthusiastic of spies, subtle as foxes, unscrupulous as Beelzebub, and as

7

mischief-loving as city lads usually are. They had this tremendous advantage over us. One by one we poor victims were exhibited before them for an hour at a time. They saw us in detail; we saw them in the mass. We were unable to say whether any particular lad we met in the streets was a pupil at the Model School or not, but each one of them could recognize a Normalite a mile away.

The picture of John Brent, chief of these amateur Bow Street runners, as first I saw him, standing before us straight as a pillar, has never been obliterated from my mind. Brent always stood as if he had just stepped from one of the pages of a book on anatomy which showed the correct human pose. He had a habit of bowing his head without thrusting forward his shoulders, making a gesture of affirmation or agreement, which reminded me of one of those squat china figures where you pull a string, and the head inclines up and down.

I can remember nothing of what Dr. Cardiff said about health, but his book on the subject of hygiene may still be purchased. An introductory lecture on natural philosophy by Professor Donovan brought us to twelve o'clock, and then the whole school poured into the street, each member of it making for his own particular licensed boarding-house. Sam and I walked together down Church Street. I began the conversation.

"I think I have seen her."

"Seen whom?"

"The girl who is causing Sidney Alexander Maurice McKurdy to break the most stringent rule of the school."

"You arouse my curiosity," replied Sam, with an

indifference which, if feigned, was very well done.
" May I know her name, or is it a secret ?"

" She was the first girl called by Dr. Darnell. Her name is Aline Arbuthnot, which sounds like the title of a heroine in a cheap novelette, but she is worthy to be the heroine of the most expensive novel."

" You interest me. I did not happen to see her. I was following your good advice, and keeping my eyes fixed on old Darnell, who pretended not to remember me. How did it happen that your own eyes were wandering to that side of the room when you had already warned me that danger followed such conduct ?"

" I don't know just how it happened. Certain reasons, upon which I may expatiate later in our acquaintance, took away the prop I had intended to lean against. So far from gazing at the headmaster, I was at great pains to avoid his recognition."

" Had you met him before ?"

" Yes."

" The plot thickens. If you can exert any influence with him you may be able to pull me out of a difficulty now and then as the session advances. With the best intentions in the world I find myself frequently at odds with the good doctor."

" I fear there won't be influence enough to go round. He called me into his room after class, and read the Riot Act. He warned me that I was to expect no mercy, and I practically told him to lay on, Macduff, and damned be both of us. All in all, I regarded it as a mighty poor beginning."

" When and where have you met him before ? Did you quarrel with him ? Nearly everybody does, so that doesn't count. He is a good man with a bad temper."

" Oh, we met under the most amiable auspices. The first night I was in town, I drifted into a social organization, and there was introduced to Dr. Darnell, and also to Rhine wine, meeting both for the first time. Not to put too fine a point upon it, I got simply garrulously drunk, and Dr. Darnell supported me to my hotel."

Sam stood stock still in astonishment.

" Suffering Peter ! you don't mean it ? Well, as my Aunt Jane says, that's a corker."

" Yes, I couldn't have had a worse introduction, but, after all, it can't be helped. I nearly fled when I first caught sight of him this morning, but getting my second wind, I decided to brazen it out. After all, I'm here to study; I don't intend to infringe any of the regulations, so what's the odds ?"

" Quite right. Oh, excellent young man, how much more elder art thou than thy looks; and, talking about looks, was this girl you speak of handsome ?"

" More than handsome. She has a dignity of bearing I never saw equalled; a mass of jet black hair, and eyes like stars of heaven, only much the more serious and beautiful."

" Dear me, dear me, dear me ! I'm not sure but this is worse than the Rhine wine as a first attack. And speaking once more of good looks, did you pay an equal amount of attention to the man who entered our class-room during old Cardiff's holding forth ?"

" Yes, I did."

" What did you think of him ?"

" The most well-favoured man I ever saw, but I didn't like him."

" You'll like him less as time goes on. He is John Brent, head of the Model. Whenever you think of that girl, think also of John Brent. He is the antidote to the sort of rhapsody you were indulging in. A stands for Arbuthnot, B stands for Brent, A.B.; you will notice that they are alphabetically easy of remembrance."

"I'm sure I don't know what you're talking about."

> "But seen too oft, familiar with her face,
>   We first endure, then pity, then embrace,"

quoted Sam. "You'll be seeing her every day, and as you may not see Brent more than once a week, let us hope out of sight will not be out of mind in this case."

"You infer that I shall seek the acquaintance of Miss Arbuthnot?"

"Well, my Aunt Jane says she has known such things done. She shakes her head when she hears talk of silent devotion; doesn't believe in its lasting qualities."

"Oh, bother your Aunt Jane."

"I have frequently done so, Tommy, my boy; indeed, I'm her chief anxiety in life."

Long before the conversation had reached this point, we were seated in our study. When the talk was interrupted by the tinkle of a bell down below, Sam jumped up exclaiming joyously—

"Come down into the basement, my son, and I will initiate you into the mysteries of our *ménage*. I am caterer this week, self-appointed. Next week the caterer will be duly elected."

"Caterer? I thought Mrs. Sponsor was caterer?"

"No. This epicurean republic elects its own president every Saturday night. You pay Mrs. Sponsor for your share of this study, and for your bedroom. This payment includes cooking and care of the rooms.

The caterer, when appointed, makes such arrangement for provisioning the citadel as he deems necessary, and Mrs. Sponsor's cook is responsible for serving up. Thus there is no growling about the food in this boarding-house, because we buy such provender as pleases us. Every Saturday night the caterer presents his account, which is summed up, and divided by eight, the number of people at our table, and each man forks over his share. Some caterers we had last year ran towards luxury and extravagance, so they were not re-elected. Others, again, fed us on lines so economical that they were not elected again. What the crowd wanted last session was moderation, and doubtless the same feeling will rule the roast now. Come on."

CHAPTER VIII

Suspicion sleeps at Wisdom's gate.
'PARADISE LOST.'

DOUBTLESS Dr. Darnell regarded me as a confirmed inebriate, but he gave no sign of wishing to snatch a brand from the burning, being more anxious, I took it, to prevent my setting alight the green sticks surrounding me. His initial distrust of me was increased by what he supposed was the unerring instinct of my wickedness which led me into instant alliance with Sam McKurdy, who had been the chief revolter against authority in the former session, and who would have been expelled from the school had proof been as strong as suspicion. The headmaster's attitude was that of a man who had now two undesirables on his hands instead of one. It filled me with dumb and helpless rage to see that he was constantly on the alert for a new outbreak on my part, knowing, probably, that drunkards may keep sober enough for a time, but are sure, sooner or later, to backslide in every sense of the word.

The first class of the day assembled each morning in his room, and it was exasperating to find his eagle eyes scrutinizing my personal appearance as if to detect signs of dissipation the night before. The quite honest and unconscious look of gentle surprise when, in the morning, he received from me a clear and concise answer to one of his questions, made me wish to cry out that I was as great an advocate of temperance as himself. It is in a case of this kind that a man has a right to expect help from his friends, but I did not receive it. Sam, with whom I consulted in our study, thought it a fit subject for roars of laughter. He perceived comic elements in the situation which were entirely concealed from my vision. Thinking that, as he knew Dr. Darnell so much better than I did, he might be able to counsel me, I divulged to him my plan of seeking the Doctor in his private room, and telling him I had never in my life tasted a drop of intoxicating liquor before the night I met him at the Lodge, and never would again, but Sam sank back in his arm-chair, and shook with merriment.

"No good, my boy," he cried. "We all know what incorrigible liars drunkards are."

One morning there occurred an incident which nearly caused a break between Sam and myself. I considered that I was wounded in the house of my friend, and he held I was lacking in a sense of humour. Dr. Darnell seemed to have singled out both of us as targets for his shafts of sarcasm. He appeared to take a particular delight in fastening on some inane remark made by either of us, and holding the same up to the ridicule of the class, and I must say that he could make a man look more different kinds of a fool in a shorter space of time with fewer words than any person I have ever encountered. Sam's replies, whenever he got an opening, were invariably good-natured, and sometimes exceedingly clever, and in justice to Dr. Darnell, it should be stated that he never exercised his authority to defend himself from a thrust which his wit could not parry. Once he received a gem from me, and I knew I had put my foot in it the moment I had opened my mouth, as Sir Boyle Roche said.

Dr. Darnell sat back in his chair, and a contemptuous smile came to his lips. He then spent a few verbal minutes in running his scalpel through the interstices of my soul. His theme was my ignorance, and the unfortunate position of the pupils entrusted to my care, I having, by my own confession, taught school for three years.

"Dr. Darnell," I said sharply, "I left the master's chair for the pupil's seat because I knew I was ignorant. I am here because I am ignorant, but, when I was a master, and met an ignorance even more deplorable than my own, I spent my time in trying to remove it, and not in making funny remarks about it."

I looked for an outburst of rage, and expected to be told to leave the room, but no shade of resentment came into the Doctor's face. Indeed, all anger and scorn disappeared from it.

"Mr. Prentiss," he said quietly, "your summing up of a teacher's duty is not only admirable in itself, but very tersely put. I shall remember that in your favour when I am making out your certificate."

Thus he disarmed me, and made me regret the vehemence I had used.

Before we had been three days under his rule, he knew the name of every man and woman in his class while the amiable and altogether charming Professor Donovan, of chemical fame, did not know one man from another even when the six months' term had ended. Professor Donovan, for all his tremendous learning and wonderful capacity as teacher, was kindly, simple and childlike, and altogether the most lovable man I have ever met. Sam was already his devoted slave, although it was quite evident that the Professor had not the least recollection of him from the session before. So fond were we both of Professor Donovan, and so greatly did we prize the knowledge which he imparted in even the most casual conversation, that we two got into the habit of waylaying him every morning, and walking up Church Street with him, discussing those matters with which his whole mind was absorbed, and so we formed a sort of impromptu peripatetic school of philosophy as if Donovan were Aristotle himself. We always parted from him at the master's door, and, walking a few steps further up the street, entered our own gate. This had gone on for months and months, and one day Professor Donovan said to us—

"You are two singularly well-informed young men. Are you in business together up this street?"

We laughed, and said we were, which was true enough, but it was evident he had taken us for clerks with a desire for knowledge, never once recognizing us as pupils of his own class.

But Dr. Darnell, as I have said, knew each one of us by name before the end of the third day, and he sometimes paraded this knowledge in a way that was disconcerting. He would put forward some question, expatiate on its simplicity, but ask us nevertheless, to think deeply before attempting to reply. He would pause for a few moments to let this advice soak in, and suddenly, beginning with the men at the right-hand row, name one after another so quickly that before the person mentioned had time to moisten his lips and get on his feet, the alert Doctor was well into the next row, and often he succeeded in enunciating every name in the room without getting a single response. Then he would sit back, fold his arms, and look at us, as who would say, " What a nimble-witted gang you are !''

Now, Sam was an expert mathematician, and he figured out Dr. Darnell's velocity as he might have done a problem in aerodynamics with Professor Donovan. He calculated that when the name of Sinclair was pronounced, a worthy but unready individual stationed five seats behind him, that by rising then, and beginning to speak when the Doctor came to Blakeley, he would just have nipped in when his own name was called. He had allowed several exhibitions of these lingual gymnastics to pass over his head, so that the class had become accustomed to them. I suppose we were rather a dull set at the beginning, and the good Doctor thought it well to wake us up, but he did it once too often. We always knew when the spasm was coming, because of his dwelling on the simplicity of the interrogation.

" I will ask you this morning," he began with disingenuous mildness, " a very elementary question. We shall be discussing to-day the nature of compound words. I take it for granted that you all know at least what a compound word is, so I may venture to ask for a few examples." Then he began with the unfortunate Prentiss, and galloped down the row until he mentioned Sinclair; then Sam began to heave into view, and when Blakeley gave way to McKurdy the latter's stentorian voice roared out—

" Bald-headed, red-whiskered, thick-pated, florid-faced, hot-tempered."

These words, so accurately descriptive of the Doctor himself, except " thick-pated," cut across the current of his volubility like a falling tree severing a telegraph wire. The Doctor smiled, leaned forward, and said—

" Nothing personal, Mr. McKurdy?"

" Oh no, doctor," replied Sam, as though he were shocked by the suggestion.

" I thought not," commented the Doctor. " Indeed, I am so dull-witted, to use another compound word, that I will call it coincidence," and with that he went on with his lecture.

The episode to which I took exception happened the morning after I had taken counsel with Sam regarding the advisability of assuring Dr. Darnell I was a teetotaler, and Sam's action seemed to resemble a breach of confidence. Once a week the Doctor read out to us certain extracts from old examination papers which we inscribed in our notebooks, handing in next morning the answers to them, written on sheets of foolscap paper in the same form we would afterwards use in undergoing a real examination. A student was forbidden to accept help from any fellow-student in preparing his paper, and he was also forbidden to consult a text-book in formulating his answers. It was during the scrutinizing of these papers that the Doctor's sardonic wit found its chiefest scope, for he had us, as it were, committed in writing, and there was plenty of time to elaborate whatever comment he thought necessary, which was an advantage he really did not need, because he was sharp enough when there was merely our verbal replies to go upon. It was most entertaining to listen to him, except when one happened to be the victim. There was always one glum man while the rest of the school was shaking with suppressed merriment. On the occasion to which I refer he held in his hand two slips of foolscap paper, and said—

"I have here the replies of Mr. McKurdy and Mr. Prentiss." He glared first at Sam then at me, as if wondering which to select as the recipient of whatever tirade was coming.

"I believe, Mr. McKurdy," he began, settling on the one nearest him, "that Mr. Prentiss occupies the same study with you in Church Street."

To my amazement Sam merely made an affirmative motion of his head, a gesture not allowed. A student was compelled to get on his feet, and answer respectfully, in a tone of voice which all might hear. This impudent, off-hand nod aroused the Doctor's ire on the instant, and indeed his ire never slept very soundly.

"Mr. McKurdy," he thundered, "I find that these two papers are almost identical in language. Which of you assisted the other, having pledged your word neither to give nor accept help? And when you answer, sir, I shall be obliged if you stand up."

Sam made three efforts to get on his feet, and finally accomplished his task with a heave of his broad shoulders, as if he cast an invisible burden from them. Then he braced his left leg at an awkward angle from his body, and clutched the edge of his desk as if to support himself.

"Mr. Darnell," he began in a thick voice, "there'sh but one c'rrect answer to *any* question; all other answers are more or less inc'rrect."

The whole school was staring at Sam by this time, and my hair was beginning to stand on end, as the Doctor's eyes opened wide.

Sam went heedlessly on—

"Necshessarily followsh that the near'r two persons come to c'rrectness, more identical their language must be. 'Sure you there was no col—col—col——'' Sam pulled himself together with an effort, and made the plunge—"collusion."

Dr. Darnell's face became almost white. After all, he was the most innocent of men regarding the vices of his fellows which he so freely denounced from his pulpit, otherwise he would have known that no human being, or at least very few of them, ever got drunk at that time in the morning.

"Sit down, sir," he said, in a quiet voice, and the despicable Sam collapsed into his seat—came down as if somebody had jerked away a prop. Dr. Darnell looked woefully at Sam for a moment, and then with a frown at me. It was impossible for me to get up and proclaim this a practical joke, so I sat there simmering. The inexperienced class evidently thought Sam was ill, but Dr. Darnell had no illusions about his condition. Luckily the gong rang, and we trooped out, all except Sam, who was absent when I, fairly boiling with rage, looked round for him in the waiting-room.

I had no opportunity of telling him my mind until we met in our study before luncheon, for he had eluded me on the way home by making a heroic dash through the forbidden passage, thus reaching our abiding-place before me. I found him sitting in his arm-chair with a broad grin on his face, holding the poker in his hand as if to defend himself, but I was in no humour for harlequin tricks.

"What, in the name of Heaven," I cried, "induced you to act the fool as you did in class this morning?"

"Why, Tom, how could I help it? It is through temptation that the drunkards fall, and my temptation was more than I could resist. Just give a thought to my reputation, and you will appreciate the position. Here am I, the black sheep of the flock held over from last session. Dr. Darnell, from the first day, shows his apprehension that this black sheep will corrupt his new white flock, but whatever his suspicions may have been of me last year, it never came within range of his wildest fear that I tampered with the flowing bowl. From the moment you told me of your indulgence in Rhine wine, the temptation arose to exhibit myself as the good man gone wrong. Here were you, a notorious drunkard, to Dr. Darnell's own knowledge, and my room-mate. His suspicion that one had helped the other in grammar gave me my tip to show him how much more potent example may be along other lines than the paths of learning. How could I let such a chance slip? You have led me astray, my boy, down the flowery road of inebriety!"

"Led your grandmother astray," I roared, with, I think, justifiable indignation, "and blow your position. Think of *my* position."

"Dear boy, I thought you would appreciate the artistic excellence of my acting. I thought the real sot would correctly assess the imitation."

"Oh, very well, I was foolish enough to tell you, in confidence, an incident of which I am ashamed. You use the knowledge, given to the man I thought a friend, further to humiliate me. The result you call a joke. I am going to leave this place, and also withdraw from the Normal School."

McKurdy at once became serious.

"If you take it that way," he said, "you leave me no option but to tell what happened after the class left the room, and to give you the real reason I acted as I did. Of course, I had no right to interfere, and when the door had closed, and Dr. Darnell and myself were left alone in the class-room, this fact was borne in upon me when I caught a glimpse of the sorrow on the headmaster's face. However, I began the attack before he had time to pull his gun. Standing up this time without needing to hold on to the desk I spoke in my soberest voice.

" ' Dr. Darnell,' I said, ' your chief blemish as a teacher of youth is not your violent temper, as you suppose, and which you constantly endeavour to keep in check, but your habit of believing the very worst of your fellow man. If there are two possible explanations of a pupil's action, you instinctively choose the one most to his discredit. We have an example in this school of the very opposite in Professor Donovan, whom perhaps you think a simpleton. He can believe nothing but good of any one of us, and accordingly we are all on our best behaviour in his room, and young as the session is, the whole class is already devoted to him.'

" ' I was never a popularity hunter,' snapped the Doctor.

" Of course I knew I had touched him on a sore spot; gruff as you may think him, he nevertheless yearns for the affection of his pupils, which he rarely receives, and which Donovan wins so easily, and indeed unconsciously.

" ' If you wish for popularity,' I continued, ' you go the wrong way about procuring it, except in a few individual cases, for there are members of your class with penetration enough to see that your sympathies go much deeper than Professor Donovan's. You are angry when you see a man misuse his opportunities; Professor Donovan is merely sorry. Your interest in us is individual. Professor Donovan's geniality spreads over the whole class. We are separate personalities to you; we are merely a mass to Professor Donovan, who does not recognize the atoms that compose it.'

" 'Humph!' said Dr. Darnell. 'We seem to be rather under the microscope so far as you are concerned.'

" I saw that although he concealed his gratification, it was nevertheless there.

" ' A few minutes ago you thought I was drunk; now you know I am not.'

" 'If you will excuse my interrupting you, Mr. McKurdy, I had a few moments ago the two choices you spoke of. I had either to consider you idiotic or intoxicated. In adopting the latter option, did I make the worse or the better choice?'

" I laughed. I saw that my interview was not going to be a failure.

" 'Now I come to the point, Dr. Darnell. You are making a mistake about my room-mate. He told me of his unfortunate first meeting with you, and his fall from grace rather weighs on his mind. He sees that it is ever present in yours, because, as I have said, you invariably put the worst construction on a man's actions. He consulted with me yesterday, proposing to seek a private interview with you, to assure you he had never tasted wine before, and did not intend to taste it again. I advised him not to seek that interview.'

" ' Why?'

" ' Because you would not have believed him.'

" ' Are you so sure of that?'

" ' Positive.'

8

" ' Well,' said the Doctor, with a grim smile, ' as was said of Macaulay, I wish I was as sure of anything as you are of everything.'

" ' No, Doctor, it needed something more pungent than a lame explanation such as he would have given, to have reached your inner consciousness. Look what actually happened. You at once believed that I was tipsy, and at once jumped at the equally erroneous conclusion that my room-mate had led me astray, while he, poor wretch, sat there with the perspiration pouring from his brow, writhing under my action, and your suspicion, yet not knowing what to say. Indeed, there was nothing to say, and, from the Medusa look he bent on me when I turned round, I have concluded it safer to avoid him until he has had time to cool down. You judged and condemned him unheard.'

" I paused here to give the Doctor a chance to contradict me, but he remained silent. When at last he spoke, it was very quietly—

" ' I think your seat in Dr. Cardiff's room is vacant, Mr. McKurdy.'

" So with that I rose and left him."

CHAPTER IX

Defer not till to-morrow to be wise.
LETTER TO COBHAM.

Who hath woe? who hath sorrow? who hath contentions? who hath babbling? who hath wounds without cause? who hath redness of eyes?

They that tarry long at the wine; they that go to seek mixed wine.

Look not thou upon the wine when it is red, when it giveth its colour to the cup, when it moveth itself aright.

At the last it biteth like a serpent, and stingeth like an adder.

Good understanding giveth favour: but the way of transgressors is hard.

I HAD been brought up to go to church, and had heard many a prayer, many a sermon, and many readings of the Scripture. So far as religion was concerned, I was an ordinary, commonplace, healthy youth, neither unduly elated at the prospect of heaven, nor exceptionably disturbed by the danger of hell. The Bible, after all, was a thing apart; to the older people, perhaps a thing of necessity, but to us youngsters with the whole world before us, with so much to do, with such chances of getting on, with constant fear of failure and poverty in our minds, the Bible somehow did not seem to apply to the practical concerns of a hard existence. This state of placid indifference had in it no tinge of agnosticism. I should as soon have thought of doubting the recurrence of the seasons as of questioning a word of Holy Writ. I would have shrunk from an acknowledged atheist as from a confessed leper. But at our academy the Bible began to take on for me a new and terrible significance, and often in class I made note in my blank book of chapter and verse, and searched the Scriptures to learn if its pages actually contained the fierce invectives made personal by Dr. Darnell's accusatory voice.

He read the Bible magnificently, as a great actor, after close study of his part, might render a scene from Shakespeare. The preachers I had formerly listened to had been but barnstormers. I was now in the amazing presence of a Savonarola, an Edwin Booth; of a Peter the Hermit, a Henry Irving. If Dr. Darnell could have maintained for the day that state of exaltation with which he read the morning lessons, we should have been in his hands simply the clay of the potter. But he was a constant victim to sudden anger, and self-reproach made him more human for a time following an outburst. Neither could he curb himself from making a keen and bitter remark, no matter how deeply it cut, and this also was gall to him when the triumph of the moment passed, and he wished to make amends. Strangely enough, our liking for him mounted higher and higher, and we loved him for his human faults rather than for his spiritual virtues. Deep sincerity was the key-note of his nature, and he believed every word he hurled at us, not for our destruction, but for our salvation. He himself chose the extracts he read to us, and followed no line laid down by Book of Common Prayer, or any other. His readings generally left the class in a state of morose gloom, with some of the girls silently weeping, and when he closed the great Book on the desk before him, it seemed as if the gates of mercy had shut with a bang.

One day, as we came out into the waiting-room, Sam, with a sickly grin on his face, pretending he had not been affected like the rest of us, said—

" Professor Donovan ought to read the Bible to us every second day. He would blunder across the Sermon on the Mount at least sometimes, which Dr. Darnell never does, but, as my Aunt Jane says, a man finds in the Bible whatever he brings to it."

The verses that appear at the beginning of this chapter were declaimed to the class the morning after Sam tried to convince the headmaster that I was not a dissipated person, and, listening to the denunciation undoubtedly levelled at me, I surmised that Sam had not succeeded in his mission. I was confirmed in this belief when I discovered that the last verse did not belong to the chapter Dr. Darnell was reading, but had been added on for my benefit. A foreboding that trouble might be brewing for me was speedily realized.

" Mr. Prentiss," came the command in Dr. Darnell's schoolday voice, nothing of emotion now in his tones, and I rose to my feet.

" You will report to Mr. Brent to-morrow at nine o'clock in the great hall of the Model School. You will be prepared to give a reading lesson to the first division immediately after prayers. The selection is entitled ' Ashore on Anticosti,' and I advise you to con it over to-night."

Sam took the risk of turning round and smiling encouragement at me.

The way of transgressors *was* hard. I, a raw recruit, should not have been forced to attack the Gibraltar of the Model School. Usually, as I knew, a Normalite learnt the ways of the Model School by being sent first to the second, third, or fourth division, the crucial test of the first division being reserved until the session was well advanced. The Model School was the purgatory through which poor souls had the spirit burnt out of them before they reached the heaven of independence and large salaries in their profession. The four divisions were the warm rooms of a Turkish bath which sweated conceit out of a man, and the first division was its hottest corner.

Every ward in the city possessed its own large, well-appointed school-house, attended five days a week by the boys of that district. The Model School stood unique and alone, the city authorities having nothing to do with it. It was the only school in the country where corporal punishment was entirely forbidden. Its teachers held the highest qualifications; its reputation, except among us Normalites, was something to be proud of. For every vacancy which occurred in its scholastic ranks there were an hundred applicants, and the headmaster therefore had a choice of the very best material on which to work. I have no doubt that the Model School deserved all the praise bestowed upon it, and I imagine that those human terrors, the first division coterie, were held under the most rigid discipline, except for one hour on certain days, when the trembling victim from the Normal School took the platform in their presence to instruct them on some subject of which they knew a great deal more than he did. Of him, if he allowed them, they proceeded to make a monkey.

The injustice of sending me to this menagerie as a first experience braced me up, and I confess I was not the least perturbed over the prospect. I had taught backwoods schools containing pupils of my own age. More than once it had needed muscle to preserve discipline. I would not be allowed to raise the cane, of course, in the first division; but, on the other hand, they were not permitted to make a bodily attack on me, as sometimes happened in a rural school, where the ejection of a teacher by his infuriated pupils was regarded by the neighbourhood as rather a good joke. So, all in all, I looked forward without apprehension to what the morrow might bring.

That evening, on reaching our domicile, the sympathetic Sam, being caterer for the week, left me at the door to visit some provision shops in the exercise of his office. On the table up-stairs lay a letter, which I thought at first was news from home; but the superscription, in a lady's hand, showed it was intended for S. A. M. McKurdy. When Sam returned, he opened it with some eagerness, read it once or twice, made an entry in his note-book, tore up the missive, and cast the bits into the fire. When we returned to the warm and comfortable study after dinner in the basement, I settled down to a satisfactory mathematical evening with Euclid. Sam sat silent in his arm-chair, pondering; taking up no book. Finally he roused himself, as if he had come to some decision, and looked up at me. Whatever he had intended to say at first was evidently not what he actually said. The sight of the book in my hand changed his mind.

"What's that you've got?" he asked.

"Geometry."

He sprang to his feet and stood facing me, something almost like a frown on his brow.

"Don't you know that you're to give a reading lesson to the first division to-morrow morning?"

"Why, of course. What's a reading lesson? That's as easy as rolling off a log. I have taught reading for several years, you must remember."

Sam drew in a long breath.

"My dear Prentiss," he began, with more impressiveness in his manner than I had ever known him to use before, "let me give you a little much-needed advice. You evidently have not the slightest notion of what is in front of you. If Daniel, instead of being thrown into the den of lions, had been sent down to the first division, he would have had something to complain about. Those lads, before whom you appear to-morrow, are ready for you. You will be alone with them in the room, and some time during the hour, you may not hear the door open, but John Brent will be there, his face adorned with a glacial smile. By that time the boys will have reduced you to a dish-rag. You will be hot, angry, and possibly dismayed. John Brent will find the pupils thoroughly out of hand, and those chaps will know by a glance at his face whether to slay you on the spot, or instantly subside into the well-drilled meekness of a Sunday-school class. If Brent has no particular malice against you, he will quell them with one glint of his eye; if he happens to have taken a dislike to you, he will stand there with a cold smile on his lips and see you flounder deeper and deeper into disorder."

"But, my dear Sam, why should he have taken a dislike to me?"

"Because it is written in the book of fate. It is in the circumstances of the case. You are not really one of us. You came with ambitions towards the University; you were determined to qualify as a civil engineer. You think it rather a come-down that you are compelled to attend the Normal School, and, doubtless quite unconsciously, this shows in your manner. You have already given Dr. Darnell several very tart answers before his class. Now, he is a man so prone to that sort of thing himself that, curiously enough, his appreciation of a clever reply nulli-fies his personal resentment at it. Besides, he usually gives you as good as you send, and in that he scores again. Still, you haven't made much way with him. He is in a state of suspended judgment about you, and you know you are gradually drifting towards the place I held last session as the dangerous person in the school. John Brent is a horse of another colour. He has no sense of humour, and he does not know what the word forgiveness means. You may lash Dr. Darnell into frenzy with a phrase, but the frenzy will not be lasting, and the phrase will not stick. John Brent will receive with a smile any retort you can make, and that retort will be treasured up against you, never forgotten, never forgiven. Nothing you can say will hurry or retard him, but when the proper moment comes he will be waiting round the corner for you with a club, and under one stroke you will pay all indebtedness."

" Well, Sam, if everything is settled, and fixed, and pre-ordained, what's the use of my worrying ? Why not enjoy a night wi' Burns, or Euclid, before marching to the shambles ?"

" I'll tell you why. There is one chance in a million that you may defeat John Brent. There are a million chances to one that you will play right into his hands. The test is temper. If you can keep your temper, you will give John a run for his money. So I implore you to suppress your anger, no matter what happens. Remember that those youngsters are nothing to you. As viewed at present, the gallows is their proper destination, but the chances are they will become our great statesmen and merchant princes and railway presidents. I'll make one prediction, which is this. During your hour of teaching reading to the first division of the Model School, you will not hear a single line of the lesson read."

" Then, in the fiend's name, what is a person to do ?"

" The first thing is to throw away that Euclid, surround yourself with dictionaries, gazetteers and what not, and get as much information into your head as you can during the short time at your disposal. For the rest, keep your temper; take whatever comes smiling."

I had already laid down the *Elements of Geometry*, and had opened the reading text-book at the page where " Ashore on Anticosti " began.

Sam vanished into his bedroom, and came out clothed in his overcoat, with his hat in hand.

" Are you going out ?" I asked in surprise.

" Yes; I attend a little "—he hesitated—" prayer-meeting once a week, and sometimes oftener."

" I never suspected you were addicted to piety."

" No, a man is seldom appreciated in his own household. My idea is that fervent supplication a few nights a week enlivens the monotony of an otherwise drab career."

" Well, if all you've said to-night is true, you had better breathe a prayer for me while you're at it."

" *Laborare est orare*. If you work hard to-night, you won't need any one to pray for you."

" That is strange advice for a devotee to give."

" Yes, isn't it? I'm devout enough, but I also believe in hard work; speaking of which reminds me that I may need to climb the pillar of the porch to-night, so if you happen to be up late studying, and hear a snowball against the pane, you might open the window, for that is easier done from the inside than from the outside, especially in a time of frost and snow."

"All right, Sam; I'll wait up for you."

McKurdy departed, and I drew a gazetteer toward me, turned its leaves and read—

"Anticosti, a barren island of British North America, situated in the Gulf of St. Lawrence, between latitudes 49° and 50° N, and between longitudes 61° 40′ and 64° 30′ W, with a length of 135 miles, and a maximum breadth of 40. Most of the coast is——"

CHAPTER X

Let not him that girdeth on his harness boast himself as he that putteth it off.—1 KINGS xx. 11.

WHEN, on the stroke of nine, I entered the great hall of the Model School, I found seated there the whole four divisions, each in its allotted two or three rows of seats, and standing on the platform the four masters; the suave Brent, the placid Jones, the severe McAlpin, and the kindly Davison, who taught respectively first, second, third and fourth divisions. The number of pupils in each division was exactly the same, and they ranged in age from six or seven in the fourth division to sixteen or seventeen in the first division. John Brent stood at the desk, and read a chapter and a prayer in a colourless, non-committal, take-it-or-leave-it style of voice. He read the Scriptures because such reading was ordained by the Board of Education, and not in that spirit of fervent, enthusiastic belief which characterized Dr. Darnell's performance of the same function. When chapter and prayer were finished, Mr. Brent turned his face to his own class, and uttered with the decisive clip of a drill sergeant, "One!" Every boy in the first division rose to his feet, as if actuated by the same mechanism, the thick red book of reading lessons held under the left arm of each.

"Two!" Every boy side-stepped into the aisle.

"Three!" The class turned right about face.

" Four !" The contingent marched off with the
precision of a German regiment, the footsteps falling
together as if one man walked. Mr. Brent, standing
upright as a grenadier, now favoured me with that
congenital inclination of the head as if a string had
been pulled. Three fellow-students of the Normal
who were to teach the other three divisions of the
school, had been standing against the wall beside me.
They were all looking rather trembly, and I confess
the atmosphere of the place had begun to oppress me,
despite my confidence of the night before.

Dismissed by Brent's nod, I followed the tail of
the first division out of the great hall, and along the
corridor to the dreaded class-room. Through the
doorway, in perfect order, the class marched, and I,
entering behind them, closed the door, turned round,
and faced the pupils.

I found myself in a room fitted up differently from
either the amphitheatre style of the University or
the single-seat level floor of the Normal. There were
four long benches running almost the length of the
room to a flight of steps that led upward opposite the
door. The first form was level with the floor, the
second a step higher, the third another step higher,
the fourth the final step higher, but the benches were
straight, and not semi-circular as was the case at
University College. There was no desk, and no
platform for the teacher, but a clear space of flooring,
perhaps six feet wide, running the entire breadth of
the room. The wall at my back, as I faced the class,
was a black-board, and up at the ceiling were fastened
oblong boxes from which great maps could be pulled
down. For a moment or two I looked at my pupils
of the hour. They were almost unnaturally silent,
and as I gazed at their intelligent faces, mostly as

immobile as that of John Brent himself, I detected here and there semi-humorous expressions of gentle expectation. The boys, instead of taking their four benches as they should have done, had jammed themselves into the two upper seats, leaving the two lower empty. They were wedged tighter than any set of sardines in a tin box, and seemed waiting for me to say something. Now, I could not know who were right and who were wrong in the positions they occupied. I knew that half of them belonged to the upper benches, and half to the empty lower benches, and I knew also that if I attempted to disentangle them and put every boy in his proper place, my reading hour would be long past before I had unravelled the snarl. Of course, at a word from me the erring half might have stepped across into the vacant places, but I conjectured that if the word were given there would result instant confusion, dispute about places, followed by hopeless disorder, during which I should receive the inevitable visit of Mr. John Brent. Now, at least I had silence, so I took the red book from under my arm, and opened it at the turned-down page. The attack on me was evidently to be physical, and I determined to treat the situation intellectually if I could. I was not going to fight the Devil with fire, but with Holy Water.

"Young men, before you open your books, I should like to ask you a question or two that I may test that habit of observance which I am told is one of your strong points. Who wrote 'Ashore on Anticosti'?"

There was no answer to my question, and indeed, a glance at the majority of faces told me that their minds were not occupied with the subject under discussion. The general expression plainly said—

"Good gracious, isn't he going to separate the sheep from the goats?"

"Doubtless you did know the answer to this question, but have temporarily mislaid it, therefore I shall give you a lead. Two distinguished writers were born in the city of Dublin within nine years of each other. Each wrote novels that were very successful; some of them exceedingly humorous, as was to be expected from Irishmen. They died within four years of one another, and to carry our coincidence still further, their names differed in the second letter only. One was Lover; the other was Lever. Which of these two men wrote 'Ashore on Anticosti'?"

To my amazement, I held the attention of the class in spite of their uncomfortable predicament. One boy chirped up—

"We're not allowed to read novels, sir."

"Oh yes, you are. This is part of a novel, as I tell you, and here and there throughout your reading-book are selections from Charles Dickens, Thackeray and others."

"May I explain, sir?" said a boy in the corner. "Love-her and Leave-her being the themes of most novels, we are too young to understand such things."

There was a compressed titter at this, and I beamed on the lad with admiration.

"I wish Lover and Lever could have heard that remark of yours, and as a token of appreciation of your puns I'll say no more about authorship, but leave this question with you, and next time I have the pleasure of coming here, perhaps you will be able to answer it. Those who discover the novel our extract is taken from, I advise to read the book. Forbidden fruit is not without its enticing quality, and if you are caught, say that your master gave you leave. We will now consider the island of Anticosti for a few moments, and then——"

" Were you ever a jailer, sir?" inquired a small voice from the top seat.

" No, I was merely in charge of the torture chamber in a Russian prison. The jailer was my chief. I'm here because the Russian government expects to get some hints from the Model School."

" This is no joke, master," gasped another. " I'm suffocating."

" I'm sorry."

" I'm suffocating too," piped another.

" The same sympathy I extended to your comrade I extend also to you, and before there are any more complaints, let me explain my position. I am sent here to teach you to read. Dr. Darnell said, ' Teach them how to read that selection entitled " Ashore on Anticosti." ' He didn't say, ' You are to give first aid to the injured.' I have nothing to do with the manner in which you have placed yourselves in class : that is *your* affair. If you have mismanaged it, that is none of *my* affair. Furthermore, I have been informed that you often place Normal School students in an exceedingly tight place, therefore don't growl when you get into a tight place yourselves. If the medicine goes the wrong way, take it nevertheless. And now no more nonsense, but to our lesson. As a very compact body of citizens you should be able to appreciate the peculiarities of Anticosti better than most people. It is a hundred and thirty-five miles long, by forty miles wide, and excepting the lighthouse keeper, there isn't a single inhabitant on the island. Think of the elbow-room there is on Anticosti, and if you feel inclined to sing the hymn, ' Oh, what must it be to be there?' I shall listen with sympathy."

" Master, I wish to appeal to your sense of justice," said the biggest boy in the class.

" Very well."

" I am seated in my proper place. Half of the class are seated in their proper places. Why should we innocent victims be punished equally with the wrong-doers?"

" Ah, my son, you open a very large question there. Why is that the case all the world over? Why are the innocent everywhere suffering from the doings of others over whom they have no control? Take for example an unjust war, where thousands of——"

" Oh, you're merely making fun of us."

" I assure you I was never more serious in my life."

" Master, I have pointed out to you a concrete injustice; you answer in generalities. I ask you instantly to remedy this injustice, otherwise I shall leave the room and appeal to Mr. Brent."

" I cannot believe that such an appeal would prevail. How do you propose to explain to Mr. Brent this jamming of the whole class into two inadequate seats, instead of into four ample ones?"

" That is not my fault, sir. I hope you accept my word that I am in my proper place?"

" Certainly I accept it. Now, perhaps some of you are sons of noted lawyers, and maybe to those I can make my point plain. If your present contention were to hold, you should have made appeal to me the moment I entered this room. You did not do so. You remained silent, expecting me to remedy the fault that had been committed. You have learned now that I have no intention of doing so, and learning

9

this, you stand bravely on the rock of Justice.   I say you are an accessory after the fact, through your silence at the proper time, and an accessory after the fact is held almost equally culpable with the actual criminal.   But what disappoints me with you boys is this.   You do not stand to your guns like men. You don't say to yourselves, ' We've done this thing, and now we'll take the consequences, whatever they are.'   That is a manly course, but you are whimpering like a lot of teething infants."

" But this is as bad as the Black Hole in Calcutta," objected one lad.

" Don't exaggerate; it isn't.   You are seated in a well-ventilated room, with plenty of good air, and if, in breathing, you thrust your chest outward, as you should, you will experience no difficulty on that score.   It is only sideways that you are inconvenienced.   The chief thing is to pretend you like it.   Why gratify me by exhibiting your discomfort? A man from the rural districts once visited his son in college, as doubtless your fathers will do when you reach the University stage.   Dining in hall, and being unaccustomed to the plate of the place, he inadvertently put two spoonsful of salt, instead of sugar, into his coffee, much to the embarrassment of his son, who knew the ropes.   They offered the old gentleman a fresh cup, but he shook his head.

" ' No,' he said, ' I always take salt; I like it.' Do you see the point?"

" Yes," they shouted.   " Tell us another!"

" Did you ever hear of the farmer, the soldier, and the crow?"

" No, let us have it."

" A company of soldiers had camped out near the estate of a crusty old farmer.   One of the soldiers got permission to go shooting, and after wandering about a bit and finding no game, he espied a crow on the topmost branch of a tree in the farmer's orchard, and promptly shot it. It happened that this was a pet bird of the old farmer, who came out, enraged, with a loaded shot-gun, which he levelled at the soldier, whose fowling-piece was empty."

" 'You've killed that bird,' he roared, 'now you shall eat it,' and although the soldier begged off and pleaded for mercy, the old farmer was obdurate, and the soldier had to do the best he could with the crow. The farmer then turned away, but the soldier slipped a cartridge in his gun, called to him, and when the farmer wheeled round he found himself looking down the muzzle of a loaded rifle.

" 'I've begun the crow,' said the soldier, 'now you finish it.' The farmer was compelled to obey, and the soldier returned to camp. Next day the farmer complained to the Colonel, who paraded his men, and asked the aged agriculturist to pick out the culprit, which the farmer had no difficulty in doing.

" 'Step from the ranks,' said the Colonel, and the soldier did so.

" 'Do you know this man?' he asked, pointing to the farmer.

The soldier saluted.

" 'Yes, Colonel,' he replied. 'We dined together yesterday.'

" Now, that's the way to take misfortune. When you meet me in the street hereafter, never say a word about the crowded benches, but remark casually, 'That man taught me reading once.' "

The boys laughed as well as their cramped position allowed, and one of them said—

"If you go on with the reading lesson, master, you'll hear no more groans from me."

The hour was now well forward, and here was practical capitulation, so I was just about to ask the boys to step into their proper places, when an unruffled voice said slowly—

"What is the meaning of this, Mr. Prentiss?"

I turned and faced John Brent. The class became more breathless than ever. It seemed a pity that he should have stolen in just when the boys and I had come to an understanding. But the delusion that the young fellows were at all ashamed of themselves, or would be true to the implied compact that if I went on with the reading there should be no grumbling, was quickly dispelled, for, when they saw their real master before them and caught his look of disapproval on me, there arose a most pitiable wail from at least a dozen of them, who appeared to writhe in the extremity of distress. I knew then that I was not in the house of my friends, as for one brief moment I had supposed.

"It means, Mr. Brent, that these boys are so badly instructed that half of their number did not know enough to take their own seats, and the other half were so lacking in any sense of fair play that they did not complain of the intrusion until too late."

"Then, Mr. Prentiss, it was your duty to supplement the defective instruction, and to see that each boy was in his proper position before the lesson began."

"I beg your pardon, Mr. Brent. The orders given me by Dr. Darnell were definite. They had nothing to do with arithmetic, algebra, geology, geometry, geography or discipline. I was to teach reading."

Mr. Brent's tone became colder and more precise.

" Your orders were to report in the great hall, and there take your class. From the moment the class left the hall, it was under your charge."

I saw he rather had me there. The boys saw it, too, and stopped their wailing long enough to chortle.

" I imagine you are right, Mr. Brent. I made the mistake of thinking my duties began when I entered this room."

" Being at last enlightened, Mr. Prentiss, oblige me by placing this class as it should have been placed in the beginning."

" No, I prefer to deal with a compact mass."

" Do you refuse?"

" I have just done so."

" Then I shall attend to the matter myself."

" Mr. Brent, you have said that the class is in my charge. It remains so until my hour is completed. You are neither my principal nor my assistant teacher. You are here simply to judge, and your present duty consists solely in estimating my value as instructor. I shall not permit you to interfere with this class in the slightest degree until my time expires."

" You will not *permit* it?"   He placed an emphasis on the word " permit " and grew a little white round the corners of the mouth.

" No. Where I taught school last, I boarded at a farm. Every evening I saw the hired man drive sixteen cows to their stalls. Each cow knew her own stall, and turned into it night after night, without a word or a blow from the hired man. That farm was on the verge of the backwoods; you are in the capital city, supposed to be the best teacher in that city, and this class, as naturally follows, should be the premier class in the land. Yet they sit here to prove that they have not so much sense as any one of those sixteen cows, and that you are a poorer trainer of human beings than that hired man was of dumb animals.''

There was no moaning in the class while this diatribe went on. Brent went whiter and whiter, but stood rigid as a statue. I had said that I would prevent his interference, and this, carried to its logical conclusion, meant that if he attempted to give orders to the class, I was bound to throw him out of the door if I could. There he stood, a perfect specimen of manhood; a triumph of gymnasium training. There I confronted him, nothing like so handsome, nor so well set-up, but my muscles attested that I was acquainted with out-door life and hard work. I knew I couldn't throw him out, and he knew he couldn't throw me out. My finger ends were tingling with anger, and doubtless face and eyes showed that I was just about to cross the line where consequences didn't matter. I had been pleased with myself for keeping my temper during all my conflict with the class, and now in an instant everything had gone by the board beyond the possibility of recall. I was simply a primitive man, thirsting for another's blood, and yet I was not far enough gone in madness but that I could see the thin veneer of civilization uncracked on my opponent, and knew that if he spoke again, instead of declaiming as I had done, his voice would not be raised a semitone. He did not speak, nor attempt to give an order. It was one of the boys who broke the silence.

''If you please, sir, it's three minutes after the hour!''

So far as I was concerned, the tension snapped. I glanced at the clock, and laughed aloud. We had been standing like two fools, at daggers drawn in a brawl that the clock had already ticked away, and as I looked from the face of the clock to the face of the headmaster, now re-installed, it crossed my mind that Sam had been wrong in one of his assertions. Mr. Brent had not smiled once since he came into the room.

"Mr. Brent," I said, waving my hand toward the living sardines, "there is your class. I bid a cordial good-morning to you, and to it."

With that I withdrew, ending a reading lesson during which not a single sentence had been read.

CHAPTER XI

The firste vertue, sone, if thou wilt lere
Is to restreine, and kepen wel thy tonge.
'THE MANCIPLE'S TALE.'

INSTEAD of following the corridor which led from
the Model to the Normal School, I passed outside into
the street, where the air was of a temperature much
lower than the atmosphere of the school-room, especially during the final minutes of my hour therein. I
walked round the large square that contained the
educational buildings, thus proving the possibility of
circling the square, even if I could not square the
circle. The nipping cold exercised a soothing effect on
my anger, and, that departing, left me face to face
with the situation my hot impatience had created.
Fully warned by my comrade, I had succeeded in
obtaining complete control of the situation, only to be
overthrown at the last moment by my own impetuous
temper surging vainly against the hard granite of my
opponent's imperturbability; he standing there grim
and silent while my eloquence put me hopelessly in
the wrong, for none knew better than I that if criti-
cisms were to be passed, I should have waited until he
and I were alone, and not have ventured to lecture
him before his own class. In the cold outside air I
saw too late how easy it would have been to carry my
triumph to the end of the hour. I might have
shrugged my shoulders, borrowed his smile, and
referred him gently to his own pupils for a reply to

the question of why they were packed like books on a crowded shelf. An even temper and a good deal of silence would have meant victory.

Round and round the square I marched, oppressed by the futility of the situation, almost determining to quit the Normal School for ever and attend instead the College of Technology, as I had first proposed. Two considerations kept this determination from becoming fixed. First, my withdrawal would seem like a desertion of Sam, whom I had come to like; and second, there was a stubbornness in my nature which shrank from the thought of running away after my first encounter with Mr. Brent. One part of the problem, however, must not be ignored. If Mr. Brent were so powerful that he could prevent me from getting a certificate of competence as a teacher, then my six months at the Normal School would be wasted. Never for one moment did I doubt that he would do all he could against me, and the accuracy of this estimate was proved by after events. Even Banquo's ghost could not have looked upon me with colder dislike, and I might have changed Macbeth's phrase into " Thou hast no mercy in those eyes which thou dost glare with." The point, then, was to learn exactly the extent of this man's power over the credentials I might expect to receive from the school at the end of my term, so I turned in at the scholars' gate, mounted the stairs to the empty waiting-room, came to Dr. Darnell's private door, and knocked. In response came a sharp " Come in," which somehow did not sound promising. The Doctor was seated at his table, revising, so I guessed, the proof sheets of a text-book he was shortly to issue, for the torment of future generations. He looked up with an expression of displeasure at the interruption.

" It is unusual," he said crossly, " to come here unannounced. If you had spoken to Boyle, as is the rule, you would have learned that I wished to be undisturbed this morning."

" I am sorry," I apologized. " If you will tell me when you are at leisure, I will return, with your permission."

" Why are you not in Dr. Cardiff's room ?"

" Because a body cannot be in two places at the same time, and my body has been tramping for fifteen minutes round this building on the outside."

" A modern Jericho, eh? and the walls of your difficulty have not fallen, I take it ?"

" You are quite right. I merely wish to ask you one question, and your answer will decide whether or not I leave this institution."

The Doctor shoved his proof sheets to one side, leaned back in his chair, and clasped his hands behind his head, a favourite attitude of his.

" Sit down, Mr. Prentiss," he commanded shortly.

" Thank you, I prefer to stand. I shall not detain you more than a minute. I want to know——"

" Sit down !" he snapped, his eyes blazing, and I sat down.

" Trouble in the Model School, I suppose ?"

" Yes."

" I'm accustomed to that; tell me about it."

I related, as tersely as I could, what had happened, and once or twice the flicker of a smile showed for a brief portion of a second on his lips, but instantly was obliterated. The anger left his eyes, which, however, could scarcely repress a twinkle as they mentally saw those young reprobates squeezed into half the space needed, and kept there.

" I am sorry you ran counter to Mr. Brent. Did it not occur to you that if you had anything to say, it should not have been said before his pupils?"

" That occurred to me, sir, the moment I got outside."

" Ah!" said the Doctor, with a long-drawn exclamation. There was a world of sympathy in the expression, which somehow served as balm to the rawness of my nerves. It was one hot-tempered man appreciating the temptation and the fall of another. After a few minutes he spoke brusquely.

" The first division of the Model School is undoubtedly difficult to manage. Many of our students here have fallen into the mistake of thinking us wrong in allowing the Model pupils so much latitude, and I see you have fallen into the same error. If a student, going down to the first division, succeeds in controlling those boys, he obtains very high marks, and proves himself a capable disciplinarian. Success in the first division means brains and self-control, and I assure you it means knowledge of the subject to be taught as well. Therefore we rate the few successful students very high. Mr. Brent, you must remember, does not resort to corporal punishment, yet you saw to-day that he held control over both his class and his temper, an example which, even from your own account, has been largely lost upon you. You may not love Mr. Brent, but you are bound to respect him, if you are a judge of good teaching. But what I wish to say is this—Although success in the first division will greatly enhance your standing at the end of the term, you may fail entirely with Mr. Brent, and yet obtain a creditable certificate through the favourable reports of the other three teachers in the Model School."

" Thank you, Doctor," said I, rising. " That's all I wished to know."

" Your walls of Jericho have fallen at last. But before you go, I should like to put a few questions to you. Have you broken any of our rules so far?"

" Not that I know of. There seems to be a good many of them, but I think I am innocent up to date."

" Have you been asked to depart from our regulations in any way?"

" No."

" I am very glad to hear it. If at the end of the session you can say the same as honestly as I believe you to be speaking now, you need fear no adverse report Mr. Brent sends up from the Model School. It is hardly worth your while attending any class till after lunch. Have you ever seen our picture gallery?"

" No, I have not."

" It occupies the upper floor of the administrative buildings, and is open to Normal School students one day a week, and as this happens to be the day, I commend it to your attention. Some of the pictures are worth your study. Good-morning."

The Doctor returned to his proofs, and shortly after, I was climbing the broad stairs which led to the picture gallery.

If every man was weighed down with a consciousness of the effect of his most casual word, I suppose we would then live in a dumb world. Some of the students called Dr. Darnell " the red man," because of the colour of his whiskers, his florid face, and his aboriginal temper, but no Indian, unerringly flinging his tomahawk at a pioneer, more effectually eliminated a useful pathfinder than did Dr. Darnell's indifferent wave of the hand as he dismissed me to the picture gallery. It was a case of instant, mysterious, and irrevocable disappearance. A potential civil engineer entered that gallery, and was never seen again. A potential painter came out. The man who went in might, perhaps, have proved a useful individual, for his hard, healthy life would have been laid in the wilderness, by forest and stream, far from civilization; the future of the man who came out was to be Paris, Rome, London, and New York. Dr. Darnell had blotted out a bridge-builder, and produced, if we are to believe certain art critics, an indifferent painter. The headmaster probably never knew the far-reaching effect of the invitation he had given me; indeed, I hold him innocent, and put the responsibility on a certain conjunction of incidents which caused the swift transformation.

It was not the beauty of art, but the beauty of nature I first beheld on entering the long gallery, and the unexpected sight brought me to a standstill by the door. The gallery was so large that although some half-dozen visitors were present, the room seemed empty. Two of those present were not looking at the art treasures. Oblivious to all about them, they promenaded slowly along the polished wooden floor, like two young women waiting for the dance to begin. Each in her own way was beautiful. A sweet seriousness was always the distinguishing characteristic of Aline Arbuthnot, but as I stood gazing at her, this sobriety of manner was accentuated by a slight frown on that fair white brow. The downcast eyes, and a certain pathetic firmness about the lips added a suggestion of distress to her arresting face. The world may have considered her companion more beautiful than Aline Arbuthnot, but such was never for a moment my opinion. Very attractive I admit this companion was; bright, vivacious, jolly; her fair hair, in numerous bewitching tendrils, framing a face which most painters would have loved to reproduce on their canvases. Her hand was laid lightly on Aline's arm, and now and then she pulled the girl towards her with impulsive, affectionate little caresses, as if to rouse the apathy of her friend, whose attitude remained unresponsive. The blonde appeared to be pleading, scolding a little, and laughing a good deal, as if presenting some case she had at heart, which the other regarded unsympathetically, if not with complete disfavour. I stood as if my feet were glued to the shining floor, gazing moonstruck at the approaching two, and perhaps it was this intensity that caused the vivacious one to look up and meet my glance. She gave a little shriek, in which were mingled pleasure and dismay.

" Talk of the devil——" she gasped, then checked herself, and those flippant words caused an electrical thrill, strange in my experience, to tingle through to my finger-ends; for, if the phrase signified anything, it meant that they had been talking of me, strange and unaccountable as this conclusion seemed. Miss Arbuthnot raised her downcast eyes more slowly, and the frown deepened on her brow, as if in response to the other's embarrassed laugh. The disapproving glance went past me, and far beyond, making me feel as if I didn't exist. The laughing one whispered.

" No, no," said she of the frown, and now Miss Arbuthnot grasped the other by the arm and accelerated her reluctant steps, but after passing me the gayer beauty looked over her shapely shoulder and smiled, while I stood like a wooden image, without even the courtesy to raise my hat at this astonishing advance.

Again the laughing girl whispered, and Aline shook herself free.

"Never, never," she cried; then, in a voice of beseechment, almost of terror, "Come home, Sally," she said, but Sally stood her ground, the smile disappearing, and a glint of anger appearing in those eloquent eyes.

"If you are a child, I am not," she retorted, and Aline, with a gasp that was almost a sob, turned and fled. The deserted Sally stood for a moment a monument of indecision, then the smile returned, and she came towards me.

"You are Mr. Prentiss, are you not?"

"Yes," I admitted.

"I wished to introduce my friend to you, but she is an arrant little coward; nevertheless a great admirer of yours."

"Really?" I said, laughing. "She doesn't look it."

"She is, notwithstanding. She thinks the way you demonstrate a proposition in Euclid on the black-board is something admirable and fine, as if you were reading a poem by Tennyson."

"Do you mean to say that you also are a pupil at the Normal School?"

Sally laughed joyously, without a touch of resentment. She was very good-natured, as I was afterwards to learn, and as I had already surmised.

"Now, that is very complimentary," she said, "and shows you have never even glanced at me in the classroom. But I forgive you; I have noticed that you had eyes for none of us but Aline Arbuthnot."

"Oh, you saw that, did you?" I stammered, too unready to retrieve my mistake.

"Even Dr. Darnell has seen it, so I warn you. My

name is Sally Livingstone, and Miss Arbuthnot is my room-mate. I hope you will appreciate my heroism in speaking to you, for I have come to rescue you from a great danger; and look ''—she spread out her hands with a pretty gesture—'' at the risk I run, while your admirer has deserted you to your fate.''

'' I think the fact that we are standing here, Miss Livingstone, shows that we are already lost.''

'' Oh, you were lost long before I spoke to you. The moment you set foot across this threshold you were done for, if discovered. What on earth are you doing in the picture gallery on this day of the week?''

'' Why, Miss Livingstone, Dr. Darnell himself sent me here.''

Sally laughed with hearty enjoyment.

'' Oh, that is *too* funny,'' she cried. '' The good Doctor has mixed up his days. To-day the girls of the Normal School are free of the gallery, and if any of the unfortunate men students so much as set foot on this forbidden ground during this forbidden day, ex-pulsion results, and no excuse is accepted. So you must fly from this spot as if it were the city of the Plague.''

'' I think the home of the sirens would be a better name, Miss Livingstone.''

'' Perhaps it would, but the result is the same in either case. Shall you tell Dr. Darnell the predica-ment in which he has placed you?''

'' I see no reason for enlightening him. I fear my confession might take on the complexion of thanks for a great pleasure bestowed.''

'' Ah, that's better, Mr. Prentiss,'' laughed the girl. '' You'll do, with proper training. I thought you were not a ladies' man, but I see I was mistaken.''

'' Good gracious ! what caused you to think that?''

"Well, you see, I have been studying you, even though you never looked my way. I am sure you think me brazen for telling you so, and accosting you thus unceremoniously, but my room-mate being so much enamoured of your mathematical ability, I naturally had my attention drawn to you, and listened with growing admiration every time you got on your feet and said something sharp to Dr. Darnell. You don't mind my devotion, I hope?"

"Ah, Miss Livingstone, you are making fun of an awkward man, who is not clever enough to hold a candle to you."

"Don't you see my higher purpose? Don't you recognize that I am training you in an art not only neglected in the Normal School curriculum, but absolutely forbidden? I shall cure your awkwardness before I am done with you. By the way, you should promptly have contradicted me when I called myself brazen a moment since."

"I do contradict you, most emphatically."

"It is too late now. You must do that sort of thing without being told."

"You underrate the charm which you exercise, and the absorbed attention that I pay to every word you utter. It is such a pleasure to look at you that I can think of nothing else."

"Oh, you'll be a credit to my teaching yet, Mr. Prentiss. So you're not going to tell Dr. Darnell that he abandoned you to the sirens without even giving you cotton-wool for your ears?"

"I suppose it would have taken too much cotton-wool; but I am glad now he omitted my deafening. I should like to see his face if he learns of his mistake."

"He is a dear man, and I love him."

"That must have been a case of love at first sight, then."

"Oh no; it has been a case of mutual esteem slowly ripening into affection. I am not a newcomer like you. I was here last session. That is why I am so bold."

"Indeed, Miss Livingstone, boldness and brazenness must not be applied to you in my hearing."

"Excellent, excellent! I knew I should be proud of you. But I must not stand here longer talking to you. The place is too public, and at any moment the terrible Mr. Brent might walk in. He would not recognize me, because we have our own Model School, where the four teachers are all ladies, and when I say ladies, I *mean* ladies. They are not spies and amateur detectives. I hope you hate Mr. Brent with that hatred which should distinguish all Normal School students."

"I not only do, but this very morning I came within an ace of trying conclusions with him in a rough-and-tumble fight. I never knew what depths of savagery there are in my nature, until I encountered and defied John Brent in the Model School this morning."

And now I was given the intoxicating enjoyment of seeing undisguised admiration in the eyes of this handsome girl. Impulsively she held out her hand, and I took it as eagerly as it was offered.

"One woman, at least, will wear your colours if it ever comes to a tournament between you; but beware of him, beware of him. Respect him, but do not trust him. And now I must run, or Aline will be in despair. As it is she thinks me deceitful and desperately wicked."

"Indeed——" I expostulated, but she held up her hand, and did not allow me to conclude.

"That doesn't need contradiction," she cried. "I am, and I admit it. My conscience seems to have left me; and, oh dear, oh dear!" she sighed, most touchingly, "at the beginning of last session I was as particular about the rules as Aline is now; as, indeed, poor man, you would be if a siren hadn't sung her song, or if Dr. Darnell hadn't forgotten the cottonwool. We are living at No. 97, Stanmore Street, this session. Last session I was in a licensed boarding-house, with eleven other girls, and although I liked it at first, later on, through circumstances that proved beyond my control, the presence of the eleven became irksome. This session I am living with my aunt. Permission is granted by the Normal School authorities where a girl has a relative, and Aline being an old friend of mine, she got permission also. Won't you come and call upon us? It is quite proper, you know, remembering the aunt."

"I should be delighted," I hesitated; "but——"

"Oh, I know what you're going to say. You are afraid of Aline. My aunt's house is large, and Aline can pursue her studies in another room whilst I am instructing you in the arts neglected by the Normal."

I had never met any one like this before, and the experience appealed to some undeveloped portion of my nature. I remembered now with scorn that I had disclaimed being a ladies' man.

"When may I come?" I asked.

"Next Thursday evening at eight o'clock, if that day and hour is convenient. Ask for Miss Livingstone, and you will be shown into her parlour, says the spider to the fly," and Sally, as usual, laughed joyously.

"That will suit me perfectly. My chum goes out to prayer-meeting every Thursday night."

"Your chum? Who is he?"

"Sam McKurdy. I look on him as by all odds the cleverest fellow in the Normal."

She gazed up at the painted ceiling, and a little perplexed wrinkle on her forehead seemed to indicate a mental struggle towards recollection, and now, as her eyes were turned from me, I could not help noting how exquisitely the mounting blush in her cheek became her.

"He is the man who gave Dr. Darnell the compound words; don't you remember? He sits several seats in front of me."

"Oh yes, oh yes," she said hurriedly, bringing down her glance from above.

"Why, you must know him. He too was here last session."

"I remember, now that you mention it. Bring him with you. Oh, I forgot—he has another appointment——"

But here she was interrupted by the flinging open of the door, and the breathless arrival of Miss Arbuthnot, who cast past me, rather than on me, one look of scorn, and cried—

"Come away, Sally, quick! Dr. Darnell will be here in a moment."

"Oh, saints preserve us!" cried Sally, in a panic; then, in a brief command to me, "Cease looking at Aline and attend to those pictures."

I obeyed without a word, and stood gazing fixedly at a huge canvas, presumably covered with paint, not one colour of which I could distinguish at that palpitating moment.

"Ah, here you are," said the well-known voice at my elbow. "I have made a mistake. This is the ladies' day in the gallery."

"Is it?" I inquired.

"Yes, yes, come along. My fault, my fault entirely. Mr. Brent has not been in?" he asked, with as near an approach to a tremor of fear as I had ever noticed in the tones of this fearless man.

"I think not," I said. "I've been interested in the——" I made an inflection of the hand that included the works of art.

"Quite so, quite so; but let us get away," and the good Doctor and I went down the stairs with some haste, as if we were companions in crime who had luckily escaped detection.

During the entrancing but forbidden interview with Miss Livingstone, all notion of time had left me. My hurried exit with Dr. Darnell had been somewhat agitated, and my talk with that good man was, I fear, rather disconnected. Clothed in innocence I had left him in his private room, but when he dragged me from that place of danger I was already steeped in guilt. I had talked with her, laughed with her, shaken hands with her, and had placed the culminating crime upon this list of villanies by promising to call on her next Thursday at eight. Dr. Darnell had encountered in his study a young man arrogant in his blamelessness, who looked him straight in the eye, and metaphorically pounded his virtuous breast and defied a censorious world, including Mr. Brent; but Dr. Darnell took from that enchanted gallery a young man, to outward appearance the same, but an ingratiating, hesitating, humble person weighed down by a secret. On a certain occasion Christian's burden of sin had rolled from his back; my knapsack had been deftly strapped on my shoulders by the daintiest of hands. Within the compass of one fateful morning I had earned the enmity of John Brent; I had pledged my faith with Dr. Darnell to keep the rules, and half-an-hour later I had forged a weapon with which, if Brent discovered it, he could annihilate me; yet the thing that troubled me most was the kindling gleam of faith in me which had lighted Dr. Darnell's piercing eyes.

I fear the Doctor found me a rather distraught companion as we walked to the street corner where we parted. My mind kept running upon the circumstances leading up to the point where I now found myself, inquiring where, after all, I had been to blame. The Doctor himself had flung me across the line, and now rescued me too late. What should I have done when the smiling girl approached me with such entrancing friendliness? I would like the grave and reverend seigneurs of the Normal to answer *that* question. Should I have turned and fled, as Miss Arbuthnot did? Should I have drawn myself to my full height, and frozen Miss Livingstone with a stare? or should I have succumbed, and then taken refuge in the time-honoured plea of man— " The woman tempted me, and I did talk " ?

Once I laughed aloud, and the Doctor stopped and looked at me with alarm. He had evidently been speaking of something serious, not one word of which had touched my consciousness. To my dismay, I found myself nearly overpowered by a desire to put the case to him, and ask what he would have done.

" Dr. Darnell," said my mind to me, " if a pretty girl came and threw her arms round your neck, what would you do?" and as the picture of the vivacious girl and the serious Doctor rose before me, I laughed aloud.

" I don't see anything to laugh at," said the Doctor sternly.

" Why, then," I replied, recovering my wits, " let

us go slower. Passers-by think we are running a foot-race; and, while I am unknown in this city, you are not."

"Oh, I see, I see," said the Doctor, slowing down. "When I get on a subject, I become absorbed, and forget the rate either tongue or feet are going. But you recognize the importance of what I am saying?"

"Oh certainly, certainly," I replied, without the slightest notion of his subject.

"Of course, thoughtless persons think the rule absurd, but you must remember that we stand *in loco parentis* to these young women, most of whom are in a large city for the first time, away from home and friends, and our responsibilities towards them cannot be ignored."

"True," I stammered, getting the drift of his theme at last. "I appreciate the position."

"If the Normal were like one of those large colleges for ladies with which this city abounds, if it were surrounded by a high stone wall, with a porter at every gate, and inside, the rigid rule of the convent, we might have a chance, and yet even there, in spite of unceasing vigilance——" He paused, at a loss, and I added flippantly—

"Mr. Pickwick gets into the Ladies' School."

"Yes," said the Doctor, his seriousness broken by a smile, for he was a great admirer of Charles Dickens. "But you see the point," he went on, regaining his soberness. "Here are a number of young women brought into daily communication with an equal number of young men in the class-rooms of our school. A certain feeling of comradeship is bound to arise. They laugh together when something humorous happens or is said, and if an injustice is done, men and women alike are drawn into one sentiment of resentment. At four in the afternoon the young women scatter to their temporary homes all over the city. It is an almost impossible situation. Here are girls, many of whom know nothing of their danger. We have no matron, and no women teachers in the Normal, and here are a number of hot-headed, unreasonable young men, coming from anywhere, everywhere; bringing with them characters it is impossible to investigate; unprincipled, some of them, undoubtedly. Although in many cases they have exercised control over former pupils, they themselves are most restive under discipline. And then," cried the Doctor, once more oblivious to passers-by, and flinging his hands towards heaven, " in addition to all this, nature herself fights against us. What more natural than that if you met here on the street one of those young women whom you have seen day after day—what more natural than that a thrill of recognition should animate you both; strangers together in a strange town? You are like the two friendly atoms in chemistry; compelled towards each other by forces you may not comprehend, and are unable to resist."

" It seems to me you exaggerate, Doctor," I had the hypocrisy to remark, for I saw now, as I had never seen before, how the situation weighed upon him unceasingly.

" Exaggerate? Do you think so? Perhaps, perhaps. Ah, well!" He stopped at the street corner, and held out his hand. " I can trust *you*, at any rate," and with that unconscious blow he strode away. I stood looking after him till he disappeared, with his nervous, friendly grip still electrifying my right hand; in all that city no such self-condemned sneak as I. I cursed circumstances rather than myself as I turned towards my place of abode.

CHAPTER XII

Whatever brawls disturb the street
There should be peace at home,
Where sisters dwell and brothers meet
Quarrels should never come.

DR. WATTS.

I HURRIED down the street and into the silent hall of
my boarding-house. Then I looked at my watch,
and found that I should barely have time to snatch a
hurried lunch if I were to return to the school for the
afternoon session. Usually when I entered our
Church Street boarding-house, my greeting was a
cheerful murmur similar to that which comes from a
hive of slumbering bees when you tap it on the outside. Sometimes this murmur was punctuated by a
laugh, and sometimes enlivened by a snatch of song.
We all lived more or less under fear of our tall, thin,
ascetic landlady, with her fishy, severe, inquiring
eyes, which more than corroborated the Prayer-book
in its statement that we were miserable sinners. Yet
it is difficult for seven or eight students to carry on
their lives in strict silence, and although a real hearty
laugh sometimes echoed through the house, threatening to turn Mrs. Sponsor into horrified stone, we were
nevertheless rather a sedate lot. Sam once suggested that we should apply to the Board of Education
to be rated the Model Boarding-house, after the fashion
of the Model School.

On returning to this haven of peace and serenity
after the most exciting morning I had yet experienced

in my educational course, the gloomy hall smote me with a great silence. This seemed to mean that either the boys had not yet come, or that they had gone.

We ate in the basement, and I walked along the hall to the door of the stairway. In the doorway I saw Mrs. Sponsor standing, tall and slim as a fence-rail, her arms tightly folded against her level breast, thin lips compressed, and an expression of Minerva-like determination on her severe, emaciated countenance. Hers was the attitude of one waiting for trouble, and prepared thoroughly to welcome it.

" Where are you going ?" she demanded.

" To the basement," I replied, coming to a stand-still.

" What for ?"

" For something to eat."

" The dinner hour is at half-past twelve sharp."

" I know that, Mrs. Sponsor, but I was detained by Dr. Darnell himself, and could not get here sooner."

" I do not keep a restaurant," pursued Mrs. Sponsor, with no sign of relaxing. " This is not a house where there are meals at all hours. There is nothing for you down-stairs."

" Oh, I am not exacting; a bit of bread and cheese will do. I must hurry back to school. Isn't this beef-steak day ?" I continued, trying to throw an air of geniality over my comments. " There must be some cold steak left, and a slice of it will do for me."

" There is nothing left."

" We are eight, Mrs. Sponsor, just one more than Mr. Wordsworth's seven. There were purchased, and doubtless cooked, portions for eight persons. Mr. Wordsworth's seven have gone, not to Heaven, but to the Normal School. Surely they did not eat my share of the lunch." As I went on with this ill-timed bogus jocularity, Mrs. Sponsor's face and form became more and more rigid.

"I have told you that there is nothing here for you at this hour," she said with great primness and decision. "I ask you to leave the house, and let me get on with my work."

"Very well, Mrs. Sponsor," I replied, with the mildness of lamb and mint-sauce, which was due next day, "this seems a reversal of the wars we read about. The besieger is starved out and retires. Luckily a rapid retreat will bring me into the bread belt, so I bid you good-day."

I was ravenously hungry, and made quick time along Church Street, and so to my old tavern on the market square. Here I received a boisterous welcome from the clerk, who recognized me as the commercial traveller.

"How's tricks?" he asked.

"First rate," I replied.

"That's good. Business looking up, eh?"

"Yes."

"Have a drink?" and I saw my reputation as an inebriate still clung to me.

"Thanks, no. I'm after something to eat. Is there corn in Egypt?"

"You bet. Make for the dining-room, my son, and they will look after you. Sure you won't have an appetizer?"

"I already have got an appetite so clamorous that my only fear is there won't be provisions enough in the house to satisfy it."

"No use in throwing petroleum on a conflagration, my boy," and with that the clerk laughed heartily, and helped himself, while I sought the dining-room and satisfaction.

Whether it was the previous hunger, or the abundant meal, I found on leaving the hotel that my thoughts turned on provender, and thinking of sheep and lamb, I remembered it was as well to be hanged for the one as the other, so I gave up all thought of attending the afternoon session of the Normal School. I prowled about the provision shops, and inquired about prices, for next day I was to enter on my first turn as caterer for the ever-hungry eight. I had learned the duties of caterer from Sam. It seemed that a permanent order was placed with a tradesman near by our boarding-house. One day he furnished beef-steak, another lamb-chops, again veal-cutlet, and so with similar variations throughout the week. We really lived very well, and the cost of cooking being included in the price of our rooms, most of the caterer's work seemed to be to add up the bills from the tradesman once a week, divide the total by eight, receive from each man his share, and get a receipt by handing over the amount to the butcher. I had examined the bills, and, even to my inexperienced eye, they seemed rather exorbitant. Inquiry at the market square proved that if I visited the down-town tradesmen with a basket every morning, I could get quite as good material at something less than half the price. We were all rather poor in purse, so I resolved to set in a period of efficiency, reform and economy. I said nothing to my comrades about this, because we had one particularly luxurious person who, when he became caterer, used to run in various delicacies which considerably increased our payments at the end of the week. I always had my suspicion that he was the poorest of the crowd financially, but he did love to dwell on the epicurean banquets he had been accustomed to, until Sam launched out with descriptions of feasts he had enjoyed, which made the dinners of Lucullus seem like a menu of a penny restaurant.   No tit-bit that our indulgent friend could mention but Sam capped it with another so much more delicious and expensive that finally the other relapsed into silence, and gloomily augmented our bills when it came his turn.   I knew if I admitted that my purchases were made at the market square in the early morning before the other seven were up, this person would at once detect a falling-off in quality, which might spread dissatisfaction, and perhaps mutiny, round our table, for no one there, except Sam, acknowledged himself poor, and none could endure the charge of meanness.

Everything went well, and there was no grumbling, but Mrs. Sponsor became more and more grim, and ceased altogether to speak to me.   It was her habit to stand exactly four feet from the table, and watch the caterer at the head do the carving, while her silent, frightened servant waited on the table.   Mrs. Sponsor bided her time, and her time came.   Although I have referred to our mid-day meal as lunch, it was really dinner.

One day we came joyously home for dinner at half-past twelve, and I, as caterer, took my chair at the head of the table, Mrs. Sponsor standing in her usual place, silent, and, if possible, more glum than ever.   I suspected nothing till the lid of the great soup-tureen came off.   Then, with a rush, memory resumed her throne; jumped on it, in fact, with a hop and a skip.   I had forgotten my duties as caterer, and, during the morning, had ordered nothing.   Of course this sort of thing had happened before, but with a standing order at the tradesman's nothing disastrous had resulted.   Now when the waiting maid whipped off the cover of the soup-tureen, I saw the dish empty. Recovering my second wind after this knock-out blow, I grasped the ladle, and dipped two helpings of nothing in the first plate. The frightened girl did not know what to do, but looked with alarm from the empty plate to her forbidding mistress, who made no sign.

"Please serve that soup," I said. "I wish to fill the next plate."

"Hello!" cried Sam in surprise, as the empty plate was placed before him. He looked at me and grinned, and down the table the knowledge of what had occurred spread. Empty plate after empty plate was handed to the bewildered boys in silence, until our luxurious comrade was served.

"Why, what's all this?" he cried in tones of disappointment. "I don't see anything funny in foolery."

"Look here," I cried. "I won't allow grumbling while I'm caterer. Shut up, and go on with your soup."

The lads entered into the spirit of the game. After all, we were very young. The empty platter that should have contained veal-cutlets was placed before me, and the same pantomime went on. I had some fear that the waiting-girl would faint, but Madam Sponsor stood stiffly in her place without saying a word or moving a muscle. When the feast of shadows was done I rose to my feet, not in the best of temper.

"But here," thought I to myself, "is a chance for suppression of ill-humour."

"Gentlemen," I said, "I thank you all for the appreciation you have shown of my efforts as caterer. There is nothing so pleasing to a culinary artist as to perceive the satisfaction of his guests. You will remember that one chef committed suicide because a king added salt to a royal dish. You have done nothing so heinous, but have taken with hilarity all that has been set before you, and so, gentlemen, I thank you. Now I ask you to be my guests down at my old tavern on the market square, where the festival opens at one o'clock, and does not close until three. By a quick march we may storm the citadel before the first course is off. Come along! Follow your caterer, and learn how much inferior the substantial meal that awaits you is to the feast of imagination I have just spread before you."

And so with cheers we trooped noisily up the stairs, and I caught one glimpse of Mrs. Sponsor. Not a muscle of her face moved. She stood in exactly the same attitude assumed at the beginning of the lunch.

When we reached the street Brushwood Smith said he, for one, would not be seen walking through the town with such an idiot as I. He proposed, therefore, that I should take my place thirty paces in front, lead the way, and not look round or pretend that I knew any of the sane people who were following me. This proposition was accepted with hilarious acclaim by the others.

"Come on, boys," I cried, "and no nonsense. We'd better hurry to the tavern than through our meal, so step lively, or none of you will get there within thirty paces of me."

I set out for the market square at a stride that would take some beating, and the rest of them followed in a talking, laughing bunch. My genial friend, the hotel clerk, was astonished to see me enter with this boisterous delegation at my heels, and for once he forgot to offer me a drink. We were allotted a table to ourselves, I, as host, occupying a chair at the head, while Brushwood Smith made an excellent vice-chairman.   Brushwood Smith consulted his watch.

" Let's do this thing methodically," he suggested. " If Prentiss is going to stand us a decent dinner we should devote at least half-an-hour to its enjoyment."

" If we do," said Sam, " we'll be late at the afternoon session."

" It all depends on Prentiss," continued Brushwood Smith. " He has led us a foot-race from Church Street to this tavern. I don't want to make any proposals that would not come naturally from himself, but I think his failure as caterer places a certain responsibility on his shoulders."

" Heavens," said the epicurean impatiently, " you'll consume the half-hour in talk, and we'll have no time at all to consume the dinner."

" More haste, less speed," said Brushwood calmly. " Mr. Prentiss is bound to deliver us in time at the Normal School. How can he do this, you ask, if we spend half-an-hour at the table? Why, by ordering two cabs to the door, each of which will hold four persons. Do you mind, Prentiss?"

" Of course not," I replied with such cheerfulness as I could muster. Then to the waiter I gave the order for the two cabs.

" Now," said John Henceforth, " there's no use doing a thing unless you do it well. It isn't every day we get a chance at a free lunch. I notice that the bill of fare does not include dessert and cheese. I am accustomed to end my dinner with cheese."

" Yes, and begin it too," commented Sam.

" I think we ought to round up with a cup of coffee," said the epicurean, " although we'll never reach that point if we don't begin soon."

" Good, good," cried the rest; " coffee, of course."

"Will you see that coffee is ready by the time we have finished dinner," I said to the waiter, and then Sam had a suggestion to make.

"I'm not a hard drinker myself," he said, "but I think it would contribute to the hilarity of the occasion if we had a bottle of ginger-beer apiece. Any objections, Prentiss?"

"Of course not," I replied. "Now, gentlemen, give your orders. I take the clear soup. Hurry up."

The ginger-beer was brought on in flagons that looked like half-bottles of champagne, and the popping of corks attracted the attention of the room to us, while the effervescence of the straw-coloured fluid gave a decidedly dissipated appearance to the feast of which my guests made the most. They sang rousing choruses between the courses, and once I saw the clerk peep in at us and smile, as who would say—

"There's that jolly dog who knows good liquor when he sees it, with his old cronies," and I heard a man at the long table reassure his neighbour by saying that there was no harm in the young fellows; doubtless University students on a spree, sons of rich parents blowing in the old man's money. The neighbour thought it was a pity to see us drink as we were doing, and Sam roared out for another round of champagne amidst riotous applause and the clinking of glasses.

"Same as before, sir?" said the waiter.

"Same vintage," said Sam. "Mum's the word, and dry's the liquid."

After the coffee, Brushwood Smith rose unsteadily to his feet, bracing himself against the end of the table.

" I give you the health of our caterer," he cried, " but this, as is fitting, must be drunk with empty glasses, in memory of our Church Street repast of to-day."

I refused to reply to this hollow toast, and whispered to the waiter, " Bring me the bill."

" It's all paid for, sir," he said.

" What's paid for ? "

" The dinner, sir, cabs and everything else."

" None of that," cried Brushwood Smith. " Prentiss is quarrelling with the waiter about the bill, and refuses to pay. Capture him, boys, and let's take him to the lock-up."

With that they fell on me, and dragged me uproariously from the room, with a " Hip-hip-hip-hooray " and much shaking of heads from the scandalized regular guests of the hotel, who wondered audibly what the country was coming to when such dissipation as this ran riot in the middle of the day. A few words from Sam outside managed to stir up the emulation of the cabmen, and we went tearing along Church Street as if engaged in a Roman chariot-race, reaching the scholars' gate of the Normal School with two minutes to spare.

That night, when I entered my study, I found a note on my table from Mrs. Sponsor, which began with the word " Sir," and went on to inform me that a week from next Saturday I must quit the shelter of her roof, and seek lodgings elsewhere. She thus gave me ten days, or thereabouts, to find a new abode, and this was generous of her, for all I was entitled to was a week's notice. Sam thought that with a little tact and some concessions, and perhaps apologies on my part, the difficulty might be smoothed over. He suggested that I should capitulate immediately by restoring to Mrs. Sponsor's favourite tradesmen the account for our sustenance. I should quit my matutinal rambles in the market, and even if our food did cost us more, peace would reign in the household; besides which the garrison would not run the risk of starvation through any forgetfulness on my part. I had no wish to leave my comfortable quarters, and I had grown to like all my comrades, so I did what Sam suggested, he undertaking to carry my most abject apologies to Mrs. Sponsor. He found her, nevertheless, unexpectedly firm. She was quite frank in telling him she had disliked me from the first, and had determined to be rid of me. She was shrewd enough to see that I was bound to end on the scaffold some day, and was determined that her reputable house should not be tainted longer by my presence. Sam did his best, but all his persuasion was in vain.

The news that I had received my *congé* spread rapidly throughout the house. Emerson says we are all wanted, but not very much, and now and then through life every man encounters the truth of this assertion. Although I pretended an indifference it nevertheless depressed me somewhat to see that my jolly companions took my approaching departure with composure. I found myself in the position of one of those reformers who sacrifices himself for the good of an unappreciative public. As Brushwood Smith informed me, each of the boys, even Sam, was absorbed in his own affairs, and no practical purpose would be served by their taking sides in a quarrel between Mrs. Sponsor and myself. He pointed out, I thought with unnecessary cruelty, that whatever Mrs. Sponsor's manners were, she was a superb house-keeper, and that nowhere in town, to his knowledge, would we be so well taken care of. I had expected this kind of talk from John Henceforth, but not from Brushwood Smith. John Henceforth said that for his part he thought I had treated Mrs. Sponsor rather shabbily, upsetting the custom of the house by deserting her cherished butcher. After all, he held, it was merely a matter of money, and the love of money was the root of all evil. He had learned by inquiry among the rest, privately, that the wish of the house was to treat Mrs. Sponsor generously, she being a widow, and this being a hard world. John Henceforth was the mystery man, if I may so term it, of our confraternity. Nobody quite liked him, or quite disliked him, although I may confess that after his talk with me on the crisis with which I was confronted, my admiration for him did not increase. Every one had an excuse to make: some of the boys drew me aside, and explained with unnecessary volubility their regard for me, but presented the hopelessness of any one standing out against the rest. Each expatiated on the comfort of the rooms, and the excellence of the cooking. Each also cordially invited me to visit him if I felt lonesome in my new habitation, proclaiming bravely that, although Mrs. Sponsor might not favour such intercourse, yet they were, nevertheless, free men who paid their way, and were not going to be dictated to regarding their choice of friends. This was meant kindly no doubt, but the result of it all was a resolve on my part to keep to myself after I bade farewell to them on Saturday week. Brushwood Smith, who, I regret to say, was addicted to the music hall, sang along the corridors and in the study, snatches of the songs he heard there, which, from the laughter they caused, seemed to have a direct or indirect bearing on my own misfortune. He would sing in a most doleful voice, " Out in the cold world, out in the street," while the rest joined in the chorus, but the favourite ditty was one supposed to be sung by a German saloon-keeper, whose customers drank, but refused to pay. As I remember it, it ran—

> "I keeps a saloon in der city,
> I opens it early and late ;
> Dem fellows, dey all come around here
> Und say, 'Put it down on der slate.'

(*Spoken.*) And I says, 'Shentlemens, you must pay cash, I don't keep sum slates round here.' Den dey say, 'Keep it in your head, and we'll come round next Saturday night, and kick it out.' I throws off my coat, and dares 'em to kick it out now, when my wife, she comes and lays her hand on my arm, and she says :

> 'Don't give de name a bad place,'
> Und she looks right into my face.
> 'You'll get some policemans around here,
> So don't give de name a bad place.'"

Every Saturday night, when the supper-table had been cleared away, it was Mrs. Sponsor's habit to sit in state in the chair of the caterer, with eight written receipts for the week's room-money before her. One by one we descended, and paid our bills, receiving in acknowledgment the signed receipt. On this particular Saturday evening, when I was to make my last payment but one, I found the frivolous fraternity, with backs to the wall, each standing on a step of the stair at regular distances from top to bottom. Each held a white handkerchief to his eyes. The top man whispered to me that it had been intended to greet me with a farewell chorus, but they were all afraid of Mrs. Sponsor, and hoped I should pardon them for their silence. I said I would, begged them to cheer up, and went down the steps to the awful presence of the lone widow, who was sitting very straight and stiff like a figure of unrelenting justice.

I paid my money, and took my receipt in silence. Sam followed, set down his amount with an ingratiating smile, and, to my surprise, said he was going with me, and therefore was reluctantly compelled to give a week's notice. Brushwood Smith followed, deplored the fact that he could not live without Sam, and so gave a week's notice. John Henceforth came next, remarked that Brushwood could not be trusted with no watchful eye over him, therefore John gave notice, and so one after another, until the eight receipts were taken up, and Mrs. Sponsor saw that next Saturday night the house would be empty, and a woman of her experience knew right well that there was little chance even of partially refilling it before the beginning of next session. She neither flinched nor said a word.

"Madam," said I, "may I suggest a compromise? These lads have made me rather unhappy during the past few days, and especially have I suffered through Brushwood's singing. Thus a certain amount of punishment has been endured. I am willing to apologize in the most abject manner, and to renounce for ever the high office of caterer."

"Will you get down on your knees?" cried Brushwood Smith.

"Oh, I'll stand on my head if you like."

"Agreed, agreed," shouted the others. "Prentiss stands on his head, and apologizes abjectly while in that posture. If he comes down before the apology is delivered, he must do it all over again."

Mrs. Sponsor maintained a rigid silence, looking severely at one after another of us until she had somehow imparted to the coterie the disturbing belief that we all should have to flit. We had expected that she would succumb at once to the threat of emptying her house, but there was not the slightest sign of surrender in mien or look of this ossified woman.

"Gentlemen," she said at last, "there is no need to remain longer in this dining-room.   There will be nothing more to eat to-night."

"There never is anything fit to eat here at any time while the wretched Prentiss is caterer," growled the epicure. "I propose he be censured and deposed."

"Agreed, agreed," was the unanimous verdict of the rest.

"I suggest further," went on Brushwood, "that we endeavour to make a decent man of Prentiss, impossible as that task may seem to you. Who can say what a beneficial effect our good examples may have upon him?"

"We'll try," murmured the others, in no very confident tones.

"Good-night, gentlemen," said the smileless lips of Mrs. Sponsor, and, not knowing what our fate was to be, we trooped up-stairs in a rather chastened spirit.

The good woman never said anything further, but she made no objection to my stopping on, although her dislike for me abated not one jot. This she took pains to exhibit by constantly reporting my delinquencies to Dr. Darnell. It was impossible for me to sneeze at a forbidden moment without the echo of that effort reaching the headmaster. But he knew Mrs. Sponsor of old, and I don't think her frequent complaints affected my standing in the school. Indeed, towards the middle of the session I had proof that Dr. Darnell no longer regarded me as the black sheep of the flock, and this incident, through the kindness of Mrs. Sponsor, had a sequel which for a time left me alarmed and helpless, though not on my own account.

One morning, after class, Dr. Darnell requested my attendance in his private room, and there invited me to attend, as his guest, a banquet given by the secret society to which we both belonged. I accepted this invitation without, I think, showing him that I had much rather have been excused. On the night of the dinner I restricted myself to cold water, and I believe my conduct was irreproachable. It was long after ten o'clock when the Doctor and I, walking down Church Street, reached my lodging-house. Bidding him good-night, I thanked him for the pleasant evening I had spent.

"Remember," said the Doctor in reply, "that if any complaint is made about your being out after hours, I shall be compelled to punish you."

"I shall take my punishment without flinching, Doctor. The night was worth it."

The Doctor laughed, and departed for his home, while I climbed in over the porch. I had not told Sam where I was going, thinking that perhaps the headmaster would prefer that such an evidence of his favour should be known only to the recipient. Next morning, after prayers, Dr. Darnell took in his hand a sheet of note-paper, and, frowning heavily, mentioned my name. I rose to my feet.

"Mr. Prentiss," he said in his best hanging-judge manner, "I regret to have received a letter from your lodging-house keeper which states that you did not return to your rooms until after midnight. What is your answer to that accusation?"

Before I could reply, Sam sprang to his feet, and to my horror I heard him say—

"Dr. Darnell, that is not true. Mr. Prentiss and I were studying Algebra together all last evening, until after midnight. Probably the disturbance we

made at that hour induced Mrs. Sponsor to think some
one entered the house.''

Poor Sam sat down with the self-satisfied air of one
who had done his duty by his friend. Dr. Darnell
did not glance at him, but looking menacingly at
me, said—

"Mr. Prentiss, I congratulate you on your *alibi*.
Sit down."

I could not now tell Sam what an appalling mistake
he had made, but at the first opportunity I sought Dr.
Darnell in his room, and implored him not to allow
this incident to prejudice him against Sam, who, I
assured him, was usually the most truthful of men.

"Oh," said the Doctor, with a shrug of his
shoulders, "I fear I am carnal enough to appreciate
a well-told lie. That touch about the final disturbance
you two studious, silent men had made after a virtuous evening with equations, rather enlisted my admiration. Of course you will say nothing to him about
it, beyond thanking a friend in need."

In this chapter I have paid no attention to the
sequence of events, desiring merely to give some
account of our way of living, thus mentioning incidents which took place subsequent to that point where
I left off at the end of the preceding chapter, to which
I now return.

CHAPTER XIII

For if she will, she will, you may depend on't;
And if she won't, she won't: so there's an end on't.

THE fateful Thursday evening arrived, when, in defiance of statutes made and provided, I was to visit Miss Livingstone at the house of her aunt, not without hope, perhaps, of making the acquaintance of Aline Arbuthnot, despite her last glance of contempt, which still lingered disturbingly in my memory. Soon as supper was over, Sam prepared for his prayer-meeting, putting on hat and overcoat, but instead of departing at once, he sat down on the edge of the study table, swinging one leg back and forwards, while I, like the dutiful student I pretended to be, got ready my books and my writing materials. We had already discussed my adventures in the Model School, and Sam had kindly refrained from saying, " I told you so."   There appeared to be something on his mind, and I caught a furtive look now and again, as if he wished to speak to me on some subject, but hesitated.   I was hoping he would either get the problem off his mind, or himself off the table, so that I might make my own excursion, and reach the aunt's house somewhere near the time that had been set.   At last, Sam showing no signs of either speaking or moving, I stopped the pretence of setting to work, rose with a yawn, and said—

" I think I'll drop in at the College of Technology, and see how the night school there commends itself to me. You remember your suggestion that I should attend the evening session."

" All right; throw on your coat, and I'll walk that far with you."

" What are you worrying about, Sam ?" I asked, as I sheltered myself against the cold.

" Oh, nothing very much. I was wondering whether there was anything else in town that might offer greater attractions to you than the College of Technology, but I think after all your own plan is the best. Come along."

" What was your proposal ?" I asked, when we were out in the street.

" On second thoughts," he replied, with a diffidence unusual to him, " I fear my plan is impracticable. I shan't say anything about it to-night, but will seek advice, and if the friend whom I shall consult shares my opinion, you will hear from me later. I rather incline to the drawing school, however; it's more along your line of march."

" Yes, I agree with you, but not the drawing school at the College of Technology. I have visited that picture gallery in the Normal School twice this week, and I find myself rather ambitious to become a painter."

" Visited it twice ?" asked Sam in surprise. " How could you do that? We're only allowed there one day a week."

" Yes, I know that now. The first day I strayed in there through error, and stopped so short a time that I saw little of the paintings."

" Well, you should be careful in choosing your day. That gallery is John Brent's favourite rat-trap.

If he catches you there during prohibited hours you'll meet trouble."

Reaching the entrance of the college, I bade Sam a cordial farewell, which he seemed to think was more energetic than the short period of our separation warranted, for he said—

" You are not going to disappear for ever into that building, are you? I suppose you will be home before ten ?"

" Certainly. I'll let you in if you're later."

I did not enter the building at all, but waited till Sam's footsteps echoed fainter and fainter, and then I bolted. I knew my way to Stanmore Street, as I had reconnoitred the locality in daylight, so there was no danger of my unexpectedly overtaking him. Putting my best foot foremost, I reached the doorstep of Ninety-seven as the city clocks were striking eight. Ringing the bell, a trim serving-maid, on my asking for Miss Livingstone, showed me into a drawing-room to the right of the hall, and the smiling Sally herself ran forward to greet me.

" Oh, how nice of you !" she exclaimed; " and just prompt on the hour."

We shook hands like old friends.

" Yes," I said, " but I had to run for it, and am rather out of breath."

" What ?" she exclaimed, with a little tremor of fear in her voice. " You were not seen coming here —you were not followed ?"

" No; any one who attempted to follow me to-night must have been a champion sprinter. It was all the fault of my chum, McKurdy. Instead of going off to prayer-meeting as he should, he kind of clung to me, and I could not shake him off except by telling him I was going to the Technical College, which was true enough, although I did not enter its doors.”

“ Ah,” laughed Sally, “ your friend probably felt some intuition of your danger. Did you tell him you had met me at the gallery ?”

“ No, Miss Livingstone. That dread secret was not entirely my own, so I did not feel justified in sharing it, even with my chum.”

“ Then that’s all right, for Aline here will never tell, even if she does not approve. Do take off your coat and sit down, and be assured of a hearty welcome from me at least.”

All this time Miss Arbuthnot was seated at the table, poring over an open book. She did not look up as I came in, and paid not the slightest heed to what we were saying. Her elbows were on the table, on each side of her book, and her open palms were covering her ears as if to shut out all sound of our contraband conversation. The room was but dimly lighted, for the chandelier hung dark; but a rubber tube, looping down, conveyed gas from one burner to a student’s lamp whose conical green shade allowed no light to percolate to the ceiling.

“ What did Dr. Darnell say to you when he found you in the gallery ? Did he suspect anything ?”

“ Nothing. That estimable man was rather overcome by his mistake in sending me unprotected into the battle line, and had hurried there to amend his error.”

“ Quite an exciting rescue, wasn’t it ? I think the rule was made to protect you poor men. You saw how quickly I snapped you up when I got the chance.”

Miss Arbuthnot gave an impatient, but scarcely perceptible, shrug of her shoulders, so I suspected that some of our conversation was filtering through between those fair fingers.

"You must not look at Aline, if you please," cried the vivacious Sally, following my glance. "It is I whom you have come to visit, and I insist on monopolizing you. What did Mr. McKurdy say when you told him of your experiences in the Model School? I suppose you confided in him to that extent?"

"Oh yes. He didn't say very much, but I think he was rather disappointed I had incurred the enmity of Mr. Brent. If I could have kept to the lines Sam laid down, I should have been all right."

"But Mr. McKurdy himself has been unable to ward off the enmity of the subtle Brent," said Sally.

"Why, how do you know?"

"Oh—well——" explained Sally, with a pretty little blush of confusion; "it was the talk of everybody last session."

"Ah, yes, I had forgotten you were here before."

"But you mustn't forget what I tell you, for, if I do say it myself, I am worth paying attention to."

"My dear Miss Livingstone, I am paying the greatest possible attention to you. Cannot you see devotion in every word I utter?"

Sally laughed, and there was another shrug from Miss Arbuthnot. Miss Livingstone was about to speak, when we heard the door-bell ring, and the next moment the housemaid announced "Mr. McKurdy," the smile on whose face became frozen as he saw me sitting there.

"Well, I'm——" he paused.

"So am I," said I, and we both laughed, joined by the frivolous Sally. Sam, with the familiarity of an old friend, threw off his coat, and placed it out in the hall.

"Hello, Aline," he exclaimed on re-entering, "studying hard as usual, I see."

Miss Arbuthnot raised her head, but it was to look at her friend, not at the newcomer.

"Sally, dear, will you tell your young man not to address me?"

"How can you suggest my doing such a thing," said Sam nonchalantly, "when I am paying my addresses to Sally?   May I introduce to you my friend, Mr. Prentiss?"

"Sally, dear," continued Aline, "will you kindly inform your young man that I have already been offered the privilege of an introduction to Mr. Prentiss, and refused it?"

"Oh, if you wish to enlist Aline's attention," interjected Sally, "you must bring John Henceforth.   She has quite recently come to the conclusion that Mr. Henceforth outshines you all."

"I wish," said Aline, "that you two would cease discussing me."

"Miss Arbuthnot," said Sam, as if shocked, "I'm amazed that you use the phrase 'you two,' because that includes me as well as Sally, therefore you have broken the rules by addressing me."

"I beg your pardon, I wasn't addressing you at all," replied the girl, without realizing at the moment that she now did the very thing she disclaimed.   Sam and Sally both laughed, while I sat there rather glum, feeling myself in a false position, yet without the ingenuity for my extrication.   Miss Arbuthnot had resolutely returned to her reading.

"By the way," said Sam to me, "how came you here?"

"Oh, I just drifted in.   Happening to be passing, I thought this was a nice house, and asked the serving maid to show me into the drawing-room, which she did. I was getting on famously until you intruded."

" I am the culprit," said Sally ; " I met Mr. Prentiss at the picture gallery, and you have said so much about him that I already felt acquainted. He was terribly taken aback when I swooped down upon him, but was kind enough to conceal his thoughts and accept my invitation to visit us."

" Well, well, well, well," said Sam. " Miss Arbuthnot and I are the only two straightforward persons in this room. This very night I hesitated long, wishing to invite Prentiss to accompany me, but his disingenuous affection for the College of Technology completely hoodwinked me. One lives and learns."

" Look here, Sam," said I, " you talk too much, as I have frequently informed you. We were perfectly happy here until you came in. You are the serpent in Eden, so just sit down with Miss Eve Livingstone there, and talk to her. This will allow Miss Arbuthnot to go on with her neglected studies; and as for myself, I'll lay my head on the table and go to sleep. Please wake me at half-past nine. I'm going home then. I'd go now, only the warmth of Miss Livingstone's invitation demands that I shall stay at least an hour and a half. Little did I dream that I was to be thrown over for the first tramp that blundered in."

During the latter part of this exordium, Miss Livingstone had me by the shoulders, and was trying to drag me from the chair over to the other end of the room.

" Oh, you poor, misused man," she cried, with mock dolefulness. " You make me ashamed of our inhospitality. Come over with Sam and me, and we'll have a nice, old-fashioned, three-cornered talk."

" Miss Livingstone, that is the cruellest blow of all. You must take me for a simpleton. I may be from the country, but I know the adage, ' Two's company; three's a crowd.' No mob law for me, if you please."

" Come here, Sam," she commanded, " and sit down beside him."

Sam grinned, but did not move.

" Go away, perfidious woman," said I, " and leave me to my slumbers. If you don't leave me alone, I'll complain to Dr. Darnell to-morrow morning, and claim protection. I thought you loved me for myself alone, but instead your affection was all for that grinning rapscallion. Go away, and leave me to my dreams, or rather, to my nightmares. Even Mrs. Sponsor, widow as she is, would not have trifled with my tenderest feelings as you have done."

Sally laughed and laughed. I always think of laughter when I think of Sally, just as I associate seriousness with Aline.

" There should," I continued gloomily, " be a printed warning posted up in the Normal School, in the waiting-room of innocent men, saying, ' Beware of the girls who were here the session before.' "

I might have gone further in this mock heroic fashion, had I not caught Aline's grave eyes fixed upon me with a sorrowful disapproval that chased from my memory the words I was about to utter. Sometimes I thought those eyes were black, sometimes hazel, sometimes one hue hardened or softened to the other, but whatever their actual colour might be, they were always fascinating, and entrancingly worthy of study, as I was already beginning to perceive.

" To every man his own session," said Sam, as if he were uttering deep wisdom. " Come away, Sally; for, remember, I, too, am an invited guest, although

12

I am making no fuss about it. Do not waste attention on a visitor who is paying no attention to you. Give Prentiss a slate and pencil, so that he may prepare his tasks for to-morrow, and come over to this end of the room, where your gifts are appreciated. I suggest that you present Miss Arbuthnot with a slate also, and the two may write sentences to one another, which cannot be considered a breach of the rules. Or, place an inkstand between them, so that they may address their remarks to it, and thus avoid Darnell's censure. Next week I'll bring a book of instructions in the deaf-and-dumb alphabet for them.''

The second time I caught the eyes of Aline Arbuthnot, the little line of doubt, hesitation, fear, or whatever it was, disappeared from her forehead, and a very slight smile curved the sweet corners of her lips.

" Are you fond of Roman history?'' she asked, as calmly as if we were old acquaintances, between whom speaking was not prohibited. As the words were spoken, Sally slipped towards Sam's end of the room, cautiously, as if the slightest noise would kill the new conversation at its beginning.

" Roman history?'' I echoed. " Yes, I rather like it. Things seemed to happen in those days.''

" Yes, decisive things.''

" Still, you haven't gone very far with Roman history to-night, Miss Arbuthnot; for I affirm that you have not turned a leaf since I entered the room.''

" Oh, you noticed that, did you? There was no need to turn a leaf; the lesson is all contained on one page.''

She shoved the open book across the table towards me, and I read the headline at the top of the page.

" Ah, ' Crossing the Rubicon!' ''

" Yes; I'm over on your side of the stream now.

I fear I put my foot in when, inadvertently, I addressed Mr. McKurdy; but now I've waded right through, haven't I?"

"There is no doubt of that. I hope you are not sorry, Miss Arbuthnot."

"I don't know whether I am sorry or glad. I should rather have done it with more deliberation if fated to do it at all, but circumstances seem to have pushed me into the stream. It would have been undignified to scramble back, yet the act of boldly pushing across cannot be counted a token of courage. I don't think the authorities were very wise when they dug an artificial Rubicon round the Normal School like the moats that circled the ancient castles."

"I'm not so sure of that."

"What, do you justify the rule, and the capital sentence of expulsion attached to it?"

"It seems to add zest to the drab beginnings of a scholastic existence."

"Was it to experience the zest that you came here to-night?"

"I came because there was a chance of seeing you."

"Well, that's blunt enough, if I could believe it. You complained that Sally had completely bamboozled you."

"I don't know about the bamboozlement; but she invited me, and I'm willing to be bamboozled over and over again, in the circumstances."

"She told you that her aunt had a large house with many rooms, and you eagerly accepted her invitation when you learned that we had separate studies."

"You quite underestimate my perspicuity, Miss Arbuthnot. Here is exactly what happened. When you two fled from the picture gallery, and Dr. Darnell took me in charge, I made a bee-line for lunch, but found I was too late, and so was compelled to satisfy my hunger at the market square hotel. By the time the meal was finished, the hour had long past when I should have reported for the afternoon session, therefore I came direct to this spot, and viewed the house of Miss Livingstone's aunt, as Ollendorf would have said. I estimated with reasonable accuracy the number of rooms such a small dwelling would contain, and came to the accurate conclusion that you two girls studied together in one room."

" And so you acted upon her invitation?"

" To be perfectly honest, Miss Arbuthnot, I would have come even if the house were as large as the City Hall."

" I thought so."

" Merely on the chance of getting a glimpse of you, remember."

" Oh, that's all very well, Mr. Prentiss. I saw how disappointed you were when Mr. McKurdy came in."

" Awfully sorry to keep contradicting you, Miss Arbuthnot. It seems rude, and I apologize, but I was not disappointed at all. I was merely surprised. If my mind had been as alert as my wisdom is deep, I might have guessed that the Man in the Iron Mask was Sam the moment Miss Livingstone said she had been here last session. I was never for a moment deluded into thinking I was anything but a pawn on the board, moved about at Sally's pleasure, and for Sally's purposes. Charming girls don't fall in love with me at first sight, even in a picture gallery."

" Oh, it takes time, does it?"

" I am not sure that it can be accomplished at all, but I was quite certain that Sally had need of me, and now the whole plot is perfectly plain. She knew I was Sam's friend and study-mate, whereas I had never heard of her, nor had I seen her in the school, which fact I was clumsy enough to mention to her."

Aline almost laughed, but stopped on this side of laughter, letting a charming smile suffice.

"And got rapped over the knuckles for it, I suppose," she said.

"Yes; deservedly. I improved rapidly as the interview went on, and became so complimentary towards the last that I earned Sally's approval, much to my delight."

"I think you are quite clever, Mr. Prentiss."

"Precisely. Now you are beginning to do me justice."

"And now, having settled the status of one young man, I want to ask you some questions about another. Is John Henceforth a friend of yours?"

"No, merely an acquaintance."

"I thought he lived in your house."

"He does, but I see him only at meal-times and in the school. Sam and I study together, but we don't visit much at the other fellows' rooms."

"Sam and you prefer to visit a study where there are two girls."

"Exactly. You could not have hit off the situation better if you had tried for an hour."

"Don't you think Mr. Henceforth very well-educated?"

"I can't say that I have noticed it. I think Sam the best scholar in the school."

"Yes, I know you do. He thinks the same of you. I often find myself wondering at, and rather admiring, the opinions you two hold of each other. There is something nice and simple and childlike about it that is rather touching in these cynical days. Still, it blinds you to the fact that there lives in your own house a man cleverer than both of you put together. He doesn't score off Dr. Darnell, as you and Sam like to do. He is very quiet, and self-contained, with a voice like velvet, but already every master in the school is afraid of him; while you two children are playing complacently in the sand together. For instance, here to-night you are seeing the girls just like a couple of farm hands going to a neighbour's house in the country after their hard day's work is done. But John Henceforth is on no such silly mission. He is up in his room, studying hard, not at to-morrow's lessons, but away beyond, in the far intricacies of his subject, where even the most advanced of his teachers must lag behind him. And yet by your look of surprise you seem not to have known this before."

She said all this very quietly, sometimes with downcast eyes, tracing a pattern on the tablecloth with a slender forefinger; at other times gazing at me with that steadfast look so characteristic of her—a fearless, absorbed look which, as I have said before, seemed impersonal, for although her eyes were on me, her thoughts were not.

"My dear Miss Sphinx," I gasped, "how old are you? Seventy-five?"

Now the look became personal, and she smiled a little. She did not smile often, but when she did the smile was very winning.

"I am so young," she said, "that your question is not now so rude as it will afterwards become. I am little more than seventeen, but I take an absorbed interest in the life about me, although sometimes you seem all as unreal as if you were figures passing me in a pageant. You cannot tell how much I enjoy talking with you—with one of the actors, as it were. It gives a reality to the procession.''

'' I have been watching the pageant, too, or at least one of the princesses in it. I'm ready to swear that since the session opened, never once have you looked across at our side of the room. How, then, can you know so much of John Henceforth?''

'' Have you not observed that I did not describe John Henceforth's face, but his voice; and if you are so fond of Roman history as you pretend, you must remember that it was a blind girl who escaped through the intricacies of ash-covered Pompeii. Seeing is believing, says the adage, and, like most adages, ti is quite wrong. Nothing is so deceptive as sight. I should not know Mr. Henceforth if I met him in the street, but I should recognize him at once if I heard his voice.''

'' Then let me bring him here next time I come.''

'' Are you coming again ?''

'' If I am invited.''

'' Very well, I invite you. You came on Sally's invitation to-night; you shall come on mine next Thursday.''

'' I accept the invitation with very great pleasure, but if you are such an admirer of John Henceforth's, why could I not——''

'' Dear me, what has given you that idea? You are a most inattentive young man. I don't admire him. I dislike and fear him.''

'' Well, that's a good beginning.''

'' A beginning of what ?''

This simple question disconcerted me. Those eyes of unfathomed depths were hypnotizing me; making a fool of me, and I stammered—

"The beginning of a—the beginning of a—a lasting friendship. At least, so I have heard."

"There could never be friendship between John Henceforth and me. He is too hard and cruel."

"How on earth can you know that? What makes you so certain? You speak as if you had been acquainted with the man from his boyhood."

"His baiting of the teachers has escaped you, then? It is done very subtly, but it makes me tingle with resentment in Dr. Cardiff's room. Dr. Cardiff is so gentle, so much a gentleman, that it seems deplorable he should be at the mercy of this savage, remorseless and without mercy. Dr. Cardiff should not have been mathematical master. He should have taught history, or philosophy, or something of that sort. John Henceforth has taken his measure, as he has taken the measure of all the rest. He is determined to humiliate Dr. Cardiff before the class, and it is only a question of time."

"Miss Arbuthnot!" I cried in amazement, "you have certainly the most wonderful imagination of any person I ever met, but I think you are unfair to the rest of us. Do you mean to tell me that this has been going on before our eyes, and we have never seen it?"

"And do you mean to say you have never known Dr. Cardiff to talk slowly against time, watching the clock in an agony of apprehension until the gong rang and stopped the discourse, all because of some quiet question Henceforth had asked him, so far beyond his knowledge and ours that the class has as yet no appreciation of the crisis? And here is the feature of the case which makes me not only dislike, but fear John Henceforth. He never tries to push his victim over the edge. I imagine him sitting there, hard and cool, with no tell-tale smile on his face, watching,

watching, watching; enjoying keenly the writhing of the condemned. Before your unseeing eyes the helpless doctor is struggling beyond his depth, and not one of you know enough to throw him a suggestion, as one on shore might fling a life-preserver to a drowning man."

" Then why does not Dr. Cardiff say honestly, ' I cannot solve this problem ' ? Why has he not the manhood to say, ' I don't know ' ?"

" Because he is mathematical master. He dare not admit ignorance to his class."

" Then, despite Dr. Cardiff's gentlemanliness, it seems unfair to students that an incompetent man should be set over them."

" He is not an incompetent man. He has all the knowledge necessary to teach us what we need to gain our credentials."

" In that case Henceforth's questions are as much out of place as if they were inquiries regarding Buddhism. Why does not Dr. Cardiff say so, and not attempt to solve problems that have no bearing on our work ?"

" Thank you. That's the point I wished you to reach. I want you to tell Dr. Cardiff to act in the way you suggest."

" Why don't you tell him ?"

" Because, man-like, he would not pay attention to what a girl said about mathematics. Up to now poor Dr. Cardiff only vaguely realizes the power and knowledge of John Henceforth. It seems to him that he ought to be able to answer everything any of the students ask him. I want you to put him on his guard. If he does not learn his danger, he will come to disaster before us all, and you will see John Henceforth step up to the blackboard with feigned reluctance, and dash off a problem that has tangled up Dr. Cardiff as if he had involved himself in an impenetrable thicket. Now, I want you to throw him the life-preserver before the waters close over him."

She leaned forward across the table, her lovely face transformed by kindly solicitude for another. Somehow I felt as if swept off my feet. I was in a strong current myself. I thrust my hand impulsively across the table, and clasped hers, quite oblivious to the fact that our acquaintance was not yet two hours old, and she seemed equally unconscious, for she returned my grasp.

"Aline," I whispered, "I am proud to be your knight-errant on this mission. May Providence add persuasion to my tongue."

And now she laughed a little nervously, leaned back, the colour overspreading her cheeks, and withdrew her hand quickly, as if she had just become aware of its position.

"You will meet no difficulty," she said. "Do it gently; beware of wounding his self-esteem. Make a protest against Henceforth taking up our time with questions that go beyond our scope or our needs. Never let on that you imagine John Henceforth is his superior. Say that you and Sam have been talking over the matter, and that you are determined not to waste your time in mathematical regions as unpractical as the Buddhism to which you referred a moment ago. Mr. McKurdy will support you."

"But Sam has no idea Henceforth is the kind of man you believe him to be."

"I dare say not. I often think of John Henceforth seated at table with you seven ingenuous boys. How he must despise you all ! I cannot imagine why he is here, when he should be studying the higher branches at the University. Doubtless it is necessary for him to teach a few years more, and he needs merely the guinea stamp on the gold of knowledge he already possesses to make it pass current. There would be something fine about that, if he did not possess the cruelty of the Indian, and love slow torture.''

" Isn't there just a possibility, Miss Arbuthnot, that you may be mistaken ?''

" You'll see before the session ends. Luckily his Nemesis awaits him. He has estimated accurately every man but one, and that one will crush him with a ruthlessness equal to his own.''

" Good heavens ! and who is he ?''

" John Brent, headmaster of the Model.''

" What, that scoundrel ?''

" He is not a scoundrel. He should be head-master of the Normal, and will be before long.''

" I am amazed to hear you say so. You surely cannot admire a treacherous wretch like John Brent ?''

" Oh, I heard you had quarrelled with him. I love him. He is an old friend of my father's and of mine. There is no man I admire so much as John Brent.''

" Well, here's a situation, if you like ! How is John Brent to spy on me and expel me without also expelling you ? If I may change the Rubicon simile, we are both drifting down the stream in the same boat. John Brent can't upset our craft without submerging you in the current. What will John Brent do then, poor thing, as we sing about the little bird ?''

" He'll upset the boat, but he'll save me some way, and leave you to perish.''

" How can you say you love a man like Brent; a man who makes himself a spy in matters that do not concern him ?''

"They do concern him. Efficiency is his religion, and he does not spare himself in promoting the efficiency of the schools, both Normal and Model, and he'll spare nobody that stands in his way."

"Well, Miss Arbuthnot, there is one consolation for me in the situation. I am delighted to hear that you run no risk. I should feel very unhappy if, through any action of mine, another person was to suffer."

"Yes, I heard Mr. McKurdy say that of you the last time he was here. I thought your determination to have nothing to do with us was entirely to your credit, and therefore I am rather astonished to find you succumbing so quickly."

"I may tell you the reason some day."

"Of course you will say that we spoke to you first," she continued.

"I beg your pardon," I interrupted. "Exactly what I shall not say."

"No, of course you wouldn't; nevertheless, Sally spoke to you first, and I made a very speedy second. Still, I should not like you to feel any qualms of conscience so far as I am concerned. It is not my intention ever to teach school. I am here simply because my father, who has been through the course, wished me to benefit by a like training, so even if Mr. Brent expelled me, such an outcome would not mean the wrecking of a career. I should be rather afraid to meet my father, that is all. But with you, and Mr. McKurdy, and Sally, the case is different, so I hope you three will be careful."

"I think we may reduce the trio to a pair, Miss Arbuthnot. Speaking for myself, I am almost sure I shall never teach school again."

"Oh, I know; you intend to become a civil

engineer? There is a friend of mine, about your own age, in our village, who has just passed his final examination in that same profession. My father has a great belief both in him and his calling."

"No, I have forsworn that ambition. The visit to the picture gallery resulted in a change of mind as well as the breaking of rules. I am eager to become a painter now, and to go east instead of west. Since I arrived in this city, everything has turned out different from what I expected. I thought to attend the University, but instead I am in the Normal School classes. I was preparing to become a civil engineer; now I hope to exhibit at the Royal Academy. I looked forward to a life in the wilderness, but, instead, when this session is over, I shall make for Paris."

"But I thought you were very poor. Doesn't Paris call for plenty of money?"

"I suppose it does; and this very morning the question of supplies was settled, which shows what a football of fate a human being is after all. A new railway did it. A young man surveying that line aroused my ambition and turned me towards engineering. Now the attorney of the company has seized on a bit of hitherto useless land I owned, and has offered me a sum that will keep me three or four years in Paris. This relieves me from the necessity of teaching school in the future; and if your admired friend, Mr. Brent, expels me, he will merely send me to Paris the sooner."

Aline Arbuthnot made no reply, for a hand descended on my shoulder, and Sam's voice broke into our conversation.

"Sorry to interrupt, Tom," he said. "Time passes more quickly here than at our own study table, doesn't it? I have often noticed that, and I see you have soon learnt the same lesson; but if we don't reach home before ten o'clock, it will be the porch and the upper window, with no one inside to help, and these cold nights the window is not easy to open from the outside."

We bade a hurried good-night, which was followed by a stealthy opening of the front door, and a cautious reconnoitering of the deserted street before we emerged; then it was a foot-race to Church Street, where we arrived just as Mrs. Sponsor was clattering the chains that held the door. She glared fiercely at me, as if I were the only culprit.

CHAPTER XIV

I care for nobody, no, not I,
If no one cares for me.
'LOVE IN A COTTAGE.'

JOHN HENCEFORTH is a difficult man to estimate
accurately. His face, nose and eyes had something
hawk-like about them, but his manners were those of the
gentle dove. So quiet and unobtrusive was he that,
although I lived in the same house with him, saw
him every day at meals, heard him in the class, I had
no suspicion of his quality until my attention was
drawn to him by another. But now, casting back
over the period of our acquaintance, I wondered why
I had passed him by as being of no particular
account in our lives. I found myself unable to say
definitely whether I liked or disliked him, which for
me was rather a strange condition of mind, for I
either hated, or loved, those with whom I came into
contact, as, for instance, Brent and McKurdy. I do
not think that envy of his undoubted capacity, his
marvellous knowledge, and his almost uncanny skill
in debate, alloyed my feelings towards him, for Sam
also was much cleverer than I, yet my liking for him
has augmented to this day. In a controversy John
Henceforth could silence any opponent except Dr.
Darnell, who never knew when he was beaten, but
Henceforth knew it, as did all the rest of us, and
when that moment came, John Henceforth would sit

back in his seat and smile, saying nothing further, but allowing Dr. Darnell to storm on in a hopeless endeavour to bluster him into the wrong. John Henceforth could silence an antagonist, but never convince him, or make him his friend. There was something in Henceforth's personality which caused those opposed to him to become his bitter enemies, despite the hard polish of politeness which one could never scratch off, or get below to the real man. Only once have I seen him discomfited, and that, to the joy of the class, was done by Dr. Darnell. Henceforth had a wit of a corrosive, biting sort, which left its victim sour and revengeful, but he had no sense of humour, and there Dr. Darnell was his superior. The young man was naturally a rebel, impatient under restriction, a contemner of law, but these qualities would not have told against him with the class had he possessed any human sympathy.

Perhaps one of the regulations at which we chafed with the greatest persistence was the hour of military drill on Saturday. We wanted Saturday to ourselves, to ramble into the country, to sail on the Bay, or to attend some athletic game, but a doddering old veteran from the war had been engaged to put us through our paces with his marchings and counter-marchings, and all that sort of nonsense, as we regarded it. The old drill-sergeant fell an easy prey to us. He was full of stories of battles and skirmishes and imprisonments, and we often grouped round him, and set him going like a phonograph, which was not then invented. One vice carried over by Sam from the last session, was the evading of roll-call. The old man possessed a sheet of paper containing all our names, and, beginning with A, he ran down the list to Z, and as long as he heard the

cry of " Present " after each call, he was quite satisfied. I have known him read the list of forty names
to less than a dozen young men, each answering
" Present " for several missing friends, and yet the
old soldier drilled the remnant as enthusiastically as
if the whole force were under his command. One
lovely spring day, which should have brought a cheering message of hope to each of us, covered the squad
with dire disaster. Dr. Darnell, from the balcony
which hung under his eastern window, looked down
for one fateful moment on the skeleton army, and in
an incredibly short time he came amongst us like
a wolf in the fold.

" Are your men all present, sergeant ?" he demanded of the bewildered veteran.

" Yes, sir," replied the sergeant, saluting.

" Give me the list."

The sergeant handed it to him, with every lad
marked " Present," and I understand, for I was not
there, that the sergeant's watery eye wandered uneasily
over the small group, wondering what was wrong;
fearing that after all there had been a miscount. Sam
and I were tracing a brook to its source ten miles
away, and we have reason to remember where it took
its rise. John Henceforth, curiously enough, was
one of the small number in attendance, and he, with
three others, was given command of nine men
or thereabouts, for whose presence on the parade
ground each was hereafter to be responsible. Sam
and I were privates in Henceforth's company, and
next Saturday, another temptsome day for lake or
country, Dr. Darnell stood grim and forbidding on
his balcony. Henceforth, seeing him there, pretended
he didn't know the words of command, and purposely
mixed us up inextricably with the other companies,

13

effectually queering the game. Dr. Darnell called him and his awkward squad to stand at ease under the balcony, sending the other three companies out of danger to a further corner of the parade ground.

" Now," said the Doctor, " you know enough to obey orders, if you haven't the sense to give them."

He lined us up facing him, and his keen eye scanned our ranks.

" Right about face !"

We turned our backs upon the headmaster, and glared toward the east.

" Quick march !" he cried, and off we set. As we approached the eastern fence John Henceforth said—

" If old Darnell does not cry ' Halt,' each one of you, who has the courage, follow me over the fence."

Dr. Darnell never thought of crying " Halt !" and must have been astonished as he saw ten men disappear from view into the city.

The next time we saw him was in class on Monday morning, and we knew by the fierce psalm which he read that trouble awaited ten of his pupils. Of course Henceforth, as the officer on duty, was the man responsible, for a soldier must go where he is led, but nevertheless the nine of us were determined to stand by him.

" John Henceforth," said the ominous voice of Dr. Darnell, and John promptly stood up, his beak-like nose eager for a fight, his attitude, nevertheless, scrupulously correct, neither defiance in it, nor too much deference.

" What explanation have you to offer for the incident of Saturday, Mr. Henceforth ?"

John Henceforth replied with an air of injured innocence—

"Why, Dr. Darnell, you yourself gave the command to march, but when we reached the fence you had not told us to halt. There was therefore nothing for us, sir, but to break through or over."

Instantly the truculence on Dr. Darnell's face departed, and he leaned forward, his enemy delivered unto his hand.

"Quite right, and admirably stated, Mr. Henceforth, but you misapprehend the point of my inquiry. I am anxious to know why you are standing here, why you are not still marching on?"

For once John Henceforth did not know what to say, and he stood there such a picture of a man nonplussed that even his own company joined in the laughter which ensued.

In writing of John Henceforth at the present time, I labour under the advantage, or disadvantage, whichever it may be, of knowing what he has done with his life so far. Intermittently I have followed his career in the newspapers, and everywhere he has been the stormy petrel of his time and place. If he had settled in a Quaker neighbourhood, he would have had the brethren at variance within six weeks. He became almost the leading legal light of his country, and that word " almost " fits him better than any other in the language. He almost invariably loses his cases before a jury, and wins them with the Judges of the higher courts upon appeal. In politics he has led his party to victory over obstacles that appeared insurmountable, only to be crushed later by his own colleagues. Never has he attained the height of his ambition in either his profession or his politics. He has quarrelled with one party, joined the other, and defeated the victors in turn, although his old followers fought him with the bitterness which most men feel when combating one whom they consider a traitor.

He is always a leader of those in opposition, but never their leader when he brings them into power. He has done things which have caused his name to be cabled round the world, and has deluded sage London newspapers into predicting that here was the coming man. When he is cast down, but never discouraged, he begins again at the bottom. There is one thing, with all his knowledge, which he has never learned, and probably never can learn, and that is the slow, irresistible, glacier-like force of the commonplace men whom he despises. On every supreme occasion they have crushed him. He has the cleverness of a thousand ordinary men condensed in his anatomy, yet he never could conceal from the thousand his disdain of them, and their dull weight always overcame his adroitness. Unsuccessful, but undismayed, he has moved from place to place, rapidly becoming the leading man in each locality wherever he stationed himself, filling with alarm the party to which he was opposed, with a result monotonous in its completeness. Where he is to-day I have not the least notion, but I never open a morning paper without expecting to come across his name. I should like to meet him again, now that the silver is in our hair, and learn whether the incandescent lava under an exterior of ice has cooled to any appreciable extent. A friendless man, I take him to be, lacking some one ingredient in his nature which would have made him a hero of the world, for his clear-sighted, coldly selfish view of life entitled him to a place he has never attained, or at least never held for more than a day or two at a time. I am handicapped in writing of him, because not once have I been privileged to hear an unbiassed opinion of him, although I have met those who knew him both in Europe and America, but whenever his name was mentioned, whether they belong to his party or the opposition, such rancour was aroused that I usually got nothing but lurid profanity. He is a man not to be ignored, and I can imagine his quiet incisive voice from the body of a public meeting being the precursor of a riot. Something in his tone rouses virulent antagonism in the human race.

To return to the time of my history, John Henceforth's record at the Model School should have filled us all with joy. If any one else had handled the first division as he did, we would have formed a torchlight procession, and placed the victor on a pinnacle, or carried him shoulder high in a chair. John Henceforth made the young lions of the first division feel, for the first time in their lives, that they were worms of the dust, and this without ever raising his voice. His knowledge of any subject was so supreme that it required a well-educated man to appreciate how far in advance of him John Henceforth was, and the youths of the first division were quite clever enough to know that there stood before them the master of *their* master. He never expressed contumely in words, but his whole bearing towards them was a sneer. He paralyzed them with supercilious disdain, and flouted them with a knowledge that made their own acquirements seem the very dregs of information. He never quarrelled with the headmaster as I had done, but with a few smiling, derisive words, exposed the limitations of John Brent to his class, and left them both as if he pitied them equally. We learnt all this somehow, but not from John Henceforth, who was no braggart, and yet his triumph was never our triumph. He was among us, but not of us. I tried to analyze my own feelings towards him, but without much success. Distrust seems too strong a word to use, so I may put it this way. If it became necessary that Sam should be in such a spot at such a moment, and I telegraphed him to that effect, I should know he would be there at the right time, no matter what the inconvenience might be to himself. If I made the same request of John Henceforth, I should know he wouldn't be there, but that he would furnish, when he saw me, absolutely incontrovertible reasons why it was impossible for him to come.

After my talk with Aline Arbuthnot I watched my comrade more and more, and wondered at my own stupidity in not having previously seen his baiting of the masters, more especially of the kindly Dr. Cardiff. As a rule the class hung together, and in a controversy between an individual and a master, the individual, right or wrong, could count on the sympathy of his fellows. John Henceforth seemingly felt strong enough to stand alone, and his case was an exception to the rule. In the incident which I have cited, where Dr. Darnell for the moment got the better of him, the laughter was louder and more spontaneous than if any other person had been the victim.

It came about that Sam, a member of his own house, checkmated him in his next attempt to embarrass Dr. Cardiff, and this intervention by McKurdy happened to reveal the fact that he and I were breaking the all-important rule, so, if Henceforth wished for revenge, he had it sooner than might have been expected.

On the Thursday following our visit to the girls, we assembled in Dr. Cardiff's room to grapple with the useful subject of arithmetic. On this occasion John Henceforth had evidently determined not to be

nullified by the time limit. He rose in his place, at
the very beginning of the hour, and asked permission
to speak. He said he had encountered a simple problem, which nevertheless baffled him, and he would
be so much obliged if Dr. Cardiff would kindly dis-
play the solution on the black-board.

Now, Dr. Cardiff was one of the most simple-
minded, unsuspicious of men. Two days before, in
pursuance of my promise to Aline Arbuthnot, I had
sought an interview with him in his own room, and
endeavoured, without wounding his self-esteem, to
make him aware of the danger that lurked in John
Henceforth's simple problems, but evidently he had
taken my words merely at their face value, looking
for no meaning underneath, for now he acceded very
graciously to Henceforth's request, and asked him
to read out the problem, which the young man did.
It seemed so innocent that Dr. Cardiff at first objected
on the ground of insufficient data, but Henceforth
said he had been assured by a University student
that the problem, as read, gave all the data a mathematician should require. Upon this assurance the
unfortunate Cardiff set down the figures on the black-
board. Probably remembering my own admonition
to him, he made a mild, semi-humorous protest
against employing the time of the class on elementary
problems, and John Henceforth, with that beak of his
ready to pounce on his victim, apologized most
humbly for the liberty he had taken, excusing himself
by saying that the solution would occupy but a few
moments, and perhaps several in the class beside
himself might be interested in its working out. With
a friendly smile, the unlucky Dr. Cardiff started
towards his downfall.

Much as I prided myself on my mathematical ability,

I knew that Sam was my superior, and now began to suspect that John Henceforth could beat us both. I looked across at him. That knife-edge profile of his had more and more the resemblance to the beak of a bird of prey. His hawk-like eyes were fastened on poor Dr. Cardiff, who already began to flounder. There was an electrical uneasiness in the room, and I glanced down our row at Sam, wondering how he was taking it. He proved to be the sole person in the room beside Dr. Cardiff who was at work, and I heard the scribble of his pen on the foolscap before him. At last he threw back his head, but I guessed from his action that he had merely run up against a difficulty, and had not solved the enigma. He rose to his feet.

"Dr. Cardiff," he said, "I should like to ask a favour."

The doctor's usually placid face turned from the black-board with a baffled expression rather pitiful to see. Almost a hint of fear shone in his eyes when he saw that the next best mathematician in the school was on his feet. He drew his handkerchief across his brow, then found courage to say—

"What is it, Mr. McKurdy?"

"I think this proposition is not so simple as it seems," replied Sam, with an air of such childlike candour that none, unless it was Henceforth himself, fathomed the fact that this was an intervention. "I suggest, Dr. Cardiff, that you give us this arithmetical puzzle for our home lesson to-night, instead of working it out now on the black-board. I believe we will appreciate your demonstration better after we have had some experience with its intricacies."

Dr. Cardiff seemed too crestfallen to avail himself instantly of this means of escape. He had somehow the pathetic air of a harmless animal that has been trapped, and knew not for the moment which of those beasts around him was friend or foe. As Sam sat down I rose, and said—

"Dr. Cardiff, I should like to support the proposal of Mr. McKurdy. I want to try a fall with this seemingly innocuous hickory knot myself."

At last Dr. Cardiff smiled.

"I think, Mr. Prentiss, you are mixing your similes a little. Nevertheless, I agree with the suggestion. Please write this question down in your notebooks, and bring me the solution to-morrow morning."

The doctor sat down at his desk, and once more drew his handkerchief across his brow. I indulged in another glance at Henceforth. There was a slight sarcastic smile on his thin lips, but he made no protest.

As Sam walked with me down Church Street after the day's session, I found him very indignant at the action of Henceforth, and in this feeling I concurred. We were talking about the matter when unexpectedly we found Henceforth walking between us, but whether he had heard anything or not, I did not know, and Sam seemed not to care.

"Well, McKurdy," he said, "you came nobly to the rescue."

"Yes, I did. Why do you wish to humiliate Dr. Cardiff?"

"Why are we given an incompetent master?" asked Henceforth, using almost the same phrase I had presented to Miss Arbuthnot.

"He is not incompetent," cried Sam hotly, "and this is a mere catch or trick, which, so far as I have investigated it, cannot be solved except by algebra."

"You are mistaken," replied Henceforth. "There are only two men in this city who can solve it arithmetically, and I am one of them. I merely wished to thank you for your salvage of the good doctor, and yet venture to inform you that it is but temporary. He will be as unable to demonstrate this on the blackboard to-morrow as he is to-day."

"Don't be too sure," warned Sam, "and as for there being only two men in the city who can do the sum, I'll lay you a wager that there will be four by six o'clock to-night."

"I'm not a betting man," said Henceforth, with his thin smile.

When we reached our study, we poked the fire, threw off our coats, and waded in. For an hour there was silence in the room, then Sam said quietly—

"I've got it."

Half-an-hour later I said, "I've got it too. I found the answer first by algebra, and although I've done it now on strict arithmetical lines, I feel as if I had had assistance."

Sam shoved over his solution to me, and I studied with admiration his legitimate work. We felt very proud of ourselves, and after supper started for Stanmore Street in a state of considerable hilarity. I shall never forget how charming Aline Arbuthnot was that evening. In class during the day I had caught one flash from her glorious eyes after I had spoken in favour of McKurdy's proposal, and now I was to hear grateful praise from her lips.

"Oh, we are proud of you two men," she cried, as we came into the room. "Your action to-day was splendid."

"Sam is the one deserving of praise," I demurred. "I simply sat like a bump on a log, and didn't know what to do. His ingenuity saved the situation.''

"Indeed, you under-rate yourself," went on the flattering Aline. "Your support was needed, and it came in just the right way at just the right time, for poor Dr. Cardiff was like a man lost in a maze; too bewildered to take the opportunity offered him. Of course the initiative belongs to Mr. McKurdy, and is to his eternal credit, but I link you two together in the scheme, and what I say of one I say of the other."

"You are quite right, Miss Arbuthnot," quoth Sam. "I needed and welcomed Prentiss's support. Indeed, I was just about to get on my feet again when I heard his voice. I expected half-a-dozen to rise up, but I suppose nobody really saw the crisis except us four and John Henceforth. How far have you got with the problem?"

"Oh," cried Sally, "we've got far enough to know it can't be done by arithmetic."

Sam and I laughed, and Aline asked anxiously—

"What about to-morrow? Has the torture merely been postponed after all?"

"Oh no," said Sam. "Prentiss and I have done it, and on our table at home the solution is beautifully worked out on two sheets of blue foolscap paper. Those will be presented to Dr. Cardiff at the assembling of our class to-morrow."

"Then the villain is foiled," said Sally.

"It would seem so. Don't you girls want to be shown how it's done?"

They both declared they did, and Sam continued—

"Prentiss, you take the post of mathematical teacher to Miss Arbuthnot, while I worry along with Sally," and thus we disposed ourselves.

Aline Arbuthnot, as I always hold, was the brightest girl in the school, and the only one of the fair section of the room who could demonstrate a problem in Euclid if the diagram were turned upside down, and 1,2,3,4, etc., placed at the angles instead of A,B,C, and D. Many of the girls studied their Euclid as they would learn a verse by Tennyson, reciting the formula glibly enough, but if even the most casual inquiry was made regarding the reason for this, that or the other, they relapsed into silence. They always reminded me of a guide in the Cathedral of St. John at Malta, who had learned by rote the descriptions of the various objects of interest in every European language, but went all to pieces if you asked him questions.

A more delightful task than to teach mathematics to Aline Arbuthnot could not be desired by any man. The reserve which characterized her reception of me the Thursday before had departed, and we were now old friends. In less than half-an-hour the girls declared they understood the solution from beginning to end. They wrote it down beautifully on their sheets of blue foolscap, and placed their names at the head of the papers. There was no prohibition against receiving help, so far as Dr. Cardiff was concerned, and he liked to see as many papers as possible on his desk.

Next day, when the mathematical class assembled, there seemed a very small sheaf of papers on the master's desk, and when the unsuspicious man read out the names there was instant silence.

"I am sorry to say," began Dr. Cardiff benignly, "that only four persons have solved this problem: Miss Arbuthnot, Miss Livingstone, Mr. McKurdy and Mr. Prentiss. I admit that the problem presents certain difficulties," continued the guileless Doctor,

" but I am astonished that more of you gentlemen did not solve it when two of the ladies were able to do so."

There were difficulties in the problem, doubtless, but these were as nothing compared to the difficulties which now confronted our quartette. I could not forbear a glance at the class. Miss Arbuthnot was looking straight ahead of her; Miss Livingstone sat very still, with downcast eyes. Most of our fellows pretended ignorance, but two or three were leering at Sam and me with broad grins on their faces. I think at that moment the Doctor was the only person in the room ignorant of the situation, for he said calmly—

" Miss Arbuthnot and Miss Livingstone, please work out the solution on your black-board, while Mr. Prentiss and Mr. McKurdy will do the same on this side of the room."

Oh, Sally, Sally; there come occasions in this life when high spirits will not see one through. Sally stood before the black-board, a white chalk crayon in her fingers, with dejected mien and drooping head, and never set a single mark on the black-board.

I worked out the problem with the largest numerals that have ever been used on this earth unless an endeavour has been made to communicate with the inhabitants of Mars. I hoped that the girls, if they found themselves in arithmetical difficulties, would glance across the room, and " follow copy," as printers say. Aline confessed at our next interview that this sign-board style of arithmetical demonstration had proved most useful in helping her over some of the more intricate places, but Sally made no attempt either to work out the question originally, or to follow the lead given by my figures. As I stood at the black-board my back was toward the class, and I did not at that time know of the partial failure at the opposite board. I worked as slowly as I could, so that the girls might have time to follow, and using such large characters I accomplished the demonstration in sections, for I continually came to an end of my figuring at the lower boundary of the black-board. At the conclusion of each section I moved on, like a house painter, from force of necessity, and also to get my body out of the way of the ornamental work I was doing on the board. By the time I had finished, Miss Arbuthnot, her work complete, was in her seat again. Sally had sunk down abashed, leaving the sombre board as blank as she found it. Sam had long since ended his task—he was always a rapid worker. When I turned round I found the eyes of both master and pupils upon me. Dr. Cardiff's face was very grave. At last it had come to his comprehension that McKurdy and I had explained this problem to the young ladies the night before. His right hand was gently stroking his long beard, always a sign of perplexity with Dr. Cardiff. He said nothing to Miss Livingstone regarding her failure, nor to the three of us did his usual word of encouraging commendation come because of our success. He simply sat there silent and thoughtful, stroking his beard. A deep silence hung over the room, and dusting the chalk from my fingers I caught the glitter of John Henceforth's inquiring eyes, and saw his crooked smile.

"Speech, speech," he whispered, but so incisive was his voice, and so still the room, that the words were heard to the furthest corner. I felt that somebody should say something to relieve the tension, so I took the liberty of addressing John Henceforth himself. In my nervousness I made a bad stumble at the very beginning.

"The solving of an arithmetical problem," said I, "should exhibit more than the mere answer required."

"I think this one does," said the quick-witted Henceforth, before I could explain my words.

Dr. Cardiff stroked his beard, rested a sorrowing eye on John Henceforth, but said nothing.

"Yes, Mr. Henceforth," I continued, "the elementary nature of your little puzzle did not require the time I have given to it. I wished to show you all the beauty of Arabic notation. The figures I have endeavoured to put down I learned from civil engineers running a railway survey. They do them in red chalk on stakes——"

"Do the civil engineers ever use a red herring as well as red chalk?" asked Henceforth with an assumption of artless inquiry. He had me on the spit, and I saw he was determined to turn it.

"The civil engineers," I went on unheeding, "do this sort of work very well, and my attempt at copying them is but a poor imitation. Nevertheless, if I have succeeded in giving a hint that a seven and a two, well drawn, contain elements of beauty, I am satisfied."

There was a little ripple of applause which intimated I had at least the sympathy of the class.

"I think the figures are very beautiful," said Henceforth, "and they have this great advantage, that they can be read from a distance."

I made no reply, but took my seat, and the study of arithmetic went on. At the beginning of the session I did not know whether I liked or disliked John Henceforth. I solved this problem and the one on the black-board simultaneously.

CHAPTER XV

WHEN we were all gathered in the waiting-room, I
observed that Sam had stayed behind, in response, he
told me afterwards, to a quiet signal from Dr. Cardiff.
John Henceforth stood apart from the rest, his customary grin on his face, knowing the spirit of the
class was against him, and not caring, I surmise.
The others regarded his remarks as so many strokes
below the belt. He was not playing the game, but
no one said anything until the door opened, and Sam
entered. I saw him, for the first time in my life,
flushed with anger. McKurdy walked across the floor
to where Henceforth stood, never flinching, or raising
his hands to protect himself, although he must have
known a personal assault was intended. Sam grasped
him by the arms midway between shoulder and
elbow, and shook him as a terrier shakes a rat.
Henceforth was a thin, gaunt man; a living skeleton
when compared with Sam, who knew little of his own
strength while good-natured, and when angry did not
know it at all. I expected to hear the slender bones
crack. Henceforth's grin froze into an expression of
extreme physical pain, and his lips went white with
agony, but he made no murmur.

"You sneaking sweep," hissed Sam, "with no

esprit de corps, and no instincts of a gentleman. You may score off me as much as you like, and if I cannot answer you with my tongue, I shall not do it with my fists, but, by God, if you attempt to show your cleverness again where a lady is involved, I'll break your d——d neck."

" You are breaking my d——d arms," said Henceforth very coolly, " and when you are quite done with them, I shall thank you for releasing your grasp."

McKurdy flung him staggering, and he would have fallen had the room been less crowded. The gong rang three times, and we went down-stairs to hear the mild Professor Donovan on Natural Philosophy.

I expected lunch that fateful Friday to prove an embarrassing meal, after what had happened, but such was not the case. John Henceforth appeared at table exactly as usual, and seemed to cherish no resentment of the treatment he had received at the sinewy hands of McKurdy. The two opponents did not directly address each other, but if a stranger had been our guest, he would have noticed nothing amiss in our little company. Indeed, John Henceforth made to me, in well-chosen words and most ingratiating accents, a semi-apology for his remarks in class.

" It is all a question of tactics," he said, " and I admit that doubtless I was in the wrong. I hold that the best course in a difficulty is to face it. Your plan seemed to be to cover it up, to ignore it, to run away from it. Lions in the path are usually chained when you march boldly upon them. The moment you four stood up to work out the solution of the problem, which it had been shown no one else in the class could do, the situation was perfectly plain to every one in the room, especially as nearly every one knew that

14

those two girls could not, unassisted, accomplish the task set to them. I now recognize, however, that your way of dealing with the case was probably better than mine, and I have no hesitation in making an apology, and begging your pardon."

" Mr. Henceforth, you miss the chief point of the incident."

" Really? What is the chief point?"

" The chief point is that it was none of your cursed business. You had no right to interfere. No one else in the class said a word, and you should have been the last to put in your oar, because the crisis in which we four found ourselves was caused either by your cruelty or your vanity : your cruelty if the problem was given merely to embarrass Dr. Cardiff; your vanity if you wished to show that you knew more of mathematics than any of your colleagues. Yesterday you proved yourself to be either mean or vain, whichever you choose, and to-day you proved yourself impertinent."

" I am afraid you are a trifle harsh in your judgment, Mr. Prentiss, but it is not for me to complain. The rule we have infringed is an absurd one, and I intend to do what I can to have it abolished. We are all in the same boat, and I think we should work together with one object in view, which is the annulment of so foolish and childish an enactment. Now, to be quite frank with you, and to place myself entirely at your mercy, I state here before you all, that Miss Clara Lane, of the Normal School, is a friend of mine, whom I visit and talk to whenever I get the opportunity."

" Mr. Henceforth, your confession is quite safe with us, although it involves another, possibly without her knowledge or consent."

" Oh, you mean Miss Lane?   She wouldn't mind. We understand each other thoroughly.   Of course, I don't intend to shout from the housetops what I have told you, and it is my purpose to give John Brent a run for his money.   I merely mention the fact to show my confidence in the present company, and to make a bid for your confidence in return."

During this talk none of the others said anything, but no evidence was forthcoming of a universal desire on the part of those present to sacrifice themselves that future students might escape the yoke of this obnoxious rule.

The same evening we were convincingly shown that news permeated rapidly throughout the large establishment to which we belonged.   As Sam and I were walking home from the Normal, we met the always handsome and dignified Mr. Brent, who paused and greeted us with his smile of conscious superiority.

" I see you hunt in couples, gentlemen," he re-marked, with prim urbanity.

" Yes," replied Sam airily, " we are brothers who dwell in unity, as my Aunt Jane always advised me to do."

" I am glad to hear it, Mr. McKurdy, and also to learn that you two stand high in the mathematical class."

" I hope we stand high in every class," I rejoined, " especially in reading."

" If one paid attention to rumour one might think that mathematics is still your strong point.   Good-evening, gentlemen," and with that Mr. Brent passed smiling on.

" News in the Normal School," said Sam, " is like carbonic acid gas.   It flows downwards."

We were just returning from the chemical class, and Sam's similes were always tinged by his latest occupation.

"You think he knows all about it, then?"

"I am certain of that. He always knows more of what is passing in the Normal School than our own teachers. He believes he could have us expelled to-morrow if he wished."

"Undoubtedly. When will he strike?"

"Just when he is ready, and not a moment before. The session is young yet. He has ample time, and he will take it. It may surprise you to know that you are not in the least suspected. John Brent's gaze was fixed entirely on me. He thinks he has got me, and, in a way of speaking, he has. This morning it never occurred to Dr. Cardiff that you were implicated. I am still the scape-goat, and it was to me old Cardiff signalled to remain behind. Cardiff is a gentleman, and will say nothing. He spoke with great kindness, more in sorrow than in anger, and implored me to quit the dangerous path of dalliance. You see, both he and Brent know that the two girls lodge in the same house, and that Sally was here last session. Cardiff imagines I visit her, and Brent is sure of it. My mathematical instruction is thus supposed to account for both of the girls sending in replies. You, with your figures of the civil engineer, are held guiltless. The only person with a true knowledge of the situation is John Henceforth. I don't understand that subtle man. I see no reason why he should round on us, yet his conduct this morning showed a mischievous determination to accentuate our difficulties. We must visit the girls to-night, and put them on their guard."

"But now that John Brent knows where you go,

isn't there a chance he may have the house watched ?"

" I rather imagine he has known where I go for some time. In any case, there's little danger of the house being watched during these bleak winter nights. It's no fun standing guard outdoors in this weather, but when the days become long, with nights sweet and mild, then espionage adds attraction to the pleasure of a starry ramble. I am convinced that John Brent is not yet ready. However much he may dislike us, there is no question that he will not allow the desire for revenge to hurry him. He is a coldly calculating man, and his plan, whatever it is, will be well thought out, and the trap sprung at precisely the right moment. To act now might possibly mean the expulsion of two or three of us, but I think Brent wants to make a big haul when he casts his net. Our downfall would frighten the rest of the school, and the trapping of you and me would be a mere incident of the session, with no influence for or against the administration of Dr. Darnell. I may be doing Brent an injustice, but I believe his aims are purely selfish, and in that case he wants to show a laxity of discipline impinging upon the very rule the authorities consider most important, as their severest punishment follows its breach ; therefore Brent desires to bag at least a dozen of us, and to do that he will not frighten the covey. He must be in possession of direct, unshakable proof, and at best the incident of to-day is no more than strong circumstantial evidence. So, my boy, if my deductions are right, to-day's affair will never even reach the ears of Dr. Darnell, and nothing will happen till after the ice breaks up in the Bay. No, we never were safer than at the present moment, so let us make the best of our opportunity by paying a surprise visit to the dear girls to-night. It is possible they may be panic-stricken, and there is enough of the spirit of the missionary in me to wish to calm the doubts of one. Doubtless you will not object to soothe the fears of the other.''

When we arrived at Stanmore Street that night, I found a state of affairs of which I had dreamed. Aline Arbuthnot was alone, sitting in an arm-chair, her feet to the fire, reading a book.

"Oh," she cried, jumping up. " We didn't expect you. Sally has gone to church.''

Sam, who had been about to cast off his overcoat, allowed it to remain on his shoulders.

" To church ?'' he echoed. " To the Centre Street church ?''

Aline smiled.

"Yes. I see you know where. That's what comes of last session, I suppose.''

" It was there I first had the pleasure of meeting Sally, and we have attended many a sermon since.''

" I wish you had come a little earlier. She has been gone only a few minutes. Poor Sally is very much overwrought by what happened this morning. She blames herself instead of circumstances, and bemoans her failure at the black-board, which, she says, caused the catastrophe.''

" Nonsense," cried Sam; " she is not in the least to blame, and the failure at the black-board made no difference, for the show was given away by us four sending in our papers together. The fault lies entirely with me. I should have known that our herd of dull cattle could not solve the problem had they been given a year instead of one night to do it.''

" It will cheer her up to hear you say that, Mr. McKurdy, for Sally is very contrite and disconsolate.

I am glad to say that Sally has come to the resolution not to meet you again till the end of the school term.''

''Quite so,'' said Sam dryly. '' She came to that decision about twenty-seven times last session. Sally used to sign the pledge and swear off regularly twice a week at first.''

Aline's eyes sparkled with indignation.

'' There speaks selfish man,'' she cried. '' Instead of helping her to keep her good resolutions you stand there bragging of her breaking them.''

Sam laughed joyously.

'' There is another thing I brag of. Hasn't Sally ever told you that we are going to be married as soon as we save a sixpence—not one sixpence, you know, but a sixpence each? Oh, we're not reckless. Why should I not see my dear girl as often as I can, in spite of all the ancient educational fogies, and their rules for the culture of old maids? We're young but once, and I for one am going to make hay while the snow flies. I'll begin my career of renunciation after I'm eighty-five. Sally and I will discuss this question coming from church. Persuade Prentiss to reform, and induce him to stop at home. I'm past hope, as my Aunt Jane says, and so good-night to you both for a time. Sally and I will be back here in about an hour,'' and as Sam went off we heard him whistling the refrain of a then popular negro melody, entitled, '' Seeing Sally Home.''

Aline laughed, and sank down in the easy-chair.

'' My precepts are ignored,'' said she; '' or, as Dr. Darnell would quote : ' Some fell on stony places.' ''

'' Yes, Sam is a hardened sinner; but I am particularly susceptible to good advice, and pay great attention to precept. May I remain until they return and listen to counsel ?''

"Yes, do," she invited encouragingly. "Take off your coat and draw up a chair."

It is odd how chance plays with us, now for, and now against. I took off my coat, and was about to open the door, and hang it up in the hall, when I thought it a pity to disturb the cosiness of the room by a blast of cold air from the unheated entry. My next motion was to place the coat over the back of a chair, but finally I walked to the end of the room, drew aside the heavy curtains which shut out a square bay-window, and threw my coat on the window-seat, that favourite chatting-place of Sam and Sally. Then I pushed Sally's easy-chair as near as I dared to Aline's, and sat down beside her, facing the cheerful fire.

Given the ordering of affairs in the universe, I could not have contrived a more blissful situation. The seated girl formed an entrancing picture. I suppose even at that time there was in my soul an appreciation of beauty which later enabled me to achieve such success as has been mine in life. She sat with her small feet on the fender, her bewitching eyes gazing dreamily at the blaze, her white hands lying listlessly on her lap. A certain relaxation in the way she leaned back in the easy-chair gave a touch of surrender to her attitude that appealed strangely to me, and set my heart beating even faster than it had ever done before. There was an air of having contended with fate, having been conquered, and now the inevitableness of it all softened defeat and atoned for it. The current of the Rubicon had proved too strong for us, and we were floating down the stream together, lotus-lured and silent, languorously happy, and peacefully content with the present, thinking nothing of either past or future.

" What do you see in the blaze, Aline?" I whispered.

I had called her Aline before, but that was in a moment of emotion; this was done deliberately. She showed no resentment and made no move whatever, but answered as one speaking in her sleep.

" I see the beauties of Arabic notation; the lovely outlines of twos and sevens and fours and threes, done artistically on a black-board. I hear a voice you cannot hear, the voice of a man trying to save the situation, speaking without the excitement he must feel, and interrupted by the waspish voice of a thin Mephistopheles, who for some reason tries to trip him into a pit. But mathematics is a dangerous subject in this room; we must avoid it, for I cannot help thinking of the scene in the class-room this morning; the deep silences, the words spoken, the gradual dawning of enlightenment upon Dr. Cardiff, and the pained tragedy of his face when enlightenment became complete. It seemed as if I had never begun to live till then, and to find myself an actress in the drama, the principal in a conspiracy, yet unremorseful, amazed me. It amazed me more to know that my impulse was not to cry, but to laugh, and I am not a laughing girl. Yet the cause of it is so trivial; you and I have talked together, that is all. If you came to my father's house, if you were sitting in our drawing-room, instead of here, what more natural and proper than that I should speak with you? Why, then, is it a crime in this city—a crime with penalty? and yet, so powerful is imagination, I experience every thrill which must come with the consciousness of guilt."

As this was said, she had partly roused herself from her listless position.

"And so in the fire you see the scrivening of the civil engineers?"

"Why do you harp on the civil engineers?" she cried, now fully alive again, and turning on me something of the same look which a few minutes before had shown her resentment against McKurdy's words. "You mentioned the civil engineers in the class-room to-day."

"Why not? Do you dislike a civil engineer?"

She leaned back again, all energy departed once more.

"No, no. The truth is, I don't know what I like or dislike. Ah, I remember now, you intended to be a civil engineer, but are going to turn painter instead. Of course, what more natural than that you should mention civil engineers? You are thinking of your first profession, even though you have turned towards your second. You, perhaps, find it not so easy to be off with the old love before you are on with the new."

She contradicted her statement about the laughing girl by laughing now, and somehow it struck me as not being happy laughter.

"I think," she said at last, "I should have indulged in hysterics after I reached my room, or I should have scolded or cried, or done something to lessen the burden of an uneasy conscience. Instead, I foolishly reasoned it all out, and now I find myself talking to you quite at random. I really don't know what I am saying."

"Indeed," I assured her, "you are speaking most delightfully, and I hope you will——"

There came two sharp knocks at the door. Aline sprang up, alert, tense, vivid. Dreams had vanished into the nothingness they are.

" Draw back your chair to the middle of the room,"
she whispered hurriedly, " and get into the bay window. That is the servant's signal warning us of a
master's visit—Dr. Darnell, or, more likely, Dr.
Cardiff."

I lifted the chair, placed it silently in the centre of
the room, and vanished behind the big curtain, thanking Providence as I sat down that I was sitting on
my overcoat.

" Come in," I heard the clear, unruffled voice of
Aline.

The door opened, and the maid announced—

" Mr. Brent, miss."

How adaptable are women. Her welcome sounded
heartfelt and joyous.

" Why, Mr. Brent, is this you? How good of you
to call on me on such a bitter night."

" How are you, Aline?" came the smooth greeting
of John Brent.

" Very well indeed, thank you, Mr. Brent."

" Are you all alone?"

" Sally—Miss Livingstone, you know—my room-
mate, has gone to church."

" You've been reading, I see."

" Reading a little, yes; but mostly sitting idle by
the fire, dreaming."

" Thinking of home, perhaps."

" Yes, my thoughts have been there once or twice
this evening. Won't you take off your coat, Mr.
Brent?"

" No, thank you. I can stop but a moment." I
heard the snapping of a watch-case. " I am due at
the Young Men's Christian Association in half-an-
hour from now, where I am to give a short address
on education."

"Well, I know of no one more capable than yourself, Mr. Brent."

"There is one man who could take my place to-night with great advantage to the audience, and that is your father, Aline."

"Yes, he is a good speaker," said the girl; "but surely not better than you are, Mr. Brent."

"He is my superior both in eloquence and information, and it is about him I dropped in to talk with you to-night."

"About my father?"

"Yes, about his ambition for you. You know, Aline, he regards me as your guardian at the Normal School. He confided to me that you were betrothed to Herbert Roscume, the civil engineer."

"No, no!" cried the girl, "I am not—I am not engaged to any one, and never have been. You are mistaken in what my father said. He could not have told you such a thing. It is not true."

John Brent's tones became cold and formal as they always did when he was contradicted.

"Your father said that Roscume was the son of his oldest friend, and that he hoped to see you married to him."

"That is a different thing altogether, Mr. Brent. I have my own life to live, and I may disappoint my father's hopes."

"I trust not, Aline. Have you told him so?"

"No, we never discussed the matter. Why should we? There was nothing to discuss. And why have you come to me now, with the name of Herbert Roscume on your lips? Why do you speak to me on a subject my own father did not venture to broach?"

"I came because of the incident at the Normal

School this morning, and I wish to say at once that I know you to be perfectly innocent. I know that this person McKurdy visits your friend, Miss Livingstone. Doubtless they are at church together at this moment."

"I assure you, Mr. Brent, that Sally set out entirely alone. Generally I accompany her to the Friday evening meeting, but to-night I was interested in a book, and so stopped at home."

"I beg you to believe, Aline, that the correctness of your own behaviour is unquestioned. I am here only to remind you of your father's equally strong faith in your blameless conduct. You know how bitterly disappointed he would be if anything happened that brought your name into notoriety at the Normal School. You are his only daughter, and it would be impertinence on my part if I referred to his devoted affection for you; his confidence in you; his unshaken belief in you, second only to his belief in his God; a severe man to all others except you; a learned and deeply religious man."

Through the interstices of his words I heard stifled sobs.

"Now, my dear girl, you must not take this hard of me. Remember I have known you since you were a toddling little child, and when I hear these baby lips say, 'I have my own life to live,' I realize how the years are passing. 'Your own life,' yes; and I speak in the hope that you may not make a mistake which in all your after life you cannot remedy. Trust to your father's judgment, Aline. He is a man who rarely makes a mistake about his fellow-men. These people in the Normal School are but riff-raff. There is not a man of brains among them."

"Yes, there is," came in faltering accents, with

nevertheless a spirit of resentment and opposition in them. "John Henceforth is a man of brains."

"John Henceforth!" ejaculated Brent, very slowly. There was a long pause. "John Henceforth," he said again. "What do you know of John Henceforth?"

"I know that he is the cleverest student in the Normal School, and the only man who can teach your division in the Model."

"Aline, who told you that?"

"I have heard him answer every question put to him, and he has asked questions that his masters cannot answer. It is said in our waiting-room that he is the only man who can hold control of your pupils."

"Ah! so his doings are discussed in the waiting-room? Has John Henceforth ever dared to speak to you?"

"No."

"I should be sorry if I thought you really admired such a person. John Henceforth is not a man, but a devil."

"Give the devil his due, then," said the now natural voice of Aline.

Brent laughed a little.

"I will, before the session is over. Now, Aline, there are no hard feelings, I hope."

"No."

"That's right. Keep to the rules for your father's sake, and mine. We are both very proud of you. Good-night."

I heard the room door open. Aline, I fancied, went out with him to the hall, for the murmur of indistinguishable words came to me. The street door opened and shut. There was a long silence, and surmising that Aline had not returned to the room, I parted the curtains and stepped out. The door was closed, and Aline stood with her back against it, head bowed deep in thought. I think she had forgotten I was there. She looked up with wet eyes, but greeted me with a wavering gleam of a smile, although she said nothing. I came forward, and took her two unresisting hands in mine.

"Aline," I said, "I am not going to give you up."

"Oh, have you also a claim upon me?"

"Aline, I am not going to give you up! If you tell me to leave, I shall do so. If you do not wish me to return, I shall not return. If you command me never to address you again until this dismal term of school is ended, I will obey you, but I will marry you at last in spite of all the Brents and Roscumes in the land!"

"You mustn't talk like that!" She pulled her hands away.

"I refuse to give you up!"

"I'm not yours to give up."

"No, nor any one else's."

"I will listen to no more of this foolish talk. You and Mr. Brent between you have spoiled my evening."

"Brent has; I haven't. We were very happy when that beastly double knock struck the panels."

"Oh, it was Sally who invented the signal, and coached the servant to give it. Once or twice during the session the Principal or Dr. Cardiff calls, one to look after the welfare of our souls, the other after the health of our bodies. And now you must go, Mr. Prentiss."

"May I not wait for Sam?"

"No."

" May I come again ?"

" No."

" Then my only consolation is to reiterate the phrase, ' I shan't give you up ' ! "

" I wish you wouldn't repeat that. It sounds parrot-like and flippant. You don't know what you are saying. You are not sincere." Then, hurriedly, " Not that it makes any difference with me. I care as little for the future painter as for the future civil engineer. I care for nobody but my father. I shall not disappoint him."

" You will marry whomsoever he chooses, then ?"

" Very likely."

" I don't believe it, Aline."

I took her hands again, meeting more resistance than on the former occasion. I felt I was losing ground.

" You don't care for that chap Roscume ?"

" No, nor for that chap Prentiss."

I laughed, and even she smiled, and looked enchanting with her dewy eyes and her sweet red lips.

" I don't quite believe you, Aline. Let us try the red litmus test."

" The red litmus test ?"

" Yes; don't you remember Professor Donovan's demonstration in the chemistry class this afternoon ?"

" Yes; but I don't understand you."

" I'll explain."

The first kiss was not a success, for she turned her head abruptly away from me when she divined the nature of the experiment, but I held her with a palpitating fervour which thrilled me with the delight of life; and somehow, without definite surrender on her part, and yet reluctant acquiescence, the next kiss came tenderly off, and she made no struggle towards its curtailment, till each of us had to breathe again. Then she pushed me away from her, and somehow my back was to the door, and she stood in the middle of the room, breathing hard and arranging her hair.

"You take an unfair advantage of me," she gasped. "My nerves are all unstrung to-night."

Before I could reply, the unexpected opening of the door almost precipitated me on my face, and Sally came whirling in, laughing like one demented. Aline's arms dropped to her side, and I saw, by her mounting colour, that she thought the frivolous Sally was laughing at us, but it was not so.

"Oh, Aline, Aline," she cried, "we've had such fun, and *such* a narrow escape."

Sam entered more soberly, while I pretended to be holding open the door for him. Aline was already as composed as if she were standing there to receive expected guests.

"What was the fun, and what was the escape?" she asked, with her customary calmness.

"Oh, the fun was being with a man you like, and the escape was a threatened meeting with a man you hate. I was doleful in church, Aline, and even the rectitude of my conduct offered little consolation. There weren't many present, and I had a pew to myself. Imagine my surprise when a man came in and sat down very close to me. 'I beg your pardon,' I said, and pulled my skirts aside, then looked up, and saw Sam's heavenly countenance, and I assure you, Aline—oh, well, some day you'll know all about it yourself."

"And be sure, Aline," said Sam gravely, "to choose a learned and cultured man, as Miss Livingstone has done."

15

Sally went on, pausing now and then to laugh so recklessly that sometimes she bent double.

"Really, Sally," protested Aline, "I have been telling these two young men that you were a penitent, and here you act like this."

"Oh, I *was* a penitent, but you can't be a penitent always. Sam and I were coming hippity-hop up the street like a pair of children, when whom do you think we saw approaching us, luckily with head bent down as if thinking deeply? No other than John Brent. Sam arose to the occasion. I was simply paralyzed with fright, when he swung me in through a gateway and up the stone steps of a splendid house, as if we were going visiting there. But before Mr. Brent had passed, the door opened suddenly, and out came a man."

Sally surrendered herself to helpless laughter again.

"Al, you should have seen Sam's face. The man said, 'I beg your pardon,' and Sam, with the innocence of the infant Samuel, inquired, oh, so blandly ! 'Does Mr. Thomas Prentiss live here ?' 'No,' replied the man, quite genially; 'Mr. Prentiss lives five doors further up. I don't know whether his name is Thomas or not, but he's probably the person you're looking for. I will show you the house.' So, closing the door, and coming down the steps, this obliging individual took us with him to the home of Prentiss. Luckily John Brent had passed on, and unluckily I had to keep from laughing if I could. The stranger was *so* kind. He ran on ahead and pulled the bell, because I was hanging upon Sam's arm, almost limp from suppressed laughter, and Sam all the while shaking me to make me behave myself. Then the stranger lifted his hat and left us. When the door was opened, Sam asked if Mr. Livingstone lived there, and was told he did not, and thus I discovered that Sam has no invention, but uses his friends' names in a pinch.''

'' I suspected all along that it was Brent you met,'' I said, when she had finished, determined to show that we also had not been devoid of experiences, '' because Brent has visited Miss Arbuthnot.''

'' What!'' shouted Sam, '' while *you* were here?''

'' Oh yes.''

'' Good Lord, you don't mean it?''

'' Is that true, Aline?'' asked Sally, fright driving away her laughter.

'' Quite true,'' replied Aline, without a smile.

'' What did he say to you?'' asked Sam.

'' Oh, he didn't say much to me,'' I replied, '' and I didn't say much to him. He's always very gentlemanly, you know, and I think I conducted myself with propriety. What else was there to do?''

'' Good Lord, good Lord!'' moaned Sam, and I saw Sally show signs of descending into the vale of penitence again.

'' There!'' she cried; '' I knew that stupid servant would not give the double knock.''

'' Oh, but she did,'' said Aline quickly.

'' Then why,'' demanded Sally, '' why on earth didn't you get Mr. Prentiss under the table, or under the sofa?''

'' I couldn't ask Mr. Prentiss to adopt so undignified a position.''

'' Good gracious, girl!'' protested Sam. '' Anything was better than meeting Brent here. Now that you two are involved, our escape counts for nothing.''

'' Oh, it's only your under-the-sofa suggestion that I object to. Why is that better than sitting in the bay window behind the curtain?'' I asked.

'' Then he didn't see you?''

"Of course he didn't. What made you think he did?"

"Oh, you villain!" cried Sam. "You two villains, in fact. You gave me the fright of my life, and that not on my own account, but on yours. Sally, this is a vile plot against two innocent persons, who came joyfully in, merely to be flung upon a snow-bank."

"I told him you were at church, Sally, and he thought you very good indeed," said Aline.

Sally rose, the colour back once more in her cheeks.

"I'll give you a shaking for this, my girl, as soon as we get these two men away," she said. "Goodnight, Sam," holding out her hand; and Sam, having confessed the situation, boldly kissed her before us, as one accustomed, but I knew that kiss was as nothing to ours.

"We'll see you next Thursday," said Sally.

"Yes," replied Sam. "If you want me before, send a note."

Sally shook hands with me, then I turned and shook hands with Aline.

"Next Thursday?" I queried.

"That was what Sally said," replied Aline.

CHAPTER XVI

WINTER relaxed, and melted into spring. Nothing happened. Spring mellowed and warmed into summer, and still nothing happened. The ice had long since broken up in the Bay, and the Lake was now picturesque with shipping. Continued immunity produced the inevitable result of making us careless. The optimism of spring was in our veins, and we took risks that would have made us shudder earlier in the year. It was a time of strong hope, noble ambition, complete confidence, and supreme content. How healthy we were, how innocent, how energetic, how penniless! I cannot believe that four such happy persons ever existed on this earth before. I often meet young people wandering about, quite evidently under the delusion they are happy, but I smile kindly when they pass; smile as one who has known the Real Thing. It is absurd to suppose that any one now-a-days can be so blest as we were. Even then it amazed me that Sam should be enamoured with Sally when he had actually seen Aline, but, to my great luck, so it was. A touch of humour was given to the situation by Sam sometimes stopping in his rhapsodies about Sally, placing his arm across my shoulder, while a sense of gentle pity came into his eyes, as he said—

" But then, you know, Aline is one of the finest girls in the world also."

Oh, the inadequacy of language! Oh, the blindness of man! Poor old Sam was as incapable of estimating the worth of Aline as he would have been of guessing the value of the Sistine Madonna had he come across it in a second-hand shop. It was my heavenly year, when all I could ever win was already in my possession, through favour of those necromancers, Hope and Confidence.

When the warm spring days came, we planned and carried out the most delightful excursions. Various railways radiated from the city, and we would choose this line or that for Saturday's wayfarings. These jaunts were accomplished with all the surreptitious fascination of an intrigue. The two girls, after an early breakfast, carrying lunches for four in two baskets, took the morning train together to the stopping-place we had decided upon. Sam and I rose sometimes at midnight, sometimes at two o'clock, sometimes at three, depending on the distance, and with a sandwich or two in our pockets, opened the window, slipped over the portico, strode along the silent and deserted streets, through the suburbs, and out into the sweet morning air of the country. Arriving, we set up a signal; a white handkerchief fluttering from a pole; and rested after our walk near the station, but out of sight of it. If, when the train came in, the girls, looking this way and that, could not see our signal, Sam, who was a fair woodsman, holding at his command most of the forest sounds, gave a bird call, and we were soon laughing and talking together.

Once, I remember, we walked all night; a lovely, mild, still summer night, for we had chosen a rendezvous far off down the Lake. Sam sang songs, and imitated the birds so well that sometimes he was sleepily answered by one of them, who doubtless wondered what her mate was doing abroad at that hour. It was an up-hill, down-hill tramp, because of the numerous ravines through which streams ran to the Lake. We enjoyed a midnight lunch by the margin of one rivulet, and drank its crystal water under the starlight; then swung on and on and on, the world empty except for ourselves, and at last arrived while it was still dark, except for the summer lightning that wavered like pale phosphorus in the horizon. The hills should have made it a fatiguing journey, but we felt only a gentle lassitude as we stretched ourselves in the warm, dewless grass under the trees, Sam exclaiming—

"Gemini crickets, this is good, as my Aunt Jane would say," that expression sharing his favour with "Gee whilikins!" except on those rare occasions when he was very angry, and needed stronger expletives.

It was hours and hours before the girls could arrive, and I said to Sam that they would be called upon to endure sleepy swains that day, to which he drowsily assented. The soothing rhythm of the waves on the sand was the only sound, and at last that ceased. When I awoke, the eyes of Aline were looking into mine. She was seated beside me, and held my hand in hers. For a moment I could not imagine where I was, but knew it must be Paradise, whether on this earth or elsewhere. The sadness which always underlay her smile, and added sweetness to it, seemed more accentuated this morning than I had ever known it to be before. Light-hearted Sally had woven garlands of flowers, festoon after festoon of which she had looped around Sam, who now, newly awakened, looked like a festive wood-god, still bewildered with sleep; then there was much laughter, which Sally did not hesitate to join.

My favourite rendezvous was a deep, wooded dell, through which a clear trout stream ran babbling to the Lake. We could see a V-shaped section of this Lake at the end of the Ravine, framed at the top by the sky, and on each side by tree-clad slopes. Often a vessel in full sail, white as a bride, crossed this wedge-shaped expanse of blue water. "There," Aline would say, "our ship comes home."

I often think of this dear girl as the spirit of the dell; the sprite of the transparent stream; the nymph of the blue Lake; with the truth and purity of the wild-wood, having no relation to any city or town. We would buy this secret dell when we became rich, and build, not a castle in Spain, but a log chalet, and shut out the world. Wealth, indeed, occupied little of our thoughts, except inasmuch as a portion was needed to buy dells and to build a summer home. I never knew any one so hopefully brave as she, with no fear of poverty in those courageous eyes, but rather a welcoming. I think Aline would have been disappointed had fame come without the welding experience of privation together, and she pictured our wandering through the lanes of rural France, too poor to pay our fare even at third class on a railway, sleeping perhaps under a hedge, like gypsies, and ever searching for the unknown romantic spot which I should make world-famous in a picture. In dire straits I should rest by the wayside while she went up the grand avenue and danced or sang to those in the big house for the crusts we needed; I sketching industriously while she was gone; she returning always triumphant, the complete commissary. She indulged in one of her infrequent laughs as she wondered what the effect would be on the French of that ditty, " Seeing Sally Home," given in a language they did not understand, with a little Plantation break-down executed on the flags of the chateau at the end of every verse. Of course we would become rich and famous long before youth had passed, and so optimistic were we that she fancied us prosperous, yet yearning once more for the road, and the days when she had to sing for our supper. But what did it matter when we were together? and here her hand would nestle into mine, if it were not already there.

The one disquieting feature to me in these conversations was her sublime confidence in my future.   Three years at most, she said, and then would come recognition, fame, and unlimited success. Sometimes I laughed at her, but more often could not trust my voice to reply, for I knew I was an untried man, and that even in sunny France the storms came. And sometimes I saw a tired little courageous creature whom I vainly attempted to shelter from the rain under the hedge. What if I should fail? But that thought I was compelled to hide, for any hint of it brought forth a noble scorn. I should paint nothing but the worthiest pictures, potent for good, and what matter if we were poor?

Like the sadness which I sometimes detected in her smile, her nature was permeated by a deep religious feeling, that unconsciously tinctured her thoughts and words, and in this I recognized the influence of her father. Aline would have inspired a clod, and my own doubts vanished in the radiance of her belief in me. Indeed, with all her human love, there was something of the nun about her, and I resolved that my first picture, when I had learned the rudiments of the art, should be Aline as a sister of charity; the dark flowing robes, the spotless band across the fore-head, and her demure face illuminated with the glow of religious fervour from within. So, hand-in-hand, we were to set out together, the sublime folly of youth more entrancing than the wisdom of the ages.

But the immediate unknown which every day occupied some portion of our thoughts was her father, and how we should deal with him. Often when we were alone together, in the ecstasy of a vision, the thought of her father suddenly smote the exultation from her face. She was torn between two great affec-tions, the old and the new, and she feared the impos-sibility of their reconciliation. Reclining on the sward of the hillside, she would abruptly cover her face with her hands, resting her head on the turf, and remain thus motionless in dry-eyed, sobless woe, shrinking from my touch, unheeding for the moment any attempt at consolation. Then the nun was upper-most, upbraiding her breach of discipline, and the dis-loyalty to her father. Then she would protest at the mesh circumstances had woven round us, talking to convince herself, for she knew I needed no convinc-ing. Why should she not meet her man before all the world, unafraid and unashamed? Why should there be any necessity for these clandestine trysts; these stolen talks? At last the saving grace of common-sense came uppermost, and the futility of blaming the fates being apparent, she would say, breathlessly—

"Let us plan. Let us plan! Surely you and I can circumvent destiny, if only for such time as will enable us to escape together," and finally we would fall to our favourite diversion of castle-building, until the structure seemed substantial and the ways and means practicable.

I had often proposed to go and see her father, and it was at such times that the chimerical nature of the career I had to offer him became most apparent. I should have gone and braved the Douglas in his hall if she had allowed me, but of course Aline knew him, and I didn't, and she said I should never win consent. He would withdraw her at once from the school, and prevent her seeing me again. She had as strong a belief in his power of beating down opposition as she had in my future, but alas, the power of overcoming obstacles was present with him, while my future existed only in the optimistic mind of Aline. So this at last we resolved to do.

At the end of the session we would be married, asking no one's permission. The day before our wedding Aline would write a long letter to her father, and post it to reach him after the ceremony. If he telegraphed us an invitation, we would visit him; if no word came, we would leave for Paris, Aline certain that he would be proud to welcome us when I, famous, brought her at last to her own home. At the thought of her father receiving this letter when he was looking instead for herself, Aline's chin quivered a little, and the rapid eyelids tried to crush back the tears, but I knew she would keep her word, and undauntingly face the future with me.

Neither of us shall ever forget the last day in the glen. Summer was then well forward, and the weather perfect. A great piece of fortune had come to Sam, and it counterbalanced the money I had received for my bit of land from the railway, an accession of wealth I always felt ashamed I had mentioned in the face of Sam's enveloping poverty. But now the inequality was more than balanced in two directions; the first through the gift of a position, the second through the welcoming consent of her parents to his union with Sally. The authorities governing a large school a hundred miles or so from our city, requested Dr. Darnell to select the most promising student in the Normal, a man who, above all things, was proficient in mathematics, and to the man so selected would be given the principalship of this school, at a salary almost beyond our dreams of avarice. Now, by rights, John Henceforth should have got this position, if educational requirements alone had been consulted, but whether it was that Dr. Darnell thought McKurdy the better all-round man, or whether the universal distrust and dislike with which Henceforth was regarded caused him to be passed over, I do not know, but McKurdy received the appointment. Sam asked, and obtained, a few days' leave, in which to visit the scene of his future activity. Sally shammed ill, and was allowed to go home for a week. She told her parents the position of affairs, and Sam, extending his hurried trip, was received with open arms by the old people and the young alike, becoming instantly popular with every one; so there was to be a wedding, with paternal blessings, and old shoes and rice. Of course, Aline and I were glad of our friends' prosperity, but I think Sam's rôle of Conquering Hero at Sally's home brought our own situation into somewhat saddening contrast, and Aline's wistful look at me now and then betrayed her thoughts, although she said nothing.

It was during the absence of Sam and Sally that we paid our final visit to the Glen, and as immunity long continued fosters boldness, I took the risk of going to the station, boarding the train, and seating myself beside Aline, much to her astonishment, and perhaps a little to her dismay. We reached our dell unseen. That morning I had received a joyous letter from Sam, full of humour and character sketching, and I kept this epistle for our dell, after hurriedly skimming it over, that we might enjoy it together. Sam would return on Monday, he wrote, and Sally would venture back a few days later, so that they need not put in a simultaneous appearance at the school, and he breathed a prayer that their coincident absence had escaped attention. He was having the time of his life, he wrote, and all in all, this was a beautiful world. Judging by his description, the school of which he was to be the head, loomed as large as St. Paul's Cathedral, and so Sam was making an excellent start in life. Lying face downward on the turf, Aline beside me, I read aloud this exuberant epistle; the only sound except my own voice being the constant ripple of the brook, and the intermittent crash of the waves on the sandy beach a few hundred yards away. I knew that Aline would thoroughly appreciate Sam's clever character sketches of the old folk and the relatives, for she was acquainted with them. I could hardly read for laughing. It seemed as good as that recent comer, Mark Twain, of whom I have remained to this day the devoted admirer.

"Isn't that the funniest letter you ever heard?" I asked when the reading was finished.

"Yes," she said in anything but an enthusiastic tone. I looked at her. Stretched at full length, she rested on her elbow. Her head was bent low, and she was pulling the grass nervously, as if something annoyed her.

"Why, Aline, don't you think it humorous?"

"Oh," she said, without looking up, "I fear I am no judge of humour. I think his description of

Sally's father and mother is a little flippant, and unappreciative. They are most excellent people."

" Why, of course; he says nothing to the contrary. Dear me, Sam is no panoplied prince, prancing down there in pomp, if you will forgive the alliteration, and I dare say Mr. and Mrs. Livingstone compare very favourably with Sam's own parents, who are not troubled with pride of race, or that sort of thing."

" Oh," she cried, sitting up, and impatiently, even angrily, dashing the tear-drops from her eyelids, " I wish my father knew you as I do, or would even give himself the chance to become acquainted with you."

" He will, never fear."

" He won't. It isn't the first man who asks Judge Arbuthnot for his daughter that will get her."

" Now, Aline," I laughed, " if that means anything, it's a reflection on the Livingstones, and worse far than anything Sam has said in his letter."

" Put away that letter," she cried. " Don't read to me—talk to me. This is my day : it belongs to me, and I refuse to think of anything but you, and myself, and happiness. If my father makes it hard for me, it is you who must be my recompense. Oh, Tom, Tom !" she cried, pulling my head down to her, which required little exertion, and resting her face on my shoulder, " it might have been so pleasant, and so straight, and so honest. I know that you would like him, and he would like you if he but gave you an opportunity, which he never will do, even after I have married you. I'm an envious little wretch, and I believe I'm bad tempered, too," and with that she wept more than I have ever known her to do before or since. At last she sprang up, held out her hands, and pulled me to my feet.

" Give me the letter," she commanded, and when
I had done so, she tore it into little pieces, scattering
them over the surface of the brook.

" There !" she cried, " it is an incantation," holding her outspread hands over the stream. " Float
out into the universe, and cast a spell over all hard-
hearted parents," and thus there was lost to the world
a most entertaining composition.

Then she made a drinking cup of her two outstretched hands, filled it at the crystal brook, and
held it out to me.

" A toast !" she cried. " Drink to the happiness
of Sam and Sally !" which, bending over, I did.

I followed her example, and she drank from my
hands, then challenged me to a race for the beach.
All bitterness had floated away with those fragments
of paper, and now for the sands and the sunlight,
after the shade of the dell.

At first Aline seemed feverishly determined to be
happy, but by and by her usual serenity returned,
and happiness came without being coerced. It was
indeed a day to be remembered, and even the little
flurry in the dell was not without its contrasting
advantages. We lingered until we had to hurry for
our last train, and then I, not knowing whether to be
glad or sorry, saw it move off when we came in sight
of the station a quarter of a mile away.

" That's what it is to carry a cheap watch," I said,
wondering with a qualm of dismay how she would
take it. She came a little closer to me, and looked
up with a smile.

" Did you do that on purpose ?" she asked.

" What ? Miss the train ? Of course not."

" I was wishing you had. It arouses suspicions of
wickedness; and oh, Tom, you are so much better

than I am, that I hoped you had done this to put us even."

"Nonsense," I protested. "Nobody in the world is so good as you, or good enough for you."

"That's nice. I hope you will always cherish such a delusion, Tom. And now let us set out."

"Where for?"

"The city, of course."

"What, on foot? You'd never reach there. Why, it would be midnight before I even could cover that distance. I can probably hire a horse, and some kind of conveyance at the station."

"Indeed, you shall do nothing of the sort. After all my talk of our walks in France, do you think I am going to shirk a journey now that the chance is offered me?"

"Yes, but we weren't going to tramp France until our money gave out. I've got money in my pocket."

"In that case I won't need to dance for our dinner. Are there any taverns on the road?"

"Yes, several."

"Good. Then we will call in at one of them, and rest, and get something to eat if they cater for way-worn travellers. Come along, Tommy, my dear. I know what you're afraid of. It will be dark by and by, but I shan't hurt you."

We walked along joyously together till the sun went down, Aline merrier than ever I had known her, with a fascinating flash of recklessness in her demeanour. When we came to lonely stretches of the road, she sang gaily, "Seeing Sally Home," and other songs, changing the name to "Aline," saying that the right word in the song was Nelly, but that any two-syllabled girl would do.

"Why, Aline," I said, "it seems as if we had crossed the Rubicon again."

She stopped in the road, and looked at me with glowing eyes.

"Do you know that's exactly what I was thinking, only you spoke first, which isn't fair to a woman."

"You're not a woman; you're just a little girl, and frivolous at that."

"But isn't it strange, I was thinking of the Rubicon? Why, Tom, we think alike already. How will it be when we are fifty?"

She said she must try over her songs in case they refused us a meal at the tavern, and that it would be all good practice for the chateaux of France. They did not refuse us dinner, however, though a somewhat scowling woman waited on us, who, probably struck by our youth, and the beauty of my companion, seemed rather curious to know who we were, and where we were going. She dropped dark hints about the dangers of the city, and I think would have tendered good advice if she had received any encouragement. She said that the taverns further along the way were most unsafe for respectable people, but left us in some doubt whether she included us in that category or not. I learned at the next place of entertainment that her own house bore no very good reputation.

I paid the bill, and we resumed our way, through the gloaming, and presently into the darkness of the night. There was no moon, but the sky was full of stars, and the country became very silent and mysterious. Aline kept close to my side, and her footsteps faltered a little, though she denied strenuously that she was in the least tired. The roads were good,

but dusty, and I am sure if we could have seen ourselves, we looked like a miller and his lass. But the
dusty road made easy walking, not hard to the foot, as
would be those of France, and sometimes we varied
the route by walking on the grass by the side,
although, in the dark, this was a more dangerous
footway than the dusty centre of the thoroughfare.
For an hour we had been seeing the light of the city a
dim halo in the sky. We fell into long silences that
had a happiness of their own, more subtle than that
of conversation.

"I am glad," she said, at the end of one of these,
"that you came from the city by train instead of on
foot."

"Let me carry you?" I suggested.

"Why do you say that?"

"Because you mentioned my coming by train,
which means you thought I should be very tired
by now if I had walked. So I infer *you* are very
tired."

"I could walk all night," she averred, "but if I
sat down to rest I'm not so sure I could get up
again."

"Let's try, and find out. If you can't, I'll carry
you into town," and despite her protests, I made her
sit down beside me under the spreading branches of a
great oak. She snuggled up close beside me, with
content, I judged.

"I wonder," she began, then paused. "Hark!"
she said.

We could hear the bells of the city, and counting,
found they struck twelve.

"Sunday morning," she cried, and once more the
same thought occurred to us, and our lips met.

" So long as I am at Stanmore Street before day-light," she said drowsily, " I don't care."

Her head sank down on my shoulder in the most natural way imaginable, as if that were the most fitting resting-place for it, and in five minutes she was asleep. I let an hour go past, and when the clocks struck one, remembering how early the light comes in mid-summer, I kissed her awake. She murmured sleepily as if she were a little child, and treating her as one, I picked her up in my arms, and strode along the road. She twined her arms around my neck, now thoroughly awake.

" I'll stay here for one luxurious minute, counting the steps as a second each, for if I stop longer, I shall fall asleep again, and then, poor man, I know you would carry me uncomplaining the whole way. Oh, this is delicious. I wonder how many steps I have forgotten to count."

" Begin now," I said, " and count till you go to sleep," but as she said sixty, she sprang from my arms before I was aware, running in front of me, crying she could see the street lamps of the outskirts, which had now become visible.

It was a little after two o'clock when we arrived at the Stanmore Street gate, she the lucky possessor of a latch-key.

" Let me look at you," I said, taking her by the shoulders, and turning her round till the street lamps shone on her face. Her eyelids drooped heavy from fatigue and lack of sleep, and the eyes she turned to me were misty with dreams, but the rather wan smile was devoid of its sadness.

" Dear girl," I said, " you are just fainting with fatigue."

"Dear boy," she murmured, "I am not. So a day begun in petulance ends in contradiction, but nothing can ever take away from us the lovely day, and the bright, still more lovely night. Oh, Tommy, Tommy, how I love you!" and then I found it took a long kiss to bid good-night.

CHAPTER XVII

But as some muskets so contrive it,
As if to miss the mark they drive at,
And though well aimed at duck or plover,
Bear wide and kick their owners over.

McFINGAL.

AN old painter writing his reminiscences has one
advantage over a novelist. I come now to a chapter
which a writer of fiction would not dare use. The
freaks of chance, which have ever made a football of
me, sometimes to my advantage, sometimes to my
undoing, play such a part in the incident I am about
to relate that such a narration would be useless anywhere else than in a true story. We had become careless, as I have said, through long-continued favour
of circumstance, and when John Brent's blow fell on
us it took us so thoroughly by surprise that for the
moment we thought we were slain. In this episode
the probity of Dr. Cardiff comes into play, and we
were given a striking example of the effect of character. Dr. Cardiff was known to all as an absolutely
truthful man, who would not lie no matter how his
own interests suffered. The only thing that saved
McKurdy on that day when Dr. Cardiff's suspicions
were aroused by the coincidence of us four standing
up at the black-board to solve a problem which had
baffled all the rest, was the fact that it was a suspicion only, but Dr. Cardiff, when he spoke to
McKurdy, warned him that if ever suspicion crystal-
lized into certainty, nothing would prevent the doctor

from bringing the delinquency to the knowledge of those in authority, even if the victim were his dearest friend. We all knew this of Dr. Cardiff, and did not respect him the less because of it, and when Dr. Cardiff gave his word regarding any fact within his knowledge, that settled the matter with friend and foe alike.

During the period of which I speak, there lived for some years in our city a great preacher, whose eloquence had caused to be built the Memorial Church, one of the largest religious edifices in this city of churches. I have heard Henry Ward Beecher, Mr. Spurgeon, T. De Witt Talmage, Dr. Parker, and other great pulpit orators, but the man of whom I speak was, in my opinion, the peer of any of them. On the night in question this gifted divine was preaching his farewell sermon in the Memorial Church, which stood facing Centre Street, at the corner of Church Street, while the Centre Street Church was several hundred yards further down that thoroughfare, and on the other side of Church Street from the Memorial. Nearly opposite the Memorial was Knox Church, an edifice that housed a Scottish Presbyterian congregation. There was thus a group of churches within a radius, say, of five hundred yards from the intersection of Centre Street and Church Street. I was never a bigoted church goer, but during my term at the Normal School I fell into the habit, attending usually the Centre Street Church, and incidentally walking home with Aline if circumstances were favourable, in spite of the fact that church-going, more often than anything else, landed victims into the net of John Brent.

On the night in question, Sam and I started out gaily for Centre Street Church. It was a lowering night, threatening rain.   I don't know whether we possessed umbrellas or not, but in any case we had left them behind, and reaching Centre Street Church, we went to the gallery, the better to gaze round the congregation below and learn the whereabouts of Miss Livingstone and Miss Arbuthnot. I can report nothing of the sermon, for my whole time was taken in a fruitless effort to find the girl I sought. When at last the service was finished, Sam whispered that if we hurried down to the door we might catch them as they passed out, if they had been, as we guessed, seated far back out of sight under the gallery. We were the first down the stairs, and stood one on either side the doorway, scanning eagerly the congregation that poured out into the street. A slight rain was drizzling down, causing a partial block at the porch, owing to every one raising an umbrella. We saw nothing of the girls, but so intent were we on the search that my heart jumped as I heard a well-known voice say—

" What, Mr. Prentiss, not afraid of a few drops of rain, I hope?" and there beside me stood Dr. Cardiff.

" Why, no," I gasped, when the more versatile Sam intervened in an everyday voice, with—

" Good-evening, Dr. Cardiff. Prentiss and I were just thinking of making a dash for it."

" Oh, don't do that, but come under my umbrella," invited the genial doctor. " It's old-fashioned, and wide enough for three. I'm passing your boarding-house," and with that, one on either side of him, the stately Cardiff walked along Centre Street towards the corner of Church Street. I had been stricken dumb by the encounter, although it was quite evident that the good doctor had not the slightest suspicion why we were waiting by the church door. I thanked my stars the girls had not put in an appearance a moment before. Sam, however, was in no way abashed, and talked to the doctor about the latest mathematical problem with all the nonchalance of a man who had never spoken to a girl in his life. As we neared the corner of Church Street we met an immense crowd of well-dressed people, and Dr. Cardiff, gazing towards the brightly-lighted Memorial Church, said—

" Ah, Doctor Spence has preached his farewell sermon to-night. I thought of going to hear him, but I knew it would be almost impossible to find a seat. I suppose he has had a record congregation this evening."

Sam, who was intent on his mathematical problem, said " Yes," and went on with his elucidation, but I, who remained silent, saw that Dr. Cardiff was mistaken. It was not the congregation from the Memorial Church we were meeting, but an unusually large concourse of people from Knox Church. It was evident from the brilliant light shining from the Memorial Church that the farewell was not yet over, but as this seemed a mattèr of no importance, I said nothing. I felt disappointed at returning home under the wing of Dr. Cardiff, instead of having some one else under my wing, and so was glum and out of humour. Being now certain that the girls had gone to hear the eloquent Dr. Spence, I regretted that we formed an escort for Dr. Cardiff, as we might have waited with more success at the doors of the Memorial Church. Indeed, though we were progressing slowly, there was still time to retrace our steps if Sam did not keep on with his tedious mathematics when we reached our door, but I found no opportunity to give McKurdy a hint which would make him realize the situation without arousing suspicion in the mind of Dr. Cardiff.

Arriving at our house, however, I was more deeply annoyed than ever at my learned friend, who had now become absorbed in the topic he was discussing.

"I am afraid, Mr. McKurdy," said Dr. Cardiff, as we all three paused in front of our portico, "I am afraid I should need to see you do that on the blackboard before I comprehended your point. I don't quite follow you."

"Oh well," cried the genial Sam, "just come upstairs, and I'll demonstrate it to you in five minutes."

There was nothing for me to say. Sam opened the door with his latch-key, and, accompanied by the Doctor, we mounted to our study. I was so disgusted at the turn affairs had taken that I bade good-night to the two of them, opened my bedroom door, entered, undressed, and went to bed. I heard the voices outside, and at last the bluff, hearty tones of Dr. Cardiff.

"Oh, I see it all now, and I think that is an excellent method, Mr. McKurdy; much better than the solution given in the key. I congratulate you, and thank you very much for the demonstration, so goodnight. What! has Prentiss gone to bed?"

Sam, who always took liberties when he knew I was cross, threw open the door.

"Asleep, Tom?" he cried.

"No."

Dr. Cardiff thrust in his head, and said in his kindly fashion—

"Good-night, Mr. Prentiss. I am afraid our chatter has disturbed your early sleep."

"Oh, not at all, doctor," I replied. "Good-night."

Sam let him out at the front door, then came upstairs and into my room again.

"Why were you so short with Dr. Cardiff tonight?" he demanded.

"Short with Dr. Cardiff? I was short with you, you ass. What the deuce are you undertaking Dr. Cardiff's mathematical education for? Those two girls are at the Memorial Church, and if it hadn't been for your nonsense, we should have been there by this time."

"Why, Tom, you're crazy. The Memorial Church had dismissed its congregation before we got to the corner."

"You're wrong, and Dr. Cardiff was wrong. That was the Knox Church mob that we met. The Memorial windows were all ablaze. I suppose the sermon was a long one, and now several thousand people are shaking hands with Dr. Spence."

"In that case it's you who are the ass. What in thunder did you go to bed for? Get up, you villain."

"I'll do nothing of the sort."

"Oh, you won't, eh?" and within two seconds Sam had me sprawling on the floor.

"Wrap a blanket round you," he cried, "and let's get back to church. Come, hustle on with your duds, or I'll drag you there as you are."

I dressed in double quick time, and very shortly we were out in Church Street again. We ran to the corner, and there, still radiant with white light, shone out the great windows of the Memorial Church. The clouds had cleared away, and the stars were shining. It was an ideal night for a walk home. Presently the great organ sounded, and people began to pour out of the church. When it was about half emptied, we saw our two girls, and they saw us. Aline took my arm, and we went on ahead together, Sam and Sally following. By this time the humorous aspect of Dr. Cardiff's intervention had become apparent to me, and I told Aline all that had happened. I was in the middle of this interesting recital when some instinct of danger caused me to look ahead, and there, under a lamp-post, stood John Brent, with two of his pupils; he was looking straight at us, and had undoubtedly recognized me. I now occupied a position where I must confront him with the light of the gas-lamp in my face. There was no escape; already that steely smile was on his lips.

" Pull down your veil," I whispered to Aline, then over my shoulder, " Pull down your veil, Sally."

Both did as I requested without asking questions, and a few moments later the triumphant voice of John Brent said—

" Good-evening, Mr. Prentiss."

" Good-evening, Mr. Brent," I replied.

" Good-evening, Mr. McKurdy."

" Good-evening, Mr. Brent," said McKurdy.

I expected that either he or his satellites would follow us, but apparently they did not. Probably they expected to make another haul before the immense congregation got past. Whether he just happened to be there, or whether his spies had tracked the girls to the church, spotted us, and then made for the rendezvous where Mr. Brent was awaiting us, were conundrums that did not interest me. The important fact was that he was accompanied by two independent witnesses who knew us, and could corroborate his statement if we disputed it. Aline and I discussed the matter as we walked to Stanmore Street. I felt certain that Brent had not recognized the girls, and so far as I was concerned, expulsion did not so much matter, but with McKurdy and Sally Livingstone this encounter was nothing short of a disaster. His expulsion meant the loss of his Normal School certificate, and the consequent giving up of the appointment on which he and Sally had counted so much. When we reached the gate, we expected to find the other two, who had loitered away behind us, in the depths of despair; but instead, their arrival was heralded by Sally's silvery laugh, always a joyous thing to hear.

"Now, Miss Aline Arbuthnot," began Sam, "everything hinges on you. If you are asked to-morrow whether or not you walked home from church with a young man, what will you say?"

"I will tell the truth," answered Aline promptly.

"Oh, hang it all!" cried Sam. "Can't you do any better than that?"

"I'll not implicate you, Mr. McKurdy, nor shall I mention Mr. Prentiss's name, but I will plead guilty so far as I am concerned. They cannot force me to incriminate any one else."

"It's no use, Sam," I said. "We can't lie out of this complication. We might outface Brent, but there's the two witnesses, remember."

"Oh, it will be all right," replied Sam confidently, "if you allow me to do the talking, and if Aline here does not give anybody away but herself. Dear Sally has promised to fabricate like a little heroine, and go to church for a week after to make up for it. You at best are an awkward liar, Tom, and even when you tell the truth, nobody believes you. But if you keep your mouth shut, I'll pull you through."

"Well, Sam, I'm overjoyed to hear you say so. I dislike losing caste in Aline's eyes, but, neverthe-less, I am free to confess that if there is anything I can do in the fiction line to help you, I'm your man."

"On second thoughts," said Aline bravely, and I saw she was determined to be no better than the man to whom she was engaged, "on this occasion I shall affirm I came home with Sally. There, that's as bad as if I had told the falsehood."

" I don't think you will be called upon. I am sure Brent was so eager to trap us that he paid no attention to you girls."

" That's what I think," I agreed. " Well, then, girls, good-night, and don't lose any sleep because of this *contretemps*."

On Monday morning we knew the fight was on as soon as we entered the waiting-room, for we were informed that the class was to assemble for prayers before Professor Donovan, who, on extraordinary occasions, read prayers in an amateurish sort of way. We met Boyle the janitor at the gate, and he handed us a note each, which curtly summoned us to Dr. Darnell's private room, and there we found the Doctor seated at his table, with a face that was painful to see. He had the look of a stricken man, and he made no response to our salutation. Beside him, erect, debonair, handsome, triumphant, stood John Brent. His witnesses were not present. Doubtless he felt there was no need to call them, for we could not dispute his charge. He returned our obeisances by that mechanical bow of his with the string attached to it.

" Gentlemen," Dr. Darnell began, " Mr. Brent states he met you last night coming from the Memorial Church, each with a lady on his arm."

" What is that, Doctor ?" inquired Sam, incredulously, leaning a little forward and wrinkling his brows.

" Did you attend the Memorial Church last night, Mr. McKurdy ?"

" Certainly not. I am a communicant at the Centre Street Church."

" Not last night," said John Brent.

"Do you mean to state, Mr. Brent, that you met me with a lady on my arm, last night?"

"Yes, Mr. McKurdy," replied Mr. Brent, with ingratiating suavity. "I met you and Mr. Prentiss each with a woman heavily veiled. I said, 'Good-night, Mr. Prentiss,' and he replied, 'Good-night, Mr. Brent.' I then bade you good-night, and you replied with the same phrase Mr. Prentiss used. You were coming from Memorial Church."

Sam drew a deep breath and straightened himself up with the air of one who says, "Oh, this is *too* much!"

Dr. Darnell was moistening his lips, and his eyes seemed to penetrate Sam to the backbone.

"You are not going to deny it, Mr. McKurdy?" suggested Mr. Brent sweetly. "I have two witnesses, you know, but I prefer not to call them unless a denial makes it necessary."

"You say you met me with a lady," murmured Sam dreamily, more to himself than to his auditors, as if he required time to adjust his mind to the proper apprehension of this absurd accusation.

"Mr. McKurdy," said Dr. Darnell eagerly, "there is, of course, a chance of mistakes being made in recognition at night, and possibly this may be an instance. Did any person whom you know see you at Centre Street Church last night?"

"Oh yes, Mr. Prentiss was with me."

Dr. Darnell sank back in his chair with a sigh of disappointment.

"Come, now, Mr. McKurdy," protested John Brent, "this comedy has gone quite far enough. You are not such a child as to suppose that the evidence of your fellow-culprit will help you. Dr. Darnell asks if you can bring forward any witness to your presence in Centre Street Church. Would you kindly answer yes, or no?"

Sam hung down his head.

"I don't know many people there," he replied slowly. "I am slightly acquainted with the clergyman, but I don't suppose he recognized us. The church was full, and we were sitting back in the gallery. At that distance I should doubt if he saw us."

"Really, Dr. Darnell," said Mr. Brent, with justifiable impatience, "Mr. McKurdy is trifling with us. He was not at Centre Street Church last night, but at the Memorial."

Sam cast a pained look at him, and at Dr. Darnell.

"I saw no one in the church whom I knew, but coming home——" Sam turned to me with a sudden flash of inspiration. "Where did we encounter Dr. Cardiff?"

"At the church door," I replied.

"What's that, what's that?" cried the headmaster, leaning forward again. "Dr. Cardiff? What about Dr. Cardiff?"

"Oh, he walked home with us. He kindly offered his umbrella. It was drizzling a little; not what you would call a smart shower," he explained in deferential tones to John Brent, whose eyes were fastened on him, and whose brow was beginning to frown, "but a gentle rain."

"Mr. McKurdy," said the headmaster sharply, "did you walk home from Centre Street Church with Dr. Cardiff?"

"Certainly, sir," answered McKurdy, as brusquely as the other had questioned.

Dr. Darnell smote a bell, and the obsequious Boyle slunk in.

"Ask Dr. Cardiff to come to my room."

Boyle hurried out.

"All that I have to say," commented John Brent, "if this turns out to be true, is that you two went back to the Memorial Church after Dr. Cardiff saw you home."

"Really, Mr. Brent, you are shifting your ground. You asked me to prove——"

"Why didn't you tell us at first," interrupted Dr. Darnell sharply, "that you had come home with Dr. Cardiff?"

"Well, you see," stammered Sam, "I was taken by surprise. I scarcely knew what to say. It is a great piece of luck that we met Dr. Cardiff. Mr. Brent stated that we were not at Centre Street Church, and, when we prove him wrong, if he is allowed to shift his ground, I claim it is not fair."

The stately Dr. Cardiff came in looking very grave, for on receiving so unusual a summons to the headmaster's room he knew something was amiss, and seeing Sam and me standing there, with whom he had parted in such amity less than a dozen hours before, his surmise that some serious delinquency had been reported was confirmed. Being a kindly man, with, I am sure, a sort of fatherly regard for us, the gloom on his face deepened. He stood silent, slowly stroking his long black beard, awaiting whatever question might ensue.

"Perhaps, Mr. Brent," began the headmaster, "you had better tell Dr. Cardiff what you have already told me."

John Brent bowed slowly, and began his recital in the measured tones of a judge pronouncing sentence.

"Last night, walking up Church Street with two of my pupils, just after the congregation in the Memo-

rial Church had been dismissed, I met Mr. Prentiss
and Mr. McKurdy, coming, as I suppose, from that
church, each accompanied by a lady. I bade good-
night first to Mr. Prentiss, then to Mr. McKurdy,
and they both replied, bidding good-night to me by
name. The pupils of the Model School who were with
me know these young men, and are prepared to sub-
stantiate what I allege. Mr. McKurdy denies the
facts I have stated; maintains that he did not attend
the Memorial Church last night, but was present, instead, at the Centre Street Church. On being pressed
by Dr. Darnell for any evidence proving his presence
there, he first gave Mr. Prentiss as his witness, which
of course was not admissible; then, after some hesitation, he remembered that they had met you at the door,
whereupon, as it was raining, you offered them a share
of your umbrella, and so saw them to their own
house."

John Brent pausing, Dr. Cardiff said—

" So far as your remarks concern me, the facts are
exactly as you have stated them."

" Before Dr. Cardiff came in," continued John
Brent, addressing the headmaster, whose expression
of belief doubtless irritated him, " I said it would have
been quite practical for Mr. Prentiss and Mr. McKurdy to have attended the Centre Street Church, and
the Memorial Church as well, granting the possibility
that the Centre Street services ended before those at
the Memorial."

" I have no wish to intervene," said Sam, with a
modesty that was almost overdone, " but your contention was, Mr. Brent, that we had not attended the
Centre Street Church at all, and proof of our presence
there was demanded. Now I contend, with all humility, that you placed upon us an almost impossible

17

task, for we are two strangers in the city, having no acquaintances outside this school, and it is only our immense good fortune in meeting Dr. Cardiff at the door that has saved us. The hesitation you refer to is very natural when one is unexpectedly called upon to prove where he was or was not at a specified time in the past."

"Quite so, Mr. McKurdy," concurred Mr. Brent icily, "but that does not dispose of my statement that I met you two on Church Street with two women, and there are independent witnesses to prove it. I unreservedly accept Dr. Cardiff's statement, and that brings you to your own door. But it was possible for you to retrace your steps the moment Dr. Cardiff's back was turned, and the distance from your boarding-house to the Memorial Church is short. Unquestionably that is exactly what you did, for I assuredly met you on the street with those two women."

My impulse was to call on Dr. Cardiff for further evidence, but I kept silence, as arranged. Sam merely shrugged his shoulders, and said not a word to jog the doctor's memory. The crushing rejoinder came at last, and with Dr. Cardiff's usual slowness.

"I did not part with the young men at their door, Mr. Brent, and I may settle the matter at once by telling you that before we turned into Church Street the congregation of the Memorial Church had been dismissed, and we met an enormous concourse of people at the corner, which delayed us somewhat. Perhaps," he said, turning to McKurdy, "you may remember my saying I had thought of going to the Memorial Church myself, but feared there would be no vacant seat, as it was Dr. Spence's farewell sermon."

"Now that you mention it, doctor, I remember your saying so," corroborated Sam.

"Aside from that," continued Cardiff, "I did not part with the young men at the door. Perhaps we should not have talked shop on Sunday night, but, be that as it may, Mr. McKurdy and I became involved in a mathematical discussion, and I went upstairs to his study, waiting there some considerable time while he demonstrated his contention. When at last I bade them good-night, Mr. Prentiss had gone to bed, and when Mr. McKurdy let me out the front door, the city was silent, and every church within it was closed."

Our evidence was so complete that it was almost inartistic. The face of John Brent was a study. He believed every word Dr. Cardiff had spoken, the latter's sincerity and truthfulness being beyond question. He knew he was defeated, but of one thing he was absolutely positive, and that was the meeting on Church Street. He was too good a sportsman to show defeat, and his face exhibited instead an intellectual curiosity to know how a cog had slipped in a case he had supposed perfect and final. I caught his eye bent upon me. The little incident of going to bed doubtless appealed to him as the last stroke of a designing villain.

Dr. Darnell's countenance was no such impassive mask as that of our accuser. It simply radiated joy. There was a long silence, then the headmaster said—

"I thank you, Dr. Cardiff. And now, Mr. Brent, I have been waiting for some expression of regret on your part."

John Brent bowed.

"Gentlemen, I hope you will accept my apology in the same spirit in which it is tendered."

Dr. Darnell shot a sharp glance at the speaker, whose tone had little that was conciliatory in it, and whose equivocal words sounded like a challenge. Indeed, we well knew that underneath them lay a determination to get at the bottom of this mystery, and as we were aware that Brent was entirely in the right, and we entirely in the wrong, our victory, perfect as it seemed, was not without seeds of disquietude. Still, even if he could have found some one who knew the exact minute at which the Centre Street church dismissed its congregation, and another who knew the moment when the services at the Memorial ended, he could scarcely have proved that we returned, because Dr. Cardiff was as completely under the delusion that he had stopped in our room for a long time as he was that he had met the congregation of the Memorial Church some minutes before.

One rainy day, about a week later, when it was too wet to play football, I wandered round the precincts of the Model School, when I met John Brent. It seemed a chance meeting, but I have reason to believe that it was designed. He greeted me with an engaging air of *bonhomie*, admitted with seeming generosity that he had spent the week investigating, but confessed himself completely baffled, and alleged he wasn't sorry. He drew me into the Model School cloak-room and closed the door.

"Now, Prentiss," he said, "as between man and man, tell me the truth of this, quite in confidence. Of course, you know I met and recognized you. Who was the girl? I pledge you my word that I will say nothing of her or to her."

At no time did I fear John Brent more than when he was genial. I glanced carefully round the long, narrow room, from whose hooks along the wall hung a row of waterproofs, reaching nearly to the floor. In two instances I saw a stout pair of boots, and the bottoms of trouser legs. He had his witnesses concealed behind the wrappers.

"You still persist in believing you met us that Sunday night, Mr. Brent?"

"Oh, come now, Prentiss, what's the use of talking like that? You know perfectly well I met you and spoke to you."

"It amazes me to hear you persist in your statement, Mr. Brent. I assure you every word spoken by Dr. Cardiff was true."

"I am well aware of it, Mr. Prentiss. Of course, I know it was the discrepancy of time that gave you your opportunity. You won't say anything further, then?"

"There is nothing further to say, Mr. Brent."

He opened the door.

"Very well. We will meet at Philippi, Mr. Prentiss."

"At Philippi, Mr. Brent."

CHAPTER XVIII

King. *What do you call the play?*
Hamlet. *The mouse-trap.*

WHEN at last the *débâcle* came, it was not through
the carelessness of either Sam or myself, although
we were both involved in the crash. John Brent's
triumph contained the odd element of being too complete. He had gone to work with a quiet doggedness
that was admirable, and the downfall he caused bore
some resemblance in its thoroughness to the rending
of the Philistine pillars by that other athlete, Samson.
Warned by his failure with us, he adopted another
method, and John Henceforth was the god in the
machine in this case. None of our masters knew
much about, or cared anything at all for sport, and so
John Brent, a stout champion of renown, had been
given charge of our out-door games, and indeed many
of us were proud to be under the instruction and
advice of such a celebrity of the field. Efficient at
everything he undertook, John Brent so roused our
enthusiasm, and coached us so well in our individual
and team play at football, that our first team was
almost invincible. From Sam McKurdy, who was a
bulwark of strength, to John Henceforth, slim and
agile, John Brent placed every man in the position
that man was most capable of holding, and when the
University eleven, which looked down upon us as
merely ephemeral six-months' scholars, not to be

compared with people who spend four years in acquiring a defective education, at last consented to meet us one Saturday, they found some difficulty shortly after in giving any satisfactory reason for their defeat. Our victory was due to John Brent, who welded the material at his disposal into a conquering, living machine. Indeed, we had some trouble in preventing our enthusiasm for him in the field from overcoming our prejudice against him in the school.

Every day, at intermission in the forenoon, we enjoyed a kick at the ball, even though the interval was not long enough to carry through a game. The ball was kept in an out-house belonging to the Model School. Sometimes a Modelite brought it on the ground, sometimes a Normal student, and sometimes Mr. Brent himself. One morning, after a night of rain, Brent came out with the ball in his hands, and cast a hesitating glance over the ground. We gathered round him.

"I think," he said very casually, "that we will spoil the turf if we play to-day."

"Oh, nonsense, nonsense!" was the instant outcry. "The ground's all right: in perfect condition," which it was.

"I think not," said Mr. Brent, in that calm way which roused the ever-latent rebelliousness of John Henceforth, who, constitutionally, hated authority. Henceforth tried to snatch the ball, but Brent, with a smile held it out of his reach.

"No play to-day," he said, "and perhaps none to-morrow, and as a matter of safety, I shall hide the ball."

Now, had we been less excited, that remark should have aroused our suspicions. John Brent was not a man to be disobeyed. If he had wished to prohibit the game he would have said so definitely enough, and then seen to it that his orders were respected without the help of a missing ball. He walked off with the ball, and disappeared among the out-buildings that clustered round the Model School.

" I'll find that ball," said Henceforth, "and we'll play a game at noon."

He set out in search, but did not find it. He spent the whole hour at noon looking for the ball in every nook and cranny, even breaking open some doors that were locked, for which he had afterwards to pay the bill.

At the afternoon recess Mr. Brent appeared, exceedingly composed, informed us of the damage Henceforth had done to the school property, said that the destruction must be made good, and added that as a punishment there would be no football that week.

There was instant protest at this unfairness. Why should the whole class be punished for the fault of one, and that one known? John Brent, impassive, stood his ground, denied the unfairness, listened unmoved to our threats of appeal to Dr. Darnell, then turned and left us smarting under a sense of tyranny which drove whatever reasoning powers we possessed temporarily into abeyance, indeed, exactly the state of mind Mr. Brent had counted upon.

That night John Henceforth recited indignantly to his best girl the facts of the case. In return she told him Mr. Brent had arrived during recess at the waiting-room thronged by Normal School girls, and had placed the football under a bench. Now, the feminine side of the Normal School building was to us forbidden ground, and Henceforth made the mistake of thinking Brent had intended to lure him thither. In this he completely missed the point of the

case, which was summed up in the two words, " Who
told?" Henceforth, confident that our appeal to Dr.
Darnell would be sustained, and Brent probably censured, and believing that his trespass would be con-
doned owing to provocation given by Mr. Brent,
marched next morning into the girls' waiting-room,
and emerged triumphantly with the ball. This we
kicked about until school was called with the same
vigour we would have used had the ball been John
Brent himself, then entered the class-room firmly
determined to stand by our rights, and act as one
man.

" Let us apply to Mr. Brent in this case," said
John Henceforth, " the tactics he has taught us to
use on the football field," and so resolutely we
marched in, still under the illusion that Brent would
be annoyed at the resumption of the game. To our
amazement, Dr. Darnell said nothing; indeed, the
day passed without anybody saying anything. To
make our perplexity more complete, John Brent appeared as usual at intermission, and instructed us
how to conduct ourselves creditably on the football
field.

Next day nothing happened, and we were still
guessing. On the third morning it was evident that
something was seriously wrong. John Brent read
prayers in Dr. Darnell's room, and then proceeded to
give the grammar lesson just as if he were headmaster.
He read a chapter in the Bible with a smug correctness
which seemed to indicate that he could have improved
the Book, had he been consulted in its compilation.
But what struck us all with amazement was the fact
that a large number of the girls were absent, while
those present displayed faces which showed signs of
agitation and weeping. Apprehension spread like a

panic amongst us. To all this John Brent paid not the slightest attention, but expatiated on the beauties of grammar in a tone at once learned and courteous. If we had been less agitated, we might have recognized that he was as great at the desk as at the goal; a perfect teacher, with something ingratiating in his address; gentle with those who gave, him wild answers, and subtly appreciative where commendation was deserved. Aline never looked at me, but I saw that at least she had not been weeping. Sally Livingstone was pale, and seemingly frightened. One girl at the back kept her head on the desk during the first half-hour, then rose and went out, but Mr. Brent took no notice. His calm accents flowed steadily on.

That afternoon, as soon as school was dismissed, Sam and I walked directly from the school gates to Stanmore Street, a proceeding which a week before we would have regarded as the height of recklessness. The girls had reached there before us, Aline imperturbable, Sally agitated. Indeed, Sally, all her levity gone, was almost in a complaining mood, for one of the first things she said was—

"It is all very well for Aline to take the case quietly. It makes no difference to her, but to Sam and me it will mean ruin."

It may as well be stated at this point that Sally's fear for her future proved unfounded, although I am not sure that her confident assumption regarding Aline was justified by after events. We learned that on the previous afternoon, the girls had been called to the headmaster's room one after another in alphabetical order. Aline Arbuthnot was the first to undergo the question. She found Dr. Darnell at his table, and John Brent standing beside him. Both seemed shocked at her answers, but of the two John Brent appeared to be the most taken aback. Dr. Darnell conducted the examination.

" Did you know that the football was hidden in your waiting-room ?"

" Yes."

" Did you tell any one where it was ?"

" No."

There was a pause, then Dr. Darnell said—

" Have you ever spoken with one of the male students in the Normal School, Miss Arbuthnot ?"

" Yes."

" By accident ?" gasped Dr. Darnell.

" No. Deliberately."

" Repeatedly ?"

" Repeatedly."

" Is your acquaintance with him still going on ?"

" Yes."

" Who is he ?"

" I refuse to answer."

Neither Dr. Darnell nor Mr. Brent made any comment, and Aline, leaving the room, gave place to another. Some of the girls broke down and cried, confessing everything; others stood stubbornly silent, but the majority admitted they had broken the rules. Down and down the alphabet the headmaster continued his catechism, and at some point he must have thrown up his hands in despair, and stopped the inquisition. Truth was mighty and it prevailed. The whole school proved to be honeycombed with disobedience.

Sally Livingstone had not been called, and so escaped the ordeal. Many of the girls became ill through fright, and most of the rest were in a state of terror. It seemed rather odd that Dr. Darnell had finished his scrutiny before he reached Miss Lane, the immediate cause of the trouble, it being she who had told John Henceforth where the ball was hidden.

The week that followed remains an ugly memory in my mind, for in spite of the fact that Aline and myself would not suffer directly, even if both were expelled, yet our sympathies were roused for the others. Every morning Dr. Darnell read from the Old Testament in his most terrible voice the fiercest passages of denunciation he could select. He took out delinquencies as something personal rather than as directed against the authority of the whole school. Never shall I forget the ringing accusation of the words from Jeremiah, " So has he dealt treacherously with me," and his culminating thunder in the last verse of the chapter, " We lie down in our shame, and our confusion covereth us, for we have sinned against the Lord our God, we and our fathers, from our youth even unto this day, and have not obeyed the voice of the Lord our God," and for the moment he almost made me believe that the drastic rule of the Normal School was made by the Lord, and not by a body of fussy old gentlemen in high places, who had forgotten their own youth, and never suspected they were contravening the will of the Almighty as expressed in the impulses of His creatures.

Little real study took place that week, either in school or at home, and every night Sam and I went to console the girls, who possessing finer sensibilities and being much more religious than ourselves, were threatened with nervous collapse under the repeated hammering of these terrible texts. Even the good-natured Sam became irritable, and roundly cursed Dr. Darnell for what he called his malignant treatment of us. He committed to memory several hair-raising passages referring to those in authority, and threatened to stand up in his place at school, and hurl back at the headmaster some of his own ammunition, but there being no need of aggravating the situation, we persuaded him to keep silent. It had leaked out somehow, and doubtless was true, that the consideration of our misdemeanour and the passing of sentence had been taken from the Normal School governors, and was now before a board of their superiors. Some of these were in favour of exacting the utmost penalty of the statutes, and expelling the whole class if each member of it was proved guilty, while others pleaded for more moderate methods. Yet the peacemakers were confronted with the dilemma that something must be done, and that if they expelled one, logically they must expel all who were equally culpable. What they wished to avoid was a storm of discussion in the newspapers, and doubtless more than one of them knew that the people at large could not be made to consider it an unpardonable sin if a young man called upon a young woman. So while the reverend elders discussed behind closed doors, we were kept in a state of suspense, with Dr. Darnell hurling scriptural maledictions upon us. The one feeble consolation left us was that John Brent had builded better than he knew, and if once the affair was made public, there was like to be an investigation by the legislature into the conduct of both Normal and Model Schools.

CHAPTER XIX

Now man to man, and steel to steel,
A Chieftain's vengeance thou shalt feel.
'LADY OF THE LAKE.'

WITH the storm-cloud hanging over our heads, none knowing which of us would be struck by the lightning or which spared, the session dragged itself miserably towards its close. Habit is a strong task-master, and we trooped as usual into the different rooms for grammar, for mathematics or for chemistry, and listlessly learned something perhaps, although each knew that further acquirement of knowledge might be futile in so far as Normal School credentials were concerned. We reversed the conditions noted in the old war song. John Brown's body lay moulder-ing in the grave, but his soul went marching on. Our spirits were broken, our souls were sickened with apprehensions, but our bodies went marching on accomplishing the routine of scholastic duty.

Only one man had dropped out of the ranks, Heze-kiah Crump, who certainly was innocent of infring-ing any rule. Crump was a loose-jointed, ungainly creature, who had obtained permission to live in some unknown portion of the town outside the radius of the licensed boarding-houses. Nature had formed him to be the butt of whatever community he joined, although he might have been a respected citizen in the semi-aboriginal district of pioneers from which he hailed. When we learned of his retreat we were all glad that the class had left him alone after it was seen how acutely he suffered, and how unable he was to reply in kind each time we tried our sarcasms on him.

Brushwood Smith had been the last man to exercise his wit on the dumb, retortless Hezekiah. This happened in the waiting-room when we were all listening for the gong. I forget what Brushwood said; it was one of his customary bucolic pleasantries, but poor Crump visibly writhed under it, blushing like a girl when he heard the thoughtless laughter and found the eyes of the class upon him. Then into the ensuing silence came one short, bitter sentence from John Henceforth, that cut like a whip. Brushwood's mouth became a straight line, and his hands clenched. He took a step toward Henceforth, who never flinched. One peculiarity of Henceforth's verbal thrusts was that the ordinary man felt himself impelled to retaliate by planting his fist between Henceforth's eyes. John distilled such venom into his barbed words that mere language in any one else's mouth became ineffectual. Henceforth grinned at Smith's truculent approach.

"*Now* you know how it feels yourself," was all he said, as he turned his back indifferently on one he had made his enemy for life. This nonchalant sentence caused those who had laughed to be ashamed of themselves, and formed an invisible shield for Crump that protected him throughout the session. We all became conscious that whoever attempted a bout with Hezekiah Crump ran a danger of bringing up on the point of John Henceforth's rapier; a *dénouement* to be avoided if possible. We were amazed to witness the development of a friendship between the cleverest scholar of the class and the stupidest dullard in its ranks; rather the development of that relationship which exists between a man and a big, faithful, adoring dog. I think that Henceforth helped Crump now and then with his lessons, and Hezekiah's difficulties must have been to John like the elementary troubles of an A B C class. On several occasions I met the shrinking, awkward man shuffling down our stairs, coming, doubtless, from consulting John Henceforth, for he was acquainted with no one else in our house. The last time I thus encountered him was the night before he disappeared. I nodded to him, but he paid no attention, and it seemed to me his bovine eyes were filled with fear.

Meanwhile John Henceforth himself grew upon us, and I, for one, readjusted my estimate of him. Under the cloud of anxiety that overshadowed us he alone stood undismayed. Now emerged upon our cognizance those qualities which were to distinguish him later in life. Born leader of a forlorn hope we discovered him, or, to change the comparison, a stormy petrel whose courage rose with the mounting and threatening of the gale. He took his place naturally and unquestioned at the head of our disorganized phalanx; the knowledge of coming conflict making him, for the time, the most persuasive and courteous of human beings. He encouraged the dejected, he strengthened the strong. He proved an incomparable stump speaker; he swayed us this way or that at his will. His hold on us became all the greater as we knew, and he knew, that he himself was doomed. Whoever escaped, there would be no pardon for John Henceforth. From the beginning of the session he had been a thorn in the flesh of the authorities, a thorn which rankled all the more because he, time and again, had exhibited the comparative incompetence alike of the professors in the Normal School and the masters in the Model. His usual point of vantage was the sill of the waiting-room window, and from this altitude he addressed us.

"Those who have dominion over us," he said, "are really in a much greater quandary than we are. If there happened to be a man of brains or decision among them, their deliberations might be ended in ten minutes. They cannot expel the whole class any more than they can indict a nation. When Cromwell surrounded several hundred levellers at Burford, he imprisoned them in the church, took out three of their number, stood them up against a stone wall, and shot them dead. Yet the rest were equally guilty, but he let them go after a lecture in Dr. Darnell's best style. The Education Committee will probably attempt to do something of this sort: select three or six of you, and expel you. That is what you must hold out against. 'None or all,' that is your battle-cry. Stand by those who are selected as scapegoats. Of course these people must expel somebody: they must save their faces. Luckily Barkis is willing. My case differs from that of any other member of this society. What you did quietly and unobtrusively, I did openly and in defiance of the law. I broke into the girls' waiting-room in broad daylight before the whole world, as it were, and spoke to at least a dozen of the girls there assembled. This gives the authorities a line of retreat. With the blowing of trumpets and the beating of tom-toms, they will fire me into the outer wilderness, as is right and proper."

"Hold hard," cried McKurdy, "we're not going to make an exception in your case. Our watchword 'All' includes you."

There was a roar of approval at this, for our

18

fighting blood was up, and we were not thinking of consequences.

"Thanks, gentlemen," said Henceforth, showing no elation at the unanimity in his favour. "I have just pointed out to you what the authorities can do, and what they can't. I now beg to inform you that there is one thing *you* can't do, and that is to save me. It is only by frankly recognizing what is impossible that success can be attained. Attempt the impossible and you lose the possible. But aside from all this, I shall have no mutiny in the ranks. I am either your leader, or I'm not. If I am your leader, you must do exactly as I tell you, otherwise I shall step out and leave the school at once. No credit is due to me for my willingness to be kicked out: expulsion matters nothing to me, for I do not intend to be a teacher; but to the majority of you here, expulsion would be a very serious matter, and Mr. McKurdy, who has just spoken so straightforwardly, has perhaps the most to lose, therefore I won't have it. Any attempt to link up my case with yours will lead to my instant departure from these delightful shores."

In spite of this prohibition, we began to work quietly and secretly in John Henceforth's favour, when an event happened which put all thought of rescue out of our reach. John Henceforth, then as now, could be depended upon to do the unexpected and dramatic thing, to the entire confusion of his followers. On the day after Hezekiah Crump's disappearance, and while the momentous decision on which our fates depended still hung fire, John Henceforth entered the waiting-room looking whiter than ever I had seen him before. There was an ugly gleam in his eye which always betokened trouble for some one, and, for the first and only time, although he spoke very quietly, there was a trace of emotion in his voice.

"Gentlemen," he began; "I am not going to speak on the impending crisis this time. I wish to say a few words about an unfortunate fellow who until yesterday was one of us. I refer to Hezekiah Crump. As Hezekiah is not here, and never will be here again, I may venture to say that I have always regarded him as one of Nature's cruel practical jokes. That a yearning ambition to succeed should be implanted in the breast of a man lacking every quality that makes for success, seems to me an instance of the general unfitness of things. His gifts are limited to a capacity for suffering, and an inexhaustible capability for faithfulness. He has lived in a hovel on the outskirts of this city, working for his board, rising at four o'clock in the morning, or earlier, to finish his tasks before the three-mile walk to the school, and I believe he was often on the verge of starvation. He is the victim of that deluding volume, 'Smiles' Self-Help,' and a tattered copy is in his pocket at this moment as he tramps northward, he not having money enough to pay railway fare home, being yet too proud to ask or accept help from any to whom he has not given value in work. I wish that in lieu of that dog-eared volume its weight in sandwiches were in his pocket.

"His record at the Model School has been deplorable. Never once in the first division has he managed to get in a word. The grotesqueness of his figure and the vacant imbecility of his face offered opportunities of comment which John Brent's pupils would be the last to ignore. Dr. Darnell sent him to the first division yesterday to teach anatomy, and goodness knows, his class had before them one of the most unique specimens of anatomy that could well be imagined. It is rather odd that he came up to my room the night before, and implored me to tell him the secret of my control over those lads.

" ' My dear Hezekiah,' I said, ' it all lies in the cussed contrariness of things. You want to be kind to them and to instruct them, and so you wish them to behave like little gentlemen. On the contrary, I hoped they would rebel if they dared, and neither of us got our wish. They are like wolves with you, and like lambs with me. They have never yet given me the chance to let loose my vocabulary upon them, and I have been waiting all the session for the slightest sign of revolt.'

" He said this was his last opportunity. He knew how badly he had done heretofore, and he was painfully anxious to retrieve. His future depended on his success the next day. In his neck-of-the-woods, in a spot so remote that it will take him a week or more to walk there (thank goodness it is the most charming out-door time of the year—he will sleep in barns and under haystacks, and will get a bite when he can screw up his courage to ask for it); well, in this neck-of-the-woods, Hezekiah is quite a man, and the people, realizing how backward they are in educational facilities, have built some sort of a school-house by the united labour of the neighbourhood, and it is Hezekiah's ambition to teach that school. His doting old mother is waiting for him, with ' See the Conquering Hero Comes ' singing in her heart.

" Well, I won't talk any more about that : I don't like to think of Hezekiah's heart-broken return. One of Crump's few pleasures in this town was the haunting of a bookshop. In this shop lay shelved a second-hand set of the *Encyclopædia Britannica,* and his greatest happiness was to dream of possessing this storehouse of knowledge some day. Now, none of us are overburdened with cash, but I ventured to pay a deposit on that set of books, and I am now going to pass the hat, hoping to accumulate the remainder of the sum. I propose to take train for Hezekiah's native bailiwick, and get there before him with these volumes. I'll drum up the neighbourhood, make them a speech, decorate the school-house, and we'll give Hezekiah a reception when that Johnny comes marching home. McKurdy, pass the hat.''

McKurdy promptly obeyed, and more than the requisite sum was flung in before he finished his round. As Henceforth had been speaking, he held in his hand a scroll, with which he gesticulated as if he were a Roman senator. He now unrolled this, and we saw it was a blazonry of scarlet and gold and black German lettering.

'' I have had inscribed here a eulogy of Hezekiah Crump, and a testimonial of the esteem in which he is held by one and all. I want the signature of each of you to this parchment done in your very best hand-writing. I shall present it to him framed, with the best wishes of his former colleagues, if you accept me as your delegate.''

This discourse for the moment raised John Henceforth to the rank of hero and champion amongst us, but he was a man who could never let well alone, and the twist in his nature, to which I have referred, drove him into the discounting of anything that told in his favour. Instead of quietly seeing Dr. Darnell in his own room, and obtaining permission to leave the school for a day or two, he rose next morning in class, and stated a determination when he should have made a request.

"Dr. Darnell," he said, "I intend to be absent from these classes for a few days."

Dr. Darnell was on edge in a moment.

"Why limit the time, Mr. Henceforth?" he inquired acidly.

John Henceforth smiled. This was a retort to his liking.

"The class of male students, Dr. Darnell, has generously subscribed a testimonial and an illuminated address of appreciation to Mr. Hezekiah Crump, lately one of us; an earnest young man, who having enacted badly the part of Daniel in the lions' den, was somewhat mauled by the brutes, and has gone home wounded in spirit, which probably hurts him more than if his outward body had been misused."

"So you," said the Doctor, very successfully suppressing his only too visible anger, "you, possessing a courage which your friend seemed to lack, fearing no lion, doubtless think, from the grandiloquence of your remarks and the impertinence of your manner, that you are a modern Marmion, bearding the lion in his den."

"Yes," said the imperturbable Henceforth; "the Douglas in his hall; the Darnell at his desk."

"Very well, the Darnell at his desk gives you permission, with this proviso, that you go down at once to the Model School, and give to the pupils of the first division the lesson in anatomy which Mr. Hezekiah Crump failed to impart."

"With the greatest pleasure in the world, Dr. Darnell," replied Henceforth, bowing, "and if I should succeed where he failed, may I plead that my hour there will be added to Mr. Crump's credit?"

"Mr. Crump having deserted his post, his name has already been struck off our list."

Again John Henceforth bowed.

"In that case I must content myself with taking whatever credit may be due. I shall endeavour to instruct those lads so well that a lasting impression will be made on them, which should be the aim of all good teachers. It is my desire that my last day in the Model will cause me to stand high in the ranks of the few who have succeeded, and I am sure, Dr. Darnell, it will give you a pleasure at least equal to my own, when you set down this flattering rating on the credentials you will bestow upon me at the end of the session."

John Henceforth smiled and made a third bow, but there was no smile on Dr. Darnell's grim face, and no answering salutation. He knew there would be no credentials from the school to Henceforth. Henceforth knew it also, and each knew that the other knew.

Henceforth must have been conscious of the feeling of uneasiness in the room while this colloquy was going on, but it is not likely that he cared in the slightest. He was ever a man to take his own line of country, irrespective of disaster to himself or others.

I had the account of his hour's teaching graphically told me by one who was present.

There was deep silence when John the elder installed John the younger into his place before the class with a courteous wave of the hand, for this lesson was by way of being an extra turn, and John Brent, under instructions from Dr. Darnell, stopped his own work to give John Henceforth the opportunity of taking his place. This being an unusual occurrence, the pupils seemed slightly apprehensive and unprepared for the intervention. Brent closed the door as he departed, and Henceforth's white and wry smile beamed like cold moonlight on the boys.

" I am sent to teach you," he said in a voice audible only because of the stillness of the room, " that lesson in anatomy which my friend, Hezekiah Crump, somehow failed to deliver. Do you happen to remember what particular section of the human body was under consideration, if I may use such a term as ' under consideration ' to describe the *mêlée* that ensued ?"

" The muscles of the back, sir," promptly responded the class.

" Thank you very much : the muscles of the back. I have not had an opportunity to prepare this lesson, so you must bear with me if I should fall into error."

The class laughed. Very well they knew that John Henceforth never fell into error.

" Beginning at the back of the head, I will name a few of the muscles and ask you to correct me if I make a mistake. Occipitalis, splenus capitis, splenus colli, levator anguli scapulæ, supraspinatos, rhomboidens, infraspinatus, teres major, serratus posticus inferior; how am I getting along ?"

" First rate, sir."

" Have I missed any ?"

" No, sir."

" Ah," said John sweetly; " I fear that the other day you were not prepared for Mr. Crump's cross-examination. One muscle has been omitted. Now, sir, you at the top corner, name the missing muscle."

" I cannot, sir."

" Next boy."

" No, sir; I don't remember it."

" Next boy."

"Tendon Achilles," ventured the third lad.

"Nonsense; you are down at the heel now, or rather, at the ankle. Come, come, I want no more fooling," but not one of the class could give the missing word.

Henceforth's smile vanished, and an ugly frown ruffled his brow. His eyes looked like live coals, and the boys began to quail. He stared at them for a few moments in silence.

"I'll give you a lead," he said at last, picking up a long, tough pointer of hickory, most bendable and tenacious of woods. He switched this lithe rod through the air, making it give out a hiss like that of a serpent.

"First boy, name the muscles which enable me to do this, and you will find among them the one we are searching for."

Several essayed the task, but none gave the list complete.

"You have been badly taught, or else your work has been shirked."

"Please, sir," pleaded one boy, "Mr. Brent places the diagram of the human body before us, and we name the muscles as he indicates them with the pointer."

"A very poor plan," said Henceforth. "I can put a pointer to a better use than that, and there is no need of a diagram when you have each got your bodies with you."

He strode to the door, turned the key, and slipped it into his pocket.

"Now, young gentlemen, I will teach you anatomy and name the muscles myself. But first let me utter a few words of warning. There are enough of you here, if you have courage, to overpower me instantly.

I dare you to attempt it, you cowardly ruffians. You shrieked with laughter when you caused an unfortunate man to break into weeping. Besides teaching you anatomy, I'll teach you to shriek on the other side of your mouths. And now for the word of warning. If any boy leaves his seat, or attempts to leave it; stands up or attempts to stand up, until I jerk him from his place, I'll knock that boy senseless with the butt-end of this pointer.''

He seized the first boy by the collar and vigorously laid on the rod, amidst howls, not only from the victim, but from several others. He named aloud the muscles he struck, then flung the weeping lad against the door.

"Sit there," he said, "and howl; then when they break in the door, its fall may utterly extinguish you. And now, you young scapegraces," he added, turning to the class, "if you have paid proper attention you will have learned that I have found the lost muscle on this lad's body, and that its name is Teres minor. Because in my list I mentioned one Teres, you forgot there was a second, and in order that there may be no waste of breath, you will from now until I have finished with you, shout the names of the muscles I indicate with this amateur billiard cue, and keep back this outcry for help which cannot be forthcoming, because this door is stoutly built, and they cannot break it down in time to save any one of you from anatomical instruction." With that he rapidly and effectually went on with his work, until pointer after pointer splintered and streams of perspiration ran down his face. Towards the end the battering at the door increased in violence without perceptible result.

When the last boy had passed under the rod,

Henceforth mopped his brow, then ordered the sobbing contingent back into their seats, a command that was promptly obeyed with exemplary docility. Without haste John Henceforth produced the key and opened the door. Mr. Brent and his three assistants stood there. Boyle and two or three helpers were holding a long bench, which they had been using as a battering-ram. Dr. Darnell came hurrying up, followed by the messenger sent for him.

"Have you gone mad, sir?" demanded the Doctor.

"Mad, sir?" echoed Henceforth, raising his eyebrows and mopping them again with his sodden handkerchief. "Certainly not, sir. I have given the class a number of good marks, and expect to receive a number of good marks in consequence. Turn about is fair play, you know."

"This is a case for the police," said John Brent with cold severity. "It is a criminal offence: assault and battery."

"You have not sent for the police?" gasped Dr. Darnell.

"No, sir; I have waited for your permission."

"Do nothing hastily, Mr. Brent. I must consider this outrage."

Brent bowed mechanically.

"Boyle, take away that bench and those men, and don't stand there gaping like a fool."

The worthy janitor and his company hastily retreated.

"May I submit, with the utmost respect," pleaded John Henceforth gently to Mr. Brent, "that this is not a case for the police, but rather one for Dr. Cardiff, and a few boxes of soothing salve, should they prove necessary. These fine lads will never forget that Teres is an important organ of the body, even though it be termed minor. Your class, Mr. Brent, has only to take off its shirt and gaze over its shoulder into a mirror, when it will find distinctive blue marks to indicate all the important muscles of the back.''

'' Sir,'' said Dr. Darnell, '' you will report to the committee assembled in my room this afternoon at half-past four o'clock.''

'' I am sorry to disobey you, Doctor; but you must arrest me now if there is a desire to accept Mr. Brent's kindly suggestion, or accept my assurance that I shall return within a few days and place myself at the disposal of the committee—or of the police,'' he added, smiling at John Brent.

'' Very well,'' assented the headmaster.

'' Good-day to you, gentlemen,'' and bowing to each in turn Henceforth left them standing there.

The case never got into the police court.

CHAPTER XX

Who giveth this woman to be married to this man?
BOOK OF COMMON PRAYER.

JOHN HENCEFORTH returned from the wilderness,
gave us a graphic account of Hezekiah Crump's
home-coming, then delivered himself up to the Education Committee, smiling sardonically when he learned
that the police had not been informed of his assault
on the first division of the Model School.

Next morning he appeared in his usual seat, but
we knew something untoward was about to happen,
because all the teachers of both Normal and Model
Schools were seated in a group on Dr. Darnell's
platform. After the fiercest prayer and chapter of the
session, the headmaster, without seating himself,
called the name of John Henceforth, who at once
stood up, straight as a pole.

" Mr. Henceforth," said our chief, " it is my painful duty to expel you from this institution, and to add
that such ejection necessarily involves the withhold-
ing of whatever credentials the Normal School might,
in other circumstances, have been prepared to bestow.
The Model School has hitherto been carried on and
the most admirable discipline maintained without
recourse to corporal punishment, and you were well
aware of the rule that forbids the use of the rod."

" Pardon me, Dr. Darnell," interrupted Henceforth,
with sweet gentleness, " but my objection to the rule
is that it contravenes the Scriptures which you read

so admirably. See Proverbs xiii. 24; also Proverbs xxii. 15, which says tersely, ' Foolishness is bound in the heart of a child, but the rod of correction shall drive it far from him.' Nothing on this earth is so foolish as the first division, so I adopted the biblical method of elimination.''

Dr. Darnell paused for a few moments, anger flashing up in his eyes, then dying down again. Silently he declined controversy and went on unheeding.

'' This rule you deliberately broke——''

'' Also five hickory pointers,'' plaintively complained John, as if some of his merits were being ignored.

Dr. Darnell, with a sigh, ended lamely—

'' Therefore I ask you to leave these precincts.''

John Henceforth quietly tip-toed to the door, his method of march showing that there was at least one art he had learned during the session. He turned facing us, and I thought he was about to make a speech, but he merely said '' Good-bye,'' and then, in Dr. Darnell's best manner, he named rapidly every student present, beginning with Miss Arbuthnot and ending with Brushwood Smith. Finally he bowed to the girls, next to us, and after a low obeisance to the masters, opened the door and departed. That was the last we ever saw of John Henceforth.

McKurdy sprang to his feet and, in defiance of time and place, shouted—

'' Three cheers for John Henceforth. I admire his pluck, and don't care who knows it.''

The cheers were heartily given, and under cover of them the masters left the room.

John Henceforth, as we were afterwards to learn, had fought our battle behind closed doors in the committee room. His discourse was described as a marvel of concise reasoning, of brilliant but restrained eloquence, of argument that no dignitary present could overturn. He pictured the perils of opening the flood-gates of publicity, holding that no man could predict what might or might not be swept away by the inundation. He offered himself for expulsion, but stipulated that the Model School episode should be the reason given. This compromise was adopted by the committee.

Yet Henceforth never took the trouble to inform any of us that he had won our fight. The moment the contest was closed, all interest in it or in us seemed to have vanished from his mind.

When we returned to our rooms, Sam brought down his fist on our study table, and said he would stand it no longer. For some time marriage licences were in our possession—and Sam and Sally had long ago proclaimed their intention of getting married at the same place and hour as Aline and I. The Rev. Mr. Morris, a kindly old gentleman, pastor of the Centre Street church, who liked both of the girls as if they had been his own daughters, had consented to perform the ceremony, they being regular attendants of his church. He knew nothing of the rules of the Normal School, and the locked doors had not yet opened to allow the recent trouble to become public. Knowing that Sally's parents had given an enthusiastic consent to the marriage of their daughter (for she had introduced him to them when they had visited the city a few weeks before), the simple old man never dreamed that there could be any objection to the marriage of Aline. Aline herself was showing signs of breaking down under the strain, despite her admirable courage. She had expected John Brent to call upon her, and expostulate, perhaps, but he had made no attempt to see her. Then she told me that she was being followed, and spied upon wherever she went, and although I tried to laugh her out of this delusion, she remained firm in her belief. Why should they follow her when the worst was known? She thought it was to trap the man whose acquaintance she had confessed, but I said that if any spying was done, John Brent must be the cause of it, and I rather fancied he now wished he had not taken such an active part in forcing the crisis, and so was little likely to engage further in the business of amateur detective.

If the bride is happy on whom the sun shines, our two poor girls were entering a life of misery, for a fierce tropical thunderstorm raged over the city when we all went to Centre Street Church together; I to be Sam's witness, he to be mine. The reverend old gentleman was awaiting us, and the empty church was almost dark, the rain roaring and lashing against the panes. The sexton had lit a few gas jets at the further end of the church. The clergyman asked us if we preferred to wait until the storm had passed. It would not last long, he said. Sally was willing, but Aline, shuddering a little as she clung to me, cried—

"No, no! Let us get it over."

The girls were near the verge of hysterics, both of them, and no wonder, with the bitter week ending in such a terrible storm. Sam and Sally stood up together first, as longest engaged. When the short ceremony was finished, Aline and I took the places of the newly married pair at the altar rail. Aline's hand was cold as ice, and when I smiled reassuringly at her, a very wan and sad smile replied to mine. The clergyman began his abbreviated exhortation, undoubtedly familiar enough to him, and when he came to the words which he spoke so mechanically, "Therefore if any man can show just cause why they may not lawfully be joined together, let him now speak, or else hereafter for ever hold his peace," there answered a voice I knew only too well, from the darkened forward part of the church.

"I object!"

Slowly towards us up the aisle, as if there was no need to hurry, came the footsteps of a man, and presently the face and form of John Brent materialized out of the darkness into the area of illumination.

"Sir," he said to the clergyman, "I represent the father of this girl."

"You do not!" cried Aline. "You have no right; no authority over me!"

Brent paid not the least heed to this protest, but still addressing the bewildered old man, who, in his long experience, had probably never met an interruption like this before, he continued in a bland, convincing, semi-deferential tone, as one addressing the cloth—

"Sir, Miss Arbuthnot is between seventeen and eighteen years of age, and when I have said that, I need not add that it is illegal for you to marry her without the consent of her father, the surviving parent in this case. If you do not accept my word as to her age, ask Miss Arbuthnot: she will tell you the truth."

"You have no right to interfere," protested Aline.

Brent did not reply.

"Has this gentleman stated your age correctly, Miss Arbuthnot?" asked the clergyman.

"Yes."

"That being so, I cannot go on with the ceremony. It would be illegal if I did."

19

"I must apologize to you, sir, for this intervention," said John Brent. "I am very sorry that it
has been necessary. I had hoped that Judge Arbuthnot himself would have been present. He should
have been here by this time, but perhaps his train
has been delayed by the storm."

As he spoke, the church door opened, and a man
entered as if driven in by the lashing of the rain. As
he came within our view, I saw a tall, distinguished
personage with the face of a statesman.

"Am I in time?" he demanded brusquely of
Brent.

"Oh yes, Judge Arbuthnot."

"Thank God! Brent, you are a true friend. I
can never repay you adequately for this."

As he turned to his daughter, face and voice
softened, and the light of a great, forgiving love came
into those eyes that were so like Aline's.

"Aline, darling," was all he said as he took her
hand.

The girl stood as one hypnotized, scarcely breathing. In her eyes was an exaltation of fear, qualified
nevertheless with strong affection. Her face, pathetic
and refined, seemed like that of one about to die.
The droop of the sweet lips was indescribably sad.
Her father, who looked at or spoke to none but his
daughter and Brent, took Aline with him down the
aisle, and they disappeared together in the dark and
the storm. I strode forward. Brent placed himself
squarely across my path. I raised my clenched fist,
only to find my arm firmly gripped by McKurdy.

"It is no use," he whispered; "it is neither
the time nor the place for violence. Chance is
against you for the moment—only for the moment,
remember."

CHAPTER XXI

A narrow compass! and yet there
Dwelt all that's good, and all that's fair :
Give me but what this riband bound,
Take all the rest the sun goes round.
'ON A GIRDLE.'

AFTER the marriage ceremony Sally went home, as the marriage certificate in her case quite obliterated all thoughts of a teacher's certificate. Sam stayed in town, waiting to learn whether he was to be expelled with the rest, or called upon to pass an examination for his credentials. Much to McKurdy's amazement, John Brent said nothing about the marriage. Sam came triumphantly through his ordeal, and became possessed of the diploma which rated his qualifications at a high valuation.

I bade good-bye to Dr. Darnell and the rest, telling them I was going to Paris. I lingered for one unhappy day, hoping to receive a letter, if Aline got opportunity to write, but in this I was disappointed, and next morning I took train to the village that had been Aline's home. I stopped there the greater part of a week at the quietest tavern in the place. Judge Arbuthnot's house stood in well-timbered grounds just outside the village; a large, plain structure of stone, not at all like the dwelling I had pictured, and it was now, apparently, uninhabited. Already an air of desertion hung about it, and it seemed rather forbidding. The iron gates were locked, and the high wall of rough stone surrounding it gave the place an air of aloofness, as if it looked down on its more humble neighbours. The high wall presented no difficulties to a porch-climber, and I scrambled over into the grounds threaded by avenues and walks of deep green gloom through the luxuriance of summer growth. I rambled aimlessly under the trees, wondering which had been Aline's favourite walk. At length I was startled by a man breaking through the thicket and accosting me.

"What are you doing here?"

"I am anxious to meet Judge Arbuthnot."

"He is not at home."

"Where is he?"

"I don't know."

"When will he return?"

"I don't know."

"Are you watchman here?"

"I am in charge of the house and grounds. How did you get in here? The gate is locked." .

"I know it is. I came in over the wall."

"You had no right to."

"I know that, but I am anxious to learn the whereabouts of the Judge."

"You can't learn them from me."

"Surely you can tell me where you forward his letters."

"They are not to be forwarded. And now, if you've quite done your questioning, I'll lead you to the gate, and unlock it."

"May I see through the house?"

"No."

"Nor the rest of the grounds?"

"No."

The man was evidently as determined as the master.

We walked together in silence to the gate; I thanked him, bade him good-day, and receiving no response, went out. Melancholy as was my mood, I could not help smiling to think that the fellow probably would not be so gruff when I returned with Aline; for that I should so return, I had at that time not the slightest doubt.

As I walked down to the village, I found myself readjusting dear little Aline herself in my mind. The place I had left was quite evidently a home of wealth, yet Aline and I had always talked of poverty, and trudging together through the by-ways of a foreign land. I, too, had never given a thought to riches, except such as Aline was so sure would come through my own brush. Ah me, one is young but once. I began to see the stern father's action in another light. He doubtless regarded me as a fortune-hunter, trading on the simplicity of a guileless girl.

I could not help hearing a good deal of gossip about him, for his sudden departure had set tongues wagging. I learnt he was respected, reputed to be the wealthiest man in the neighbourhood; a strict church-goer, kind to those in need, but not exactly popular, for he was one who kept much to himself, and lacked that friendly affability which wins votes.

One day I caught a glimpse of Sally, surrounded by girl friends. She was laughing heartily, and so were they. I remembered that here was Sally's home as well as that of Aline, but I shrank from a meeting at the moment, and this proved to be the last time I was to see the sprightly Sally. The day before I left the village, I read in the local newspaper that Judge Arbuthnot had resigned his office. There was a sketch of his career, but no information regarding his whereabouts and intentions. On the following day I saw a large printed poster at the gate announcing the estate for sale. I took the next train for the city, called at my former boarding-house, was met by the grim Mrs. Sponsor, who eyed me with cold dislike as she said there was no letter for me, and closed the door in my face.

I often wonder why it is that such a commonplace, colourless person as I am succeeds in inspiring such royal hatred in certain men and women. I cannot account for that woman's calculated malignity towards me, and the relentlessness of it arouses almost an admiration, for at that moment she held in her possession the letter from Aline I so eagerly sought, and she broke not only the seal, but the law, to learn its contents. That, perhaps, has often been done before, but she held the letter for three years, then posted it to me, knowing it to be useless. It reached me in a hospital in Paris, and all but completed the work that illness and privation had begun. She sent it to mé when my name was appearing in all the newspapers as the painter of the successful Salon picture of that year. Thus she got my address.

Baffled at last by the trivial fact that my only address was in the hands of the enemy, spending time and money without result, realizing that day by day my chances were lessening of doing with my future what Aline and I had planned, I at last reached Paris, and took the cheapest top studio at No. 9, Rue Falgarie, in the Mont Parnasse quarter. I worked with a desperate industry that should have earned reward, but did not. I lived frugally, and got the reputation among my acquaintances of miserly meanness. My comrades, however, began to show more and more respect for my painting, whatever they might think of my generosity, and this respect of his fellow-crafts-

men often buoys up a man to bear the indifference of
the public, and the refusal of the dealers. I never
lost confidence in my ultimate success, but there grew
upon me a depressing, fatalistic belief that the success
would come too late; that I should never see Aline
again. It was during these dejected hours, after I
had become in some measure an adept at my profession, that I painted the picture since known as " The
Interruption." This is not the name by which I should
have called it. My other pictures came back with
unfailing regularity from the Salon, and also, indeed,
from the smaller exhibitions to which I sent them.
It has been said that the fame of " The Interruption "
was newspaper-made, and not brush-won. Some
widely circulated journals printed romantic stories of
the picture; accounts founded on studio gossip that
went wide of the mark, but aside from this I think
that the painting itself must have arrested attention
not only because of the beauty of its subject, but also
from the fact that it was produced under great tribula-
tion of soul. As I worked at it, I closed my eyes,
and saw the model before me; Aline, as she stood
that black day in the old church at the moment her
father came in. There was no background to show
where the girl was, only dark colour that made face
and figure stand out like a carven statue; in her
splendid eyes the sudden fear; in her sweet face the
radiance of those ideals for which, together, we were
to strive.

When it was finished I had no money to buy a
frame, so I tacked the canvas upon the door, the head
at the height of Aline herself as she stood with her
back against the door, the night I first kissed her.
The studio door was overhung by a green baize
curtain, sliding on a rod at the top, thus no one but

myself ever saw the picture. If any visitor entered, it was hidden behind the curtain. The picture became my friend, my lover, my inspiration. When evening came on, and I was safe from interruption, I used to draw back the curtain, and solace myself by gazing at her image, as if I were a devotee before the image of my saint. My mind retains but a hazy recollection of the few days that preceded my illness, yet I remember being startled at finding myself talking to her, and hearing her voice, and when I roused myself, I knew this should not be. On the last day in that studio, McKenzie, who occupied the first floor, had invited me down to dinner. A number of the painters round about were coming, and I think McKenzie rather suspected that my own larder was empty, for the good fellow had tried to press some money on me a while before, which I told him I did not need.

It was now three years since I had seen Aline herself. She had become a dearly remembered dream, and the picture grew more and more into the reality. I felt too ill and depressed to go down the long stairs, and the idea came to me that Aline would be lonesome without me. I drew back the curtain, and, instead of the picture, there stood the girl herself, with her serious eyes looking sorrowfully upon me. Never was my mind clearer. Never was I surer this could be no illusion. All at once I knew that my past doubts were nonsense, and that this was exactly the way Aline would come to me; that she had stolen up the stairs and hidden herself before her own likeness. It was the most natural thing that had ever happened in the world, and perfectly logical. Why, then, did she look so sad?

"Aline, Aline!" I cried, and flung my arms about her; then the world went out like a snuffed candle.

It seems that, in falling, my hand caught the canvas, and tore it from its fastenings; and when, some time later, McKenzie came bursting in to learn why I had not appeared, the door struck against my body, and he nearly fell over me in the darkness. He picked me up and carried me down the long stairs into his studio, where the group of young fellows were singing and drinking.

"Run for a doctor, Smithers," he cried, and Smithers ran.

McKenzie placed me on a couch, and tried to force some brandy between my set teeth. One of the students took up the canvas which lay face downwards on my breast. McKenzie says he held it up, crying—

"Ye gods, boys, look at this! Has he done it? I never thought him capable of such work," and there was a chorus of approval of the picture, and expressions of belief in the artist.

"There's no use in wasting brandy on a dead man," cried the one who hadn't believed in me. "Don't you see how it is? This is a case of suicide. There's no model like this in Paris. She belongs to him. Something has gone wrong, and he has died clasping her in his arms."

McKenzie admits that this interesting theory staggered him for a moment, but the arrival of the doctor speedily set that rumour at rest. Nevertheless, the absurd story got into the papers, and the true account of the circumstances, printed later, never quite overtook it. I was driven away to the hospital, and there passed through a long illness, which has left little impression on my mind beyond nightmare intervals of consciousness.

McKenzie caused the picture to be framed, labelled it "The Interruption," and sent it to the Salon, where it was accepted and hung in the chief place of the principal room. I suppose I was the only intelligent man in Paris who remained ignorant of the fact that I had become the painter of the moment.

My recovery was slower than the nurses and the doctors had expected, and we were well into the summer before I was allowed an easy-chair on the balcony of the hospital. I learned of my success in the Salon, and the news produced a moderately cheering effect, which was enhanced by the financial results that the shrewd McKenzie brought about for me. I was uneasily aware that my expenses at the hospital were liquidated by the generosity of my comrades, none of whom were too well provided with funds, excepting McKenzie, who was fortunate enough to possess a private income. He was somewhat taken aback at first by my refusal, which he characterized as stubborn, of all the surprisingly generous offers made for the Salon picture itself. He said I could easily produce a duplicate, and undertook to stipulate with the purchaser that the painting itself should remain in my possession until this was done, but I knew I should never paint another such picture, either as a replica or as an original. Besides, there were other reasons, into which I could not enter even with so close a friend as McKenzie. However, with much more acumen than I possessed, he manipulated the disposal of the various canvases in my studio, and, all in all, it seemed rather a joke on the public that they should now pay exorbitant prices for work which, six months before, could not be given away. Thus it began to appear that I need no longer dread an encounter with hard times when once I got upon my feet again.

One day McKenzie brought me from the studio a

letter which had been addressed to me there. It bore
a foreign stamp, and the handwriting was unknown
to me. I threw it on the table, unopened, until my
friend had gone. There was no scrap of writing
inside resembling the superscription on the envelope,
but I pulled out an opened letter which bore the crest
of the French Transatlantic line. My heart jumped
as I saw the handwriting, and for one blessed moment
I thought she had learned my address; but when I
saw that the date was three years old, temporary
oblivion came, and Mrs. Sponsor's revenge was within an ace of becoming complete. At last I read the
pencilled lines, evidently hurriedly scribbled under
fear of interruption :

" Dear, dear Tom,
        " I had a presentiment we would not be married
to-day. After all, in spite of licence and clergyman,
it would not have seemed right to me unless my father
were standing by. Oh, Tom, even at this moment we
must not forget that I never even gave him an opportunity of saying ' yes ' or ' no,' and he learned of my
resolve abruptly by telegram from another than his
own daughter. I tell you this, Tom, instead of con-
soling you, poor boy, so that you will not think
harshly of my father. The young can wait, but the
old have few to love, and a loss means a greater
wrench, perhaps, and is more irreparable. Do not
think I am under surveillance, or am being unkindly
treated. He simply asked my word that I should not
leave him if the chance offered, and I gave it. He
trusted me completely, and the bonds, if silken, are
as strong as steel. Of all places on earth, Father is
taking me to Paris. Oh, Tom, think of that, when
I expected my first sight of it would be in company

of some one else. I am under only one prohibition. He will not allow me to speak of you and refuses to listen if I attempt to broach the subject of our acquaintance, friendship and love. He is very tender and gentle with me, as if I had been miraculously rescued from some almost fatal disaster, or had recovered from a mortal illness. I am under no restrictions, and he has not even forbidden my writing to you, but I think this comes from his supreme confidence in his own ability to keep us apart. He will descend to no petty device, but his resolution will not falter. Yet how illogical is man! He recognizes that his daughter will not break her word, but he does not dream that her resolution may prove as strong as his own. Why should I be like him in one quality and not in another? Ah, poor deluded Tom, it's a determined wife you'll get, so beware in time.

" I have an intuition you will see our house before you see me. I fancy you taking the railway journey with Sally, who was going home as soon as she was married, and I think her talk will cheer you up. You know you always liked Sally, but I shall feel jealous of that railway journey to the end of my days. I wonder if you will think to tell the man in charge that you are a friend of mine, for then he will let you into the house, and you will see my father's fine picture gallery, which I had been keeping as a surprise for you, believing in the beyond of my heart that this would be my last trump—that sounds like the Judgment, doesn't it? but I mean cards—to win my father round if he proved long obdurate, for he is a connoisseur in art, and a correspondent with many great painters of the day, whose pictures he buys. How, then, could he hold out against my famous Tom, with pictures in every Salon? Why, we'd raise the price on him, dear, and if he held out, you'd be the one painter he couldn't buy. Oh dear, oh dear! I'm trying to write frivolously, for I fear my poor boy will be gloomy, and I love to think that this letter will hearten him. And now, listen to my plan. You must come to Paris by the next boat. As soon as Father and I are settled, I shall steal out to the Poste Restante, and there deposit a letter for you, giving our address; but perhaps it will be better that you should not write to me at the Hotel, but use the Poste Restante also. I shall let a week go by, during which time I shall be the most devoted daughter in Europe. Then will come again the breaking of rules. I hope the police won't begin to notice a foreign girl stealing day by day to the Poste Restante. Father will be seeing many painters in Paris, and we will be visiting galleries day after day; studios also, I suppose; and he shall have no reason to complain of his daughter's lack of interest. Thus we may plot against the poor man, who thinks his daughter aspires to marry a schoolmaster ever so far away. Tom, he never even looked at you in the church. He would not know you if he met you to-day. You must get acquainted with some one who will introduce you to him, and then, dear Tom, be as nice to him as you were to me. Be your own self, and I've no fear of the result, only don't expect him to succumb to your fascinations so quickly as I did.

" And now, dear Tom, good-bye for seven or eight days. You will find a letter from me awaiting you, telling you what hours of the day will be most convenient for me to keep any appointment you make. I suggest some spot in the Tuilleries Gardens, for Father thinks of going to the Hôtel Continental, which he tells me is opposite. And now, dear Tom, with a thousand kisses, forgive me for saying that after all this is much better than a clandestine marriage. I see clearly we are on the right way, although still plotting."

Poor girl! poor courageous little girl! I saw her going back and forth between her hotel and the rude building at the end of the Tuilleries Gardens which at that time housed the post-office, before the new post-office was finished. I wondered when her brave heart had sunk under hope deferred. To think that we two were in Paris together, and that Chance, which had made such sport of us, never brought us face to face. I got no sleep that night, for whenever I dropped off, I saw a dejected figure before a post-office window, and awoke, crying, " Aline! Aline!"

The doctor was in despair the next morning, and McKenzie in a state of Celtic wrath, thinking I was to blame for the relapse.

" This will never do," he cried. " What have you been bothering your head about? Was that a bill I brought you yesterday? Why fash about bills? Haven't you money enough, you miser?"

" Bills," I retorted irritably. " How could I incur bills? Nobody trusted me."

" Nonsense, we all trusted you," but at that the doctor pushed him out of the room.

I rallied quicker on this occasion. I had an incentive. As McKenzie said, there now was plenty of money, and I need no longer be tied by the leg to a squalid studio in the Rue Falgarie. Surely I could soon discover the whereabouts of Judge Arbuthnot.

Seven days after receipt of the letter (I was struck by the coincidence) McKenzie brought in the English paper published in Paris. I was out on the balcony again.

"That ought to interest you," he said. "You must hurry up and get well, for the Salon closes in a few weeks, and we are determined you shall visit it before the end."

I took the paper, and scanned the heading of the article he pointed out:

"The Original of the Salon Picture." Then, with increasing eagerness, I read the item:

"Most celebrated paintings exhibited in the Salon year by year containing the human figure carry no secret regarding the model who posed for it. She is either one of the professional class, or perhaps a *grande dame* of society. Every painter has his favourite model who appears year after year in his tableaux, but the model who stood for 'The Interruption' remained unknown, until a correspondent, writing from Switzerland, whose letter we published, stated that he believed the original of the picture to be the only daughter of Judge Arbuthnot, then stopping at Interlaken. We made inquiries, but found that Miss Arbuthnot had been with her father in Germany during the year the picture was painted here in Paris. Yesterday Judge Arbuthnot arrived with his daughter from Switzerland, and they are staying at the Hôtel Continental. He was kind enough to receive our reporter, and in answer to his questions said he had never even heard of the Salon picture, and of course had not yet seen it. He knew nothing of Prentiss, the painter, and regretted to learn from our reporter that the young man is still in hospital. This should dispose of one of the many erroneous items floating about regarding the popular painting in question. The reporter did not have the privilege of meeting

Miss Arbuthnot, and so can make no statement regarding the coincidence of likeness. Judge Arbuthnot will visit the Salon to-morrow at eleven, escorted by the President of the Artists' Society."

" Are you acquainted with Judge Arbuthnot?" asked McKenzie.

" No."

" He is one of the few collectors who appreciate what they are buying."

" What, do you know him?"

" Oh yes. He bought a pair of my statuettes about a year and a half ago, and has been in my studio several times since."

" Not at the Rue Falgarie?" I cried.

" Yes. What do you find astonishing in that?"

" Was his daughter with him?"

" I think she was. I don't remember."

" Good heavens, you *know* whether she was with him or not? What's the use of talking like a blabbing idiot?"

" Look here, Prentiss, you're temporarily suffering from lack of outdoor exercise. Is it fame that's doing this, or money? Am I dealing with a haughty celebrity, or a bloated millionaire, or both combined into a despot? Well, your majesty, I imagine the girl was there, and now that your irritability has stimulated my memory, I may say that her presence accounts for something familiar I noticed in your picture. Was she up in your studio, too, and is that how you managed to get her likeness into your painting?"

" No, no. Excuse me, Mac. As you say, I'm becoming an unbearable beast."

" Oh, I didn't go quite so far as that. I'll give you an introduction to Judge Arbuthnot if you like."

“ Thank you. I’d be ever so much obliged.”

Aline’s plot was running through my mind—her plot of three years ago.

“ I’d like to get a glimpse of him first. I’m going to be at the Salon to-morrow at eleven o’clock.”

“ I wouldn’t chance it if I were you, my boy.”

“ Oh, there’s no danger. Summon a cab for me at half-past ten, or thereabouts.”

“ I’ll take you for a drive, Tom, but I’m hanged if I’m going to lead you through those hot and crowded rooms.”

“ We’ll see how I feel when we get there. I’m all right, I think. Then we’ll drive to the Hôtel Continental, and you’ll introduce me to Mr. Arbuthnot when he returns.”

“ Very well, half-past ten sharp. I’ll be here and take you out, doctor and the weather permitting.”

There was a great crowd round the picture as I slunk past on McKenzie’s arm. I did not see Judge Arbuthnot, nor any one else my eyes sought, but the picture itself seemed to recognize me. The face changed as I looked at it.

“ Here, here,” cried McKenzie; “ brace up, brace up, old man. These rooms are too hot for you. Let’s get outside again.”

“ Wait a minute, wait a minute,” I pleaded.

I saw the hands in the picture grasp the side of the frame. Her face was smiling now that she had recognized me, and I divined at once that she intended to step down and come to me. The crowd vanished from my sight.

“ Stop !” I shouted. “ Stop ! Don’t attempt that, Aline. Wait, I’ll help you ! Aline, Aline !”

But she came running towards me with a cry—

“ Oh Tom ! oh Tom !”

20

I saw with impatience a man trying to hinder her advance. I heard McKenzie mutter a curse. That McKenzie should make a ridiculous pretence of supporting me aroused my anger, and I tried to shake him off, but some one else came to his assistance and firmly grasped my other arm. My hot temper was passing, and I began to feel like a man awakening from a sleep, wondering what he had been doing.

" I'm McKenzie," I heard my friend say. " I don't know that you remember me, Judge."

" Oh yes, I remember you very well. Is this Mr. Prentiss ?"

" Yes, gone clean dotty. I shouldn't have brought him out, but he *would* come. Stubborn devil when he takes it in his head."

" Quite so," said the unemotional voice of the Judge. " I rather sympathize with that state of mind. Let us get out of this. We're attracting too much attention. Mr. McKenzie, will you give your arm to my daughter? I'll look after Mr. Prentiss. My carriage is outside."

" I'm all right, Mr. Arbuthnot," I said, in a tone intended to be very conciliatory. " I never felt better in my life."

" Of course you're all right. Will you have a nip of brandy in the refreshment-room ?"

" No, thank you. I never drink spirits."

The Judge led me along. I dimly suspected I was not quite *compos mentis*, yet felt an inordinate desire to talk, and prove that I was perfectly sane.

" Talking of brandy, Mr. Arbuthnot, did Aline ever tell you about my encounter with the Rhine wine ?"

" No," said my conductor shortly. " We won't talk of anything, please, till we're in the carriage."

Arriving at last at the carriage, I saw Aline sitting in the front seat, and hoped she wouldn't vanish this time, as she had done before.

" Father," she said, " Mr. McKenzie is telephoning to the hotel."

" That's right. I understand," said her father, helping me in. It was an open carriage. He sat down beside me, and gave the order to drive to the Continental, and we rolled along the smooth streets of Paris.

I gazed at Aline opposite, those hands that had grasped at the sides of the picture-frame resting on her lap. It seemed to me that natural, easy conversation, rather than profundity, was my rôle.

" Nice town, Paris," I said, smiling at her; then I saw I was wrong. Her eyes filled with tears, and her nether lip trembled.

" Would you like to sit here, Aline?" asked her father.

" Yes, father, please," said the girl.

They changed places. Mr. Arbuthnot rested his arm along the back of the seat, and watched the people we were passing. His was a fine profile, I thought.

" There is something strengthening in your father's face. I felt encouraged when he caught me by the arm just now."

The man, seemingly, did not hear. Aline surreptitiously grasped my hand, and at once I knew I was talking foolishly. Silence was my cue. I leaned back, and did not speak till we were in the courtyard of the hotel. The lift took us up to a cosy parlour on the front, looking out on the Tuilleries Gardens. I sank into an arm-chair, Aline standing beside me, and thus her father left us. She threw her arms around my neck, kissed me, and sobbed as if her heart would break.

"Dear Aline," I said, now thoroughly myself again, "don't cry. I never heard you cry like that before."

"No, Tom," she sobbed, "that's something I have learnt in Europe, but this is the last, I hope."

The door opened with somewhat unnecessary rattling at the handle. Mr. Arbuthnot appeared. Aline had sprung away from me, and stood looking out at the Tuilleries Gardens. Parental authority was still strong.

"The doctor has arrived," said Mr. Arbuthnot. "Come away, Aline, for a few minutes."

Aline turned from the window, hesitated before me for a few moments, then sank to the floor, resting her wet cheek on the hand that lay on my knee.

"Oh, Tom! oh, Tom!" she cried.

"Send the other doctor away, Mr. Arbuthnot. I'm in consultation with a rival a thousand times more potent than he."

Judge Arbuthnot smiled, and closed the door.

THE END

UNIVERSITY OF TORONTO PRESS